T0366120

Sarah's BLESSING

Jerald Beverland

Archway Publishing books may be ordered through booksellers or by contacting:

Archway Publishing
1663 Liberty Drive
Bloomington, IN 47403
www.archwaypublishing.com
1 (888) 242-5904

ISBN: 978-1-4808-4941-9 (sc)
ISBN: 978-1-4808-4940-2 (e)

Library of Congress Control Number: 2017910820

Print information available on the last page.

Archway Publishing rev. date: 08/29/2017

The Lost River Valley was beautiful in the spring of 1876. It was the McCrumb family's first spring in the exquisite mystery of the valley. The winter's snow had given way early that year to a warmer spring according to the Lemhi Indian tribe; the McCrumb's new Valley neighbors. The blessings of such a captivating valley and the wonderful spring weather was a God send to the weary and beleaguered McCrumb family.

The McCrumb's trek from Alma Kansas to the Idaho Territory had been accomplished in old western covered wagons that are only found today in history books of the old west. That hazardous journey had begun a little over one year earlier. It was on March 17, 1875, when the McCrumb's began their perilous journey from Kansas into the mysterious American western frontiers with its much-uncharted lands that had never been seen by the white man. By 1875 prairie schooners (covered wagons) would dot the western landscape like the armada of windjamming ocean schooners that were being launched daily from the shores of Europe and the British Isles towards the new Americas.

The prairie schooners were a relentless sight from the vast lands of Texas to the California coast that was bordered by the immense Pacific Ocean. The prairie schooners could be seen traversing the raw wild lands of the Colorado and Utah Territories pushing their way onward to the great American northwestern territories of Oregon and Washington. The American West was becoming a 'land lock sea" of prairie schooners. The prairie schooner was more commonly referred to as covered wagons by the more sophisticated easterners along the Atlantic coast. But Lucy McCrumb called them prairie schooners until the day she passed away in 1951 at the age of 92.

The McCrumb's journey to this magical valley had been challenging at times with dangerous periods of heart-rending moments that caused the Kansas pioneers to question their decision to go west. Maybe now the McCrumb's could start a new life in this beautiful valley that God had shaped during His creation. This magnificent valley was five miles above sea level and was surrounded on three sides by the majestic Idaho Rocky Mountains. Those spacious mountain peaks were towering several thousand more feet above the valley floor, desperately searching and reaching upwards trying to find the pinnacle of heaven. The "Pioneer Range" as it was later named, was the tallest range of the Rockies in the Idaho Territory.

The McCrumb family had begun their long and difficult journey to this largely unknown and mysterious valley a few years after the final canon shots of the devastating War Between the States were silenced. That war was a time in John McCrumb's life that he had desperately tried to forget. It was nothing more to him now than just a passing whisper in history. He had left behind the horrors of that war and was moving on to the future with his family. Discovering the Lost River Valley was truly a gift from God and the McCrumb family was firmly convinced that was a divine truth. If only his beloved Sarah was here by his side. She would have loved the beauty of this valley. Sarah's pioneering love of nature's wonderments would have brought a unique blossoming beauty to this valley.

The mysterious "Lost River" gave the valley its ominous name. The river's headwaters were almost a hundred miles north, deep into the gold-laden Challis Range of the Rockies. The rapid torrent of the river as it cascaded south toward the valley caused the river to cut wild eddies, raging whirlpools and twisting swirls like a snake traversing through the graveled terrain of the land. The churning waters created wide cuts in some areas, then narrow channels in other parts of the craggy rocky landscape. The river would finally terminate it flow at the southern end of this virgin valley, into an open dessert of many thousands of square miles of land that was covered with nothing but the ever-present mysterious Idaho sagebrush.

Eighteen miles to the west of the seemingly never ending sea of sagebrush and just a few miles southwest of where the valley floor ended laid thousands of acres of mysterious and ominous appearing sea of lava rock from the flow of tripartite ancient volcanoes. The menacing appearance of the volcanic lava beds and the perverted sculptured lava creations were a new and sometimes a frightening experience for the McCrumb's. That type of landscape could always be a danger to a novice pioneer trying to explore the never ending lava flows. The flow of the volcanoes was constant in a couple of direction over one hundred miles wide. Many unfortunate adventures had gotten lost in the jagged landscape and cave cones only to vanished and never be heard of again. Even the native Indians of the valley had learned to avoid the "evil spirits" of the land of "death".

The "Pioneer" mountain range of the great Rocky Mountains surrounded the valley on three sides and then abruptly ended at the beginning of the vast covered sagebrush desert, leaving the southern end of the valley with no mountains to inhibit the pioneers for almost a hundred miles leaving an easy access to its fertile southern landscape of the valley.

The "Lost River" ended its dynamic energetic course after many tantalizing twists and turns in its seventy mile battle with earth's unforgiving elements from high in the Challis Mountains and finally winding through the floor of the valley until it suddenly terminated a few miles into the vast open desert. As the final roar of the river subsided and the waters of the river calmed, an insignificant large shallow lake, only a foot or two deep appeared, which had absolutely no outstanding defining characteristics. The lake just suddenly appeared; never growing any bigger or any deeper. Strangely very few fish could be seen in the shallows of the lake. Upstream the river was a fisherman's paradise for catching huge Rainbow Trout and Whitefish.

The lack of fish just added more mystery to the strange nature of the shallow lake bed that mysteriously swallowed up the immense volumes of the water from the "Lost River". Just as fast as the waters of the "Lost River" terminated into the lake, the lake waters vanished and disappeared into minute gaps and fissures in the ground.

The folks in the valley would later refer to the enigmatic lake as "the sinks". The clear waters of "the sinks" would slowly and mysteriously disappear into the undetermined belly of the earth. No one knew for sure where the waters from the "Lost River" would finally end its improbable journey. Some guessed the disappearing water from the lake would eventually find its way into the huge and thunderous "Snake River" which was over one hundred mile to the south of the valley.

John McCrumb stood on the banks of the "Lost River" on that beautiful spring day in 1876 as its rushing waters prepared for its final journey to "the sinks" and then monstrous Snake River. John's mind started to drift back into time as he surveyed the beauty of the Lost River Vallery. Memories of the past year and the journey from

Alma Kansas in 1875 to the present in 1876. Sarah, his precious wife, and her death clouded his mind as if time was about to just stand still.

………………………………………………………………………

John McCrumb had settled his family in western Pennsylvania in 1858 after following Mormon missionaries from their Scottish homeland far across the Atlantic Ocean. He and his wife and young daughter homesteaded a small portion of land near a farming community called Moravia, which was near the larger hamlet of New Wilmington. Their small farm was situated not far from the Beaver River near the far western boundary of Pennsylvania. Over the next few years John's wife, Sarah, gave birth to two sons and a second daughter. Their oldest daughter Lucy was birthed during their treacherous sea journey from Scotland to the promising new land of their future. The life-changing adventures of the McCrumb clan were on the cusp of a fantastic journey that would take them from the Highlands of Scotland to their new adopted land of America.

In 1861 the devastating civil war between the northern and the southern American States erupted under the newly elected President, Abraham Lincoln. John McCrumb was 44 years old when he and his younger brother James enlisted into the 134 Pennsylvania Volunteers in August 1862. They both felt it was their duty to fight and defend the northern cause against the wayward southern states. They would have defended their homeland of Scotland at any cost and now America was their new home and they would defend it at any cost.

Both brothers were engaged in the 1862 Battle of Richmond Kentucky. James was taken prisoner during that three-day battle.

He managed to escape five weeks later and was reunited with his union comrades by Thanksgiving of that same year.

John was wounded in his right hip on the first day of the battle for Chancellorsville May I, 1863. The bloody battle at Chancellorsville raged on for three more days and John managed to continue fighting even with his painful wound. John was not able to be treated properly for his bullet wound because of the close proximity of the raging three-day battle. He survived that dreadful battle without being killed or captured by the rebel army. The harrowing and confusing retreat of the dispersed Union soldiers hindered him further from adequate medical treatment; he had no choice but to eventually leave that rebel's bullet where it had found its final resting place in his hip. When John eventually died at the Seattle's Old Soldier's Home in 1906 that "damn rebel's bullet" (as John referred to it) had worked its way down his leg to almost his ankle. His family and friends always referred to the bullet as John's "badge of courage".

Both John and James were mustered out of the Union army on May 26th, 1863. Reflections of those dreaded days in the two civil war battles would revisit John in disturbing dreams many times during his life. It is hard to forget when you kill another human and indeed John never forgot. Those stories are for later pages in this dialogue.

In the spring of 1864, John and Sarah decided to sell their small Pennsylvania farm and head further west to the state of Kansas. John purchased 160 acres of fertile ground near Alma Kansas. Alma was few miles west of the largest city in Kansas called Topeka. Alma was almost due north of the Wild West city of Wichita. John built a fine home for his ever-growing family. Everything fell in the proper place for the McCrumb family during those Kansas years. John and Sarah had two beautiful daughters and a couple of handsome strapping sons. The weather seemed to always be in their favor and their yearly crops brought in high yields. Their herd of cattle grew and offered a handsome reward every two years when the cattlemen from Wichita come to buy.

But, after a few years, a few dark clouds appeared on theMcCrum's future horizon; Sarah's health seemed to wane and the ever call of the new western frontier would sound off in the remote winds of their minds.

The allure of the western frontier lay heavily during many evening conversations around the McCrumb supper table. It was usually one of the two McCrumb boys that would ignite the Wild West talks during the evening supper meal.

"Poppa", Jerald, the oldest of the boys, 14 years old to be exact, brokered the conversation on this night, "Jacob told me today that his pa was taken his family to California and he was gonna hunt for gold."

"Ummm, is that right?" was John's reply, knowing what was coming next. So John decided to beat his son to the point of the story.

"Yep, the Silvers are heading for California, but they won't be looking for any gold son. Arron, Jacob's Pa told me his family will probably leave in a month, just after the last snow. He'll be working on a big ocean schooner for a big Pacific coast fishing company."

"Wat's a schooner pa?" The 13-year-old Jacky mumbled with a mouth full of food.

"Jacky, You know better than to try to gag words out with a mouth full of food." Lucy quipped. "ain't you ever going to grow any manners?"

Lucy was the oldest of the McCrumb young'uns. She was seventeen years old and had been born on board of the three mastered schooner during the treacherous voyage from Scotland to the Americas. Lucy had inherited the will and determination of the strongest of a Scottish heritage. She had a wanderlust for adventure and an enduring drive for nature's knowledge. All of the McCrumb children were strong willed, hardworking, and never dodged a chance for adventure or a warranted or even an unwarranted confrontation; mental or physical. But Lucy was just a mite step above the others in her tenacity of determination. It was because of her exerted and steady labors that kept her siblings in check during the grueling and arduous voyage from their home in Kansas to the Idaho Territory. She was a tomboy for sure and definitely a daddy's girl. She always addressed her father as "pap".

Jacky took a big gulp trying to swallow the lump of food in his mouth as he retorted to Lucy's mocking comment. "My teacher sez there ain't no setch word as "ain't"! Ain't you ever gonna learn how to speak proper?" He was trying to out-do his sister.

Jacky felt gallant with his quick comeback against his sister, but all of the time realizing he was wrong trying to talk with a mouth full of food. Sarah, his ma was a woman of higher ideals for her children. She was continuously trying to form their good character in religion, education, and manners. And, talking with a mouth full of food was not endured by his mom.

Sarah was a soft-spoken woman with a deep Scottish belief of the philosophy, "Live and let live." Her strength of character was one of sincere devotion to her husband and to her children. Her passion was her husband and her children.

Sarah only stood a little over five foot tall, but her love of others, her will for life and her tenacity of judgment demonstrated the heart of a giant. But Sarah knew that her life was slowing ebbing with time. Ever since the McCrumb family had reached the shores of their new country Sarah's health seemed to grow a little worse each year. But, for the present, her life was dedicated to making a new home for her family in America.

Back at the supper table, Jacky had totally forgotten about his schooner question. Jerald continued quizzing his poppa about California, gold and the West. "Poppa, are we still gonna move somewhere out west like ya said? Is there really a lot of gold in the mountains? Jacob said that gold was everywhere, in the rivers and streams; all a person had to do was just pick it up. Are those western Indians really wild, and do they really paint their faces before they scalp the hair from pioneers folk's heads? Jacob said they do."

Jerald's questions were coming so fast that his father had lost track of the first two questions.

"Slow down Jerald", his father demanded, "One question at a time, if you please."

His mother looked at him with her familiar understanding smile. She knew and understood the children's anticipation on the possible move to the western frontier. She and John had discussed the possibility of moving the family out west for some time now at the nightly supper table. The family's discussions of building a new future in the West had become more frequent of late.

The discussion around the supper table that night seemed to be more probing than normal. Sarah and John's attitudes were noticeably uneasy and tense.

The discussions of moving west between Sarah and John had been more interwoven with substance when their young'uns were not around. They did not want to excite the children about a western movement before a move was imminent and a date of departure secured. The McCrumb's were a very friendly neighbor, but also a very discreet family when it came to their private lives. Sarah and John did not want any gossip or speculation drifting from mouth to ear around the Kansas farming community concerning any moves they might have been planning to travel west.

The lively discussion around the table came to a blunt halt when fifteen-year-old Amy, the McCrumb's second daughter softly pleated to her Poppa, "Poppa if we move out west will the Indians really cut our hair off?" The chill in her voice gripped everyone's attention. What had been a lively conversation now turned to one of troubling concern.

John quickly glanced over at Sarah and immediately caught the nervous tension in her eyes. Sarah was desperately looking at him trying to determine his reaction to Amy's question. A complete conversation was transpiring between their two nervous looking stares. Each completely understood the other's unspoken words. It was time to tell their children that the McCrumb family's future would be revealed in the American western frontier.

On November 5^{th,} 1874 a most important decision had been made and the children were told; after the last snow of the 1874 winter and the first sign of the 1875 spring, the McCrumb family would begin their adventure to the west and a new life.

By the end of February of 1875, John had sold the 160-acre farm, the house and all of the out structures, which included the large cattle barn, a corn crib, ice house, chicken coop, good size hay barn and a number of horse and cattle corrals, and a three-holer outhouse. With the sale of the farm went ten milking cows, thirty-two beef cattle, a bunch of chickens, four goats, five horses, three mules and all of the rats a person could ever want.

It took John, Sarah and the four young'uns two weeks to pack their two medium size covered wagons with all of their worldly goods that they were taking west with them. Sarah had packed with the greatest of care her cherished fine china, her handmade quilts, two of her mother's handmade Scottish quilts, two cedar chests full of personal keepsakes, beloved family photos, and precious family memories.

Sarah also wanted to make sure that there was plenty of paper and soft cloth material for her and the girl's personal hygiene. She wanted to make sure that the girls were properly prepared for their individual menstrual times of the month. She knew that it would be a problem on the trail for their feminine and personal female essentials. She also made sure that there was a convenient space in the chuck wagon for the girls when they needed to use the waste pot for personal matters. The boys and men could relieve themselves anywhere in the wide open and nobody would care or notice. But she and the girls needed their own delicate privacy.

John made sure that the families' two large Scottish furniture heirlooms were safely packed. The only other items he was concerned about was his arsenal of protection and hunting weapons. One his favorites was the 1862 Henry 44 caliber repeater; the same rifle that took him through his service in the cause of the northern states. His 1873 Winchester was always saddled to his horse. He had two shotguns, a 12 gauge Parker Brothers and a 16 gauge Winchester. His army 45 Colt sidearm was always close by or sometimes holstered to his side.

John also cut and prepared different size cuts of lumber for repair to the wagons in case they were damaged somehow during the long journey to the west. To be further prepared for any trail damage to the wagons he chose a variety of small iron bars and narrow iron plates for strength repairs. He bundled and stored a number of wheel spokes for the trip. He attached two extra spare wagon wheels under the floor of each of the wagons with leather straps.

Lucy and Amy delicately wrapped their personal wearing finery in white sheets and properly packed wooden trunks. Their individual favorite items such as a handmade quilt that they both had quilted together, their needlework, dolls of many sizes, buttons, and bows and of course Lucy's own 22 caliber Remington rifle were placed in the wagons with care.

It didn't take Jerald and Jacky long to pack their belongings in the wagons. Mostly all they cared about were their hunting rifles and pocket knives; each had a 22 caliber rifle and a 12 gauge shotgun. Jacky had his favorite cowboy hat and Jerald his buckskin coat. They left all of the other unimportant stuff for their mom to pack; stuff like clothes, shoes and wearing necessities.

Each covered wagon was being pulled by two of the families horses. Each of the boys would take turns during the long journey west by riding their own horse or by driving one of the covered wagons. Lucy and Amy's small ponies would trail behind the wagons while they drove the chuck wagon.

Throughout Lucy's life, until the day she passed away, she would tell her children, her grandchildren, and her great-grandchildren how proud she was at being a teamster (a prairie schooner driver) at the age of seventeen. She always referred to the covered wagons of the old west as prairie schooners. She would refer to herself as a teamster, not just to an old ordinary wagon driver.

The sisters called their special covered wagon the, "eatery chuck wagon" because it had all of the food for the journey stored in it. Lucy even had made a bright sign that she had attached to the back of the wagon that read, "Lucy's Foods and Chuck Wagon". Sarah and John had prepared an ample supply of dried choices of beef, pig and deer meat. Of course, they could also kill other meats on the journey. Dried beans, rice, and corn were kegged for the trip. Flour, sugar, salt, coffee and other food staples were sufficiently prepared.

Also trailing behind the wagons were eight extra field horses, three cows, the proud bull, a mule and four family dogs. The cows, bull, and mule were tethered together and fasten to the back of the chuck wagon with a long rope. The horses by nature herded together.

The anticipation of their dreams that might be at the end of their western journey and their sincere fears of the unknown that they might encounter on the long pathway ahead of them weighed heavily on the McCrumb families hearts and minds.

John and Sarah continued to pray that they were making the right decision by taking the children into the unknown wilderness ahead of them. They continued to ask "GOD" for guidance. Lucy and Amy tried not to show any sign of outward fear or consternation so as to worry their pa and ma. They did talk to each other about those fears and uncertainties. They found great strength in each other's courage. All Jerald and Jacky could see ahead of them were exciting adventures. They dreamed of killing many Buffalo, taking the hides of the giant grizzly, fighting off the savage Indian, finding the biggest gold nugget and climbing the highest mountains. With those two boys, all seemed well with the world, but deep down their mental uncertainties were very real. They were about to learn many difficult lessons of life before this journey was finished.

Three days before the McCrumb's were to embark on their western journey two unrelated incidents occurred on that same day; one that seemed strange at the time and the other only Sarah knew about it. Both of these events would significantly affect their journey to the western frontier.

John and Sarah had said their "good by" to all of their Alma, Kansas neighbors. The girls had cried farewell tears with all of their girlfriends and managed to tell a couple of boys their feelings after a few giggles. The brothers were still hyping how they were going to conquer the west. They also managed to reclaim friendship with all of the guys whom they had had fights and disagreements with in the past.

Early on that morning while John and the children were out tending to final preparations for the journey Sarah had collapsed to the bedroom floor with excruciating stomach pains. She had experienced these types of pains before, but not with this intensity and distress. These pains had become more frequent than they had been in the past few months. She was reluctant to tell John about the pains reoccurring nature.

She knew that John was deeply concerned about her health and she didn't want him to worry even more than he had, or put the journey out west on hold. Especially not after selling the farm and laboring for weeks in preparations for the move. Sarah had been passing spots of blood for almost a year.

In the past 12 months, John and Sarah had made two very difficult long and exhausting trips by horse and wagon to doctors in Topeka Kansas. The medicine that the doctors in Topeka gave her did reduce the pain, but the symptoms were ever present. At times more apparent than other times. John wanted to call the western journey off, but Sarah convinced him that she was feeling fine and there was no need to worry. The doctors were very concerned with Sarah's condition, but couldn't quite pinpoint its cause. One doctor thought it might be her kidneys; the other was more convinced it was caused by female problems. Sarah had her own sentiments but kept them to herself. She did not want to alarm her family. Anyhow, there were doctors in Salt Lake City that could help she reasoned; if and when they reached that point. Salt Lake was a determined destination for the McCromb's, but not a confirmed one. Not as yet, anyway.

As the pain subsided Sarah managed to regain some of her composure. She slowly got up from the floor and made her way to the bed. She sat on the edge of the bed for a few moments then walked to the kitchen to make herself a cup of tea. There she would relax and regain her emotions. She convinced herself that this episode was not one to tell John. If it should happen again then she would confide in him.

The children were in the large front yard finishing arranging the contents in the two covered wagons. John was down next to the big corral discussing some boring last minute questions from the new owner of the McCrumb's ranch.

During his thoughtless answers to the new owner's questions, John had noticed a lone rider on horseback in the far distance riding toward the ranch from the north. After about twenty to thirty minutes of mundane questions and useless answers, the lone rider had finally managed to reach the opposite side of the corral that John and the new owner were having their conversations. The stranger dismounted his distinctive palomino horse and leaned on the fence rails with his back towards the two conversing ranchers.

John could not contain his curiosity any longer. The only people that ever visited the ranch were neighbors and occasionally Kiowa Indians. John had a good relationship with the Kiowa tribe. He would trade a couple of horses and maybe a cow or two for buffalo, beaver, and bear skins. He could sell or trade these items to his neighbors. The rare trading occasions with the Kiowa kept John and his family secure from marauding renegade Indians. Now the question was, who was this stranger who rides in big as you please; and seemingly from nowhere.

John endeavored to size up the stranger in his mind as he slowly walked to where the strange visitor stood. John figured the rider with the ruddy complexion was at least six foot one or maybe six foot two. John stood five foot eleven and that was with his cowboy boots on. He was pretty sure the stranger worked in the sun because of his ruddy complexion and was probably a wrangler or a cowboy of some sorts. The guy's clothes were worn and rugged in appearance.

Through all of John's observations of the fellow, the one thing that caught his attention the most was the long barrel six shooter that hung from the stranger left hip. John also detected the heavy wear on the gun's holster. He determined the stranger to be about thirty years old, give or take a couple years. It was hard to tell because of his sun-baked face and hands.

John approached the stranger with a measured and cautioned demeanor.

"Howdy", John said in his most familiar and friendly expression. "My name is John McCrumb. And, who do I have the pleasure meeting on this fine day?"

"Jake", was the stranger's reply, but only after a few seconds of silence. "Jake Banks". Those last two words seemed to just slowly trail off in the distance... His facial features stayed stoic as if he was anticipating an unfriendly response.

John stared at this stranger desperately trying to recognize anything familiar about him. He reached far back over the years in search of anyone who he might have crossed paths with. There was something….. Something……. But he just couldn't pull it into focus.

"Well, Jake Banks, what brings you to this neck of the Kansas woods?' John finally managed to ask the question after a couple of moments of silence.

"If you're looking for work I'm afraid I can't help you. You see, we just sold this farm. Maybe the new owner over there….." John turned and pointed to the new owner on the other side of the corral". "I could talk to him and maybe….."

"No sir, I don't want work." Jake cut into the center of John's sentence before he could finish it. "I heard you and your family was heading further west in a few days. I'm here to ask if I can travel with you."

The statement and question from this stranger caught John by surprise and his astonishment was demonstrated by the serious scowl on his face. What was this stranger asking? Why was he asking? What was the stranger purpose in going out west? Why did he want to travel with the McCrumb's? Who in the devil was this person standing next to him? All of these questions were frantically racing through John's mind.

It took John a few minutes to regain his composure. "Son, I'm not sure just what you're asking. Hell, I don't even know who you are!........ Or, where you come from……… I don't know a thing about you. You ride up out of nowhere and ask me a question like that……. Son, I don't think we have too much more to talk about"

John turned to walk away, and then a strange sensation made him stop and slowly shake his head. He turned back to face this Jake Banks, "Jake, I'm sorry, but just who in the hell are you anyway!"

An ever so slight grin faded in and then out on the rugged face of this stranger who had mysteriously entered the McCrumb's lives.

"You know me, Mr. McCrumb,........You know me." Jake's answer was in a soft voice, almost a whisper.

....

Jake Banks was born in 1842 to Joan and Jedidiah Banks in a share cropper's shanty on the outskirts of Pittsburgh Pennsylvania. His ma died in childbirth and his pa died the next year in the devastating Pittsburgh fire of 1845. An aunt, his mom's sister whom never married, took the young boy to be her own after the death of his dad.

Life was never easy for Jake, so when the Civil War broke out in 1861 he determined that maybe service in the Union Army could be his calling; a soldier's life. He was sixteen years old when he joined the ranks of the Pennsylvania militia. From the latter part of 1861 to the early months of 1863 Jake had been in some slight battles, but mostly he had served as an orderly and a runner for the Northern Armies command staff. By January of 1863, The Union forces had lost many of the battles and the Northern cause was in despair for the soldier on the front lines. General Robert E. Lee and the rebel army seemed to be everywhere. The Union soldier's moral was at an ebb low and so was Jake's. He didn't feel like he was adding anything to the northern cause. He finally got up enough nerve to ask for a transfer to a front-line regiment.

It was General Hooker himself who OK'd Jake's transfer to the 105th Regiment Pennsylvania Volunteers. Jake was about to experience many reasons why he might have wished he had not asked for that transfer. His first real test in a deadly conflict and a bloody battle was the battle of Chancellorsville on May 1st, 1863.

....

"You do know me, Mr. McCrumb, You do know me," Jake repeated the words almost word for word. "I was in the battle of Chancellorsville Mr. McCrumb. You saved my life"

Before Jake said anything else he gave John the opportunity to study his face, and reflect back to the days of that horrific and bloody civil war battle.

John stared hard into Jake's eyes as his mind drifted back thirteen years. Thirteen years to a place in a time he had tried hard to forget.

As John's mind slowly wandered back through the haze of forgotten memories of years gone by suddenly he found himself back in the thick wilderness east of Chancellorsville Virginia on May 1, 1863.

The memories of that four-day battle became a vivid flashback in his mind's eye; cannons belching fire and coughing iron dragons in the shape of black iron balls of destruction. The screaming sound of musket balls and bullets were whizzing in every direction around him. Confusion and mayhem, blood and death were everywhere within his grasp, he could even have touched them. More than once, with death surrounding him, he had asked "GOD" would he ever see his beloved Sarah again.

General Hooker's Army of the Potomac, 130,000 soldiers strong, had crossed over the Rappahannock River and encamped in a seven square mile area around the northern and northwestern edge of Chancellorsville, Virginia. They were entrenched in a dense expanse of trees with heavy underbrush and choked thickets. It was difficult to move in any direction because of the density of the woods. It was even difficult trying to keep in close contact with fellow soldiers. John realized that trying to fight an enemy in this cluster of vegetation would be difficult and challenging.

There were times during those three days of battle he had regretted that he and his comrades had ever crossed over the Rappahannock River the day before the battle raged. He should have stopped at the smaller Rapidan River and turned back towards home. All of a sudden he realized that he was not fighting for a cause, he would be fighting for his life.

When the battle began in earnest on the first day John's detachment was near the "Wilderness Church" west of Chancellorsville. They were to hold that position until they received further orders, but they were quickly overrun from the west by the rebel army. John and his Union comrades made a muddled and wild retreat back towards Chancellorsville and the "Turnpike". They had to make their way through thick stands of trees and tangled underbrush. The soldier who was running next to John fell to the ground dead with a rebel bullet to the back of his head.

A strange panic overtook John and at that same moment a rebel soldier came out of some underbrush from his right side and they collided sending both men plummeting to the ground. Both men had dropped their rifles because of the collision and both men became entangled in the undergrowth. John could see the rebel soldier trying disparately to retrieve his musket. John had ended up on his back and his rifle was under him. He realized he wouldn't have time to untangle himself and maneuver himself into a shooting position before the rebel could reach his rifle and shoot it. By instinct John pulled his 45 caliber six-shooter from its holster and with one shot sent his adversary tumbling backward; dead. His panic now turned into a mode of survival. He can't quite remember how, but he did make it back to his Union company without any other encounters with the enemy. The rebels had gotten what they wanted; the "Wilderness Church" position.

The main body of the Union forces was entrenched just outside of Chancellorsville between Fairview and Hazel Grove. John was out of breath, shaking with fear and relieved all at the same time when he reached his comrades in blue. John didn't know it at the time, but Lee's command was less than half the size of Hooker's army of the Potomac. He would have sworn that those figures were reversed. There seemed to be reb's everywhere and every time they charged in battles they would let out the strangest soul-cuddling yells that would scare the devil himself.

That first day of fighting was intense and constant, the rebel forces just would not let up. Hooker's forces were dug in around the "Grove" and "Fairview" with nowhere to go. It was impossible to see where the enemy was because of the dense woods; at times they were completely surrounded by the men in gray. Half of the time they were shooting at shadows and strange images.

The only hand to hand combat the first day was the one that John was involved earlier that morning. Just before nightfall, a rebel regiment charged a short distance towards where John was hunkered down in a shallow ravine. The barrage of muskets firing left the air reeking of the smell of gunpowder and smoke. John, not sure if the rebs were going to continue their charge decided to fall back to a stand of large trees. Before he reached the safety of the trees a rebel's musket ball smashed into his right hip. The force of the bullet sent him reeling to the ground with a sharp grinding pain. At first, John wasn't sure where his wound was; only that he had been shot. The pain seemed to be everywhere. Two of his comrades pulled him to the safety of a large tree. Other fellow soldiers lay dead just a few feet away from where John laid.

Fire belching cannons and the flare from muskets tore the dark of night into reds, yellows, and strange other colors all night long. The soldiers in blue were pinned to their position without much movement allowed. Because of those many difficulties John did not have a doctor that could tend to his wound that night.

With the first light of day of the next morning, a strange and thick haze of red colored smoke laid heavy in the trees and underbrush. A person couldn't see the sky for the smell of gunpowder in the air and in their eyes. It was a scary sight with many mind-bending interpretations. John was never able to purge his mind of that smell and the visions of that bizarre morning.

One thing he did know, he was still alive! Everything that had happened in the past twenty-four hours seemed unreal to him. It seemed like he had been in this jungle of trees and twisted underbrush for days, not hours. He wasn't sure who was winning the battles. He was sure of one thing; there were a number of battles being fought in different areas around Chancellorsville. No matter in which direction a person's ears were tuned, he was sure to hear the rage of gunfire; both big guns and small guns. Scuttlebutt was the enemy was attacking from all directions and many of the Union forces were being overrun with screaming rebels. His unit had so far been stationary in their battle with their enemy until new orders were given.

A couple of hours after sunrise John's commanding officer did order the men to fall back further to the northeast a couple of hundred yards. Moving wasn't easy for the men because of the heavy foliage and the trees. Any movement for John was excruciating. The bullet wound to his hip had not totally stopped bleeding and the pain was still sharp and agonizing.

During the early hours before dawn, a couple of his buddies had poured whiskey on the wound, heated up a knife over a small fire and pressed the hot blade to the wound three different times for a few seconds each time. After the third time, the blade was applied to the bullet wound more whiskey was poured over the wound. John had put a fairly large twig between his teeth before the knife blade was placed on the wound. With the first touch of the hot blade, the exhausted soldier passed out. When he awoke later the bleeding had stopped.

The second day of battle for John and his company heavy rebel artillery attacks plagued them most of the day. Their movement was minimal. Musket fire was steady, but not overwhelming. It was the Rebel's cannon barrages that kept John and his comrade's hunkered down during the second day of the battle. The trees and area surrounding John's company's entrenchment for hundreds of yards looked as if a massive tornado had ripped through the forest of trees. Trees were splintered like twigs. The exploding cannon balls were leaving massive gaping craters and deepen cavities in the landscape. The explosions had taken a devastating toll on human life in the Union Army. Soldiers with wounded torn bodies laid everywhere a person's eye could view. Many more soldiers would be killed before this day would end. Some of the dead John knew, many he did not know. More than once John thought what a stupid way to fight a battle and even a more stupid way to die.

"When is this hell going to end? Where in the hell is General Hooker and his 130,000 Union Soldiers? Why can't they stop those damn rebel's cannons? I can't even see the enemy I'm fighting. Why can't they get us out of these forsaken woods? GOD, please help us!" All of these thoughts kept running through John's mind hour after hour.

By nightfall of the second day John and his companions were exhausted, fatigued and bewildered with the continuing onslaught of the rebel resolve. Again, the scuttlebutt was the enemy had overrun many of the other Union positions and many of his comrades in blue were frantically retreating. Both John and his fighting partners were puzzled why their company had not been overrun by the southern forces. That perplexing question would be answered early on the third day in the battle of Chancellorsville.

....

There was an eerie and unnerving awareness that flowed thru the ranks of John and his army buddies the night before the third day of fighting. Something else odd was happening that night; many stragglers from other Union Regiments who had been displaced from their units because of rebel advancements were finding themselves lost in the dense forests around Chanslervillie. Many of these stragglers from other Union regiments were finding their way into the entrenchment of John's company.

John could hear battles raging in every direction. The skies were aglow with the charges of cannon and musket explosions. The glow and confusion of not knowing what was coming next played heavy on the minds of the Union soldiers. Also, the deafening silence coming from the rebs that had been battering John's unit for two days was extremely troubling. What was happening or what was about to happen was on the mind of every soldier in blue.

Much of the time the pain in John's hip was forgotten because of the fear of being killed during the battle. But now, with the deadening silence of his immediate enemy that pain once again played havoc with his hip. Nothing he could do would relieve any amount of the pain

Even at midnight, the silence in the camp was frightening. Movement among the Union soldiers was scarce, not knowing what the Rebs were up to. Anyway, there was plenty of noise coming from other areas around Chancellorsville to keep one's mind occupied.

Sometime a few hours before dawn John heard someone call his name from in the dark. Not wanting any of his adversaries to pinpoint his location John whispered as loud as he thought necessary to be heard.

"Over here' I'm over here by the cook's tent," John answered. "Be careful of the wagon debris, it's a real tangle mess."

John could see three figures making their way towards him in the dark. He soon recognized one of the figures as Bill Bentley, a Union Sargent. Another one he recognized was his Captain, Wesley Jordan. The third figure he had never seen before. It was a young kid who looked to be younger than 20 years. But, it was hard to tell because of the darkness and the guy really looked dirty and ragged. It was hard to determine any detail features of his face or anything else about him.

"John, this guy has something you desperately need, Morphine." The captain emphasized.

"Thank GOD!" John felt a surge of relief. "Where did he get it?" John's voice was trembling with thankful anticipation? Now, maybe the pain will decrease dramatically.

"He is from another unit……. about a mile from here. They were overrun….. by the rebs." Sargent Bentley said in a hesitating and low whisper. "He was carrying some medical supplies from their hospital tent to another area with wounded men when his unit was overrun by the enemy."

"I was just about to reach the wounded men……… when everything around me lit up like the 4th of July." The young newcomer piped in, as he was pushing the hypodermic needle with morphine into John's hip.

"It seemed like there were at least a thousand rebel soldiers shooting and screaming all around us. I fell to the ground and crawled into some underbrush." The new guy was now crying as he told this part of his story. "Our guys were falling everywhere…….. It was horrible……. I stayed hiding in the brush for seemed like hours………. I was afraid to move……….. I waited for the reb's to move on………… Then I took off in the direction I was facing……….Not even knowing where I was going. I did manage to keep all of the medical supplies in my shoulder bag"

Tears were still streaming down the kid's cheeks when he poured some whiskey on the needle and John's wound. He had poured from the same bottle before he stuck the needle in John's hip.

"Look, kid," John trying to reassure him, "It's OK to cry. Hell, this battle has made a lot of grown men to cry, including me!"

John felt immediate relief from the pain in his hip; the morphine was doing its thing. But the danger of infection was still a physical threat. John knew that possibility was real and continued to pray for a doctor and some type of treatment for the possible infection. In the meantime, his only choices were being dictated by the current circumstances happening right then and in real time.

John thanked the kid, Captain Jordon, the sergeant for their help and then faded into a shallow troubled slumber. This was the first time he really experienced any meaningful sleep for the last forty-eight hours.

After two hours of sleep and just before dawn on the third day of fighting for the control of Chancellorsville John was roused by the sound of heavy activity in the encampment. There was a lot of confusion and frantic movement on all sides of him. He asks the guys that were close to him what was going on. No one seemed to have any knowledgeable answers, just more confusing and panic answers. Within minutes all of those questions would be answered. It seemed as if the doors of hell had been blown open and hell's fire was being unleashed.

As the sun peeked in the eastern sky and the night's darkness began giving way to a new day John's enemy had awoken and was about to bring massive destruction to General Hooker's Army of the Potomac. Rebel battle cries and the deafening exploding muskets shattered the morning skies seemingly from all directions. This third day of the battle for territory around Chancellorsville would be the second bloodiest day of the Civil War and John was in the middle of it.

John managed to grab his rifle, his ammunition pouch, and his bowie knife. His forty-five caliber Colt handgun was still attached to his service belt. He was one of the more fortunate soldiers in this campaign, he had a new 1862 44 caliber, Henry, repeating rifle. He had purchased the repeater the year before, just before he enlisted in the army. Most of the southern soldiers had the old type muzzle loading muskets. Those old muskets put them at a threatening disadvantage against John's Henry repeater. There wasn't any time for John to think about what he should do during this massive attack from the enemy. He just had to react to what was happening right there in front of him.

The hand to hand fighting was fierce with numerous casualties on both sides. John and his comrades were taking a pounding from the southern troops, there were just too many of them. The engagement between the two adversaries continued off and on for hours. The rebels would pull back, regroup and charge again. This plan of attack was working well for their ultimate goal of claiming all of the battle for Chancellorsville as won. The Union soldiers knew that this battle was a lost cause and the only way to gain anything from it was to retreat and find a safe distance away from the rebellious enemy.

Now the fighting for John was not for claiming new land and maintaining possession of it, the fighting now was for the preservation of one's own life. It was the struggle of finding an escape route from this senseless chaos of kill or be killed. John and about fifty or sixty of his comrades had struggled with minor resistance making their way to the north for maybe four or five hundred yards. It had been tough going because of the trees and underbrush, but the underbrush was also a blessing because the rebels pursuing them were also having a difficult time making any progress through the tangled muddled mess.

In their retreat, they had come to a small open clearing of about an acre or two with a narrow dried up creek bed dividing it. Fearing that they could encounter other southern militia in the direction they were heading they decided to take a stand in the creek bed. The banks of the creek were two to three feet high and would give them ample cover from their pursuers. They also would have the advantage of surprise; the rebs wouldn't see them until it was too late. They didn't have to wait very long before the outline of the enemy was visible. After the rebel's had advanced maybe six or seven feet into the open clearing the Union muskets, rifles, and handguns began to belch fire and brimstone into their charging adversary. Those poor rebs in the front of the charge didn't stand a chance; every man one of them either fell dead or wounded. The guys behind that first group didn't fare much better. After that first and second volley of gunfire, there were fifty or so men in gray that lay in the clearing either wounded, dying or dead.

The southern combatants just kept on coming out of those woods yelling and yelping like screeching banshees. Ten, twenty, thirty or more went to the ground while others rushed the creek bed with muskets blazing death and bayonets slashing through the air. The hand to hand fighting was brutal, neither side giving any quarter; it was killed or be killed. The rebel's outnumbered those in Union blue three to one. John had emptied his Henry repeater of its ammunition and had drawn his Colt forty-five. The dead and the wounded from both sides were blanketing the grounds around the creek bed. John had also drawn his bowie knife, he knew once he had exhausted the bullets in his Colt forty-five the knife was the only weapon he had left to fight with.

John wasn't sure how many enemy soldiers he had killed; his only concern was the fact that he was still alive. He had been hit twice with the butt of rifles, a flesh wound to his shoulder caused by a musket ball and a bayonet wound to his left side had left John in a panic of self-survival. As he was looking where to place his next shot from his Colt revolver he saw a comrade taking a bayonet to the side of his back and another rebel slamming his musket butt to the same guy's head. He used his last two bullets sending both of those rebels sprawling to the ground in mortal pain.

John managed to make his way over to where his fallen comrade laid when a third rebel that was near him drew a musket bead on the fallen warrior. John dropped his revolver and lunged at the rebel soldier before he could pull the musket's trigger plunging his bowie knife deep in the guy's gut. Both John and his wounded adversary stumbled to the ground with John fearing that this might be his final act on this earth.

When John had regained his mental capacity he endeavored to right himself in a setting position. Something dramatic was happening all around him, but he just couldn't quite figure out what was causing all of the commotions. He leaned over to see if the young Union soldier was still alive.

He was!

John had to take a double look at the guy he had just saved from certain death. It was the young kid with the syringe and the morphine. How strange is this John thought, the same kid who had helped John with his hip pain? John managed to stand and then fully realized what was happening around him. The rebels were scattering in every direction. The flaming burst of muskets discharging was everywhere around John. He finally realized that he was in the midst of much larger battle than he had been in just moments ago. But this time the Union forces were in command and the rebels were being routed. There were Union blue uniforms everywhere. John picked up his revolver and withdrew the Bowie knife from the dead rebel's belly, then carried the young wounded soldier to a protected area from the gunfire. When he was satisfied that the kid was going to be OK, John grabbed his Henry repeater, then endeavored to find out where these new Union forces had come from.

He saw Captain Jordan not far from where he stood him barking orders with a loud commanding voice, a voice that was music to

John's ears. When the captain saw John he came running up to him with a satisfying look on his face.

"Glad we got here when we did", he shouted over the roaring noise of the barking guns. "We got the orders to pull back to the Rappahannock, but not everyone was able to get the communication. Too much confusion……..too many men had been separated during the bewilderment of the rebels early morning charge…….. but glad to find you and your men."

"Captain you and your men are a blessing……….a gift from God", John sputtered! "We wouldn't have lasted much longer. How in this world did you find us?"

"John, we weren't looking for ya or anyone else for that matter. It's just a miracle we even came this way. We just went in the first direction we thought best."

Captain Jordan paused took a quick survey of his surroundings. All he saw was Union blue, the entire enemy had scattered in different directions into the woods. The night would be on them in a couple of hours and the fatigue of the day had drained every body and soul that was still able to stand. Not much could be done for the dead. The wounded were attended to and the camp was called for the night.

John had gone back to check on the young boy he had saved. The kid was awake and his wounds were being taken care of.

"How are ya doing kid?" John asked in his normally soft voice.

"Pretty good sir. Thanks for helping me out today". The kid was tired and showed his weakness from the battle. "They gave me some pain killer…." He managed to softly say, "I think I'll just get some rest", with that the kid fell into a sleep of exhaustion.

Sentries were posted around the perimeter of the camp and many of the men fell into troubled sleep.

All night long cannons could be heard belching their destruction in the distance. By dawn, the dreaded sound of muskets firing was closing in on the Union encampment sending a familiar fear through the minds of the Union soldier.

Captain Jordan called for his troops to move out, "With Haste?"

The fourth day of this horrid battle was spent by the Union soldiers trying desperately to retreat to safety. They met some moderate resistance from roving bands of Confederate troops that were trying to cut the escape routes from the retreating Union army. Under Captains Jordan's leadership the Union troops that John was with managed to fight their way back to, and over the Rappahannock River to safety.

The battle for Chancellorsville was a total disastrous defeat for the Union Army and President Abraham Lincoln. Two months later the battle at Gettysburg would turn the tide of the Civil War in the favor of the North. Chancellorsville would be John's last major campaign; his wounds would keep him out of any other major battles, just minor scrimmages. He was mustered out of the army at the end of May, just three weeks after the battle of Chancellorsville. That damn bullet was still in his hip and there it would stay for the rest of his life.

After crossing the Rappahannock River he said goodbye to the kid he had saved and they both went their separate ways. It later occurred to John that he never did learn the kid's name. The kid went on to fight in the Gettysburg battle and much more before the war ended in 1865. He ended up serving President Lincoln as a personal courier with the rank of sergeant. He was at the Fords

Theater the night Lincoln was assassinated. He was there outside the burning barn with pistol drawn when John Wilks Booth was killed.

....

John's mind was in a flurry of emotions as he continued to look into the eyes of Jake Banks on that spring day in 1875. Slowly John turned and put his face into his cupped hands. After a few moments, he slowly turned to face Jake. Tears were softly trickling down John's cheeks.

"You're the kid with the morphine!" John finally managed to say, with quivering lips and chin. Jake Banks just smiled and extended his right hand towards John.

Three days later the McCrumb family and Jake Banks began the difficult and dangerous journey into an unknown western adventure. Jake had been adopted into the McCrumb family with open arms and heartfelt acceptance. As far as Sarah and the children were concerned Jake was a treasured hero. To John, he would always be like a brother.

The McCrumb family's initial travel destination was the City of Salt Lake which was in the vicinity around the "Great Lake of Salt", which was west of the Colorado Territory and just south of the Idaho Territory. Pioneers of the Mormon religion had settled the land around the great lake of salt in 1841. To reach their target destination John and his company would first have to travel to the city of Denver in the Colorado Territory, then north by the "Overland Trail" to the "Mormon Trail", which spanned the bottom part of the Wyoming territory.

Their plans were not only ambitious but very dangerous. All of the lands they planned to cross to reach Salt Lake City were occupied by Native American Indians of various different tribes. Many of these Indian tribes were either at war with each other or having conflicts with cavalry troops or just resenting the white man who in their mind were assaulting their culture and invading their holy lands and sacred hunting grounds. History had recorded numerous deadly "Indian Wars" between neighboring tribes. Constant conflicts involving white settlers and the Indians was a matter of increasing concern in all of the western territories. A continuing fear of those Native Americans spread like wildfire through white settlements every time there was a story of a massacre, or raids, which included Indians and the white man.

Many of those stories of a massacre or Indian raids on the surface were true, but the complete details of those stories were seldom accurate. Sometimes it would only be five or six renegade Indians doing the raiding and not hundreds as the stories would retell. Many times there would not be any deaths in those repeated conflicts and not dozens that the stories would report. Other times the stories would be absolutely correct and hold many chilling truths. None of the retold stories of the conflicts between the Indians and the white man could be believed for any accuracy. The truth was always hidden somewhere in the confusing retelling of the event.

John felt confident that the Kiowa Indians wouldn't bother them because of his strong relationship he has had with them for years. But the other tribes had him very concerned. There were constant reports and rumors of escalating raids by the Pawnee, the Arapaho, the Ute, the Cheyenne and the Lakota. John's concern proved to be valid, especially with the Pawnee and the Ute tribes.

Both John and Jake had figured that the two wagons could travel, without any hindrance, about twenty to twenty-five miles each day. John was hoping to reach Abilene, Kansas in three days. Once in Abilene they could rest and make sure all of the provisions they needed were accounted for. It would also be a partial test on the condition of the wagons after three days of travel. The next small settlement after Abilene would be Salina, Kansas, about a day's journey from Abilene. At Salina, they would have to cross over the Smoky Hill River. After Salina, It would be many days before they would have contact with any other helpful settlement or trading post. Hays City, Kansas and Fort Hays would be the next gainful stop after Salina for the western travelers. It would be almost two weeks before they would reach the safety of either of those stops.

On the 17th of March, 1875 the McCrumb's and Jake Banks uttered the now famous western words, "Wagons Ho"!

That spring sunny day the two covered wagons rolled off of the farmland in Kansas and the trek to the West would begin. The last of the preparations had been accomplished the day before. All of the vegetable and miscellaneous crops seeds for their future settlement were stored in cans, buckets and then situated in the wagons. Jockey boxes dangled from the sides of the wagons, along with buckets of axle grease for the wagon wheels. Tool boxes for repairs were placed in handy storage areas. Twenty-five-gallon wooden slat kegs that had been filled with fresh drinking water were attached to the sides of the two wagons. All was ready for the "Wagon HO!"

Sarah was commanding Mike and Molly; the two loved family horses that were pulling the wagon that Lucy had dubbed the "chuck wagon". Both of the girls were sitting along side of their mom. Scout and Barney, two young stallions were pulling the other wagon that was being driven by thirteen-year-old Jacky. John was on his horse

Thunder, riding as wagon master, while Jake and Jerald, on their horses, were riding watch and keeping the life stock in line.

The small two wagon caravan began the journey west on the ancient "Smoky Hill Trail". This trail was first blazed and traveled by Native Americans next to the Smoky Hill River in the early 1800's. When gold was discovered at Pikes Peak in the Colorado Territory and the area that later became Denver, Kansas residents, and other eastern gold hunters, not wanting to challenge the high peaks of the Rocky Mountains used the Smoky Hill Trail through the state of Kansas to reach the Colorado gold fields. It was a harder trail to travel, but there were no dangerous mountains to cross. Another problem traveling the Smoky Hill Trail in the 1850's and 1860's were the marauding Indians that lived along the Smoky Hill River banks at that time. By the time the McCrumb's had set their wagons rolling on the Smoky Hill Trail in the spring of 1875 much of the Indian danger had faded. The Kiowa had taken care of that problem.

The first two days of their travel went satisfactorily with no surprising events. Early on the second day, they did see a small band of Kiowa far off in the distance, which John figured was a scouting or hunting party. At midday on the third day, the little wagon train rolled into Abilene, Kansas. They did some purchasing and trading before they prepared to camp just outside of Abilene for the night. The wagons rode the trail with no problems.

Early on the morning of the fourth day, the McCrumb's two wagons started rolling just as the sun was rising in the east. It was mid-morning on that fourth day when they saw that small band of Kiowa again. This second sighting had John just a little curious. But he quickly passed it off as just a coincidence. Two more days passed with no reasons for any concern. The journey so far was succeeding on schedule, in fact, it was going better than John had expected. In those first six days, they had traveled about one hundred and thirty miles. John figured they had about one hundred and seventy or so miles left before they would be out of Kansas. That would put them in Colorado Territory in about nine to ten days. Those calculations agreed with John and Jake's original travel plans.

Early on the seventh day of their journey, the small wagon train met with an encounter that could have turned deadly. This was the type of encounter they had prayed to avoid. Jacky had taken the reigns of Scout and Barney and Jerald was now riding watch with Jake. Jerald was keeping the trailing horses in line with the wagons when he noticed a band of Indians to the north of the rough and rocky wagon trail. The wagons were still about fifty or sixty miles east of Fort Hays. Because of the distance between Jerald and the Indians he could not tell if they were Kiowa. He continued to watch them for five or ten minutes. The Indians seemed to be purposely riding parallel with the two wagons, not getting any closer just staying the same distance away. When the Indians veered off their course and started to ride towards the wagons Jerald decided to tell his dad. He spiked his horse Joshua with the heel of his boot and rode to where his dad was scouting the trail. John was about a quarter of a mile in front of the wagons. He had not noticed the Indians; he was too busy making sure there weren't any large rocks in the trail that could have hinder or damaged the wheels of the wagons.

The terrain of this part of Kansas was large rolling hills and it was extremely rocky. There were large boulders and smaller rocks the size of dinner plates and various size pebbles dotted the landscape and the trail. Anything moving in the distant hills could only be seen if the object was on the crest of one of the hills. The object would be obscured if it was in one of the valleys or gullies between the hills.

When Jerald told his dad that he had seen some Indians, everything with the two wagons came to a screeching halt. When John and Jake visually searched the horizon to the north of them they spotted no movement except natural movements caused by the ever-blowing wind.

"Are you sure you saw Injuns?" Jake asked. Everyone was taking this possible sighting with somber anxiety. Nothing could be overlooked with any possibility of Indians close by.

"Jerald, just where did you see them?" Now it was John's turn to question his son.

"They were right over there......... maybe on the top of that second hill.......not on top of that first hill......but that second hill." Jerald pointed to the spot where he had last seen the Indians on horses.

"John!" Jake yelled. "There they are over there coming through that ravine."

"No God, Please..... Not Pawnee!" John retorted. The tragic sound in John's voice told the complete story.

They rushed back to the wagons to prepare for the imminent and savage attack. The Pawnee were fierce warriors without any fear of death. John told Sarah and the girls to burrow down as deep as possible in the bed of the wagons between any items they could squeeze themselves. John and Jake already had their sidearms strapped to their belts. Jake got his Winchester 30/30. John grabbed his Henry repeater and his Parker shotgun. The boys armed themselves with their twenty-two caliber rifles and both had a loaded shotgun.

After letting the animal stock lose each of the men took a position underneath of the wagons and waited for the charge. John reminded everyone to be calm, aim careful, don't miss their objective when shooting and don't waste ammunition. John understood in his heart that this day could potentially end tragically. Driving off the attacking Indians would be almost impossible. He started to doubt his own intelligence and judgments about this trip to the west. How could he be so stupid as to put his family in this seemingly impossible situation? If anyone survived this mayhem how could he possibly face them either on this earth or in heaven; if he even made it to heaven?

John's last conscious words out loud were, "God, Please help us!"

It looked to be a war party of about thirty to forty Pawnee Indians with their faces and bodies painted in weird frightening designs. It was unusual for Pawnee to be this far south. This part of Kansas was Kiowa territory. The Indian riders were driving their horses at a full gallop out of the gulch straight towards the covered wagons. Their war whoops were blood-curdling.

Both McCrumb boys were close to peeing in their pants. In fact, one of them did pee in his pants but he managed to hide it from his brother. Neither one of the boys had ever experienced this type of intense fear. Physical death had never been this close to a reality in their lives. Now they could imagine what their dad and Jake had gone through during the War between the States. They didn't want to die, at least not like this. It flashed through Jerald mind the possibility that he and Jacky could be scalped.

"Do you think its hurts to be scalped?' He asked Jacky as a few tears trickled down his cheeks.

Jacky was too terrified to answer. All he could do was shrug his shoulders.

When the Pawnee had gotten within about 200 feet of the wagons both John and Jake fired their weapons. Within a matter of seconds, five of the Indians were shot from their horses. With that first blast of firepower from their dad and Jake's rifles both Jerald and Jacky began firing their guns. Jacky fired his shotgun as fast as he could. He did manage to bring down one warrior and wounding another one. The wounded one dropped his rifle and it was trampled by some of the other charging horses. Jerald was sure that he had hit a couple of them, but wasn't sure to what extent. The Pawnee ran their horses at a full gallop within yards of the wagons firing their rifles and sending arrows into the wooden side boards and the canvas tops of the wagons.

Sarah and the girls were hunkered down in the chuck wagon between trunks, boxes and anything else they could find for cover and protection. It was a frightful situation for them not being able to see what was happening outside of the wagon. Sarah tried to calm the girls, reassuring them that everything would be alright.

She also knew that this day could possibly end in sorrow, but she mustn't let the girls feel her anxiety. It was the blood-curdling screams of the Indians that sent Sarah and the girls into a new panic of fear. Lucy wanted to get out of the wagon and help her "pap" fight off those rowdy Indians. Sarah had to get stern with Lucy to quiet her down. Amy was lying next to her mom crying and shaking. She was shaking almost uncontrollably. Sarah was holding Amy tightly in her arms, while silently asking God to help them. When the shooting started a new fear that was overpowering and a terrorizing feeling enveloped Sarah and her daughters. When Lucy saw the first arrow that slashed through the wagon's canvas cover she buried her head and cried as she had never cried before.

The Pawnee stopped their steeds about a hundred yards passed the wagons. They regrouped for their counter attack. This time the charge would end at the wagons with hand to hand fighting.

John knew what was coming next. He knew that the Indians would not pass them by the second time. All he could think about was his precious Sarah, the girls, and his sons. This was not the way their lives should end. He was supposed to protect them from this kind of life. What if the Pawnee takes Sarah and the girls, rape them or makes them trophy squaws for the Braves? Tears, caused by fear and anger began to well up in John's eyes. Why would God let this happen to them, that question kept racing through his mind. In what might be his last moments on this earth he was determined to kill as many of those bastards Indians as possible. If the Indians were victorious that day he was going to make them pay a dear price for their victory. He would not stop defending his family as long as he had the breath of life that God had given him.

As the Pawnee staged their final charge back towards the wagons, their numbers had been reduced by at least ten. Those ten Indians had either been killed or wounded during the initial charge. The Pawnee leader thrust his rifle high in the air, yelled as in triumph and started the charge back to the wagons. Suddenly, the shrill war cry's stopped. The charging Pawnee brought their horses to an abrupt halt. In a matter of seconds, the Pawnee had reined in their mounts and turned their direction to the north, towards the first of the high Kansas hills. They whipped their horses into a frantic sprint up the steep incline towards the first hill's knoll. It was all happening so fast even John couldn't figure out what was going on.

It was Jacky that yelled first, "Poppa…. look!…. Look who's coming……..I think it is our friends….. the Kiowa." Jacky thought he recognized the Indian on the front horse.

Indeed it was the Kiowa. They had been shadowing the little wagon train for days. When the family left the farm seven days earlier the Kiowa were watching. Now, the Kiowa were defending the McCrumb's in a battle against the Kiowa's hated Pawnee enemy. Not only were they defending the McCrumb family, the Pawnee had violated the Kiowa territory and now the Pawnee had to pay the price for their trespassing ways.

The Kiowa war party had over sixty warriors and was being led by the Kiowa chief, "Big Tree". It really wasn't a war party that the Pawnee wanted to engage in battle. As the Pawnee reached the top of the knoll they realized that the Kiowa had them trapped. Half of the Kiowa braves had positioned themselves half way up the opposite side of that first hill. Other Kiowa were riding towards the Pawnee from their flank. Then there were the Kiowa they had almost met in battle on the side of the hill where the two covered wagons were. A tragic and major defeat were about to befall on the scalps of that renegade group of Pawnee.

It was almost an hour before the Kiowa chief "Big Tree" and his braves rode back to the wagons of the grateful McCrumb's. Five of the Kiowa braves had stayed behind with the McCrumb's while the rest pursued the Pawnee. During that hour Sarah and the children had time to calm their nerves and rid some of their fears. The initial reaction from John and his family were tears of joy and many hugs of love. Jake was included with those tears and many hugs of relief. It was a Godsend for relief to the pioneer travelers, a relief to be alive and safe.

It was a rare experience for the McCrumb girls to be that close to the Indians. They were always in the far background when their pa did the trading with the Kiowa. Lucy was fascinated with how handsome the Braves were. She timidly offered some of them cookies that she had baked for the journey. When they accepted her kindness she was overwhelmed with pride. She wanted so much to be friends with them, but she knew that would probably never happen. Maybe, she wished, there might be other Indians in her future that she could befriend. They couldn't all be like the Pawnee. And, in her future, that wish would come true.

The boys were intrigued with the handmade knives, Tomahawks, bows, arrows, and beadwork on leather items. Both of the boys were stunned when they were both offered gifts of a knife and a beaded sheath. Each of them was given a bead work pouch and bear claw necklaces. One of the smaller Braves handed Jerald a beaded handled tomahawk. Each of the girls was given some beadwork items including a beaded necklace. Lucy's favorite was a beaded pouch from one of the young braves she had given a cookie.

John thanked "Big Tree", the Kiowa chief for saving his families lives. They exchanged personal and private conversations for a few moments. Then the chief gave John and Jake some trophies of the battle, which included a number of Pawnee items. Two of the gifts were scalps.

Sarah was given a special necklace from the chief, made of silver, abalone shell, and small nuggets of gold and bear teeth. These were treasured gifts that would never leave the McCrumb family. They were reminders of a time in their lives when unknown friends of a different race had saved their lives. It was a very valuable lesson learned by the McCrumb and Banks families.

Before the Kiowa departed from the area where the Pawnee had attacked the small wagon train they helped the McCrumb's to round up their scattered life stock. One of the trail horses had been killed by a Pawnee bullet. John gave the Kiowa two of the trail horses in gratitude for their life-saving help. John still had five trail horses, plus the wagon horses and their riding mounts. The trail horses could be used on the wagons or for mounts if needed.

Both John and Jake agreed that it would be best if they made camp for the night. It was getting late and everyone needed the rest after such a traumatic day. It was not only a physical rest everyone needed, everyone really needed an emotional rest. It was important that Sarah and the girls were allotted time to calmly talk about their emotional fears and anxieties from the day's terrible events. The boys also needed to be reassured by their pa and Jake that the fear and the terror they had experienced that day was normal and did not make the boys in any way cowards. The talks were not as critical for the boys but were definitely needed for the girls.

The conversations around the camp fire that night were emotional and extremely intense. The discussions were not only beneficial but very supportive for everyone. Before they had decided to call it a night Jerald had asked his pa if he, Jake, Jacky, and his pa could ride over the hill to where the Kiowa had encountered the Pawnee. At first, John declared a quick, "NO"! It was a resounding and adamant "NO".

He didn't think it would be a proper scene for the boys to experience. After a few calm moments of discussions, Jake convinced John that the boys were old enough and should see that kind of a tragedy. It would be a valuable life lesson for the boys. Lucy also wanted to go, but John said no. She just could not understand why it was all right for the boys to go and not her. She reminded her dad that she was much older than the boys. John reaffirmed his unyielding "NO", but Lucy was not about to give up her request. It was Sarah that finally put a blunt stop to the conversation. Lucy was staying with the wagons!

The last decision that was made that night before everyone found sleep was; the wagons would roll again the day after "tomorrow".

Jake, John, and the boys had their horses saddled at dawn. Each one had secured their weapons either on their side or on their horse or both. It took them almost a half an hour to reach the knoll of the hill where the Kiowa and the Pawnee fatal battle had been fought. The spot they were looking for was a half mile further to the east and down in the valley between two hills. John could make out two dead horses and maybe a third. The bodies of the Pawnee braves were harder to distinguish at that distance. The Kiowa had taken all of the Pawnee ponies that had not been killed.

Their ride to the area where the deadly fighting had taken place the day before was slow and cautious for the four cowboys. The closer they rode to that patch of land where the dead Pawnee laid the tragic reality of death set in for the McCrumb pioneers. John was having second thoughts about his decision in allowing his sons to witness such a horrific tragedy.

The four of them dismounted their horses about twenty feet from the nearest corpse. At first glance, John could tell that the body had been gravely violated. Neither John nor Jake counted the bodies; it looked to be about eighteen or twenty in all, which meant that the Kiowa had taken some of the Pawnee as prisoners.

Jerald and Jacky were very cautious in approaching the first dead Indian that was nearest the brothers. When they were close enough to get a really good view of the corpse Jerald suddenly turned, went to his knees and began to puke. Jacky just stood there for a moment in a stupor type trance of disbelief. Then he turned and ran back to his horse. He fell to his knees and vomited. That was a moment in their lives they would never forget. It was a life learning lesson that would later strengthen their resolve for humanity.

Most of the bodies had been disfigured to different degrees. All of the eyes had been gouged. Some had their private parts disfigured and others had been damaged in the area of their hearts. Not all of the Pawnee had been scalped. John and Jake spent a couple of hours or so examining the area in the hopes of learning important details that could be helpful in any future encounters with other Indian tribes. There was evidence that some kind of wild animals had visited the field during the night. Before the four rode back to their camp both of the boys had managed to find new courage and joined their pa and Jake in exploring the ill-fated battlefield. As they explored the carnage neither Jerald nor Jacky had noticed the different items that their pa and Jake had gathered from the field where the deadly conflict had occurred. All of those items were carefully place in a large black leather bag that had a handle and a key lock. It would be much later in their lives before the brothers would learn the secret contents of the large black leather bag. John also made the determination that Sarah and the girls would not see the black bag's contents.

While the men were searching the battle area on the other side of the hill Sarah and the girls among other chores, were fixing food for the men's return. The mental terror of the day before was still a troubling problem for Lucy and Amy. Behind their cheerful façade was the memory of yesterday's terror still lurking just beneath those cheerful smiles? Sarah was doing everything she could to keep hers and the girl's spirits high.

That night was spent in preparations for the continuing journey the next morning. The evening's conversations were void of any reference to what had occurred that morning exploring the area of the Pawnee and Kiowa battle that had occurred the day before. Lucy was the only one who tried to get answers about the morning findings where the Pawnee's had been killed. Sarah finally had to take Lucy aside and demand that she be quiet. No one wanted to talk about the massacre in front of the girls. Sarah had some reoccurring pains during the day and she was anxious for the camp to go silent.

Sarah's physical problems were never far from her. The pains that troubled her would come and go giving her off and on discomfort. When the pain would reach a level where she couldn't disguise it in her facial expressions she would make an excuse to be by herself. Her constant worry was what would happen to her family if she wasn't there to love, comfort and take care of them. Sarah was a realist; she knew that her illness could separate her from her beloved John and children at any moment of any day. Sarah was very religious and that became her greatest comfort; she put her life and the fate of her family in the "Hands of God!"

The afternoon and late evening of the eighth day out from the start of their pilgrimage west by the small group of pioneers finally came to an end. The night would bring relief to all. This night John found comfort in the sounds of the prairies midnights magic music. As he lay next to his beloved wife he thanked God for their blessings of the day. He didn't tell his family about one of the private conversations that he and the Kiowa Chief had the day before. Chief "Big Tree" had told John that a band of his Braves would shadow the two wagons until they reached the Colorado Territory. That was a great mental relief to John as he lapsed into a deep and sustaining sleep.

The McCrumb's and Jake were well on their way west at the crack of dawn on the ninth day of their journey from the Kansas farm. John was hoping they could make Hays City in two days. The little wagon train might be able to do it if they had two long days of travel time without any incidents. He figured that Hays City was between fifty or sixty miles in front of them. There they could get more supplies or anything else they determined they might need for their continuing trek west. They also could seek any available traveler's information concerning the journey into and through the Colorado Territory. Or, maybe they could obtain some news of other wagon trains traveling to the Great Lake of Salt. Maybe the Army Commander at Fort Hays could supply them with possible travel information, or at least inform them of any locations of cavalry posts in the Colorado Territory. There might even be a doctor in Hays City that Sarah could see concerning her physical problems.

John had heard that Hays City in its infancy was a desperado's city of choice. In about 1867 the Kansas Pacific Railroad had temporarily established a cattle station there. It wasn't long before cattle tramps and low life riff raft made it to the town. In the late 1860's the city hired a notorious gunslinger as a special marshal to help stop the killings and clean the human trash from Hays City. But Wild Bill Hickok, the new marshal, just made matters worse. After killing two soldiers from Fort Hayes Hickok dramatically left the city before he was confronted by the military. Hickok's next stop would be Abilene, Kansas. By the early 1870's the railroad company moved the cattle business in Hays City to another location and the human trash followed, leaving the city a much safer place to live. John also heard that the famous William "Buffalo Bill" Cody had something to do with the town's founding, but wasn't quite sure what it was. All he really cared about now was the fact it was a safe corn growing community where he and his family could buy and maybe trade for their continuing journey west.

The next two days on the bumpy and rocky Smoky Hill Trail was completed without any difficult incidents, but Hays City was nowhere in sight. John had somehow miss-calculated the distance and their travel time. Now, he wasn't sure how far they were from Hays City or the Colorado Territory. His only option was to just keep moving west until Hays City came into view.

The next morning the wagons came to a spot where the Smoky Hill River ran its banks not far from the wagon trail. The fresh clean water was appealing to the girls. Sarah and the girls begged their poppa to stop the journey for some bathing time. Sarah told John that this would be a good location to wash a bunch of dirty clothes. The pioneers needed fresh drinking water and there were other female personal reasons to stop. The boys quickly joined the ranks of the begging. It didn't take Jake long before he was singing the girl's song in begging to stop. John didn't stand a prayer of a chance in winning this argument. Deep down he already knew that he was going stop anyway.

The girls followed the river on foot to where there was a sharp ninety-degree bend in the river. That extreme bend in the river would give the girls complete privacy except for any prying four-footed animal eyes. Where they decided to bathe wasn't very far from the wagons and was within shouting distance of the men. After shedding their smelly clothes the men used the river waters that were next to the trail and wagons to bath their dirty and stinking bodies. Sarah had told the men that she would give them plenty of notice before the girls would make their way back to the wagons.

Sarah and the girls had their garments peeled off faster than the guys did. The girls were having a great time being able to bath naked in the cold river water alongside their mom. During the concern of bathing one's self there sure was a lot of splashing games being exercised and enjoyed between Sarah and the girls. Both of the girls were tall, slim and comely just like their mom. The girls had their mom's physical beauty, curves, and shapes, all in the right places.

Their mom and pa never knew that back at the Kansas farm the girls would saddle their horses and ride far out into the hay or corn fields and take their clothes off and run naked through the fields. It was a freedom for them that they totally controlled as they wished. They were almost caught a couple of times by their brothers, but they just laughed it off. They didn't consider their brother smart enough to even realize what the sisters were during. Boys were just too dumb at times, they thought.

After all of the cleansing and bathing, Sarah and the girls washed all of the dirty clothing. The wooden water kegs were drained and fresh water replaced the old. All of the stock was refreshed. The men went upstream and caught a mess of fish for supper. After a few hours, the small wagon train was again moving west.

There still wasn't any site of Hays City on the twelfth day of travel which caused some genuine concerns for John. He felt that Hays City would surely appear on the thirteenth day after leaving the farm at Alma. So far the weather had been pleasant without rain or too much wind. There was still a lot of snow on the mountain tops in the far distance. The wagons were always halted and the stock situated and cared for before dusk of each night. When dusk would finally gather into darkness the evening supper was served and singing or word games were played until it was time for slumber. There was always that uneasy feeling of apprehension of what the night's unknown message could bring to the camp. It seemed that the McCrumb's and Jake had been traveling for weeks, not days.

Just before the dawn of the next day the two wagons and their teamsters were once again heading west. After traveling for hours there still wasn't any indication or site of Hays City. John's anxiety was slowly turning into a modest panic. He didn't make any outward appearance of panic, he didn't want to cause alarm for his family. Jake had the same worry and concerns as John. About an hour before dusk they finally saw the outline of buildings on the horizon.

It was Hays City! Finally!

As they neared the town two riders on horseback were making their way towards the wagons. John could make out the shape of a shiny badge on the jacket of one of the riders.

"Good evening folks. I'm Bill Tibbets the sheriff of Hays City and this is my deputy Mike Burrows. Have you been traveling long?"

"A little over a week" John answered. "And we are very glad to see you and Hays City."

"Where do you all hail from?" Was Mike Burrows' question after John's response.

"We're from Kansas, Alma Kansas, on our way to Salt Lake City." John was quick in answering the deputy's question.

"Well, welcome to Hays City folks," The sheriff appeared to be very sincere in his words of welcome. "We don't get many visitors to our city anymore and when we do they are surely our welcomed guests. Follow us and we'll show you where you can place your wagons. How long do you plan to stay?"

"Not sure, maybe a day or two." John responded, "We're going to need some extra supplies and a doctor if you have one in Hays City."

"We have both supplies and a doctor for your needs." The deputy reassured John.

With an ongoing conversation as they rode towards the town John and Jake related to the sheriff and his deputy their encounter with the Pawnee and how the Kiowa had helped them. Both the sheriff and deputy were surprised and somewhat bewildered that the Kiowa had intervened on the side of the white man. John explained that his family had a long-standing relationship with the Kiowa. Even that revelation stunned the two lawmen.

During the continuing conversation, John and his family followed the sheriff and deputy to a suitable spot to camp the wagons. The sheriff suggested they eat supper at the local eatery. He also volunteered to get them clean rooms for the night at the local boarding house where they could have a refreshing bath. The boarding rooms and the eatery were in the same building. Everyone enthusiastically agreed that was a great idea.

The sheriff reassured John the wagons and their contents would definitely be safe through the night. This was the first real feeling of relief John had experienced since leaving the farm. After their second bath since leaving Alma Jake and the McCrumb family eat a hardy meal in the Hays City's best eatery. John had the biggest steak the cafe' could find. Jake had the next biggest steak. Sarah wasn't very hungry, but she ate anyway so John wouldn't worry. She hadn't let on in front of John the extent of her pains.

John Knew! She couldn't fool him; he knew she wasn't feeling well. They would see the Hays City doctor on the morrow. The children enjoyed their meals, especially the berry pie desserts.

Early the next morning Jake and John checked the contents in the wagons; all was still in place and secured. The sheriff walked John and Sarah over to the doctor's office, which also severed as the doctor's home. He was an older gentleman who had been doctoring for over forty years. John figured if the doctor had been in Hays City for that long of time he probably had patched up a whole lot of bullet holes. The examination consisted mostly of questions and some finger thumping. He gave Sarah some home remedies for pain, sickness and a possibly a far-reaching cure-all for everything else. They all tasted like medicine. He didn't charge them anything, just wished them well on their trip to the west. John decided to stay in Hays City for a couple of days to give Sarah a chance to rest and relax.

The residents of Hays City were extremely helpful to the small caravan of folks from Alma, Kansas. The ladies of Hays City were especially pleasant to Sarah. They engaged her in caring conversations and provided her with sincere heartfelt comfort. The McCrumb girls made quick friends with some of the girls that lived in town and a couple who lived on farms near the town. And, both girls managed to find time for a couple of flirtation gestures towards some of the boys in town. Jerald and Jacky managed to capture the imagination of the town boys with their fascinating story's about the Pawnee raid and the Kiowa items that were given to them.

John and Jake purchased the needed supplies plus extra ammunition for their weapons. They re-examined the wagons for any small items of damage that they might have missed after the Pawnee raid. They inspected the wheels, wheel spokes, and grease casings and found them in good condition. They checked the axles, back bolsters, wheel brake blocks and made sure the wagon tongues had no cracks or breaks. Everything was checked and readied for their return to the Smoky Hill Trail after spending three days in Hays City. The wagons would roll again on the seventeenth day of their journey to the west. The sheriff and some of the Hays City residents bid the caravan "God's speed" on the morning of their departure.

John didn't have the slightest idea what day of the month it was when the two covered wagons once again began the journey to their western destination. He didn't know if it was the last week of March or the first week of April. He had forgotten to inquire while in Hays City and he had misplaced the ragged calendar he had been using to mark off the days. The calendar would turn up sooner or later he kept reassuring himself.

The night before they departed from Hays City John diligently went over all of the information he had gotten from Fort Hayes. He knew that some of the information just might be old and not precise or accurate. Any information or communication to be had in the western territories at the best was days old, if not weeks old. There was constant sordid news of Indian raids in the Colorado Territory where white settlers were massacred. There were also reports that some of these raids resulted because white merchants and ranchers had attacked the Indian villages. Then there were reports of the Cavalry and Indians engaging in battles with each other. The commanders at Fort Hays had told John that it was mainly the Ute Indians to worry about. If John and his family could reach Denver and the Overland Trail north without incident with the Ute Indians the rest of the journey to Salt Lake City would be fairly safe. "*Without incident*", were the two significant words that really troubled John.

Historical recorders had indicated that the Ute Indians had lived on the lands of Colorado, Utah and southern Wyoming Territories for hundreds of years, maybe thousands of years. Before the white man showed up on the scene the Ute tribes were primarily farmers growing corn, beans, squash, and potatoes. They were one of the first Indian tribes to utilize the use of the horse. Over the early years, they had developed expert horsemanship. With their agile ability on the horse, the buffalo, elk, and deer became an extensive source of food and fur for the Ute, not only for their own use but also for trading with other tribes.

With the wide-ranging use of the horse early in their history the Southern Ute in Arizona began trading with the Spanish. They would raid other Indian tribes and capture prisoners to trade to the Spanish for horses, guns and other items. The Ute gained a reputation as fierce warriors.

The major disruption to the Northern Ute, those in the Colorado, Wyoming and Utah Territories came with the influx of Mormons to the area of the Great Salt Lake. With the arrival of more Mormons every year from 1850- 1860 the Ute were continually being pushed further back off of the land they had claimed for centuries. Finally, many of the Ute resisted with raids against whites settlers they considered interlopers. In the 1870's the US Government interfered and began designating Indian Reservations for the Ute to live on. Some of the Ute resisted and fought back against living on a Plot of ground designated by the white man where a Ute could and could not live. At times the raids became vicious and deadly. The more the Indian raided whites and killed women and children the more the white man fought back, and with greater numbers and superior firepower. On many of the raids where the white man was engaged, the Calvary was also involved. Sometimes the raids on the Ute were instigated by white renegades and loose minded soldiers. These types of raids usually ended up with the killing of Indian women and children. Of course, the Ute would retaliate with savage revenge.

A lot of this type of back and forth fighting was happening in the late 1870's in the exact spot, at the exact time in the Colorado

Territory where John, Jake, and the McCrumb family would be traveling in just a few weeks. This was that "*Without Incident*" that John was worried about!

John had calculated that the Colorado Territory was still seven or eight days of travel time from Hays City. That calculation was of course without any unforeseen incident that might hinder their journey. They would stay on the Smoky Hill Trail which was next to the Smoky Hill River. Both the river and parts of the trail went all the way to the boomtown of Denver in the Colorado Territory. The river would keep them and their stock in fresh water daily.

The source of the Smoky Hill River originated in the high plains of the eastern Colorado Territory at the foothills of the Rocky Mountains and just above the growing town of Denver. The river flowed east into western Kansas, then to central Kansas next to Hays City and the city of Salina, Kansas. It was at Selina Kansas where the McCrumb's began their journey on the Smoky Hill Trail. After flowing by Salina the Smoky Hill River would disappear into the larger Kansas River.

The days came and went unimpeded for the small group of pioneer travelers. It was on the twentieth day after leaving the farm that both John and Jake thought they caught a glimpse of a band of Kiowa that had been promised to shadow the small wagon train. After conservations between the two, due to the sighting, they concluded it was the Kiowa. They were thankful that they had not encountered any other Indian tribes. They were sure it was because of the Kiowa that no other Indians had bothered them. The next day was the twenty-first day of traveling from Alma and fresh meat was getting low. John decided the men should hunt for fresh meat. Dried meat was getting old to the taste buds. They had plenty of fish from the river and rabbits that were killed along the trail. Now was time for fresh meat from larger animals.

It was early morning when the men started their hunt for wild game food. They parked the wagons next to the Smoky Hill River. Jerald went with Jake while they hunted for larger game and Jacky went with his pa. They agreed not to wonder any further than a mile or so from the wagons. John left his Parker shotgun with Sarah for protection. She was to fire it if the girls needed help. They had other rifles to use if needed.

The guys saw plenty of rabbits, a couple of porcupines, but no large game. Not even a wild razorback hog. After a couple of hours, the empty handed hunters were becoming discouraged with their lack of success. All of the sudden the quiet late morning air was shattered with multiple gun shots that were all coming from the direction of the wagons. The gunshots lasted less than a minute, and then there was complete silence. John and his hunting comrades were momentarily paralyzed with fear of the unknown. They all started to run at the same time back towards the wagons. Harsh and terrifying thoughts were pouring through each of their minds. Each feared the worst; hostile Indians.

They were a little more than a mile from the wagons when they heard the gunshots. The faster they ran through the trees and underbrush the farther away it seemed the wagons were. What seemed like hours were only a few minutes before the wagons came into view. At first glance, Sarah and the girls were nowhere in sight. No Indians were in sight either. Everything seemed strange and vacant of any life. When the guys got close to the wagons they could hear the girls, but still, could not see them. As they came around the wagons the reasons for the gunshots became visibly explained.

Sarah and the sisters were standing a few feet off of the trail with shotgun and rifles still poised for direct action if need be. Between the girls and the river lay the biggest black bear Jerald or Jacky had ever seen. Everyone just stood in place, stunned, petrified, and absolutely in total disbelief.

Jake was the first to move from his rigged position. Very slowly he approached the bear with increased caution. There wasn't any movement from the bear that Jake could detect. He got about five feet from the bear when a spontaneous muscle spasm jerked the bear's legs. Everyone liked to have peed their pants because of the instant fright. In fact, the two sisters did or already had a slight accident in their panties.

After that initial shock wore off everyone started to laugh. Actually, it was only a halfhearted laugh. Jake turned towards John and slowly uttered some profound words.

"John, this poor damn bear didn't stand a chance with all of these bullets holes in him."

Everybody had cautiously moved closer to the bear.

"Damn Sarah, this is one of the biggest bears I have ever seen" That was John's second comment after hugging and kissing her. His first comment was just after he had taken her in his arms, and said, "Thank God you're alright!"

"Next time John," Jake lamented," we should send the girls out to hunt for meat and we'll stay close to the wagons."

Jacky and Jerald were all over the bear claiming trophies.

"I want the bear's head", Jacky snapped.

"So do I." was Jerald's quick response.

They both claimed an equal share of the bear's claws and teeth.

John joined the fray with, "Hang on there guys, you can't take out the teeth and keep the head too. It's either one or the other."

"Hey,….. all of you guys,..…just wait a darn minute here." Now it was Lucy's turn to control the discussion. ""Who killed that there bear anyway?........... I didn't see either one of my brothers doing any shooting………. Did you see them doing any shooting at the bear momma?"

Sarah just smiled, shook her head and said, "No."

"Well, Then!" Lucy snapped. "That settles it! ………….I guess that means momma, Amy and me gets the bear teeth and claws………And, we just might give you each a claw or just maybe a tooth, ……….if you ask us really nicely." With that said both Amy and Lucy started to laugh and dance around the bear.

Sarah explained to the men just what had happened. After the men had left to hunt for game Sarah and the girls went down to the river to look for pretty rocks or anything else they could find that appeared to be interesting. After the rock excursion, they decided to dangle their feet in the river for a while. They lost track of time until one of them mentioned that the guys might be coming back to the wagons soon. They put their shoes back on, picked up their guns and started back towards the wagons when they heard this horrid grunting noise. That's when they saw this huge bear lumbering on all fours across the river thirty or forty feet downstream from where they had been standing. Within a split second, they all started running back towards the wagons. When the bear reached the same side of the river the girls were on the bear started to run towards the area where the girls had been standing. When the bear did reach the spot where Sarah and the sisters had been dangling their feet in the water the bear rose on its hind legs.

Later, the girls would boast that the bear must have stood fifteen to twenty feet tall. Actually, the bear probably stood maybe seven or eight foot tall. It was a big black bear, but not overly big for this part of Kansas.

After the bear stood upright it took a few steps forward toward the girls, but the kid's dogs kept the bear at bay with their barking and nipping at the bear's feet. Sarah was not about to take a chance that the bear might eventually leave and all would be well. The Pawnee didn't get her family and neither was this hairy bear. She told the girls to start shooting those guns and aim for the bears head.

The bear story would get bigger and better each time it was retold around the camp fires.

It took Jake and John the rest of the day to skin the bear and cut away the desired parts for food. They extracted the bear's claws and its teeth. It would have been impossible to preserve the bear's head because of time and decay. They buried the head along with the rest of the bear's carcass. They put large rocks on the covered grave in hopes of keeping other animals from digging up the bear's remains. The dogs were rewarded with choice parts of the bear for food.

Jerald and Jacky would have taken credit for all the skinning of the bear if they thought they could get away with it. The girls took the claws and teeth down to the river and washed them clean than they laid them out to dry. The two boys tried their best not to show how irritated they were with their sisters. Under their breaths, they plotted how they could finally end up with the majority of the teeth and claws. To say they were upset and infuriated would have been an understatement.

By nightfall, everyone was ready for more bear stories. The bear skin had been stretched for drying, the bear meat was salted down, claws and teeth dried and food had been prepared for the evening meal. It really had been an unusual day for the traveling pioneers. John made the comment that he would have many exciting stories to tell his grandkids someday.

Any calming sleep that night was difficult to be had, because of bear stories, bear dreams, possible bear noises, and of course some male frustration for not having any bear claws or bears teeth in their possession.

At dawn on the twenty-second day into their journey, the Alma Kansas pioneers were ready to roll once again. Stories about the day before still took command in the general conversations. Jerald and Jacky were still grumbling about their sisters and the fact they did not own any of the bear claws and bear teeth. The sisters were all smiles and giggles at ever chance they had by dangling bear claws and bear teeth in front of their brothers. Sarah was thankful that everyone was safe and well. John and Jake were focused on the journey and the task ahead of them.

Sarah found the beat-up old ragged calendar and everyone agreed that this day in their journey was the 7th day of April 1875. It was also agreed that Sarah would now take charge of the calendar and mark the days off. If John's calculation were anywhere near correct the two wagon train caravan should be rolling into the Colorado Territory on or about the 12th of April. Neither John nor Jake expected any major problems or difficulties while still in the state of Kansas. Both were worried about what was before them in the Colorado Territory. They still had a couple of small rivers, really just streams to cross, and they shouldn't be any hindrance.

While the wagons were rolling either John or Jake would scout ahead of the teams of horses and whichever son wasn't controlling a wagon team he would be driving the life stock. Jacky would be on the wagon one day and Jerald the next. Sarah would take turns riding on the wagon with the girls one day and the boys the next day. Depending on how she felt other times Sarah would rest in one of the wagons. John had arranged a place where she could lie down. So far the weather had complemented their trek to the west. There hadn't been any rain and the temperatures were still mild, cool at night and in the mornings and not too hot during the afternoons. That would change in a few weeks.

They had only seen a couple of very small buffalo herds in Kansas, but they were sure that would change. There had been reports that there was still large herds of bison roaming in the Territories of Colorado, Wyoming, and Montana. At least that is what was told to John back at Fort Hays.

In the 1850's and 1860's Kansas had hundreds of thousands of buffalo roaming the state. As Kansas was being settled by the white man from the east the buffalo was being pushed, slowly at first, pushed farther to the west and to the northwest. By the late 1870's that part of Kansas where John and Sarah had settled most of the buffalo were gone. There were still small herds here and there, but even they were vanishing. Kansas farmers and buffalo hunters were killing buffalo for two reasons: one, the Buffalo was destroying farmlands in the farmer's opinion; two, there was a huge eastern market for buffalo hides, buffalo skulls, and buffalo bones. The hides were made into coats, the skulls were displayed as trophies and the bones were crushed to make fertilizer, buttons and in some cases dishes.

The Alma pioneers had seen a few small herds way off in the distance during their twenty-one-day journey so far. John was hoping to personally witness one of those monster herds he was told existed in some of the western territories. It wouldn't be long before his wish would be granted, but not in the way he wanted it to happen.

The 12th of April came and went without any celebration ceremony. There wasn't any way to establish just where the small wagon caravan was; Kansas or the Colorado Territory. The landscape all looked the same in all directions. If there was going to be some kind of a Colorado Territory celebration it would have to be at a time when they actually knew where they were. And, this surely was not that time.

It had been a number of days since anyone really had the opportunity to take a refreshing bath or any kind of an occasion to half way clean themselves. John figured it was time to do just that. It had been about four days since the river had come close to the trail to even be seen by the travelers. John informed everyone that the next time the river came into view and if there was an easy access to the river the wagons would stop so everyone could refresh themselves with a clean bath. Actually, it was not John who made the decision for the bath stop, it was Sarah's decision. Sarah did not ask John if he would stop the wagons, she told John that he was going to stop the wagons so she and the girls could bathe themselves. She told him if the men wanted to stink and smell like a pig pen that was fine with her, but she and the girls were tired of smelling like a barnyard.

Sarah also wanted an opportunity to wash out some clothes. Some of those clothes that needed to be washed were private garments suitable to just ladies. It wasn't easy for ladies and young girls on these long wagon train journeys. Especially when it involved their personal hygiene or personal relief of natural body functions. All a man had to do was find a spot behind a horse or tree to pee. He could go behind any old bush almost anywhere and squat to poop. And, nobody would say anything or even really care. A lady or young girl couldn't get by with just a tree of a bush. They demanded a more secluded privacy. Sarah had procured a couple of medium sized tin buckets back in Alma for her and the girls to use in the wagons when needed. It wasn't always pleasant when they had to use them, which was every day, but it was all they had. They surely weren't going to go behind a horse or squat behind some dirty old dusty bush. It was even embarrassing for the girls when they had to empty the tin buckets at night. They were sure the boys, or their pa, or Jake was surely watching them when actually none of the guys had any idea what they were doing. Most of the time it was the guys who were worrying about the girls when the guys were trying to find a sheltered spot to pee or poop at night. The girls did know what the guys were doing, but never really cared.

On the 13th of April, 1875, on about the twenty-eighth day on the trail after leaving the farm in Alma, two very important events occurred. Both events were important to the traveling caravan of two covered wagons and the seven pioneers. Each event had a different degree of importance to each of the travelers. The first and probably the more important event happened early in the morning of that day. It was the sighting of the Smoky Hill River and its proximity in relationship to the trail; only a few yards away and with good access from the trail. The girls were extremely delighted. So were the boys but to a lesser degree.

The second important event was declared by John and Jake!

"Listen up everybody!" That was John in his most official sounding voice. "Jake and I wish to officially declare that of right here on this day, we are in the lands of the Colorado Territory. We're over half way to our planned destination and everybody has done a really good job at getting us this far on our journey."

After a couple of congratulatory yells, everyone prepared themselves for the river event.

From where the caravan was at this point the trail was becoming more challenging to recognize causing travel time difficult. The landscape had dramatically changed from large rolling hills, trees, rocks of all sizes and bushes that were typical in the State of Kansas to a vast open expanse of flat prairie land as far as the eye could comprehend. It was a different kind of a world to the travelers. There were no places to hide. There were no places to find shelter. Way out there on the western horizon, they thought maybe there may be the faint outline of a range of mountains. Even that was elusive. This part of the vast Colorado Territory was void of any defining character. It was a strange land to these new visitors.

John and Sarah thought Kansas was void and desolate when they first settled there, but this new country was far more void and desolate of life than Kansas ever was. Kansas was a Garden of Eden compared to this new strange territory of desolation. Jake and the children didn't know what to make of this new landscape. They didn't have anything to compare it with. Scouting a new trail would not be all that difficult. But making sure there were no holes, gorges or things to impede the wagon wheels was the important aspects of scouting for a reliable trail. There would be streams and maybe rivers to forge. They could handle that type of problems when and if that time came.

The Smoky Hill River would always be in close proximity and in the sight of the two wagon masters. Jake had been promoted without fanfare with a new title of assistant wagon master, whatever that meant. No one seemed to know when that promotion occurred, or if it was ever announced.

The two wagons were now rolling west-northwest towards the town of Denver. The small wagon train was about one hundred and fifty miles from Denver. John was not sure just how far away Denver was from this point in theirs travels. He couldn't even make an educated guess. Maybe two hundred miles, maybe, he thought? The total miles from Alma to Denver were approximately four hundred and fifty miles. But there were no official calculations in miles from one point to another point in 1875. Everything in traveling time or distance in the western territories was just a matter of a good guess or old misused information from some trapper or miner.

Crossing the vast prairie of the Colorado Territory was slow and rigorous because of the rough and bumpy landscape. The wheels had to be checked every night for fractures or loose connections. The men were always finding loose bolts and wagon body parts that had separated or were separating. It was a constant effort in keeping the wagons in good rolling conditions. If one of the wagons should lose a wheel on the trail that could put the small group of pioneers behind schedule for days. At this point, they couldn't afford the loss of time. Supplies were getting low and everyone was weary; with both mental and physical fatigue.

On the 15th of April, the small band of travelers woke up to an unwelcome surprise nor one they would ever forget. The night before they made camp Jake had mentioned to John that the land and terrain appeared different somehow. The sage brush and foliage were gone in both directions of north and south which left a barren area of a couple of hundred yards wide and just as desolate as far as the eye could see in the other two directions. John agreed but didn't think any more about it.

The thunderous sound that shattered the still morning air on the 16th of April in 1875 sent a terrifying and frightful chill through the pioneer travelers from Kansas. The deafening roar abruptly woke everyone up in the camp. It sounded and felt like one of those tornadoes that the McCrumb's had seen and witnessed in Kansas. That was Sarah and John's first thought; a tornado. That was until they looked to the south and saw what was really causing that menacing sound.

It was Buffalo! Thousands of stampeding buffalo, "maybe millions of buffalo", Jacky later lamented! As far as the pioneers could see in any direction; it was buffalo!

John and Sarah quickly scrambled everyone into the second wagon and told them to hold on tight. Jake scattered the life stock towards the east out of the way of the main path of the trampling herd of bison. The wagons were on the eastern fringe of the Buffalo herd's powerful path to the north. If the wagons became involved in the middle of the main charge of the bison herd both wagons would undoubtedly be destroyed and anyone inside the wagons would be trampled to death.

A single thought that was running through both Sarah and John's mind was, "Pawnee, bears and now buffalos." Also, another thought did pass through their minds momentarily." We could be home in bed on the farm!"

The charging of the behemoth animals was causing the ground under the wagons to rumble and shake like a massive earthquake would cause. The ferocity of the vast numbers of pounding hooves was causing extreme anxiety and genuine terror with the Kansas pioneers that were cowered in the covered wagon. At times the Buffaloes were charging on both sides of the two wagons. Part of the eastern edge of the buffalo herd was brushing against and dangerously close to the wagons. Every time a buffalo would slam into a wagon there would be crashing sounds and the wagons would shudder against the massive weight and size of the bison's power. There were times when John thought the wagons would collapse under the weight of the charging animals. Jake and John were continuously trying to calm everyone that everything would be alright.

Jerald kept asking the same question.

"Pa won't this ever stop?........They're going to tear the wagons apart and we all will be killed!"

Everyone had gotten into the second wagon away from the stampeding buffalo. The first wagon would give them protection if the charging hoard of buffalo became too much for the wagons to withstand. The Buffalo would crash into the first wagon leaving the second wagon somewhat protected. Everyone thought the thundering noise and creaking wagons would last for hours. Sarah was convinced there were millions of buffalo stampeding around the wagons. Everyone was afraid to take a chance to get up and look outside of the wagons. The girls were in tears as were the boys. It must have been twenty or thirty minutes before the thunderous clamor of snorting animals began to diminish. Finally, the trembling ground became an eerily motionless emptiness and the sound of beating hooves was vanishing in the distance.

Movement in the wagons was practically non-existent. Fear had gripped everyone and it seemed the only thing to do now was to wait for the next deluge of stampeding bison to slam into the wagons. Slowly, very slowly, each person in the wagon made an effort to look outside of the wagon to see if the buffalo were really gone. John was the first to chance a look. He could still see the tail end of the herd as the bison made their wild stampede toward the north. Eventually, after everyone had finally managed to find a degree of courage to leave the wagon, one by one they each managed to stand on the trampled ground that the wild buffalo had churned. They all just stood in dead silence, gawking in amazement. There was a sense of bewilderment at what had just occurred. It was like a terrifying and strange dream. But this wasn't a dream, it was strange, it was very terrifying, but it was very real and definitely not a dream. There was an awesome and overwhelming silence before anyone spoke.

The first sound that anyone heard was the "nanneee" sound the goat was making. Everybody started to laugh seeing the goat running towards them at a horse like a gallop. The goat's quest ended at Amy's legs wanting to be petted. The bull and cows were not far from the wagons all huddled together. Mike and Molly, two of the wagon horses were making their way back to the camp. More of the horses could be seen in the distance. The scattered stock would be rounded up later.

Now Jake and the McCrumb's could see just how close they had come to death's door. John knew that the herd of buffalo had at times encircled the wagons during the stampede, but he was amazed at just how far the wagons had become part of the bison's charging corridor of destruction. It was a miracle the wagons withstood the onslaught as well as they did. He could see some damage to the front wagon, but it would take some close observation before they could determine just how much damage had been done. The width of the damage that the Buffalo had caused to the landscape was at the least two hundred yards wide. The earth within those two hundred yards was chewed up as if it had just been freshly plowed. It was an awesome sight for the Kansas Pioneers to envision.

Jake was the first to notice what looked like a buffalo lying on the ground in the distance, or maybe it was one of the horses that had gotten itself trampled to death under the buffalo's stampeding hooves. John told the boys to make sure the saddles and items they had thrown under the wagons were still all there and still in one piece. He told the girls to help their ma clean up around the wagons. John and Jake made their way toward the animal Jake had spotted. As they closed the gap between themselves and the downed animal they could tell it was a buffalo. But, a bigger surprise awaited them; it wasn't just one buffalo, it was two buffalos; a damaged cow and a very young calf laying next to her. The calf didn't make any effort to move, just laid there and made a kind of whimpering sound. The cow made a halfhearted effort to get up, but couldn't.

"Look at that leg." The sound of Jake's voice was a voice of concern. "It's broken in more than one place. I think her neck might be broken too…… John, this cow is dying."

John's answer to Jake's statement was determined and to the point. He took his forty-five caliber revolver from its holster and put a mercy bullet into the buffalo cow's brain.

"Now what? What are we gonna do with the calf? Do we kill it?" That was Jake's quick question after John had put the young female buffalo out of her misery.

The gunshot had alerted everyone back at the wagons. The boys started to run towards Jake and their pa. Sarah half-heartedly told the girls to stay where they were. They weren't having any part of that. If the boys were allowed to see what the shooting was all about so could the girls.

Both John and Jake just stood there scratching their heads seeking an answer to Jake's question. The boys, Lucy and Amy solved the answer to Jake's question the second they saw the buffalo calf. They made a sudden stop just a couple of yards from the dead cow and her calf. Both their mouths and their eyes were wide open with expressions of excitement. Within seconds Jacky was on his knees hugging the calf. Jerald was only a second behind Jacky. Lucy and Amy were just seconds behind both boys.

The McCrumb kids were all over the calf with loving touches and hugs.

"I guess we're gonna keep It........, Right John? I really don't think you have much of a choice, do you poppa!" Jake quipped with a broad smile on his face.

"What in the hell are we going to do with a baby buffalo?" John quizzed while shaking his head.

"We'll make him part of our family." Lucy pleaded to her pap.

"What do you mean... Him?.... What if it is a girl?" Jake questioned, jesting with Lucy.

"If it's a girl then she can be another sister in the family." Lucy shot back thru a big smile on her lips.

John, in his sternness voice possible, but still keeping an understanding and compassionate flavor to the sound in his words, warned the two boys and the two girls of rules concerning the buffalo calf.

"That little fella doesn't belong to anyone of you!. He can be a friend too........." John stopped in mid-sentence. He turned to Jake with a red face to ask the delicate question.

"Jake," is it a boy or girl buffalo?" Now, it was Jake's turn to become little red faced.

"How would I know?" Jake stammered as he tried to shuffle the question elsewhere.

"Well, can anybody tell me if it a boy or girl buffalo?" John asked the question again. His face had returned to its natural color by now.

Everyone just stood there looking at each other. The silence was deafening.

"OH for crying out loud, can't any of you big brave men tell the difference? Somebody pick the baby up so I can look. I can tell if it is a boy or girl buffalo." Lucy enjoyed not only being in control of the situation, she also enjoyed putting her pap and Jake, also her brothers in an embarrassing situation.

"Well, come on." She demanded, "let's see if he has a "peedee" or not!"

Jerald, with a flushed face, managed to get up and then picked the little buffalo up high enough that everyone could see the gender.

It was Lucy again, laughing and shouting loud enough for her mom to hear back at the wagons. Even the prairie dogs heard her.

"Well look at that guys!" She was laughing so hard she could hardly get the words out of her mouth. "It doesn't have a "peedee" guys, I guess that means it's a little girl buffalo. Ain't that sweet?"

John had just about enough of his daughter's gleefully digs at the men.

"OK Lucy," John acknowledged her little digs. "That's enough. We're all getting your point. Don't buy back the farm!"

John continued, "Now let me finish what I was about to say a minute ago before Lucy had her fun with us. "The little girl buffalo doesn't belong to anyone of you, but she can be friends with all of you. OK? NO fighting over her. And, all of you are going to have to take care and feed her. If you don't do this I will do away with her. Now carry her back to the wagons and show your mom."

Jacky picked the calf up then he and Jerald headed back to the wagons.

"Pap, you really wouldn't shoot this poor little creature, would you?" Lucy stammered with tears welling up in her eyes

"Poppa, you can't kill our new friend." Now it was Amy turn with tears starting to flow.

John regretted that he had used those harsh words. He really didn't intend to kill the calf. He got down on his one knee and hugged both of his daughters, drawing them close to his chest.

"My sweet and beautiful girls….. NO……. I promise you both that I will never hurt your new friend……... I promise!" Now, John had tears rolling on his cheeks. "Now go with the boys and find some cow milk for your buffalo friend. Jake and I have some work to do on this cow… now get."

The girls kissed their dad on his cheeks than left to go back to the wagons.

Lucy turned and threw her dad a hand kiss, "I love you pap, and I love you this much." As she made a gesture with her arms outspread.

"Their pretty special girls John, you're a very lucky man to have three beautiful women in your life," Jake commented as the two men watched as the girls running hand in hand back towards the wagons.

"Yeah, I do know that they are very special and I am truly lucky." John agreed.

John did know how fortunate he was. He thanked God every day for the blessings of his family. He was so proud of his two sons. Jerald and Jacky were becoming men far before their age. Jerald always took responsibility with a sincere determination and dedication. Jacky did also, but Jacky was more deliberate than Jerald. Jerald was quicker to antagonism, Jacky was more cautious, but just as dangerous when pushed too far. Both sons would stand hard when confronted with adversity, difficulties or danger of any degree. And no one had better touch their mom or their sisters, for if they did, they would never touch anyone else.

Both brothers had many battles royal against each other, and that was OK. But, if either one of them was being confronted to battle with anyone outside of the family, both brothers stood together to make sure the fight was fair. Every boy back in Alma, Kansas understood it was not a good idea to confront either of the McCrumb brothers. And God help anyone if they ever touched one of McCrumb sisters. When Jerald turned 17 Jacky was already a full inch taller than him and Jacky was still growing.

Lucy and Amy were John's two beautiful princesses. Lucy was the bold one and Amy the shy one. Both of the girls were delightful and beautiful like their mom. Lucy was two years older than her sister. The sisters were best of friends and trusting confidantes. Both girls stood about five foot five inches tall, with a slender body carriage. In the bright sunlight, their hair seemed to turn a little sun glow red, other times their hair was a radiant auburn. Each had a number of secrets from other family members, but there were no secrets between the two sisters. Both were very intelligent and quick with a ready response to any question or situation. Because of Amy's shyness, she relied on Lucy's boldness to talk to boys or grownups. And, most of the time, even though they would hesitate to admit it, they loved and admired their brothers.

Sarah was John's queen and she could do no wrong. No women could be loved more fervently than Sarah was loved by her husband and her children. Sarah was the thread of strength and the foundation of faith in the McCrumb family. Her health had been fragile since giving birth to Lucy on the long and sometimes violent boat voyage from Scotland to the Americas. After landing in the new world she gained some of her health back for a while, but in the last couple of years, her health had begun to decline once again. Sarah knew that her health was failing, and she accepted the reality that her days on this earth with her family were fading. And, because of her strong faith, she would leave that final day of departure to her God. She was doing everything in her power not only to prepare John and the children for that day but also to give them the strength of faith to endure when that day came. Her legacy would be the character of her children and God's blessing to her beloved John. But right now she was here, and that was all that mattered.

John wiped away a couple of tears and turned to Jake telling him they needed to take the hide of the buffalo and harvest some buffalo steaks before dark settled in.

They hadn't gotten too far into the skinning before Jerald and Jacky showed back on the scene. The brothers wanted to help their pa skin the bison. It didn't take the four of them long to skin the hide from the buffalo cow. They carved out some buffalo steaks, rump roasts and some meat for the dogs. The boys salvage the horns so each one could have one. Jake kept the tail and John some of the teeth. John told the boys that they needed to gather the stray stock that hadn't wondered back to the wagons. But, before he could finish his statement Jerald grabbed his pa's arm and pointed towards the wagons.

"Pa, isn't that a man standing next to the wagon?"

John whirled around and squinted, to get a better eyeball focus on the wagons and the girls. There was a man standing next to one of the wagons, a really big man. John's adrenaline surged. He told Jake and the boys to leave the hide and meat and then he started to run back to the wagons. Jake and the boys were right behind him. The man was talking to Sarah and the girls. They didn't appear to be in any kind of difficulties or danger. Sarah motioned to John that everything was fine and they were not in any danger. When John got close enough he could see two pack horses and a riding pony. John thought that this big guy must be a mountain man who was following the buffalo herd. He was really a big man, well over six feet in height. He had a heavy beard and his clothes were all made of animal hides. Even his shoes were built with the leather of some kind of animal.

This strange looking man in animal skin clothes nodded his head with a friendly gesture towards the girls then turned to face the approaching men. The harsh feeling to defend or attack had lessened in the frantic attitude of John's defensive instincts. He now realized this man of the mountains was not a threat to Sarah or his daughters. His fast pace had slowed to a casual walk as he approached this new visitor. The large man took a few steps toward John with his right arm extended.

"Howdy, my name is Jeremiah Austin." His deep resonating voice matched the hulk of his size. "I have been following these "Buffs" for about a week now. Never expected to run into any white folks on this hunt. Indians, maybe. White folks, no."

"I'm John McCrumb." John tried to sound in control without giving away any indication of fear or anger. As he placed his hand into the welcoming palm of Jeremiah's hand he was astounded at the size of this man's hand. He guessed that Jeremiah stood at least six feet seven or eight inches tall. Jeremiah's demeanor radiated the manner of a gentle giant. At least gentle as long as he wasn't agitated or pushed to anger.

"I see you folks got trapped in the "buff's" wild stampede this morning. You folks are really a lucky people. Those "buff" can really do damage. I see'd them take out a whole Indian camp in the Wyoming Territory once. It was a small band of Ute Indians that started this "buff" stampede."

John could tell right away that this big man was a talker. Maybe it was because he hadn't seen any white folks for some time, or maybe it was just by nature that this big man liked to talk. Whatever it was, John wasn't going to tell this giant to shut up. Let him talk John thought to himself, just let him talk. Jeremiah still had John's hand firmly buried in his huge fist.

"I was hunting the "buff", and taking some down too when the Ute butted into my hunt. That's when I knew I would have to track the "buff" down again, after the stampede. After a stampede like this one, there is always a few of the buffs who get themselves killed in the rampage. I salvage those skins too. I see you got one out there now. I hunt the "buff" and the "Grizz" for their hides than I trade the hides for guns, ammo and food staples. Been doing this for over twenty years. I speak Ute, Lakota, Comanch, and a couple of others Indians."

After that salvo of words, the big man finally lets John have his hand back. This is the kind of a man you want as a friend John thought to himself. John noticed that Jeremiah's two pack horses were loaded down with buffalo hides. Maybe this mountain man had just about as many hides as he could handle? Maybe Jeremiah was almost ready to call his hunt for the "buff" hides finished? Maybe he would consider sticking with John's family on to Denver and then to the Mormon Trail? Maybe?

It was getting late afternoon and John and Jake, with the help of Jeremiah, finished the skinning of the Buffalo and the taking of some choice buffalo steaks. Jeremiah also cut out the buffalo's tongue and liver; it was good eating he insisted. Jeremiah looked for the kidneys, but Jake had already captured the kidneys for his own "Bon Appetite" delight.

"Jeremiah." John asked, "Would you stay on if Sarah and the girls cooked us up some supper? And why don't you spend the night here in camp with us."

"Thought you'd never ask." Was Jeremiah's quick reply?

"Good!" John felt better now. After supper, John would ask Jeremiah the most important question of staying with the wagons on to Denver.

"Jeremiah!" It was Sarah's time to ask a question. "Just how do you prepare a Buffalo's tongue so you can eat it?"

"Ma'am, allow me to show you how that is cooked. Maybe the girls would like to taste it." Jeremiah started to laugh with a large smile; he looked towards the sisters with a very large grin.

"Maybe?" was Lucy's questionable reply.

Both girls had strange and doubtful looks on their faces after considering Jeremiah's offer of buffalo tongue. Both sisters loved to cook. They loved to prepare and cook different food dishes for the family when they were back on the farm. But buffalo tongue? UGG!

As the meal was being dished out by Sarah and the girls the boys politely refused the tongue meat. John and Jake tried a small piece of the cooked tongue and found it to be quite tasty; tasty enough to ask for seconds. Sarah passed on the meat, not knowing what effect it would have on her health condition. Both Lucy and Amy asked for a small second slice. Jeremiah had an amusing time watching the girls trying to be all grown up and proper while not at all enjoying the taste of the soft but somewhat grainy tongue meat.

"Well, pilgrim gals, how do ya like that buff tongue?" The question from Jeremiah was a sincere one. Both girls smiled and shook their heads in the affirmative. Jeremiah wasn't sure to believe them or not. But, it didn't matter, because he found the sisters to be beautiful and thoughtful young ladies.

Jeremiah had christened the group as the Kansas pilgrims.

Early the next morning the men, including Jeremiah began repairing the damage that the buffalos had caused to the wagons during the stampede. The extra wood and iron pieces that John had stored in the wagons before leaving the Kansas farm made the repairs much quicker and simpler. The major damage was to one of the wagon tongues. It had cracked under the weight of a buffalo falling on it.

While repairs to the wagons were being completed Jerald and Jacky rounded up the remaining horses that had been scattered during the buffalo charge. The goat, bull, and cows had come back to the wagons on their own. The wagon horses and all of the personal riding horses had also made their way back to the wagons, it was only the five extra horses the brothers had to capture and herd them back to the wagons.

By noon on the 18th of April, thirty-three days out from Alma Kansas, the two wagons, the livestock, Jeremiah Austin and the Kansas pilgrims (as Jeremiah called them) were once again ready to roll.

Jeremiah had figured it would take the travelers about six to seven days to reach Denver. The big mountain man had traveled to Denver many times before from many different directions to trade his furs and hides. It might take longer if they encounter bad weather or Ute Indians. He was more worried about the Ute then bad weather. He knew where all of the watering holes were and that was a huge plus for the McCrumb's and their two wagons because John had no idea when or where water might show up. He was relying on chance, luck and the occasional sighting of the Smoky Hill River.

Jeremiah wasn't fond of the Ute; he considered them treacherous and barbaric. He had had three different encounters with them in the past. The first time was during a trade. He traded two horses for ten buffalo hides, two knives with sheaths and a cavalry coat. The Indians called Jeremiah, "Big Mountain with Hair on Face".

The second encounter was a day later when four of the Ute tried to ambush him. They were attempting to recoup those ten buffalo hides that they had traded to Jerimiah the day before. Late that day Jeremiah found a good camp site for the night, it was near a high rock wall cliff formation and a small stream of water. He positioned his camp sight and a fake bedroll next to the rock wall anticipating a possible second meeting with the Utes. Jeremiah's instincts were right on target, the four Ute had followed him from a far distance. After he had made camp they followed the glow of his camp fire. The Ute staked their horses about a hundred yards from Jeremiah's camp. They skulked those hundred yards in true Ute style in an attempt to surprise Jeremiah or possibly catch him asleep. The Ute gave him more than enough time to settle in before they attacked.

Jeremiah had anticipated something like this just might happen. He had made a false bed roll with the buffalo hides and placed it next to the fire. He situated his real bed roll in the dark just out of the glare of the light from the campfire. It was a little after midnight when the four Ute attacked the false bed roll. Jeremiah was still awake and waiting in the dark shadows of the rock wall when the four Indians started shooting at Jeremiah's empty bedroll. The Ute moved very slowly towards the buffalo robes that they had anticipated held the sleeping mountain man. One of the Ute put two more rifle shots into the bedroll making sure in his mind that the mountain man was indeed dead.

Jeremiah had used the dim shadows of the rock cliff and the dark of night to maneuver to a more advantages position behind the four Ute Indians. Jeremiah let out a blood-curdling scream then shot two of the "raiding bastards", as he later called them. During the confusion caused by Jeremiah's earth shaking screams, and the barking of his rifle, the bewildered third and fourth Ute lost their lives to the blade of Jeremiah's long knife. It wasn't much of a struggle. His size was hard to overcome and those two Ute found that out the hard way. When all was said and done, all four Ute Indians had not only lost their lives they also lost their horses, their rifles, and their scalps.

The next morning Jeremiah located their horses and claimed them for his own. Two of the Ute had Winchester rifles. These were excellent items Jeremiah could trade in Denver. Plus there were bear claw necklaces, chest plates, and beaded items all would do well in trading.

Jeremiah's third encounter with the Ute was during the same buffalo stampede that had almost destroyed the McCrumb camp. Jeremiah had been tracking the buffalo for miles taking his time to position himself in the right spot to take a clean shot while not scaring the herd. He had already brought down two of the buffalo and was preparing to shoot the third when out of nowhere "those damn red skins showed up and stampeded the whole damn heard". The only times that Jeremiah used the phrase "damn red skins" was when he was really annoyed with Indians. The Ute never saw Jeremiah hunting the buffalo or if they did, the buffalo were more important. The only thing left for Jeremiah to do after the Ute outburst was to follow the buffalo's trail and salvage any trampled "buff".

Jeremiah had warned John and Jake to be on the lookout for any signs of the Ute because he was certain they would show up sooner or later. A wagon train had been attacked a couple of months earlier by the Ute. That wagon train was saved by a small cavalry patrol. The folks in a larger wagon train before that one had been massacred to the last man, women, and child. Most of the attacks were by small Ute raiding parties, not the main Ute nation. The larger Ute bands of warriors were either defending themselves or raiding other Indian camps or fending off the cavalry. It was a time in the American west's history when the Native Americans were desperately trying to keep the white man or other Indian tribes from claiming their holy lands. Jeremiah reiterated his warning to make no mistake, the Ute are always close by in this part of the Colorado Territory.

For the next two days, the Kansas pilgrims and Jeremiah's journey was uneventful except for a late afternoon heavy rain on the second day. The rain lasted little less than a half an hour. Long duration rainstorms on the Colorado prairie were a rarity. The wagons were camped early because of the downpour. A larger than usual campfire was built. They used dried buffalo chips to start the fire and wood that had been stored in one of the wagons to initially feed the flames. Sagebrush was an easy burn after it was thrown into the blazing fire. The hot intensity of the fire was used to dry wet clothes and other rain-soaked items that had gotten wet in the downpour.

Sarah and the girls fixed a hot meal for everyone. The night was going to be a cold one and a good hot hardy meal was a welcome comfort for the weary travelers. Everyone positioned themselves around the campfire to dry out, get warm, and swap stories, and ask questions. Most of the stories were told by Jeremiah about his encounters with Indians and living in the rugged Rocky Mountains. Most of the questions were also directed to Jeremiah.

"Jeremiah," Jerald was the first to question Jeremiah. "Is it true that the Indians don't like to be around crazy folks?"

"Well, I guess it depends on what you call crazy folks, Jerald." Jeremiah smiled as he responded to the young McCrumb's question. "Some Indians are crazy. In fact, sometimes I think all Indians are crazy. Now and then I wonder if I'm not crazy" Now Jeremiah began laughing with that deep robust voice of his.

"But is it true Jeremiah? Indians really don't like to be around crazy people? Poppa told Lucy and me that Indians are afraid of crazy people. Is it true?" It was Amy who quickly re-asks her brother's question. Amy had a genuinely concerned look on her face when she asked Jeremiah the same question that her brother had asked.

Jeremiah could hear the real anxiety in Amy's voice and a troubled look on her face. He realized this was not a joking matter with the girls. He recognized it was time for him to get serious.

"Amy, the Indians are very religious and superstitious at the same time, not like the white man. They believe that spirits live inside of things. Things like even rocks, trees, the mountains, the Buffalo, the wind, and people. They believe a crazy person has an evil spirit that lives in their heart and that evil spirit can and will bring bad luck to the Indian tribe's camp. They won't kill a person they think is crazy, because if they do then that spirit will escape and enter the heart of the one who is doing the killing. That's why they'll banish and not allow anyone they feel has an evil spirit in their camp." With that said, Jeremiah reminded everyone it was time to break up the camp fire powwow and get some rest.

"Time to get some sleep pilgrims." With those last words, Jeremiah got up and walked towards the night.

Sarah and the girls slept in the driest spot they could find in the chuck wagon, while the guys found the most convenient dry place they could find. It turned out to be a long cold miserable night for everyone.

Early the next morning on April 21, 1875, Sarah and the girls were busy cleaning up anything wet in the wagons and putting away the fire dried clothes of the night before. The men wiped down the saddles and were cleaning up any mess the rain of the day before might have caused to any of the equipment.

When the wagons began to roll Jeremiah had a bad feeling towards the direction they were heading. It was the correct direction, but he felt it was the wrong day to be traveling it. He didn't say anything to John or Jake, not yet anyway. He continued to look for those tall tale signs of nearby Indians. He didn't exactly see any signs, but in his gut, he felt those signs were there.

Just before noon, Jeremiah's fears metalized off in the distance. It was a small band of the Ute ten or fifteen braves. Jeremiah couldn't tell if it was a raiding party or a scouting party. He knew for certain it wouldn't be very long before he would find out. He told John and Jake to stop the wagons. The band of Indians stayed their distance from the wagons not making any threating moves just strangely getting on and off of their horses.

"Jeremiah, what are they doing? Jake quizzed the big man.

"I don't know.........." Jeremiah was slow to answer. "Maybe they're just messing with us........or maybe they're waiting for reinforcements...........could be sizing us up.....or waiting for the right time to............" He never finished that last sentence.

"What do we do if they attack?" was John's question.

They're not going to attack us......... not enough of them......... the party is too small" Was Jeremiah's answer. "Looks to be only about eight to twelve of them." "They won't take that kind of a chance to attack unless more show up........... I'm not sure what they're up to."

After about thirty minutes of the riddle of "on a horse, off of a horse, what, when, and where", was about to be concluded.

The band of Ute Indians had turned toward the caravan of two wagons and the eight pilgrims. Jeremiah told John to make sure all weapons were within easy hand reach. He told Sarah and the girls to stay in the cover of the wagons and out of sight.

He told John and Jake that the Ute were obsessed with white women. He told Jerald and Jacky to stay on their horses next to the wagons and don't show the first ounce of fear. Also to make sure their guns were in full view for the Indians to see.

When the Indians got close to the wagons, within a couple of hundred feet, Jeremiah told John and Jake that the three of them were going to ride out to meet the Indians. Jeremiah told both men not to show the first ounce of fear, always look the adversary square in their eyes and let him do all of the talking.

"If you see that I am going for my guns pull your guns and start shooting, blaze away with your weapons until all of those bastards are dead." That was Jeremiah's last words before riding out to meet the Indians.

There were ten Ute Indians in all. None of them had face or body paint, which meant they were not a war or marauding party. They were probably either a hunting or scouting party. A hunting party would have been much better than a scouting party. A scouting party would perhaps return to their home camp and return with more hostile intentions to do damage.

The Indians had stopped their horses, but the three men continued until they were less than fifteen feet from the Ute before they brought their mounts to a halt.

There was a moment of deafening silence. Jeremiah did not speak first, it was his choice. Finally, the lead Ute said something that Jeremiah later interpreted for John and Jake.

"Big Mountain with hair on face, we know you and your many adventures". That was the first word spoken at the beginning of the mid-afternoon parley between the ten Indians and three white men.

The conversation between Jeremiah and the Indians was all in the Ute Language and seemed calm and not in the least bit threating as far as John and Jake could make out. When the last words were spoken the Indians turned and rode back to where they had appeared. The three men rode back to the wagons without a word being spoken. Before Jeremiah dismounted from his horse he seemed disgruntled.

"We haven't seen the last of that bunch," Jeremiah's words were harsh and challenging. "They're smart enough not to come at us face to face but dumb enough to try something when they think we're not paying any attention.

"Damn bastards". Jeremiah spoke in a menacing tone.

The two wagons started to roll again among a lot of silence. Jeremiah rode a distance out front of the wagons by himself while John and Jake rode one on each side of the wagons. Everyone was taking Jeremiah's attitude as a warning of something imminent happening. Sarah was driving the chuck wagon horses, Mike and Molly. Lucy and Amy were in the back of the chuck wagon cautiously talking in almost whispers. Jerald was driving Scout and Barney, the other wagon horse team. Jacky was riding his horse "Wind" next to the wagon talking to his brother of things that might happen.

Without any warning, Jeremiah would at different times drive his horse at a gallop off in the distance where any sight of him would almost disappear. Then he would ride back to the trail almost a half of mile ahead of the two wagons.

An hour before dusk Jeremiah cautioned John that it was time to find a site for night camp and prepare for a likely long night. After camp was established Jeremiah took the men aside and a plan of action was discussed and responsibilities were determined.

All of the horses were to be tightly tethered to the wagons. There would be no fire, darkness was essential. All weapons were to be placed within hand reach of the owner. Night watch would be divided among the five men for every two-hour intervals. Jerald would take the first watch and Jacky the second. Jeremiah wanted it this way so the three men would take the most vulnerable hours between midnight and dawn. At the slightest sight or sound of danger, the person on watch was to immediately fire their weapon!

There was very little sleep accomplished that night by any of the pilgrims. All eight of the pilgrims were in a high adrenalin rush and danger alert. The only worrisome sounds during the night were the occasional howls of coyotes and wolves.

In the morning Sarah and girls cooked a quick breakfast for everyone. After the men had checked the wagons and the surrounding countryside the wagons were ready to roll. John told everyone to be cautious and observant of their surroundings. The morning was very hazy and the clouds were hanging close to the earth. Visibility for any distance sight was poor at best. Everyone on a horse was staying close to the wagons. By afternoon the haze had abated but the clouds were still hanging close to the earth. The distance visibility was much better which gave everyone a better view of the horizon.

Jeremiah could feel the presence of the Ute; he knew they were out there somewhere close by. His instincts were right on the mark. The ten Ute Indians had been following the wagons since the parley of the day before. The Indians had in their possession cavalry binoculars that had been taken during an engagement with a small cavalry patrol. The Indians had been watching the wagons from a far distance most of the day. Jeremiah was watching the horizon for any sight of the Ute with his own binoculars.

By nightfall, there hadn't been any sighting of the Indians, but there wasn't any doubt in anyone's mind those devil Redskins were still out there somewhere. Darkness came quicker than usual because of the darkening of a rain threatening sky. Jeremiah called for an early camp and warned everyone to prepare for rain and maybe some thunder and wind. It wasn't unusual for this time of year to experience these sudden on the spot short thunderstorms on the prairie. A person traveling on the prairie could see them anytime in the far distance almost every day.

This was the 37th day on the trail for Jake and the McCrumb's. It seemed like they had been traveling for months not days. Jeremiah figured they still had four days of travel before Denver would be sighted and that was too many days to be able to dodge the Indians. Everyone feared that this night was going to be a bad one. Preparations were made to battle both the storm and an enemy if this was what the night would bring. The regular schedule for the night watch was underway, Jerald first than Jacky and so on. About an hour before dawn a gusty and thundery and rainy storm deluged the two wagons and the eight shivering pioneers. The raging prairie storm would last less than an hour and would end at the first light of dawn as it filtered through the eastern sky.

The storm was not a good omen for the McCrumb's and their two friends. But the storm could give the Indians the cover they would need if they were to execute any plan of attack, which was really not an attack, but a plan to capture. The Indian's initial strategy was a night time hit and run raid, possibly making off with some horses. But with the ominous threat of a coming storm, their strategy changed. The storm would give the Indians the cover they needed for a much greater prize than just horses. Even though their numbers were small at only ten braves a violent storm and a very dark night would give them a huge advantage over their targets. And those targets would be the white women in the caravan.

As soon as the night brought darkness the Indians divided their numbers; eight of the ten set out towards the wagons on foot with the remaining two Braves staying behind holding on to the horses. The eight approached the wagons with careful attention not to be seen by any of the people in the wagons. Two of the eight Indians were positioned about hundred feet from the wagons. Those two were to start shooting if anyone from the wagons followed the six remaining in the raiding party. The remaining six Indians continued to move forward and settled within a few yards of the chuck wagon. Each small group of Indians had a very important part of maneuvering if this raid was to be successful.

The Indians settled in their positions until it was the right moment to execute their plans. The Pioneers had readied themselves as best they could to combat whatever force might threaten their safety during the night, whether it was the storm or whether it was Indians.

Lucy and Amy were huddled in the back of the chuck wagon. Sarah was asleep or attempting to sleep in the front part of the chuck wagon. The boys were in the other wagon struggling to go to sleep. Sometimes, Jeremiah, Jake, and John would walk the area around both wagons searching for any small signs of trouble. Other times they would just set in the night's darkness talking, but always alert to any encroaching danger. When the ravaging rain, the wind, and the thunder finally did burst from the dark sky the three men headed for the wagon where the two brothers were huddled.

That first burst of rain and ear deafening thunder was all the Ute Indians needed to finally execute their plans of taking the white women captive. All of that preceding day they had watched the McCrumb women's activities with the captured cavalry binoculars. They knew the women were in the chuck wagon. With that first burst of thunder, the six Ute rushed the wagon they thought the women were in.

The Ute used their knives to slit the canvas open at the back of the wagon where Lucy and Amy were sleeping. The Indians didn't see Sarah and they didn't have time to look. They hurriedly grabbed both of the sister's, lifted them over the back part of the wagons gate and out of the wagon. The sisters were caught totally by surprise and were jolted awake out of a tired and disturbing sleep. Just by human nature, the sisters started resisting the efforts of the Ute Braves. They resisted just by human instinct. The Indians clinched the palm of their hands over the girl's mouths than they quickly disappeared into the night and the pouring rain. The brilliant flashing of the lightning in the sky and crashing thunder were the Ute's unintentional accomplice in their plans.

The whipping wind drove the rain through the wagons cut canvas and on to Sarah. She awoke from a stressful sleep realizing that something was terribly wrong. She saw the outline of the cut canvas whipping in the wind and could see that the girls were gone. She crawled out of the chuck wagon and ran screaming to the other wagon. The men couldn't hear her screams until she got to the gate end of the wagon. All five of the men came out of the wagon with guns in their hands.

When they got to the back of the chuck wagon their worst fears were realized. Lucy and Amy were gone. Their first instinct was to give chase into the dark prairie in front of them. They couldn't see more than six feet in front of their face because of the darkness and the blinding rain. They were tripping over the sage brush they couldn't see. The two Indians that had stopped fifty feet from the wagons opened fire in the direction of the wagons hoping to hit or at least stop the men from following the six who had kidnapped Lucy and Amy. One of the men from the wagons gasps with a sound of pain. Somebody had been hit with a bullet. Jeremiah shouted to everyone to go back to the wagons.

Sarah was panic crying; John was trying to calm her down while a flood of tears was rolling down his cheeks. The two boys were crying and shaking with fright. Jake had a flesh wound to his shoulder from a bullet from one of the Indians who was shooting. Jeremiah was cursing the very ground that the Indians walked on.

Everybody wanted to follow the Indians right then and bring Lucy and Amy back. Jeremiah finally got everyone to calm their emotions to a point where he could reason with them. He finally did convince them that nothing could be done in the darkness of night and in a driving rain. Also, he reasoned that the Ute were going to also have a problem traveling at night in this kind of weather. He promised the hunt for the girls would start at the first break of daylight!

He told Sarah that she would have to stay behind with the wagons, but he promised her that the girls would be safe and they would be coming home. Jeremiah also worried that there was a slim chance the Ute could double back just to get Sarah while the men were scouting for Lucy and Amy. He knew it was only a slim chance, but there was that chance. He didn't mention that possibility to the other men, he kept it to himself. He needed all of the men with him when they found the raiding party, so he would just have to take that chance of the Indians not doubling back for Sarah.

By the first light of dawn, the horses were saddled and the five men were riding on the open prairie in pursuit of the savage Indians.

Jeremiah was a seasoned tracker, as good as and in most instances better than Indians. Tracking the Ute was made easy after the rain storm. He counted ten horses in the raiding party's tracks; none had left the raiding party. That was good news. It meant none were doubling back to the wagons. Jeremiah's tracking ability told him the Ute were only about an hour ahead of the five men. He could also tell the girls were being made to walk. He didn't tell John that, he didn't want him to worry. The Ute could not travel as fast as Jeremiah, Jake and the McCrumb's because of their two captives. That would give the pilgrims an advantage.

By noon the skies had cleared which gave Jeremiah and his group an edge in searching the horizon. It was mid-afternoon when Jeremiah saw something that made his heart stop. In the distance, he could see a form that looked like it could be a human body lying near a clump of small mahogany trees. He couldn't tell if his eyes were playing a trick on him or if the thing moved. He told John and the rest of the group to stay put because he wanted to do some scouting ahead and alone. John didn't like the sound of Jeremiah's request, but he would honor it. John was getting a bad feeling as he watches Jeremiah riding off and without a better explanation for going by himself.

The closer Jeremiah got to the object he saw lying in the shade of the small mahogany tree the more his stomach churned and the harder it was for him to breathe. It was what he had feared. It was one of the McCrumb girls, but he couldn't tell which one it was. Whichever one it was she was still in her nightgown and the gown was covered with blood mixed with mud.

....

Both Lucy and Amy were exhausted when Jeremiah had called for an early camp because of the possibility of a rain storm. They were so tired neither of them even wanted anything to eat. All they wanted was some decent rest and sleep.

After the girls said their prayers Lucy hugged Amy. "I love you Amy, and we're going to be alright. Pap won't let anything happen to us, I promise." Lucy knew that Amy was really terrified and she needed some reassurance that everything was going to be OK.

Lucy was just as frightened as Amy, but she was trying not to show it, even though she knew it was obvious to everybody. Everyone on the wagon train had their own level of fear resulting from the threat of Indians and nobody could really hide that intense feeling.

Both of the sisters fell into a very daunted and vulnerable sleep.

When that first clap of deafening thunder shook the wagon and when the torrential rain beat against the wagon's canvas top and the violent wind started howling and rocking the chuck wagon, both Lucy and Amy were jolted to a half awake consciousness. When the Ute Indians had grabbed them and was lifting them out of the wagon the girls thought maybe the wagon had been hit by a lightning bolt and the wagon was being overturned. Within seconds the girls realized what was happening to them. They both started to scream and struggled to resist their captor's kidnapping efforts. There wasn't much they could do, two girls against six Indians.

The Ute carried them into the darkness, into a cold driving rain. Both girls were freezing and their thin wet cloth sleeping gowns were sticking and forming to their bodies. They couldn't see their captors, it was too dark to see much of anything. They knew it was the savage red skins that had been following them for the past few days. All they could do now was continue to kick, scratch and scream. They knew no one in the other wagon would be able to hear them because of the rain and thunder. Within seconds the piercing sounds of guns firing were happening within feet of where they were. The girls couldn't tell if it was the savages shooting or if it was coming from the direction of the wagons.

With the driving rain and the girls resisting their captors it was difficult for the Indians to make any headway from the wagon where they had abducted the girls. When the Ute did reach their horses they found it even harder to get their captives to cooperate in getting on the horses. Finally, the savages gave up trying to get the girls on a horse. They decided to tether both girls at their wrists and make them walk behind a horse. That made traveling even more difficult. Most of the time both Lucy and Amy were being dragged by the horses. It was difficult for the sisters trying to walk over and through sagebrush; they were constantly tripping and falling over the brush. They were also barefooted which made walking very painful.

Finally, the Indians stopped and dismounted from their ponies from anger. They cut the leather tethers, grabbed both girls by their hair and pressed knives to their throats. The girls thought they were about to die right there in that rain storm. The savages didn't want to kill the girls, they were displaying a menacing rage in hopes it would scare the sisters to get on the ponies so traveling would be made easier. Their scare strategy worked. Both of the girl's feet were bleeding and their bodies were being ravaged from being dragged over the harsh bushes. Now, both of the girls were willing and eager to get on a pony.

Just before dawn, the rain stopped. Both of the girls were cold and exhausted from the trials of the past two hours. The girls needed to urinate but were afraid to say anything, so they just peed in quiet while riding on the back end of a horse.

It was about noon when Amy started to have severe stomach cramps. The cramps had started the evening before. She knew it was that time of the month for her menstrual period. She thought maybe she could use this time of the month to her advantage. When she finally got Lucy's attention, she pointed to her stomach and grimaced as if in pain, then pointed to the area between her legs. Then Amy pointed to her own head and made a twirling motion at her temple indicating the crazy sign. Lucy knew immediately what Amy's gestures meant but she wasn't sure just what Amy's intentions were. Lucy smiled and nodded her head in approval to whatever those intentions were.

Amy's menstrual periods were always followed with a heavy flow of a discharge of blood. The blood of her monthly had already started its flow and was enhanced because of the stress she was going through. Both girls were dirty and they're bodies were bruised and bleeding because of being drug in the dirt and over bushes. The bleeding from the cuts and gashes that they had suffered covered their bodies. Their hair was dirty and matted. Their nightgowns were filthy and torn. With a little effort from Amy along with her already disturbed and anguished appearance from the rough treatment from the Ute Indians and covered with lots of blood, Amy was going to go for the performance of her life.

Amy started to scream and whirl her arms in the air as if she was out of control. Then she purposely fell off of the horse and started to roll around on the ground. During the ground performance, she was endeavoring to get as much blood as possible on her clothes, face, and arms.

Lucy jumped off of the horse she was riding and started crying. She fell to her knees and raised her arms in the air as if she was praying. The startled Indians were taken by total surprise by the sister's dramatic and sudden actions. Some of them dismounted and stood in utter disbelief watching Amy in her torturous and shuddering motions on the ground. Suddenly Amy stopped, slowly got to her feet and with a piercing scream and pointed dramatically at the Indian she had been sharing a horse with. She stomped her feet and started spitting and wheeling her arms in the air.

Lucy decided to help Amy in her performance. She approached Amy as if to comfort her. Amy made use of Lucy's movements; she screamed at Lucy and made threatening gestures toward her. Amy grabbed hands full of dirt and threw the dirt at Lucy and up into the air.

Amy had managed to use her menstrual blood completely to her advantage. But, by doing so her exhaustion and her loss of blood were having a major effect on her strength and endurance. She was near the point of fainting. In one last grand gesture of insanity, she dropped to her knees and began to skulk forward towards the savage she had been riding with. She managed to cause saliva to dribble down both sides of her jowls. Her appearance was one of complete disgust; filthy dirty, torn clothes, disarrayed hair, cuts, and bruises and covered with blood. The closer Amy crawled towards the Indians the more confusion the Indians exhibited. She pounded the ground with her hands and started to spit and throw dirt at the Indians. She put dirt in her mouth and rolled in the dirt. She stood up and growled as she stomped her feet and charged toward the Indians. She fell with contrived spasms and began to kick wildly, then all of sudden she became absolutely quiet and still.

The Indians had become completely discombobulated and quickly backed away from Amy. They were demonstrating absolute fear, confusion, and extensive panic. Amy's performance was brilliant and had the effect she had prayed for. Lucy's face exhibited total panic, while silently thanking God for Amy's acting ability and for her safety.

The Indians quickly put Lucy back on a horse and made a quick retreat away from a possible dead and crazy white girl. Amy waited until the savages were out of sight then she slowly went into a curled fetal position on the ground. She was near an exhaustive faint. After a few moments of rest, she managed to crawl to the shade of a small clump of mahogany trees. Now she needed rest, lots of rest. She fell into an almost trance of a deep sleep, under the protection of the mahogany trees.

Amy was aware that it would be easier and safer for her Poppa and the others to save one girl than trying to save two girls. Now Lucy had a better chance of being rescued and that was Amy's reason for her performance. Her brilliant performance had worked!

....

Jeremiah wasn't an everyday religious man, he did believe in an "All Mighty God", just didn't think about it much. As he was looking down at one of the McCrumb girls his mind was begging God that she was alive. He hesitated before getting off of his horse, he was fearful he would find the girl dead. How could he tell John that one of his daughters had been killed by the Indians? Jeremiah was close to tears.

It wasn't often when tears or chills of joy could overcome the giant mountain man, but tears came to Jeremiah's eyes when he heard those soft words coming from the girl on the ground.

"Jeremiah, I'm so glad you found me. Lucy needs your help." Amy had rested and was gaining some of her strength back.

Jeremiah knelt beside Amy and hugged her in his massive arms. Both he and Amy were crying tears of joy.

"Everything is going to be OK Amy! We will find and bring Lucy back to safety. I'm making you that solemn promise. Now, you just lay back and rest for a while." With those words spoken Jeremiah went out in the open where the other men could see him.

He was waving his arms frantically for the other to come on. John's heart started to race and it felt like his heart was going to pound right out of his chest. He was sure that Jeremiah had seen something out there, but didn't want to tell John what he thought it was. Amy had gotten to her feet and walked out to Jeremiah's side. When John saw Amy he couldn't stop the flow of tears streaming down his cheeks. Jake was crying, the boys were crying, everybody was crying; Amy had been found alive and now was safe.

Amy ran to her poppa's arms and didn't want him to ever let go of her. When she finally did regain her composure she calmly related to the men what had happened to her since being taken captive earlier that morning. She was worried about Lucy's safety and begged the men to find Lucy. Her poppa was very proud of his daughter's strength, courage, and character.

It was decided that Jerald would take Amy back to the wagons and to her mom. She was still in her torn nightgown. The boys and her poppa gave Amy some of their clothes to make her more comfortable. She used some of the clothes to help make her monthly period more tolerable. The men had given Amy the privacy she needed to make the changes. John told Jerald to stay with the wagons and give comfort to Amy and his mom.

The four men now with a greater resolve rode after Lucy's captors with a more intense determination in getting her back safe and striking a harsh blow of retribution. John was determined that the raiding band of Indians who had abducted Lucy and Amy was going to pay a high price for their evil intent.

Jerald made the ride back to the wagons as easy and comfortable as possible for his sister. He knew she was tired and hurting.

Amy asked him a hundred questions, how was her momma and was her horse Ok. Did the storm do any damage to the wagons? Did any of the cows or horses run away? Is the goat OK? Are the cats and dogs OK? And of course, how is the baby buffalo? Jerald smiled at each question and was very happy to answer each one of them.

Sarah was still in a daze of grief and a motherly panic for her daughters. Her eyes were swollen from her continuous crying. As strong as Sarah was the thought of losing her daughters was almost more than she thought she would be able to endure. Especially if she was left knowing that Lucy and Amy were being raped and mistreated by savages. Living with that reality was almost not a choice she wanted to live with.

Sarah had spent most of the day scanning the horizon for any signs of riders. Her desperation over the girls was slowly turning into despair and hopelessness. All of a sudden she realized she was by herself, all alone and the thought of being all by herself scared her. The night would be all round her in a couple of hours and that loneliness would be magnified with darkness. She dreaded watching the sun inching its way towards the western horizon.

For a moment she thought she saw something moving way out there on the horizon. No, maybe it was nothing, just her wishful imagination. Yes, it was something! Or, was it? Now Sarah started to doubt her own judgment and wondered if maybe she was starting to hallucinate. She rubbed her eyes and closed them for a couple of minutes. She wouldn't look towards the horizon for a minute; she would give her eyes a rest. Maybe it was the strain of staring so long at the vacant landscape that might be causing her a blurred vision.

Now, she was afraid to open her eyes. How would she mentally respond if she saw nothing but a vast vacant expanse on the horizon when she did open them? She asked God to help her cope with any disappointment if all she saw was a vacant prairie. Slowly Sarah opened her eyes; she hesitated for a second before she lifted her head to that hope of seeing riders on the vast wasteland of sagebrush and loneliness. She wasn't hallucination; there was a rider, a lone rider.

She fell to her knees and the tears started to rush almost in an unstoppable flow. There was a rider, no; there were two riders on just one horse. Sarah tried to imagine what two riders on one horse could mean. Could it indicate tragedy or maybe it could suggest hope?

As the riders got closer Sarah recognized Jerald. She couldn't tell who the second rider was, except that rider was wearing men's clothing. It wasn't until the second rider started to wave that Sarah recognized her daughter Amy. A massive emotional weight was lifted from Sarah. She ran as fast as she could to meet the two riders. Amy jumped from the horse and fell into her mom's embrace.

When all of the cryings, hugging and kissing was finished Jerald carried his sister to the chuck wagon. She still didn't have shoes on and her feet were sore with cuts. Jerald took care of his horse and then tended to the stock. Sarah started a fire so she could heat water for Amy's bath. Sarah took the hot water and soap to Amy's cut and bruised body tenderly caring for her youngest daughter as she had when Amy was a baby. After Amy was bathed and finally clean of the physical misfortunes of the day Sarah gently rubbed balm on Amy's cuts and bruises. After her the bath, Amy happily put on some clean clothes. Sarah fixed the three of them a hot supper. Jerald lead the baby buffalo over to his sister. The little bison lay next to Amy as she stroked its wiry fur. During the supper, Amy recounted to her mom what had happened that day up to the time Jeremiah found her.

The relief Sarah felt having Amy back safe and sleeping next to her was reassuring, but the anxiety of not knowing what was happening to Lucy was causing Sarah to have a fretful mental malady. No matter how hard she tried to relax sleep was evasive and vague. Horrifying thoughts continued to race through her consciousness. All through the night, her silent sobs went from thankfulness for Amy's return then to sobs of anxious prayers for Lucy return.

John and his avenging companions were hot on the trail of the Ute captors. They were less than an hour behind the savages that had Lucy. Jeremiah suggested they stop now before the late afternoon turned into the dark of night. The search party needed to plan and figure out their strategy of action when they finally would confront the Ute. The utmost importance of that strategy was the safety of Lucy during the encounter. Freeing Lucy was their goal, but keeping her alive and safe was the ultimate results of that goal. If the Ute assumed their escape was in jeopardy they would definitely kill their captive. Any attempt at a rescue was going to be perilous and dangerous. Jeremiah was stumped on how to proceed. There were just too many of the Ute and that had to be challenged. He knew they could not attack the Ute out in the open during the broad light of day. That would give the Indians too much of an advantage. The rescue attack would have to be at night, but how? John's main concern was the safety of his daughter.

The answer to Jeremiah's and John's dilemma was just about to be answered but in an absolutely strange and unpredictable way. It was

John who warned Jeremiah of approaching riders from the same direction they had just ridden from. Jeremiah recognized the riders as Indians and they weren't Ute. He could tell by experience that these Indians were not a raiding party nor were they prepared to attack the four white men. There were five Indians in the small band riding towards them. Jeremiah wasn't quite sure but he thought the Indians could be Kiowa They weren't painted for battle; they were probably a scouting party hunting for game. John did recognize them; they were some of the Kiowa from Kansas. He knew the lead Indian, his name was "Two Elks". John knew Two Elks from their trading days on the Kansas farm. John had traded beef parts and staple foods a number of times with Two Elks in exchange for animal hides.

John walked towards the riders and welcomed them when they got close. They were the same five Kiowa that had stayed with the wagons while the other Kiowa braves chased and massacred the Pawnee that had attack the McCrumb's two wagons a couple of weeks before. It was the same five Indians that Lucy had given her homemade baked cookies too.

Two Elks had an elementary command of understanding and speaking the white man's language. He told John that he had heard from another scouting party that the Ute were following the McCrumb's wagons. That could only mean one thing; a raid on the McCrumb's wagons was imminent. Two Elks told John he wanted to help his friend from Kansas. The friend that had given Two Elks' family food during a server winter when food for Indians was scarce.

Jeremiah was able to speak and understand much of the Kiowa dialect. He explained to the five Kiowa braves how the Ute had abducted Lucy and Amy and now he and the other men were planning an attack to free Lucy. The five Braves made it known that they wanted to help free the girl who gave them the “round sweet bread”. They also would be delighted to take back ten Ute ponies to their camp in Kansas.

With the help of the Kiowa braves a plan of attack against the Ute in freeing Lucy would now be much easier, but still very dangerous. The safety of Lucy was still the most important part of any attempt to free her from her abductors. Jeremiah was pretty sure the Ute would make camp around dusk. He also knew that his group would have to stay a safe distance behind the Ute so not to be detected. Two Elks was certain that the Ute would leave at least one; maybe two of their braves behind, maybe about a mile to watch for following white men. If any followers were spotted the brave would warn the rest of the Ute and Lucy would surely be killed.

Before a successful rescue of Lucy could be affected the Ute Lookout brave or Braves would first have to be killed. With the enemies, lookout guards eliminated the remaining Ute would be unprepared for a surprise attack. Two Elk told John that he and another Kiowa brave would hunt for the lookout watchers and kill them. After the lookout sentries were eliminated then the remaining kidnappers would be surrounded and attacked.

It was decided that the rescue party would ride for a couple of more hours, then stop and camp an hour before dusk. They would wait until midnight then execute their plan to free Lucy. The time to kill the Ute Lookout could be accomplished any time after dusk had settled in on the prairie and that was Two Elks plan.

....

Lucy was certain that her pap and the other men would find Amy and tend to her hurts. Lucy prayed that her pap would eventually find her too. She turned for the last time trying to catch a glimpse of Amy before the horses had traveled too far to see her anymore.

Lucy was scared for her life and terrified of what the savages might do to her. Jeremiah had told her and Amy at one of their evening suppers back at the wagons that many Indians would only rape women captives after the squaws of their camp had stripped the captive of their clothes and had beaten them with sticks.

Riding on the back end of the Indian's pony had cause sores to Lucy's rear end and her thighs. She was afraid to hold on to the Indian on the pony. She held on the best she could to the blanket he was sitting on, but at times that wasn't enough.

She had fallen off of the horse twice. The second time she fell off the horse her head hit a small rock and she came close to losing consciousness. The Indians were anything but caring and they treated her harshly. That second time she fell off the horse the savage she was riding with yanked her up from the ground and threw her against the rump of the horse. She landed on the ground again. This time he grabbed her by her hair and shoved her back on the tail end of the horse. He took her arms and wrapped them around his waist. He was screaming at her. She couldn't tell what he was saying, but she knew he was really angry.

Lucy was on the verge of believing she was going to die not ever seeing her wonderful family ever again. She was terrified of what these savages were going to do to her. She thought about grabbing one of the savage's knives and killing herself. Because of her fatigue and mental distress Lucy's mind was losing its rational thought process. If she could only lie down for a while she thought, maybe everything would be alright. She was afraid they would kill her if she fell off of the horse again. She was so tired she involuntarily urinated and she could feel the warm urine running down the inside of both of her legs. She was afraid that they all would rape her and then leave her to die on the prairie. If only she could go to sleep, and maybe never wake up.

Lucy fell into a semi-trance on the back of that horse, she was no longer aware of her surroundings. Hitting her head on that rock when she fell off of the horse the second time turned out to be a minor blessing. It had caused a slight concussion that allowed Lucy to drift in and out of reality. It allowed her some needed mental rest.

She regained many her mental faculties when she was being lifted off of the horse and placed on the hard ground. She soon realized the Indians were making camp. Her vision was a little blurred at first, but with a few blinks of her eyes, she gained all of her vision back.

There was still some light in the sky, but night time was just a few minutes away. A small fire had been lit, but it wasn't close to her. She was cold and wished that the warmth of the fire would soon reach her. She tried counting the Indians, but something was wrong, she could only count eight of them. She knew that there were ten on horses. After counting three different times she concluded just eight Indians were in the camp. She wondered what had happened to the other two. She tried to move into a more comfortable position. Every part of her body was hurting, aching or throbbing. She still had her nightgown on and that pleased her.

She wondered if Amy was alright and safe. She was worried about her momma. She knew her momma would be sick with worry. She wondered if her Pap would ever find her. She missed the dogs and the little girl buffalo. She couldn't stop the tears from running down her cheeks. She knew that her cheeks were dirty and that bothered her. She was convinced that she stunk and she could smell herself and that upset her.

That Scottish heritage was starting to invade Lucy's disposition. She wanted to walk over and spit in the faces of all of the savages. She determined that she would not collapse to their barbaric whims. But, she must be careful and try to outwit them was her prayer. She was emotionally terrified and afraid for her life, but now she must stand fast as a McCrumb. That was her only hope of survival, at least her mental survival. But she knew that claiming mental strength might not be enough to withstand what could befall her physically. These were savages and they were capable of carving up a human being while they were still alive. Lucy wanted to close her eyes and go to sleep, but she was afraid of sleep.

It was totally dark and there was very little light surrounding her from the fire that had been started. All eight of the Indians were still squatting around the fire. They were eating something that looked like dead rats to Lucy and talking in low monotone voices. One of the Indians got up and walked over to where Lucy was and threw something on the ground next to her. She figured it was a piece of whatever they were eating. It was ghastly looking and made Lucy's stomach to turn sick.

The Indians fireside conversation went on for a couple of hours. Lucy hoped they had forgotten about her for the night. But when two of the Indians got up and moved towards her those terrifying fears she had felt when the one Indian threw her against the horse were once again being resurrected. They picked her up by her arms and dragged her over near the fire. They made her stand in one spot for a long time while all of the Indians stared and pointed fingers at her. One of the savages grabbed her by her hair and then put a knife to her forehead. Lucy could feel her knees starting to wobble as if they were going to collapse and send her to the hard and unforgiving ground. Her heart was pounding both in her throat and in her ears. She could feel urine rolling down her legs. She was shaking so hard she thought she could hear herself shaking. Tears were starting to blur her vision again. When she thought everything was coming to an end the savages all started to laugh and slapping themselves on their legs. The one with the knife took the knife and made Lucy hold it. But, she was shaking so bad her fingers just couldn't grasp hold onto the knife's handle. That made the Indians laugh even more.

The Indian picked up his knife up and shoved Lucy hard to the ground. He grabbed her hair yanking her back to a standing position. This was the same Indian that Lucy had shared a pony with. This was the same Indian that had knocked her to the ground after she had fallen off of the horse for the second time. Lucy wondered why this Indian seemed so angry towards her. She tried to understand what his reasons could be. Maybe, she thought it was because of losing Amy and only having one hostage now and not two. She was shaking so hard it was hard for her to stand. She was afraid if she fell he would cut her with the knife.

The smirking Savage ripped Lucy's nightgown from her left shoulder to just above her left breast. She could tell that her breast was not exposed. He took his knife and made a six inch cut just above her left breast. Lucy's body became completely numb. She couldn't feel her hands anymore, but her fingers were strangely tingling. She was trying hard not to fall or pass out. The Indian glared at her and a made a gesture as if he was ripping her heart out.

Lucy passed out. She crumpled to the ground in a lifeless clump.

The Savage grabbed her by one of her arms and dragged her back to where she was originally laid. Lucy's lifeless body just laid there motionless. It was if she had died and her body was recklessly tossed in a heap to decay. She laid there for moments without any movement. When she did regain her consciousness and fully recognized her surroundings the sharp pain near her left breast and the frightening feeling of warm blood oozing down her left breast caused Lucy to lapse into a mild state of shock. She was afraid that she might be bleeding to death. She was fearful of touching the knife wound. Her first reaction was to grab earth and any live or dead foliage on the ground with both hands and press the debris as hard as she could over the knife wound hoping the bleeding would stop. The cut was not deep and she did manage to stop the bleeding.

Lucy started to cry as she had never cried before. She tried hard not to cry out loud because she was afraid it would anger the Indian even more. The thought of, "why are they doing this to me" kept racing through her mind. Her prayers to God were more fervent than they had ever been. "God, why are You allowing this?" Was a constant question. "What have I done to deserve this?" Was another one of her pleas to God?

It was late and the Indians were finished for the night. They all positioned themselves next to the fire with their weapons close to their bodies. Lucy was afraid to shut her eyes in sleep. All of her body was still shaking from fear. She was ashamed and embarrassed for herself for peeing down her legs in front of these savages, even though it was involuntary. In her current dilemma, Lucy was trying to understand why these Indians and the Indians that had attacked the McCrumb wagons were so vicious. The Indians back at the farm and those that had helped to fight off the attack on the wagons were so nice. All of these thoughts had become jumbled and they were very confusing to Lucy. Her mind was whirling with fatigue, it needed rest, a lot of rest.

She thought, if her Pap didn't find her soon she would surely die at the hands of her captors. She knew that her father was worried about her safety and was frantically searching to find her. She wanted to believe that her Pap would come soon and save her. Lucy gathered enough strength to crawl farther into the darkness away from the sleeping Indians.

....

While Jeremiah, John and the rest of the men were making camp waiting for nightfall Two Elks and his companion departed on their mission of hunting down and killing the Ute lookouts. After they had tracked the Ute to their campsite, the next place Two Elks looked for was a location where he thought the lookouts would position themselves to watch for anyone trailing the captors. He was hoping he and his comrade would arrive in that area first and then surprise the lookouts after they had reached the same area.

The Ute band of raiding abductors were convinced that they had evaded and outwitted their pursuers. They knew that the men in the wagons couldn't track them in the storm. The Ute had crisscrossed and attempted to destroy any trail that an enemy might follow. They had sent lookouts to backtrack and watch for anyone that might be following them. Their size in numbers gave them a false sense of security. The two lookouts were just a matter of an obvious safeguard. They hadn't reckoned on an experienced mountain man or five Kiowa braves in the equation. They figured they were just dealing with a couple of inexperienced stupid white men from the east. They had dealt with this kind of white men before and white men always make many mistakes when dealing with the Indians, which was a major miscalculation on the part of the Ute.

When Two Elks had identified the area he was searching for the two Kiowa warrior's camouflaged themselves behind sagebrush. They were on foot; they had left their horses back at the camp site. Two Elks' experienced guess was the right guess. He had picked the exact area where the Ute were placing their lookouts. The Ute were using two of their braves to make sure the captors were not surprised and ambushed by any white men that might be searching for their female captive. The two lookouts moved to a position about a hundred yards from where Two Elks was hiding. At dusk when darkness was settling on the prairie Two Elks and his Kiowa companion slowly maneuvered their way within yards of the two Ute Braves. With very little effort and in complete silence both Ute Indians were silenced by deadly Kiowa knives.

Back at the McCrumb's campsite, Two Elks gave in detail the location of the Ute camp where Lucy was being held captive. Her rescue was just a few hours away. Jeremiah and Two Elks both agreed that any attempt at a rescue should take place a couple of hours after midnight. It was agreed that the Kiowa Indians would approach the Ute camp from the west and from the north. John and Jacky would make their entrance from the east. Jeremiah and Jake would make their attack from the south. The signal for the attack would come from Jeremiah and his deep thundering voice.

They would approach the Ute camp on foot. When they were about fifty yards from the enemy's campsite they split up and surrounded the eight sleeping Ute Indians. The campfire was still burning giving the rescuers a clean view of the sleeping captors. When they got close enough to the camp the first thing John and the others tried to do was scan the lighted area in hopes of seeing where Lucy was. They couldn't see her anywhere near the fire.

John was getting desperate, wondering if the Indians had her tied and hidden away from the camp site. Jacky was moving as quiet as he could close to the perimeter where the light from the campfire met the dark of night. A Chill almost stopped his heart when he heard a low whimper that sounded like a cry of a hurt animal. He couldn't see anything, but whatever was making that noise was really close. After he had crawled a couple of feet more he could make out a form that was silhouetted from the light of the fire and it looked like a human body laying on the ground.

"Could it be Lucy?" That was his first and wishful thought.

Jacky wasn't sure what he should do. Should he try and communicate with his sister, if indeed it was Lucy? If it was Lucy, how would he let the others know that he had found her? In a very soft murmur, Jacky whispered, "Lucy......... Lucy is that you? This is Jacky......... Lucy.....if you hear me be real quiet......Can ya hear me, Lucy?........ Lucy...... can ya hear me?" Jacky was whispering as low as he could not wanting to wake any of the Indians.

The low moaning noise had stopped and there was nothing but dead silence, only the crackling of the fire could be heard. It seemed like hours before Jacky heard the most beautiful voice in the world.

"Jacky...........is that really you?.............Is pap with you?......... Are you ....are you going to......save me?..........Please, Jacky.............please.......save me" Lucy could hardly get the words out over her choking on her tears.

That did it for Jacky, he couldn't stand it anymore, hearing his sister's sobs through her tears was just too much for him to bare. He knew that he had to do something or he would explode with excitement.

He made hs decision!

He stood straight up and started screaming, ready to kill the first Indian that got up from the ground.

"I FOUND HER!..... I FOUND LUCY!..... SHE'S ALIVE……KILL THOSE BASTARD SAVAGES!"

Nothing more was needed to be said. Seven avenging men, one avenging father, and an avenging brother descended on the eight Ute Indians like the worst tornado that had ever hit the State of Kansas. Those eight Ute didn't stand a chance of survival. Their chances of escaping death in a buffalo stampede would have had been better odds than where they were that night. Gunfire, knives and thirty seconds were all it took to send six of those Ute Indians to their mystical happy hunting grounds. It took another three minutes for the seventh Ute to join the six. The eighth Indian would later wish that he had been sent to the happy hunting grounds with the seven.

Jacky ran back to where he had found Lucy. He gently picked her up and placed her in her pap's arms. When John saw the condition that Lucy was in the tears of anger and joy cascaded down his cheeks. He was almost crushing her chest because he was hugging her so tight. Neither Jake nor Jeremiah could hold back their tears seeing this God given reunion. The five Kiowa wasn't holding back their emotions either. This was the gracious white girl that had given them her friendship with round cookies.

When John finally set Lucy on the ground he turned to face one of the surviving Indians. John's glare of hate could not be misunderstood, his anger of seeing his daughter in this condition was just too much for him to contain himself. John looked back at his daughter and for the first time saw the bloody gash and matted blood across Lucy' chest. He turned back to face the Indian and without a word plunged his hunting knife into the savages belly and twisted it before he withdrew the blade. Nine of the Ute were now dead.

When the last Ute was made to stand Lucy recognized this one to be the one who had mistreated her so badly. Just the sight of him caused her to start shaking in fear, this same fear of seeing him caused her to urinated on herself again.

"No!", she thought, "he cannot hurt me again because my pap is with me now."

Lucy was still dazed with fear and anxiety of just seeing this wicked Indian standing in front of her were causing her to have a slight seizure and she began throwing up. Her pap had stopped crying; now he was worried for his daughter's mental safety. She had been severely weakened from the trauma of the past twenty-four hours. She didn't dare to sleep after the eight savages had finally gone to sleep and after they had tormented her for hours. She was terrified that the mean one would come for her again. Now here he was standing in front of her. She couldn't control her frightful shaking. She didn't want to be sick and heaving up in front of her pap. Lucy grabbed her pap's hands and started to pray, "Thanking God for her rescue".

Lucy needed rest, but first, she needed something else from her rescuers. She wanted this cruel and cold hearted savage to never forget what he had done to her. Lucy asked her pap, Jeremiah, Jake and Two Elks to kneel close to her so she could ask a favor of them. She was so weak she could hardly speak. When they surrounded her she whispered her requests.

"The four men looked at each other in astounding bewilderment at the wishes she had requested. "Lucy, you are a beautiful McCrumb princess, your requests will be granted. Am I right men?" Jeremiah bellowed the words so loud it woke up all of the coyotes on the prairie. All four men agreed that Lucy's perplexing requests should and would be granted no matter how weird they might sound. The four men were all laughing at Lucy's bizarre and strange requests, especially Two Elks who was very pleased with Lucy's wishes. He told John that Lucy would always be a Kiowa sister to the Kiowa nation because of her bizarre way of punishing an enemy.

Lucy lapsed into a fatigued sleep. Now she was safe. Now she was in the safety of those who loved her.

It was day 39 days since the McCrumb's had left their farm in Kansas. It was early morning and there wasn't a cloud in the western sky. Lucy was still very sound asleep from her ordeal of the past forty hours. Her pap, her brother Jacky, Jake Banks, Jeremiah the huge mountain man and the five Kiowa braves were all watching this beautiful young girl as she slept. She was safe now and seemed at peace with the world. These nine grown men, well eight grown men and one boy marveled how someone so frail could have endured what Lucy had agonized through for the last forty hours. Her power of will, her mental capacity, and her physical stamina had been challenged far beyond a normal person's breaking point. Lucy survived and she would continue to survive any and all challenges the rest of her long life.

Her pap was worried how the horrible events of the past couple of day would affect his daughter's mental stability in the days ahead. Lucy was strong of body and had been strongly willed of mind, but now, what about now? Only time would answer that question.

John wanted to let Lucy sleep so she could gain back her strength. He decided not to wake her, just let her sleep until she woke up her on. He told Jacky that he needed to ride back to the wagons and let his mom and Amy know that Lucy had been rescued and that she was safe and well. Two Elks told John that he and his four Kiowa companions would accompany Jacky most of the way back to the wagons. The Kiowa were taking the ten Ute horses and their weapons back to Kansas with them and the wagons would be close to the trail back.

John told Two Elks and the other four Kiowa braves that he considered them as his Kiowa brothers. John thanked them for both their invaluable help against the Pawnee and for helping to free his Lucy from the Ute. Two Elks grabbed John's hand and made a gesture with his other hand that signified, from his heart to John's heart.

"I wish all white men were honorable like you, my pale brother." Two Elks spoke in broken English. He took a parfleche bag from his horse and handed it to John.

"Tell my pale skinned sister Lucy, that she is now called, "She, the Strong Eagle of the Sky". "Tell her that I am honored to give her this remembering pouch that holds her three requests. Tell my sister that I do not agree with her fourth request, but it has been granted as she wished. Tell my pale skinned sister that Two Elks did not kill the Ute savage as she asked, tell her that Two Elks left him to wander the empty prairie forever without moccasins or loin cloth and with the two body "hurts" that she had requested for him to remember her by."

Two Elks smiled a very broad smile; Lucy's requests had amused him, and at the same time they had delighted him.

Two Elks had good words with Jeremiah and Jake. They all would be brothers until the sun would set at life's end. The Kiowa rounded up the Ute ponies and their rifles for the journey back to Kansas. After Jacky had gathered his instructions from his poppa he and the Kiowa rode off towards the wagons. John watched his friends as they rode off to all of their tomorrows. He was glad Jacky would have traveling companions most of the way back to the wagons.

John wondered if Lucy would even remember what she had requested of the men the night before. Her requests were strange, especially for a girl. He could understand why a person might make those kinds of requests giving what Lucy had endured from the Ute. John snickered under his breath and wondered what Two Elks had done to the savage that had treated Lucy so badly. He wondered if Two Elks and the other Kiowa braves had really taken the Ute Indian and set him free, naked and without moccasins in the middle of the prairie. That was Lucy's fourth request. She didn't want him to be killed; she wanted him to suffer in shame as she was made to suffer in humiliation. John started to laugh to himself thinking, I bet Two Elks did just that and somewhere out there in the huge expanse of the prairie there is this lone naked and really sore Indian trying to walk in a straight line.

It was almost midday before Lucy finally woke from her enabling sleep. Her pap was sitting next to her waiting for his beautiful daughter to open her eyes. When she finally did open them and saw her pap sitting next to her she threw the coverings off of her and crawled into his open arms. Her tears of joy seeing her father couldn't be controlled, nor did she want them controlled. Jake and Jeremiah stood close by waiting their turn with the hugs. When she had calmed down and the hugging was completed Lucy was quickly becoming herself once again. Her questions came faster than one of those newfangled Gatling guns could shoot.

She wanted to know if Amy was safe. She asked about her mom. She wanted to know where Jerald and Jacky were. She asks her pap if she had really seen other Indians rather than just those who had kidnaped her. And, if she did where are they now. She quickly looked around to see if her Indian tormenter was still there. When she didn't see him she turned back towards at her pap with a frighten and quizzical look.

"Pap......where are the Indians.....the Indians that....that took me from the wagon? ....Where's the one that hurt me? ....Did they...Pap....did they all get away?" Tears were starting to well up in Lucy's eyes. She started to shake a little bit.

"Lucy, everything is OK." Her pap wrapped his arms around her for comfort. "There isn't anyone left to hurt you.......No....none of them got away........They'll never hurt anyone else.......Never again Lucy!........I promise you.....none of them will ever harm you again."

Lucy hugged her pap and kissed him on his cheek. Now, everything was starting to come back to her about the night before. She remembered Jacky softly whispering her name. She remembered her brother standing up and yelling something. She couldn't remember exactly what he was screaming about. She remembered the fighting. She remembered somebody carrying her to her pap.

"Pap.....didn't you hit one of those horrible Indians?

"Yes Lucy, I hit one of them because he was mean to you." John didn't want her to know that he had killed that Indian with his knife. He would tell her later what had happened to the eight Indians that had kidnapped her from the chuck wagon. He would tell her when she was stronger of body and mind. If she asked about the tenth Indian, he would tell about that one too, but only if she asked.

"Can we go back to the wagons now……I want to see momma……..
the little buffalo…….I want to feel "Buster" licking my face………..
and all of the animals……Please pap…..can we go now?

Lucy slowly stood up and cautiously walked over to Jeremiah and Jake. She wanted to give each of them another big hug and a kiss on their cheek. John had given her his shirt to wear over her nightgown.

"Jeremiah?...... I remember now…….I remember you were making me a promise….. Do you remember doing that?"

"Ya……….. I remember that promise………..Do you remember the promise, Lucy?" Jeremiah was trying his best not to bust out laughing.

Lucy got a strange expression on her face as she watched Jeremiah's funny wide smile.

"I do remember!" Lucy blurted out.

Her facial expression changed to a tortured look, a look of fear and anger. She turned towards her pap, with a look of apprehension. There was a question she wanted to ask but was almost afraid to ask it.

"Pap……what happened to that Indian……the one who hit me……..and made me stand……the one who made me stand alone….all by myself." Now the look of fear turned to one of anger. Lucy's jaw clenched and her eyes narrowed.

"Pap……what happened to that bastard that grabbed me by my hair………and cut me…….and caused me to pee down my legs……..in front of ….in front of those savages?"

None of the McCrumb's were known to use bad language, at least not very often. Sarah wouldn't allow bad language used in the house. Lucy and Amy never uttered foul language. For Lucy to use it this time, she must have been really hurting in her mind and heart.

Lucy just stood there with that McCrumb determined look waiting for an answer from her pap. Her demanding look told John that Lucy would settle for nothing less than an honest answer. He told Lucy that Jeremiah and Two Elks had fulfilled all four of her requests. Lucy vividly remembered what each of those four requests was.

"What's two elks?" Lucy demanded. "I don't know what two elks is. I didn't know anyone named Two Elks."

John explained to his daughter who Two Elks was. He told her of the Kiowa involvement in her freedom from the Ute Indians. She was delighted to learn that Two Elks and the other four Indians were the same Indians she had given her homemade cookies to at the wagons. John told her that Two Elks had called her his "pale skinned sister" and gave her the Indian name of, "She, the Strong Eagle of the Sky". When John had finished telling her all about Two Elks and what he had done and said about her, Lucy beamed all over herself with self-satisfaction.

John walked over to his horse and retrieved the parfleche bag from his saddle bags that Two Elks had given him earlier. He handed the parfleche to his daughter.

"Sweetheart, in this bag is the fulfillment of three of your four requests you made. Two Elks put them in his personal handmade parfleche bag and ask me to give it to you.........It was Jeremiah and Two Elks who made your requests come true." John prepared himself for a barrage of more questions.

Jeremiah and Jake were waiting anxiously to see if Lucy was going to open the bag. They were both wondering if she did open it what would be her reactions. They were anticipating her next question.

"OK pap……..or either of you two?" Lucy turned towards Jeremiah and Jake. "Where is that horrid Indian……the one that hit me and cut me?"

All three men just stood there looking at each other. Each of them was waiting for one of the others to say something, just say anything. Nobody wanted to be the first to adventure a very embarrassing answer to a very simple question. Finally, it was Jeremiah that broke the silence.

"Lucy…….I doubt that Indian will ever hurt any other lady as long as he lives…." There was a long silence before Jeremiah started talking again. "Lucy……he's all alone……..he's naked…….without moccasins and uh…………uh…...minus some of his important parts of………uh……..well….parts of his personal belongings…… OK?.......He's somewhere out there in the prairie all by himself……… and plenty sore and hurting………he's a hundred miles from uh……from nowhere!"

Lucy could tell that Jeremiah was not only having a difficult time trying to explain an answer to her question but his embarrassment showed all over his reddened face. Lucy decided to let Jeremiah and the other guys off of the hook for an answer that was embarrassing for them. She understood what the answer was so she interrupted Jeremiah's stammering speech.

"I want to thank all of you for saving me…" Now Lucy was smiling, knowing where that awful Indian was and how he was not dressed for that big wide open desert. She didn't quite understand all of the meaning of Jeremiah's words like, "quite sore and hurting" but she understood enough to knowingly smile. She eventually would appreciate the complete story. Once again her attention went back to the bag that her pap had handed her earlier. She slowly examined the bag, turned it around and then turned it upside down and then back right side up. She put the bag to the side of her head and gently shook it. She never opened it, just examined it real close and then smiled.

"It's a very pretty bag." She declared as she looked at the guys and smiled. "Have all of you seen what is inside of it?" All of the guys blushed and shook their heads up and down. Lucy got a bigger smile on her face. "Is what I hope that is inside this here pouch in it...... are they really in this pouch?" Now, Lucy was having some fun with the guys over her questions.

The three men couldn't help but smile with satisfaction. They all answered Lucy in the affirmative. That made her smile in the affirmative and with personal satisfaction. She was satisfied knowing that her tormenter will always need something covering the top of his stripped head and more importantly, he will never father any more babies. She patted the pretty pouch and told the men she would treasure it forever. She didn't open the pouch then; she asks her pap to put it back in one of his saddlebags.

Lucy's mind was still a little foggy from her fatigue and exhaustion of the past forty hours. As she gained physical strength the potency of mental capacities became clearer and the quicker her memory would return. Her pap told her it was time to go. He assured her that her memory would be perfect by the time they reached the two wagons.

John and the other two men made ready for the ride back to the wagons. Lucy would ride with her pap. Jeremiah figured it would take maybe five hours to reach the wagons if they rode at a good pace. That would put them back before dark.

....

The Kiowa wished Jacky good health and then rode towards Kansas with ten new horses and other captured Ute treasures. Jacky watched them for a long time, and then realized he needed to move on. He wasn't very far from the wagons. He knew his mom would be happy to see him and the good news about Lucy.

When he got close to their camp grounds he could see someone moving around the wagons. The dogs were the first to see Jacky and his horse coming in the distance. All four dogs went charging towards him at the same time. The dogs were Buster, Lucy and Amy's dog, Tubby and Kick, Jerald and Jacky's dogs, and then there was Ammo, Jeremiah's huge bear-like dog. When the dogs got to Jacky and his horse the barking and the jumping gymnastics around the horse almost became circus-like. None of the dog's barking or antics bothered the horse, he had it and heard it all before.

All of that barking brought Sarah, Amy, and Jerald out to see what was causing all of the commotions. When Sarah saw it was Jacky her heart started beating extremely hard, almost too hard. It felt as if her heart would burst if it beat any harder. Her stomach had a terribly empty feeling right down in the pit of it. Prayers for Lucy were cascading through her mind. She finally realized that she was squeezing her hands so tight that both of them were hurting. Jacky had a big smile that has to be good news she wanted to believe.

When Jacky got almost next to his mom he jumped from his horse and ran to her open arms.

"We found Lucy and she's OK! Momma, Lucy is alive and OK!" Jacky was crying, Sarah was crying. Both Amy and Jerald were crying. Sarah was trying to ask questions through the myriad of tears and nothing she sputtered made any since. But, nobody really cared, they were all so overjoyed with the good news about Lucy. After they all had regained their composures and was walking towards the wagons Jacky started laughing at the little buffalo who was bounding towards him, jumping up and down in a playful mood.

"Look, Momma, the little guy thinks he's a dog." Jacky quip, trying to get his mom focused in a more exuberant mood. He knew she was extremely concerned about Lucy.

"Yes he does, doesn't he?" Sarah responded, not really thinking about the buffalo or what Jacky had just said.

"A little "she" momma, "she" is not a little "he", "she" is a little girl buffalo" Amy had a big smile when she corrected her mom. Amy was also trying to get a smile on her momma's face. She realized that Jacky was trying to do the same. She knew that her momma was very distressed and concerned about Lucy and nothing else mattered to her at the moment. Especially subsequently she had a lot of questions to ask.

"Jacky, when are your father and Lucy coming home?" Sarah had many questions for Jacky and she didn't want to be sidetracked from asking them.

Jacky knew he might as well get all of the questions over with because his mom wasn't going to stop until she had them all answered. He decided to answer the two most important questions before she even asks them.

"Momma, Lucy is fine. She's been through a very bad experience, but she is well and not hurt. Poppa and Lucy are on their way here right now. They'll be here sometime before dark" Jacky tried to answer her the best he could without upsetting her.

"What time before dark?" Sarah almost demanded an answer. She didn't like the words, "sometime before dark".

Jacky didn't know what to say. Almost any answer he was going to give his mom was just going to agitate her. Amy tried to come to Jacky's rescue. She had to get her momma off on to another subject.

"Momma, I think Jacky is probably really tired and hungry, don't you think maybe we should……"

"Amy!" Her mom broke into Amy's question! "Jacky is tired and hungry. We need to fix supper so Lucy will have something to eat when she gets here. All three of the kids were relieved to get their mom thinking about something else, anything else. Cooking would do the trick.

Sarah's mind was groggy and fatigued from so much worry of the events of the past forty-eight hours. Her physical body was exhausted, mainly caused by stress and worry for her two daughters. Sarah was not at all well. The frustrating experience of losing Amy then Lucy to the savage Indians had placed a major burden not only on her mind but also to her body. She hadn't slept for almost three days and the emotional part of her psychic was slowly trying to shut down. But Sarah's strong will was constantly fighting against any kind of a mental shut down and that in itself was facilitating the shut down even faster. She was close to a nervous breakdown.

After the food was cooked and readied for Lucy's return Sarah and her three children sat on the back tailgates of the wagons anticipating the arrival of John, Jake, Jeremiah and of course Lucy.

The sun was slowly disappearing beyond the western skyline when Jerald started to jump up and down and pointing to the far off horizon.

"There they are momma....there they are...Lucy's coming momma......I can see Lucy.." Jerald really could not see his sister; he did see the three horses. He was just trying to get a smile on his mom's lips.

Sarah did smile and Jacky helped her down off of the wagon. Now Sarah could see the three horses and on one of the horses, there were two riders. Her eyes were beginning to well up with tears. Her body was starting to shake. Jacky put his arms around his mom to help steady her body from trembling. Sarah wanted to run to the riders, but Jacky held her firmly in his arms while talking softly to her with comforting words.

"Lucy, my precious Lucy.....I see our precious Lucy." Sarah was almost convulsing while she was trying to speak. If Jacky hadn't been holding her Sarah would have gone to the ground. Amy came to her momma's other side trying to calm her and reassure her that everything was all right.

John took his oldest daughter from the horse very gently lifted her to the ground. When Sarah saw Lucy standing alone without any help she became a little calmer putting her outstretched arms for her daughter. Both John and Lucy hurried over to Sarah; it was obvious that Sarah was in some kind of emotional distress. Everybody's tears were flowing for joy. Lucy was back with the McCrumb family safe and sound. Sarah did not want to let Lucy out of her grasp. Finally, John gently forced Sarah to let go of Lucy and they all walked to the wagons, still crying, but now the crying was being mixed with good laughter. Sarah was beginning to relax to the relief of her family because some of Sarah's laughter seemed to be dancing on her lips.

Lucy, you are a MESS! .....We need to get you cleaned up......... why do you have your daddy's shirt on.......we need to get that old sweaty thing off of you before YOU start stinking like your pa." Sarah was smiling now as she turned to look at John. She almost started laughing.

"John.......you know better than to put one of your old sweaty stinking shirts on your daughters." Sarah knew why Lucy was wearing her pap's shirt. She just wanted to make a joke out of it. Now, everybody was laughing along with Sarah and her jesting.

John and Jake took some of the extra canvas that was used for the top of the wagon covering and made a four sided private area for Lucy to bathe and clean up. Sarah and Amy had heated water for Lucy's bath. When the number five tub was full of hot water Sarah helped Lucy to shed her pap's shirt and the dirty torn nightgown, the one she wore when she was kidnapped. When Lucy had all of her clothes off Sarah started to cry softly.

"Dear God Lucy, look at all of them cuts and bruises..........My poor baby, how you must hurt." Then Sarah let out an appalling gasped and put both of her hands to her opened mouth. There was a long silence as Sarah stared at the six inch cut over Lucy's left breast. "Why?...What?.........Lucy.....how did that happen?"

Lucy grabbed her momma's hands trying to calm her after seeing the six-inch cut. Lucy got into the tub and told her momma to set down and she would tell her everything that had happened to her.

Lucy knew that her momma had been and still was very upset and very anxious over her last two days as a captive. It took some time, but Lucy described in delicate words and explained to her mom what had taken place up until she arrived back at the wagons. By the time Lucy had finished her story the hot water in the number 5 tub had turned to lukewarm water.

"More hot water, NOW,...... LOTS OF HOT WATER! ....Lucy wants more hot water" Sarah yelled in her most demanding voice and all the time there was a warm smile on her lips. Sarah was satisfied with Lucy's detailed explanation of her trials for the past forty hours but she was still tightly holding on to Lucy's hands.

After Lucy's bath and the cuts and bruises had been taken care of tenderly with balm and a mother's love she was properly dressed. She accompanied her mom to a well-prepared and welcomed feast of food that was enjoyed by the whole group of the Kansas pilgrims.

John decided that day 40 of their travels would be a day of rest and recuperation. Everybody was exhausted and fatigued from the events of the past couple of days. Both Lucy and Sarah needed a lot of rest. Amy had partially recovered physically from her ordeal. She was extremely sore from the cuts and bruises. She was having some mental problems at night because of her experience with the Ute Indians. She has asked her poppa if he would sleep near the wagon that she and Lucy were sleeping in. She either consciously or unconsciously stayed near one of the men during the day. If she had a chore away from the wagons she would ask one of her brothers to accompany her. The girls would learn later that the men were sleeping in a circle around the girl's wagon at night.

They needed to replenish their water supply but that could wait until the next day. Jeremiah knew of a watering hole (a small river) that they could easily reach by noon on the morrow. Jeremiah still figured they were four or five days out from the city of Denver by wagon. Jeremiah told John that he was going to ride ahead to Denver. He wanted to round up some cowpokes to help bring the wagons in. He could be back with help in a couple of days. John was agreeable with Jeremih's"s plan.

The McCrumb's caravan of two covered wagons renewed their journey early on the morning of April 26th, 1875. It was Jerald's birthday, fifteen years old and already a man. They came to Jeremiah's watering hole (a small river) about noon that same day. The water kegs were cleaned and refilled with fresh water. John, Jake and the boys took quick semi baths in the cold water of the river. Sarah had taken a hurried bath in Lucy's second round of hot water the night before. Lucy had noticed some blood on Sarah's clothing. Sarah tried to hide the blood stains from Lucy's sight, but she wasn't all that successful. Lucy didn't ask her momma about the stains because of her mom's present emotions caused by the past couple of days. She would inquire later when their lives were calmer and emotions were more relaxed.

Sarah and the girls used this opportunity to wash clothes in the river water and clean items that desperately needed cleaning. Sarah was having a considerable stressing pain between her stomach and her pelvic area. It was more of a nagging pain, but she was able to conceal it in her facial expressions.

Amy was doing well except for some recurring nightmares she was experiencing some nights and the fright of feeling alone. She couldn't really say she was having nightmares, but her dreams were quite disturbing. Lucy was doing surprisingly well considering what she had been through. Physically she was very sore and relatively stiff in her joints. She had more abrasions and bruises than Amy had suffered. The biggest physical problem Lucy was having was whether she was going to have a permanent scar where the Indian had cut her over her left breast. That was bothering her more than anything else. Mentally Lucy was coping relative well, especially after what she had been through both emotionally and physically. Her Scottish heritage of strong-willed ancestry was serving her well during this very difficult time in her life. She had called upon her McCrumb Scottish heritage during her capture to help give her strength to endure. It is that same Scottish will power that was serving her now. Amy did not have that same kind of tenacity of endurance that Lucy possessed.

Lucy was very concerned about her momma. She wanted to confront her mom about the blood stains on her undergarments but just didn't know how to do it at such a delicate time. Maybe, she thought, maybe she would ask her momma about the stains when they got to the city of Denver.

Lucy had taken great care of the Kiowa parfleche bag that held three of her four requests she had asked of Jeremiah. She hadn't opened the bag yet, but she knew what it held. She would pick the bag up and a large grin would encompass her with immense self-satisfaction. As long as that nasty Indian lived he would always remember Lucy McCrumb. She decided not to open, nor look in the pretty painted bag until a time when she could do it without the hate she now felt. She kept the bag with her most prized requested positions in the corner of a small cherished trunk that had been given to her on her seventh birthday by her pap.

The McCrumb's were not quite ready nor were they prepared to grasp the magnitude of the booming city of Denver. That part of the Colorado Territory was mostly mountains, small gold mining towns and a bunch of ghost towns where the gold had petered out and disappeared. In the minds of the McCrumb's the city of Denver was just another small gold mining town. But in just two short years from1875 to 1877 Denver would become the capital city of the thirty-eighth Star on the American Flag; the State of Colorado. By the time the McCrumb's would reach Denver the population had reached almost 38,000 characters of all sorts; the upper of the upper class to the lowest of the rift-raft.

Denver City had its beginning in the late 1840s and early 1850s. Denver was named after the Territorial Governor of Kansas, James W. Denver. By the 1860s the gold fields in the lands around Denver had petered out and disillusioned individual gold miners were leaving the Denver area daily by the hundreds heading to find newer and greener gold fields. Then some guy discovered a motherload of silver in the mountains around Denver. With the discovery of silver, the enrichment of Denver future bounced back bigger than ever. By 1870 two different railroads companies had parked their trains in the middle of the city of Denver and by the 1890s Denver had become the twenty-sixth largest city in the Union.

That evening after the camp had been set up and everyone was settled the McCrumb's and Jake had a small birthday celebration for Jerald. There wasn't any cake but there was plenty of love and singing. In about two more weeks Jacky, on May fifteenth would have his fourteenth birthday. He was also becoming a man at a very young age.

The next afternoon Jeremiah showed up at the wagons from Denver with three young cowpokes. He also brought a side of beef to help feed the newcomers. Jeremiah told the Kansas pilgrims that Denver was only a day away. He did all of the introductions leaving no one out. The cowpokes were very well mannered, especially towards the ladies. They had been handpicked by Jeremiah and well warned how to behave under the shadow of the mountain man's six foot seven inch two hundred and ninety-pound body. The youngest cowpoke, twenty-year-old Henry Edwards took an instant fancy to Lucy. Every time he looked her way his face would flush from pink to scarlet. He tried hard not to look in her direction. Both Sarah and John caught the color changes. Lucy did too and she managed to enhance her girl charms and pretended not to notice. That made matters even worse for the poor cowpoke. Jeremiah just smiled and was amused but not surprised at Lucy's antics.

Sarah and the girls prepared a fitting meal for their guests. That side of beef really came in handy. The food supply in Lucy's "chuck wagon" was getting mighty scrimpy; the cupboards were getting vastly bare.

John had asked Jeremiah to search out prices what cows and horses were selling for in Denver. Jeremiah told John it was a sellers' market right now in Denver. Prices were high, it would be a good time to sell. John could reap well over what a working man's year of wages would be just with the stock he had to sell. The high prices solidified John's decision to sell the stock. John and Sarah had sold the farm in Kansas at a premium price. Financially they would be well secure for a long time in the future if they were very careful and frugal with their money.

After supper and when everyone was settling in to call it a night Lucy asked her pap if she could talk to him about her momma. She asked him what was wrong with her momma. She asked him if he knew what the blood stains were all about.

John decided it was the time he told his daughters that their momma was a very sick woman. He told Lucy to go and bring Amy back to hear what he had to say. Sarah was sleeping soundly in the chuck wagon. John didn't want her to know that he was telling the girls of her physical problems. Both girls were dreading to hear what their father was going to tell them. They could tell by the look on his face that whatever it was, it wasn't good news. He tried to explain Sarah's condition to his daughters as best as he understood her condition. It was either a kidney problem that was causing the blood or it was a very bad female condition causing the discharge of blood. Either condition could be very serious and life-threatening. He told his daughters that there was a big hospital in Denver that could help their mom and hopefully, she would get better.

Before noon on May 1st, 1875, the two covered wagons were in sight of the western city of Denver, in the Colorado Territory. The Jeremiah named "Kansas pilgrims" had journey forty-five grueling days to reach this point in their quest for a future in the territories of the great America West. What had been only forty-five days seemed to have been months or at least a year to the McCrumb's. They had given up the many comforts of a farming life that had been happy and fulfilling for them only to venture into a new life of the unknown in the western frontier. As far as John was concerned Sarah needed that change to help cure her worsening health difficulties. The doctors in Topeka had recommended the change for Sarah the last time the two were in Topeka seeking help for her. The fresh air of the mountains and especially the new hospital in Denver is what those doctors had recommended.

John had known for the past few years that Sarah was in failing health. He had refused to face the inevitable possibility that Sarah could get worse and leave him and the children someday. Not his Sarah! She was too strong to ever die! But John knew better and that thought would crush his spirit. Sometimes back at the farm in Alma while riding his horse Thunder in the fields John's emotions would get the best of him when thinking of the possibility of losing his beautiful wife. There were times when he would be crying so hard he would have to get off of Thunder and sit in the fields to regain his composer.

He would kneel in a prayer to God begging Him for Sarah's good health. As Sarah's health worsened John would kneel to God again and again in prayer, at times asking why his prayers were not being answered. John would never lose his faith in God, but prayers were confusing to him at times. John never let on to Sarah or his children that his real reason for selling the farm was in the hopes that the hospital in Denver could make a difference in Sarah's health. He just continued to pray that it wasn't too late to help his beloved wife. Should he have sold the farm sooner? That question will always dog him.

Jeremiah had gone ahead of the wagons once again, this time to hunt for a place to park the wagons in Denver until they were again ready to roll. If and when they left Denver John wanted to hook up with a large wagon train that was heading north on the "Overland Trail". Every week or two a new covered wagon train would roll out of Denver traveling north on the Overland Trail either heading to the Mormon Trail to Salt Lake City or the "Oregon Trail" to the Northwest Territory. That decision would be made according to Sarah's health. Her health could cause a severe change in John's plans at any time.

Jeremiah had found the best upgrade livery stables in the city to stable the riding horses while everyone was in Denver. John had told him not to spare the cost. The animals were important to John. The livery stables also agreed to take care of the dogs. They would be boarded in large safe pens. Everyone thought it was a hoot boarding a baby buffalo. Everybody in the stables wanted to take care of the buffalo. The two wagons were put in a large barn under lock and key. Jeremiah had set up a time for John to meet with the people who were buying cattle and horses. As luck would have it, Jeremiah met a hide and fur buyer who wanted to purchase all of Jeremiah's buffalo hides and at a really good cash price.

John had persuaded Jeremiah to stick with Jake and the McCrumb family to wherever the future would take them. John suggested maybe the vast and unexplored Rocky Mountains in the Idaho Territory. That mountainous destination really fascinated and tingled Jeremiah's adventurous side; "Yea, the Rocky Mountains of Idaho", Jeremiah would, bellow. John was also considering maybe a couple of cowpokes joining the McCrumb clan on their journey to their future when they left Denver.

John and Sarah took a hired buggy from the livery stables to ride into the city of Denver. The owner of the stables had recommended to John and Sarah the best up-scaled boarding houses in Denver. John wanted Sarah to choose which place she preferred to stay while they were in the city. On the way, John chose a bank where he would put their money for safe keeping. Sarah made her choice of living quarters; the living area had a large parlor and two bedrooms. John and Sarah would stay in one of the bedrooms and the two sisters would stay in the other one. Jerald, Jacky, and Jake had chosen a good size room in the back part of the boarding house. Jeremiah chose to sleep near the wagons under the stars.

John insisted that he pay for Jake's and the boy's room in the boarding house, but Jake didn't think that was right for John to do that. Jake had saved the biggest part of his army and cow punching wages for years. He was very prudent with his money. Jake never drank liquor, gambled or partied with the crowds. His one goal was to go west someday and perhaps grow a family. He had always kept tabs on where the guy was who had saved his life during the battle of Chancellorsville. When he got news that John McCrumb was heading west with his family it was time for Jake to meet his hero for the third time.

That evening John and Sarah invited everybody including the three cowpokes to have supper with them at one of Denver's best home-style eateries. Amy made sure the cowpoke Henry Edwards sat next to Lucy. She wanted to watch his face turn different color shades of red each time Lucy would look at him and smile. She also wanted to watch her sister execute her well planned girlish charms on Henry. For years the sisters had talked about doing something like this to boys for fun, but it had always just been girl talk. But now it would be real, they could see if their female allures and wiles really worked. Anyway, it would be all in fun. Even the cowpoke Henry would enjoy it, even if his face did blush different colors of red, purple and pink.

The men all ordered their favorite meal, large beef steaks. The three cowpokes didn't order until they were told to go ahead order steaks. Here lately their meals had been mostly beans and bread. Money wasn't easy for them to come by. None of the three cowpokes smoked nor drank any alcohol beverages. All three of them were lifelong friends from the state of Tennessee.

Tennessee was not a rich man's state, mostly poor folks digging a meager living from the soil of the earth. According to one of the cowpokes, the only real way to make money in Tennessee was moonshining. The three friends wanted a better life then grubbing up old dried dirt or dying in the woods fighting over some stupid moonshine territorial war. They had heard the stories of men getting rich overnight finding gold in the creeks and rivers in the west. The lore of gold and riches overnight was just too much of a dream to pass up. They had come to the Colorado Territory to line their pockets with some of that easy gold they had heard about back in Tennessee. They had worked long and hard hours in Tennessee to save enough money to buy railroad tickets to the land of milk, honey, and gold. It didn't take them long to realize that their dream was just that; a dream. Broke and sleeping out in the open they worked at different odd jobs in Denver, mostly shoveling cow and horse poop. Now they were just trying to make enough of a poke to get train tickets back home to Tennessee.

Everyone enjoyed the supper, especially the three cowpokes, it was so much better than just plain beans. Amy enjoyed watching Lucy weave her girl charms in ways to make Henry uncomfortable. Sarah caught on to what the girls were doing. It did amuse her for a while, but she decided that she would help poor Henry out of his embarrassing predicament and put Lucy on a hot seat for a change of humor. She could see that Henry was fidgety because of the sister's antics and Lucy was just enjoying herself too much.

Sarah started a conversation with Henry. He was very polite and seemed to be well educated. She learned that he and his three friends had attended one year of schooling at a university in Tennessee. Then she made some inquiries about of his family.

"Henry, do you have any brothers or sisters in Tennessee?"

"Yes ma'am, I have two brothers and one sister." Henry tried his best to speak proper English. He was glad that Ms. McCrumb was asking him questions. He was rather shy in starting conversations.

"How old is your sister Henry?" Sarah wanted the conversation to continue, mostly for Lucy's consideration.

"She's nineteen ma'am. "Bright" is a sweet and wonderful sister ma'am."

"Bright? ....Your sister's name is "Bright", Henry?" Sarah was intrigued why anyone would name their daughter such an odd name as "Bright".

"Yes, ma'am, "Bright" is her proper name. You see Ms. McCrumb "Bright" was born partially blind, so, you see Ms. McCrumb, she brought such a "Bright" light into our lives.

Sarah looked over at Lucy and could tell now it was Lucy's turn to squirm.

"Lucy, what do you think of the name "Bright?" Sarah was hoping that Lucy was learning a very valuable lesson in this conversation concerning humility.

"It's a very beautiful name momma." That is all Lucy could muster up at the moment. She knew that she had just been taught an "on the spot" momma lesson.

"Amy, What do think of the name, Bright?" Sarah figured Amy needed the same lesson as Lucy.

"Henry, I think your sister has a God-given name and it is a wonderful name." Amy got her momma's message loud and clear. This was one of her momma's "on the spot momma moments".

Sarah would now let the conversation take its natural course between the sisters, Henry, and the other two cowpokes. All three young men joined in a pleasant conversation with the sisters.

Henry finally got up enough nerve to inquire of Lucy how she and Amy had gotten so many cuts and bruises on their arms. He was truly concerned with her wellbeing. His concern made Lucy feel real special; her antics during the supper had left her with embarrassment. By the end of the evening, everyone knew each other just a little better. John told the three cowpokes if they weren't too busy in the morning he would pay them if they would help Sarah and the girls with the rearranging and cleaning of the wagons. They could help carry whatever the ladies needed from the wagons to the boarding house. The ladies would need clothing and personal items. Sarah could have them pack whatever she needed for a longer stay in Denver.

John had located the hospital at 6th and Cherokee Sreet. The new hospital had been constructed in the second half of 1873 at a cost of $4000. The staff showed John the facilities and he was assured that Sarah would be welcomed and well cared for. By the morning of the next day, everyone had settled into city life, or settled as best as could be expected for being new residents. The girls had their clothes hung and personal items displayed in their proper places. The boy's items were heaped wherever they threw them.

Sarah and John ate breakfast together and then made their visit to the hospital. Sarah was surprised at the modern look of the hospital. Everything was so clean and white. The nurses were all in starched white uniforms and funny looking little white starched caps on their heads. Everyone was so polite. The city of Denver was anything but clean and modern looking. The streets were dirt and dusty and many of the building were weathered beaten and quite sad looking. Some were painted, but many were not painted. Sarah just thought the hospital would have the same look as the town; dark and dingy looking. She was really pleased with the hospital.

Sarah knew that her health had gone from bad to worse in the last couple of years. The trip from Alma, the Indian raid and the kidnapping of Amy and Lucy had also taken a toll on her health. Her family was safe and she was prepared to accept whatever the future would bring. She was proud of her two strong and beautiful daughters. Her sons were just boys, but in truth, they were very strong and upright young men. Her John was her next breath, her strongest heartbeat and she would always be with him as long as he was alive. God had given her a blessed life.

By 1875 there were many doctors practicing medicine in Denver. Some of them had gotten their MD degrees from fancy colleges in the Northeast Yankee states. Places like Philadelphia, New York, Virginia and even Boston. In just a few more years a much larger hospital was built in Denver with many more doctors migrating to the western frontier.

John and Sarah met with three or four different doctors that first day. The first doctor was Dr. Bancroft. He introduced Sarah to other Denver doctors as they visited the hospital from their daily office practices. After three hours of consultation with different doctors, it was decided that Sarah would check into the hospital the first thing the next morning. She should be prepared for a hospital stay of a few days while examinations and test would be conducted.

That evening while everyone was enjoying a hearty supper in Sarahs' favorite eatery John informed the gathering what Sarah's plans were for a hospital stay. Everyone knew she was going to the hospital that day, but no one was prepared to hear about a hospital "stay". The kids couldn't get the questions out quick enough. Neither Sarah nor John was able to answer any questions because with everybody asking at one time they couldn't even understand the questions. After the questions started coming one at a time either Sarah or John would attempt to answer them as knowledgeable as possible. The only answer that everyone really understood was the only question that could logically be answered; Sarah was going to have to stay in the hospital for a spell.

The next three or four days were uneventful for everyone except Sarah. She was having a variety of tests daily. Some of the tests were very invasive, embarrassing and uncomfortable. Sarah at times was filled with nervous anxiety and tinges of fear. The examination by male doctors was very disturbing and discomforting for Sarah. The doctors were professionally understanding and made sure that there were nurses with Sarah during every examination.

During those three or four days, John spent most of his time going in and out of the hospital checking on Sarah. Lucy and Amy like their father were constant visitors during hospital visiting hours. The boys spent their time between exploring Denver with Jake and Jeremiah and visiting their mom in the hospital. Sarah didn't tell anyone of her displeasure with the examinations. The examinations were an important part of hers and her family's future and they were a necessity that she and she alone must endure. She didn't want to cause any more apprehension and worry for her family.

On the fourth day of Sarah's hospital stay, the doctors called for a conference with Sarah and John. The news was not good news. Sarah had a cancer of her Cervix and a tumor on her Uterus. The options were an "Ablation" procedure and or a "Hysterectomy". Both techniques were radical and carried risks. Hysterectomies were being performed in the big eastern hospitals on women daily to rid them of the danger of female cancer. Sarah and John were informed that Sarah's "Cervix" cancer was advanced cancer. A successful outcome was in the realm of doubt. It would be Sarah's decision if any procedure was to be performed. The diagnoses did not surprise Sarah. She had felt for some time now that her bad health was cancer driven and it went as far back to or even before the time they moved to Alma.

Sarah was concerned about Lucy, Amy, Jerald, and Jacky. She told John that the children needed to be told and educated what her medical problems were. She wanted the children to set with her, John and the doctors and learn about and asks questions about what the future held for Sarah. In Sarah's mind, that was the right thing to do. The children were mature enough and strong enough and should be treated as adults, especially with something this serious. That is the way Sarah had reared them and that was the way it was going to be!

The next morning the McCrumb family and two doctors met in Sarah's hospital room to discuss her condition. The atmosphere in the room was glum, except for Sarah's loving smile. The sisters were more sensitive and anxious than the boys. The girls had a deeper empathetic understanding of Sarah's dilemma than the boys could ever grasp or imagine. The boys loved their momma just as much as their sisters did, but female and male hormones made that love just a little difficult to the understanding of those two very complex words.

The doctors explained the complexities Of Sarah's physical conditions. They tried to clarify in the simplest of understandable terms what choices their momma had and what the consequence of those choices involved both medically and physically. A radical operation would be dangerous to Sarah's physical ability to endure and overcome its trauma. Ablation would help, but to what extent was an unknown. An operation or the Ablation procedure would mean weeks or possibly months of pain and weeks in the hospital. Neither was really recommended by the doctors. It was Sarah's choice, it was her body.

After the doctors had left the room Sarah tried to reassure her family that she was comfortable and extremely happy. Her deep faith in God, she told them would sustain her through any difficulty that this earth could throw at her. She impressed on them that she wanted to be with them, but she was also OK being with God. Everybody in the room, including two nurses in their starched uniforms, was fighting back the tears. Lucy and Amy crawled on the hospital bed with their momma and wrapped their arms tightly around her. The boys were crying and seemed to be cemented to their chairs. John was silently thanking God for his beautiful family.

"Hey,….. everybody,……..it's time to smile," Sarah told everybody to smile than she started to laugh a soft laugh. "I'm still right here with my beautiful family…….. I haven't gone anywhere yet……. And, I don't plan on going anywhere anytime soon……. OK?"

That was the strength that this small Scottish lady was passing on to her children. This was the strength that Sarah had welded into her family's structure. This was the strength that helped build the west and a new nation.

"Now family,….. Listen to me….. I want you to see if there is the church of Christ in this booming city of Denver…… and if there is all of us are going to church this coming Sunday morning…... Now, tomorrow morning after I leave this hospital we are going to have breakfast in our favorite Denver eatery."

With that said Sarah told everybody to go do whatever they had to do, she was tired and needed some rest. When everyone was gone Sarah turned to the nurses and told them how beautiful her family was and how much she loved them. Sarah's body was exhausted and fatigued from the experience of traveling almost fifty days in a covered wagon. Four days of physical examination had worn her down. Jacky's birthday was only two days away on the 15th of

May and Sarah wanted to give him a small birthday party. Now, she must sleep and regain some of her strength back for that party.

Lucy and Amy found the sheriff's office and dared to go inside. They wanted to know if the sheriff people knew of a local church of Christ in Denver. One of the deputies knew of a small one, not far from the boarding house where the girls were staying. The weird looking deputy drew a map on a scrap piece of paper that he had taken out of the waste can. Lucy thought that was very rude of the deputy, but he didn't look very bright to her anyway, she just shrugged it off as he is an ignorant uneducated Duffus. The girls followed the directions on the "waste can map". Lucy was still irritated at that Duffus deputy. The map lead them to a small building near the edge of town. The front door was wide open so Lucy charged right in through the open door. Amy followed Lucy's lead. There were two older gentlemen sitting and talking on the front pew.

"Good afternoon, sirs, my name is Lucy McCrumb and this is my sister Amy McCrumb. We are new visitors to your city of Denver. Our momma is in the Denver hospital for some examinations. Our pap and two brothers are also here in your city. We have two friends that are traveling with us." Lucy was trying to get all of her words out at once. Amy decided to slow her down.

"Lucy, slow down. Ask the gentlemen what we come here for to ask." Amy was just a little flustered and aggravated at Lucy's aggressiveness.

The two men were charmed by the sister's lively attitudes and their smiles were turning to guarded chuckles.

"Well now young ladies, what can we do to help you on this beautiful day? Oh yes, my name is Deacon Benjamin and this is Elder James."

"Elder?" seemed to be a strange name for a man, but who was the girls to question it? Of course, it was not the man's first name, it was a biblical title as was the word "Deacon".

"We want to come to Sunday morning services if it is Ok with you." Amy continued to carry on the conversation.

"That would be wonderful, are you all members of the church of Christ?" Elder James was asking the question.

"Well, sir, we were all baptized in the name of Jesus". Now it was Lucy taking the lead. "We were baptized three years ago in a river near our home, or what used to be our home, in Alma Kansas. Momma, pap and our two brothers were baptized all at the same time. Pap is our father."

"That's wonderful." Deacon Benjamin was speaking. "Who baptized you?" he continued.

'Well, three years ago this traveling preacher came by our house on a summer's day and he wanted to know if he could preach to us about God and His Son Jesus Christ. Momma and Pap said absolutely sure." Amy was beaming with that information.

"We all had our bibles". Lucy said. "Momma always has us kids read a portion of the good book every day. The preacher stayed at our house for almost a whole week teaching us about our Lord and Savior Jesus in the Bible. So, we were all baptized like Phillip baptized the Eunuch in the river. That is found in the book of Acts of the Apostles in the Bible, you know."

Lucy finally stopped to take a breath or two.

The two men just stood there looking at each other, sort of dumbfounded.

"Amazing!" One of them finally uttered.

"We'll see you all Sunday and bless you and your family". The other gentleman said as he smiled and bowed his head to the sisters.

Lucy and Amy were so very proud of themselves for finding a church of Christ building. The building was really small; it might be able to hold twenty or so worshipers. The size of the building didn't matter to Lucy or Amy. They had never worshiped in a building before. There was no church of Christ building in Alma. For the first time, the McCrumb family could worship together with other people on Sunday and in a real church building. They both noticed that there wasn't a piano or organ in the small building and that is what the traveling preacher said, there should not be one in a building of worship. You just sing and make the melody from your hearts. The girls just couldn't wait to tell their momma that they had found a church of Christ.

Jeremiah and Jake heard of a possible new small gold strike in a canyon west of Denver and north of the major goldfields that had petered out a few years earlier. News of a new canyon that might reveal undiscovered gold lying around was not being taken seriously by the old veteran gold prospectors and seasoned gold hunters in the Denver area. As far as they were concerned it was just another fairy tale by some "sun baked and brain dead" old fart trying to get an easy poke of money for whiskey. It was the same old fart that been haunting the mountains around Denver for years with other faded and fabled stories of elusive gold just around the next mountain and in the next canyon.

An undiscovered canyon just didn't seem possible or logical to the territory's old time gold hunters. Jeremiah and Jake had talked at length with the old prospector with the lost canyon story. The old guy was sun baked alright and his brain could also be partially cooked, but the old prospector's brain was definitely not dead. Jeremiah tried over and over to buy him whiskey, but the old man did not want whiskey. All the old codger wanted was a grub stake or partners in a gold exploration. Jeremiah had a respectable mountain man's perception about this old fart and his strange canyon story. Jeremiah was impressed that there was more to the old prospector's tale than the old fart was letting on.

Jeremiah and Jake told John about their conversation with the old codger. The three men sat around the table drinking coffee and discussing at length the possibility of a hidden canyon and the validity of a new gold find. All three of them came to the same conclusion; anything was possible. But, did the old prospector's bizarre story of an undiscovered canyon seem very plausible. Their conclusion; stranger things have happened, like the "Old Lost Dutchmen" mine in Arizona. Jeremiah was persuaded that the old prospector had indeed found a hidden canyon but he was not sure about the gold.

John told the two men that Sarah was getting out of the hospital in the morning and he wanted to be with her all that day. He told them of her condition and that they were going to stay in Denver so her illness could be monitored by the hospital and the Denver doctors. John reasoned that the girls could stay with Sarah while he and the others could at least examine the old prospector's wild claims. Sarah wanted to see Denver and shop the city's dress and woman's stores while she had the chance. It was settled then, John, Jeremiah, Jake, the boys, and the old codger would leave the day after tomorrow to either discover a new gold find or just another one of the thousands of Colorado Territory gold busts tall tales.

The men decided to leave separately early at daybreak on the 16th of May, the day after Jacky's birthday get-to-gather. Sarah had planned the birthday party and she demanded that everyone attend. Of course, everyone wanted to be in attendance for Jacky's big day. He was fourteen years old and going on a gold hunting trip as a birthday gift from his pa, Jeremiah, and Jake. At least, that's how he looked at it. Jerald didn't agree with Jacky persistent story, but Jacky didn't care what Jerald thought.

As the sun was rising on the morning of the 16th of May each man, not wanting to attract any attention left from a different location and at a different time. They agreed to meet at a point where Jock, the old prospector had designated. It was a huge old rock wall with ancient Indian drawing high on its surface. The wall was about four miles northwest of Denver hidden in unusual and strange rock formations at the eastern edge of the majestic Rocky Mountains. From there Jock and his donkey would lead the way to gold or to just more of Colorado Territory dirt.

The mountain terrain was rough going and at times the men had to walk and lead the horses through narrow passageways. At times the men did doubt Jock's sanity. After about an hour of tough going, they came to what appeared to be a blind pass. Jeremiah was getting aggravated. Jake questioned Jock's soundness of direction. It appeared that the gold hunting party would have to turn around and head back in the same direction where they had just traveled. Jock didn't slow down he just continued to forge ahead. It appeared he was heading straight into the canyon wall. He disappeared into a large stand of twisted mahogany trees. The men followed him through the warped ancient hundred year's old tortured looking trees. The stand of trees was actually much larger than it first appeared because the back section of the trees was on a decline. In fact, the decline was rather steep and rocky. It was a little difficult to maneuver without your feet sliding out from underneath a person. At the bottom of the decline was a large natural fissure in the canyon wall.

On the other side of the large gap or hole was what appeared to be a continuation of the same canyon they were just in. The five men stood beside Jock in utter amazement. It may not be a new large gold field, but the old goat did know what he was talking about when he said there was this new undiscovered canyon. Of course, the canyon wasn't new, it was as old as the mountains themselves. Jeremiah figured this particular canyon had just been overlooked and neglected because of other earlier and larger areas of gold and silver discoveries.

They explored a small part of the valley in the canyon for a couple of hours. They found signs of early Indians writings on parts of the canyon walls. The land appeared to be virgin and untouched by any humans in recent times. There was a medium size waterfall cascading out of a large crack in the side of one of the walls of the canyon. That waterfalls looked to be very interesting and could be very promising for further exploration. The small stream that the waterfalls had created on the floor of the canyon ran across the valley floor and then disappeared into the crevasse of rocks and small holes in the earth next to the opposite wall of the canyon. When it was late afternoon John decided they needed to get back to Denver before nightfall. They had grubstaked Jock with all the food and supplies he needed for two to three months. It was Friday, they told Jock they would be back early Monday morning to help further explore this new valley for that possible mother lode. Of course, nobody expected any mother lode.

Nobody had really expected to find the kind of an adventure that they did find that morning. They had not been prepared for the kind of a discovery they had made after following Jock through the maze of twisted mahogany to the large crack that separated the two canyons. So, maybe, just maybe a mother lode could be possible. Not really very plausible, but who knows? They had been surprised and amazed so far.

Now they would have Saturday and Sunday to prepare for a four or five-day exploratory encounter in Jock's canyon. It wasn't going to be easy keeping their new adventure a secret. Especially if they did find gold. If by some far fetched chance gold was discovered they would have to stake out a legal claim and everybody would know within days for hundreds of miles in all directions. But, that would be Ok, if their claim was the big one.

Jacky's small birthday party was a fulfilling success for him and his mom. Especially for his mom! His pa, Jeremiah, and Jake had a birthday present for both Jacky and Jerald. Jerald didn't get a present on his birthday, so this was a good time to give both brothers a birthday gift. Both of the brothers were given Colt 45 Peacemakers side arms with holsters. Their pa, Jake, and Jeremiah always wore their side arm revolving six shooters. Their mom's only rules were, not in the house and not in a church building.

Jeremiah, Jake, and the cowpokes agreed to go to church with Lucy and Amy that first Sunday morning. Of course, by Sarah's words, "No guns were allowed in God's house". Elder James and Deacon Benjamin were at the front door to welcome any and all who came to worship that beautiful May morning. Both men were totally surprised to see so many visitors to this one Sunday service. There was normally always twelve to fifteen member of the church at each Sunday morning service. This morning the building was going to be filled to capacity.

"PRAISE THE LORD!" Elder James would shout, not just once, but three or four times. And a couple of times more after that.

At eleven o'clock sharp Deacon Benjamin told everybody to get a song book or share a songbook in today's case and start singing. The books were old and ragged. The church people were a really loud bunch of singing worshippers. Lucy, Amy, and their Momma joined right in and got loud with them.

"Walking on the Promises of God!" That was the first of three different songs they sang that morning before the preaching. After the three songs and just before the preacher had his say, two men passed around a tray with little pieces of what they called unleavened bread. Each person was to take one of those little pieces of unleavened bread and eat it. The Preacher said these little pieces of bread represented the body of Jesus Christ when He died on the Cross for our sins.

Everybody was singing Amen!

Then the same two men passed around little paper cups filled with red grape juice. Everyone took one and drank the grape juice contents. The grape juice represented the Blood of Jesus Christ that He had shed on the Cross for the sins of men.

Everybody was singing Amen again!

Elder James reminded everybody to give back to the Lord what they could for all of their blessings. The giving tub was inside the building next to the front door. All of the giving was to be done after the preaching and singing. That way no one was embarrassed in their giving. When the girls walked out after the services they both noticed there was a lot of money in the tub.

"There must be some rich people that worship God here!" Amy was whispering to Lucy in a very low voice.

The preacher was brother Cody. He was a large man with a strong voice. He spoke for about fifteen or twenty minutes. He talked about the love of God, the punishment for sins, the need for baptism and the grace of Jesus. After services everybody just stood around and talked, they were real friendly. Two of the young girls befriended Lucy and Amy right away. The same two girls also made glancing eyes at Jerald and Jacky. There was one boy the same age as the McCrumb brothers. Sarah was so happy to finally worship God with other ladies. She had made some new lady friends and she knew they would be her friends for life.

Sarah decided to invite two of her new acquaintances to lunch. She knew that John and the men were going prospecting for the next three or four days. She would fill her days with shopping and new friendships. Clara Baskins and Pearl Squibb both accepted Sarah's generous offer of Lunch on the morrow. They would meet at Sarah's favorite eatery at twelve noon sharp. And, maybe after lunch, the ladies would do a little shopping for some ladies fineries.

The men left Denver Monday morning at staggered times; just before sunrise and right after daybreak. They planned their departures at different intervals so not to be noticed. They were to meet at the rock wall, the one with Indian drawings. Their plans were to leave the wall by 8 AM. That would put them at the gap in the canyon wall somewhere around 9:30 or a little earlier. They could meet up with Jock by ten o'clock.

They reached the gap in the canyon wall at 9:15. They spent the next thirty minutes trying to locate Jock. They found his camp, but he wasn't there. Jeremiah wanted to start examining the waterfalls and all of the waterways in the valley with or without Jock. He was certain Jock would turn up sooner or later. It was agreed that Jeremiah, Jerald, and Jacky would start their new adventure at the Falls and John and Jake would map out all of the waterways in is this part of the valley. That would include all streams, ponds, small lakes and anywhere there was water seepage into the ground.

There wasn't any way to get up to the opening where the water was cascading out of the canyon wall, so Jeremiah, Jerald, and Jacky started their explorations at the spot where the water from the falls collided with the canyon floor. The water from the crack in the canyon wall was surging downward with enormous force by the time the water reached the canyon floor. The size of the pond that had been created by the falls was forty to sixty foot wide. They would explore the depth and sediment of the pond another day.

The stream that was allowing the water to escape from the pond was ten to fifteen feet across from bank to bank, depending on where you were standing. The deepest part of the stream at any point was only three feet deep. Most of the stream was gentle rapids rolling over small rocks and pebbles. The water was cold and crystal clear.

Jeremiah wanted to walk a couple of hundred yards of the stream. He wanted to look at the topography surrounding the pond and the stream. He told the boys to look for anything that seemed strange or out of place. He explained that the landscape around the pond and stream just might produce some clues of importance.

John and Jake had found some interesting small water pockets. They weren't sure what had caused them; there was no evidence of geysers or any water seepage from the ground. The seepage could be hidden in the middle of the pockets. They did find numerous places on the canyon walls where there was water seepage through cracks in the rock walls. There was no other stream in any of the areas they had explored. They did find another small lake. It was about an acre and a half in size.

They discovered a cave behind a thick Mahogany stand of trees and some kind of large wild berry bushes. The cave was well hidden from normal sight. It could only be seen by maneuvering around the branches of the tree and climbing through the massive bushes. Jake wanted to explore the inside of the cave but John said they would do that later. He reminded Jake that they would have to make some oil torches to be able to see in the darkness of the cave. The cave's entrance was mystifying and intriguing. John wasn't sure but there appeared to be some kind of strange markings just inside on the walls of the cave. He couldn't be sure it wasn't just a shadow playing tricks on his eyes. He didn't say anything about the markings to Jake. Jake saw the same marking but didn't say anything to John.

Jerald found a small geyser producing bubbles in the middle of the stream about a hundred feet from the waterfalls. Jeremiah didn't have an answer for that one. There was fish in the stream, looked to be Rainbow Trout; big Rainbow Trout. Jeremiah did have an answer for the trout, Eagles and bear food. When Jeremiah mentioned the word bear that got Jacky and Jerald's attention real quick. Their eyes dilated and got really big. They both put their hands on their side arms and made a quick 380 degrees adjustment with their heads and eyesight. Jeremiah started laughing and slowly walked over to a funny looking tree to take a leak. Now, both brothers had to relieve themselves, after the mention of bears.

Jeremiah walked straight back from the funny looking tree into the center of the stream. He knelt down and started to shuffle the rocks and pebbles around. His shuffling became a rather frantic motion and just as fast as he had started to move the rocks he just as quickly stopped and just stared down at the water.

"Jeremiah …………what's wrong? ………Are you hurt? ……..What is it?" Jacky was the first one to question the big man's actions.

Jeremiah just knelt there motionless for a few seconds, then he motioned for the two boys to come over to where he was kneeling. Both brothers were very cautious in their movement towards the big mountain man. They were not certain what was causing the big man's constant gaze at the water.

"Come on,………get over here you two! Hurry up!" Jeremiah was visibly agitated. The sound of his voice commanded a quick response. And, a quick response is what he got. The brothers almost tripped over themselves getting to Jeremiah's side.

"Don't move,………… let the water settle." The boys did as Jeremiah demanded. They stood absolutely still. "Now look real close and tell me what you see!"

Both Jerald and Jacky strained their stare in the direction where Jeremiah was pointing. After a few seconds of looking really close, neither one saw anything unusual, just a lot of small rocks.

"Well?' Jeremiah repeated himself. "What do you see?"

"All I see is a bunch of rocks, Jeremiah." Jerald was almost afraid to answer the big man.

"OK, what color are they?' Jeremiah's tone was softer now.

"Well, there is a red one……. there's a black one,……. a gray, a …..white and…………….that tiny one down there is a gold color." Jacky had hit the why of Jeremiah's stare.

Jeremiah gently picked the tiny gold looking stone up and put it in the palm of his hand.

"Is that….. Jeremiah is that……gold? Is it really gold?" Jerald was stammering all over the word "gold".

It was mid-afternoon on Monday when Jock got back to his home camp. For the past three days, he had been exploring both of the canyon walls. He and his mule "cactus" had walked almost five miles of the walls looking for signs of ore vanes that could be gold related. He had spent the weekend examining and chipping samples of rock surface from both walls of the canyon. He wanted to eliminate the possibility of any vanes of gold running through the rock formation of the walls. Finding no trace of gold he and his new partners could now focus on the valley floor.

Jock had found traces of gold in the valley, just enough gold to get excited over. He was getting old and the valley was just too big for him to scour all by himself. Plus he didn't have the money to continue searching his dreams of finding the elusive gold. He was tired of being ridiculed by every other gold hunter in the country as that "crazy old fart" with dreams of Canyon gold. He had been digging in these mountain canyons for almost fifty years. He had found gold in the past. But they were just a little gold claims that had kept him searching for his dream of the mother lode, always praying that maybe the next canyon would be the fulfillment of that dream. This was his last chance. That was his main reasons for taking on partners and grubstake money.

It was never the riches that drove Jock; it was always the hunt and the adventure of the find. He just knew that this valley held gold and treasure somewhere; he could feel it in his bones. He had never felt this way before about a possible strike. There was something about the valley that was different. He just could not pinpoint what that difference was. But eventually, he would, he swore he would map out that difference. The closest he could come to determine the difference in his mind was the strange way the water in this valley was dissimilar from other canyons. The water seeping from the ground was unusual for this part of the mountains. The small water geysers were not common to the area. Some of the rock construction and formation in the canyon was weird. It seemed to have been caused by some kind of volcanic disruption, but no volcanic evidence was anywhere. Then there was that strange cave and how it was situated. Somehow that cave was out of place. He hadn't explored the cave yet, but he also had seen those strange markings and they were not carved in the wall by Indians.

The stream that had been created and carved by the water gushing from the crack in the canyon wall traveled a perfectly straight course to the other side of the canyon. That in its self would not be unusual except for the fact the water in this stream seemed to be flowing slightly uphill. Jock was positive it was flowing uphill. Jeremiah had the same sensation when he first saw the stream that the water was flowing vaguely uphill. Jeremiah would later test his sensation and found that the stream was indeed slightly traveling on an uphill course.

The stream also gave the appearance of being a continuation of a larger river that was inside of the mountain but was now partially flowing across the open valley and then disappearing underneath the opposite canyon wall. If it was a continuation of a similar river it was now following underneath the next mountain. The strange water pockets found in the valley were not found in any other valleys in that region of the Rockies. The small lake, the one John and Jake saw didn't seem to have any visible source of it. All of this and other anomalies led Jock to conclude the valley was certainly different and could hold many other fascinating secrets, including gold.

Jock came upon John and Jake as they were investigating the shores of the acre and a half lake. The three of them headed back to find Jeremiah and the boys. It was getting late and early enough to make a camp for the night.

Jeremiah, Jerald, and Jacky were still in the middle of the stream moving rocks and pebbles around. Jacky had found a small gold nugget about the same size of Jeremiah's. Jock was not surprised at the trio's small gold fine. He hadn't paid much attention to the stream. Not yet anyway. He spent all of his time with the canyon walls first. He took the nuggets and examined them very closely. He seemed to be extremely satisfied with their size and structure. He kept smiling and nodding his head up and down. Finally, he spoke.

"Gentlemen, these two little pieces of rocks are a great clue to this valley. I feel there's gold in this valley, lots of gold!" Jock smiled and nodded to the other men. Jock had another surprise for his new partners.

"I think we are going to find that this is an enclosed valley caged in by four canyon walls or three canyon walls and another mountain range. Cactus and I have walked every inch of this canyon valley and we didn't find any other entrance. It wouldn't surprise me if the only entrance to this valley is the one we use. That's why no one has ever discovered this valley before. We could be the only white men to ever walk in this valley. We know the red man has been here and

I wouldn't be surprised maybe the Spaniards were here at one time. I know that the Ute Indians traded with the Spaniards a hundred years ago" Jock sounded real sure of himself.

The six men made camp for the night. Before they crawled into their bedrolls and after they had eaten they went over the day's discoveries and then plotted their priorities for the next day.

Sarah had lunch with her new friends on the same day the men rode off to their new canyon valley. The three ladies enjoyed getting to know one another. Clara Baskins' husband was vice president of the Mercantile Bank in Denver and Pearl Squibb and her husband Samuel owned the livery stables where John had stabled the wagons and the horses. Pearl had heard about the baby buffalo at the stables. She told Sarah everybody at the stables loved the little darling. Sarah told the two ladies about the buffalo stampede and how the tiny animal came into her family. Sarah told them of her family's harrowing experience with the Pawnee Indians and the kidnapping of Amy and Lucy by the Ute.

Elder James of the church of Christ had told the ladies that Sarah had been in the Denver hospital. The two ladies inquired concerning Sarah's health. Sarah told them of everything that had transpired in the hospital. Sarah told them that she was going to let God handle her sickness in His way. Both ladies were sad and happy at the same time. They were amazed at Sarah's courage in facing her future, knowing that her life was in the balance and her life was being cut short. The three ladies used one of the stable buggy's to show Sarah the city of Denver. At the end of the Denver tour, they took her to the city's most exclusive shops of ladies garments.

During the evening while John and the boys were gold hunting Sarah and the girls would either talk way into the night or read and study their Bibles. Some nights they would entertain their lady friends or other members of the church of Christ.

Lucy and Amy spent the day with their new found friends, Clair Squibb and Mary Holcomb. The two Denver girls were fascinated with Lucy and Amy's wagon train stories. They had hundreds of questions about their capture by the Ute Indians.

At the beginning of the discussions the questions the two Denver girls really wanted to ask they didn't. They were either afraid to ask, too shy to ask or both. But after getting comfortable with the ongoing conversation Mary Holcomb finally asked the bomb question.

"Lucy, did those Indians make you take all of your clothes off?" After Mary got the question out of her mouth her face turned scarlet in color. Clair's eyes got almost as big as hen eggs as she anticipated Lucy's answer.

"Well, I think they wanted to........they did talk.....but I couldn't understand them..........NO.........they really didn't...But they did tear my nightgown" Lucy wanted to add just a little suspense in her answer.

"Let me show you what they did do to me!" Lucy's eyes narrowed and her lips tightened as she spoke.

"Lucy!" It was Amy who interjected a faint sort of a protest. She really wanted Lucy to show them. She was just putting a little dramatic pause in Lucy's expression. "Do you think you should really show them?" Amy halfheartedly questioned Lucy. Then Amy turned to the two girls, "if she does show you and I don't think she should, you have to promise not to tell anyone."

Both girls shook their heads and promised not to say a word to anyone. Of course, neither Lucy nor Amy believed them.

Lucy slowly unbuttoned her blouse and pulled it and her petty coat blouse down around her shoulders to where the tops of her breasts were showing. Both girls uttered chilling gasps and frantically drew their hands up to their opened mouths. The five to six-inch scar that the savage Indian had sliced across Lucy's chest just above her left breast with his knife was scabbing over and it appeared hideous and grotesque to look at. It frightened both girls to tears. It was really just healing and healing quite well at that, but still looked hideous enough to shock the girls.

"Oh Lucy, you poor dear girl." Clair was crying. "Why did they do that?"

"Well........He made the motions as if he was going to cut my heart out." Lucy was helping the drama along with her statements.

Now Mary was also crying along with Clair. Both girls got real close to Lucy trying to focus on that "devil made scar" one of them sobbed.

"Will it always be there Lucy?" Both girls were asking at the same time.

"My momma thinks it will always show. It was a pretty deep cut." Lucy wanted them to think it would always be there.

It really was upsetting for Lucy to talk about that frightful night she had experienced with the Ute Indians. But, in some strange way talking about that torturous night even with the dramatic highlights that the McCrumb girls were adding to the event were helping both Lucy and Amy to cope with their horrible experience. Both girls were still having some emotional problems. Small conversations such as this one with the city girls allowed both Lucy and Amy to vent some of their lasting fears and anxieties' caused by the two days of being kidnapped and ill-treated. It was a type of therapy that the girls really needed and they did feel spiritually renewed after talking about the event even with the drama added.

Both of the city girls looked at Lucy and Amy as worldly and mature ladies because of what they had been through. That pleased the McCrumb sisters to absolutely no end. They were pleased to have this opportunity to experience this once in a lifetime of adulation. In a strange and inexplicable way conversations like this one gave the sisters an opportunity to cope and heal from the tragedy of their kidnapping.

Clair and Mary were intrigued how Amy maneuvered her escape from the Indians by using her monthly period. That was something they just could not imagine ever doing. A young lady's time of the month was something that folks just did not talk about. Even mothers and daughters only discussed it in hush whispers. Both Clair and Mary found it to be very refreshing to be able to engage in a conversation about such a secretive subject out in the open with other girls. It had been an extremely educational day for the two city girls. They felt just a little more grown up, more open minded with a greater understanding of the secretive parts of their female anatomy after talking to Lucy and Amy.

The four girls spent a lot of time together during the next week. Their discussions were mostly girl talk about their dreams, aspirations, and marriage. They talked about things like what they would wish for in a husband, how many children they would want to birth, even the pain in birthing. They talked about God and their faith in the word of God. Their conversations were real; they were the conversations that young ladies rarely uttered in a group setting for fear of embarrassment or maybe violating the "good book". The four young women were maturing in a Victorian age. The Victorian culture that had been given birth in merry old England had traveled across the Atlantic Ocean to the Americas and in many ways was at odds with the American culture. The further west those Victorian beliefs traveled the more they really collided with the most open culture of the American West.

....

After two days of searching for possibilities that the newly discovered box canyon might be offering the inexperienced explorers, Jeremiah decided that he and Jerald would ride back to Denver for some much-needed staple supplies and a couple of unusual supplies that would be needed to furthers their search of the canyon. They needed more lanterns and coal oil to fuel the lanterns so they could explore the cave and especially the strange cave "bubble room". Jeremiah would bring his packhorses back with him to the canyon loaded with the supplies. It was also agreed that the dogs and the baby buffalo should be a brought to the canyon. The dogs could watch and warn the prospectors of impending danger from unwelcomed wild animals or unwanted human vermin. The little buffalo would be entertaining.

The second and third day in the canyon was spent in exploring the rocky stream to determine if there was more gold in its waters. By the dawn of that third day, the color of gold was still avoiding the gold pans of Jock and his partners. Late on the fifth day, Jeremiah rode back into the canyon with lanterns, supplies, dogs and a buffalo. He was met with disappointment and a mindset of displeasure among his prospecting companions. There were only traces of gold found in the stream so far.

Jeremiah told John that Sarah looked well, maybe just a little tired. When John was alone with Jerald he asked his son how his mom was doing.

"How's your mom feeling? Is she enjoying her new friends?" John didn't want to sound alarmed with his questions. John wanted to get back to Sarah.

"She said she really likes her new friend's papa. They all went shopping last Monday and Momma bought everybody some new clothes. Her friends come over to the boarding house almost every day, sometimes even at night." Jerald could sense that his pa was worried about his mom. "Lucy and Amy's friends are at the house a lot." Then Jerald kind of wrinkled up his brow with a slight frown. "Pa.... I don't think momma feels very good.....she didn't want me...... or us to worry about her, but...I think she hurts somewhere."

'I'm going back to Denver tonight son. I'm going to be with your momma for a while and I'm not sure when I'll be back here to help Y'all, maybe in a week. You be careful here and watch over Jacky. Maybe by the time I get back, you'll have some gold for me...OK?" John was smiling at his eldest son and he gave him a big hug.

"OK pa. We'll do our best on finding that treasures before you get back." Jerald smiled, hugged his pa, but wasn't sure about the promise of treasures.

John left for Denver after he had helped Jeremiah unload the lanterns and other supplies. The days had gotten longer during the summer months in the west. Even at eight thirty or nine thirty at night, the sun was just setting in the western sky, which made for a long work day. By ten o'clock on this night all of the men were snoring in their bedrolls; they wanted to get an early start on the morning of the sixth day of gold hunting.

Digging and shifting through the rocks in the small river was a tiring task; it was also tedious and boring. It was difficult inspecting every stone and every pebble in the stream. Shovel after shovel of stones and pebbles of all sizes were examined and scrutinized for that elusive color of gold. It seemed that all that was being accomplished was just another shovel full of more rocks of all sizes were being taken from the river. There was always that fear of missing that one important gold stone.

If Jerald and Jacky found an oddly looking stone or one that had an unusual shape or color they would toss it upon the banks of the stream. A few of the stones were quite pretty in a blaze of colors while other rocks had fascinating color combinations. Their shapes were never ending. These were the types of stones that would wind up on the dry land next to the stream.

Jerald hadn't found that one particular rock that he really wanted to put in a collection for a while, but he did capture one that really intrigued him. It was almost in the perfect shape of one of his mom homemade bars of lye soap. It wasn't a particular pretty rock, in fact, it was an ugly color, it was rectangular in shape, about an inch thick and six inches long and three inches wide. It had a strange greenish and light yellow dirty mossy tinge to it and it was really heavy compared to the other rocks. He had never seen a rock like this one before. It wasn't even a pretty color so he threw it back into the water. But something kept nagging at him about its peculiar irregular shape compared with the many other really odd shaped rocks so he decided to keep it with his other collected rock specimens. He retrieved it back from the water and threw it on the river bank along with the other rocks he had accumulated.

Jeremiah was shifting through the rocks in the stream a few feet behind Jerald and Jacky. Jake and Jock were behind Jeremiah doing the same thing and at times exploring with the same stones. If something valuable was missed by one person maybe the next guy would find it. They planned on doing the complete length of the stream in this manner, even if it took weeks. They wanted to make sure the stream had been examined carefully and thoroughly before they moved their gold hunting attention to other parts of the canyon. Jeremiah had come out of the cold water to take another leak. It had been agreed that no one up-river would pee in the stream. Jeremiah was walking along the river bank to his favorite tree when he spotted an object on the ground that caught his attention. Jeremiah picked the thing up and examined the object with a kind of a suspicious deliberation. He could tell it had just come out the water.

"Who threw this up here?" Jeremiah held the object up in the air so everyone could get a good look at it.

"I did!...........Why? What is it?" It was Jerald's flat bar of soap size rock. "Where in the world did you find it?" Jeremiah was now getting everyone's attention.

"Back there a few feet." Jerald turned and pointed to the spot behind him.

"Good heavens boy this is a manmade bar of gold!" Now Jeremiah was almost exploding with excitement.

Everybody was scrambling out of the stream to get a good look at this incredible find. The excitement was overwhelming. Jock was dancing a jig, exclaiming loudly that he knew there were gold treasures in this canyon. Jake was dancing the jig with Jock. Jeremiah picked Jerald up and held him high over his own head while turning and dancing in circles. Jacky was just standing there holding the bar of gold in front of his face and gazing into its mystical powers of hypnosis.

It took a few minutes for everyone to calm down. When calm did once again reign, and then came the avalanche of mystifying and baffling questions. Questions like; how did it get into the stream, who put it in the stream, who brought it and how did it get into the canyon, how old is it, when was it brought to the canyon and where did it come from? And then, will the prodigious question ever be answered; is there more of these in the stream? All wondered if any of those questions would ever be answered?

Jock gently cleaned the gold bar while his partners quietly watched. There was some kind of greenish colored slime on the bar. The gold bar had probably been buried in the sediment in the bed of the stream underneath the stones for over a hundred years. Jerald unknowingly placed his spade just in the right position to bring the bar to the water's surface. That might indicate that other bars of gold could have been passed over because of the bad positioning of the spades.

Jock's homemade saddle soap was doing a good job of bringing out the fascinating color of gold in the bar. When the bar's cleaning was completed an indented symbol was distinctly stamped on one side of the gold bar. None of the men had the slightest idea what the symbol meant or represented. Jock thought the mark might be Spanish or Portuguese. He had seen some Portuguese symbols on gold bullion when he was a young man prospecting down near the country of Mexico. He had taken a few ounces of gold dust to an assay office down there the same time some Mexican government guys were weighing gold bars with a funny symbol stamped in it. As best he could remember the symbol maybe resembles the mark on this gold bar Jerald found. Jock guessed the gold bar weighed somewhere between one and two pounds.

"Well gentlemen, we have an important decision to make." Jock's tone of voice tone was serious in its delivery. "We start over, go on and then start over or work our way backward. "What will it be? I would suggest for the rest of the day we dig in the area where Jerald found this bar, and then tomorrow we make the decision where to go from there."

"I say we dig where Jerald found this one." Jake was expressing his choice of action.

Jeremiah and the brothers agreed. Where there was one bar maybe there will be another one. If there were a number of gold bars tossed in the stream at this location the current of the stream would not be strong enough to move them any further than where they initially landed. They sectioned off a small area of the stream and placed themselves where they would not be in each other's way.

Jerald had found the bar just after lunch, which gave the men at least another five or six hours of daylight to shift through rocks and sediment. The only times a break was taken were pee breaks. Everybody wanted to find that next gold bar if there were any other gold bars hiding in the cold waters of the small steam. If there were any more of the gold bars they would be buried deeper in the water's sediment. After four hours of continuous shoveling, it appeared the day would end with only one lonely, but a very valuable bar of gold. Just when everyone had all but given up hope for any other discoveries for the day Jeremiah went to his knees and frantically started digging in the rocks, separating rocks from sediments, tossing the debris to his sides. With one final gesture with his large hands, he brought two more gold bars up from out of the water and lifted them high into the air. The canyon walls shook with the resounding shouts of the jubilant and astonished gold hunters.

It was immediately decided that Jake would ride to Denver on the morrow, tell John of the discovery and make an inquiry of the three cowpokes if they wanted to be part of the gold hunting party.

The quarrying of stones and the splashing of the water of the stream was terminated for that day. Everyone was too excited to dig any further. The partners wanted to examine the latest discovery. The two gold bars were the same size as the first one. They also had the same strange marking, except on different areas of the bar. Jock cleaned the two bars of gold with his same homemade concoction he had used to clean the first bar. The bars bright and shining glow brought smiles to the faces of the euphoric gold seekers.

"Jock.... are we rich? How ....rich is we, I mean.... are we?" Jacky had a puzzling look on his face when he asked Jock the questions, all in one gulp.

"Son,...... we're going to be realllllllyyy rich...before we leave this canyon." Jock's smile was accented with craggy aged wrinkles caused by years and years of failed empty dug holes, disappointments and condescending jokes at his expense.

"Who in this world put these gold bars in this tiny creek?" Jeremiah was shaking his head back and forth in disbelief. "Jock......did the Spanish come this far north?.........I was told once by a Lakota tribal chief that his people had an iron headpiece from their ancient times. He told me it was from a strange people who wore iron clothes and rode the horse before the horse roamed the prairies. I thought the head piece was probably some kind of an iron helmet......... Jock, it has to be the Spaniards."

“It was the Spaniards!... I’m sure of it!” Jock had a sly smile as if he knew something the rest of the group didn’t know. “Tomorrow morning I want to show Y’all something I discovered when I first found this hidden canyon.” His smile took a turn to a serious frown. “Gentleman, this valley is full of Spanish treasures............All we have to do…..is find them!” The smile returned to Jock’s craggily face.

“What kind of treasures, Jock? Things other than these gold bars?” Now Jake had a muddled and confused look.

“Yes!” Jock’s smile broadened.” Maybe gold and maybe even silver things, things like necklaces and jewelry, swords, even rare diamonds. Maybe, and maybe much more?.”

The five men talked and pondered treasures well into the early morning hours of the next day. Sleep was not on anyone’s minds. The three shiny gold bars and what new information tomorrow might bring kept popping up in everyone’s wild thoughts.

Jake went straight to the boarding house the next morning to give John the exciting news of the three gold bars. He had left the canyon at sunrise. Sarah was more excited with the good news then John seemed to be. She wanted to know why Jake didn’t bring one of those gold bars to show them. Jake displayed a big smile and then pulled one of those treasured gold bars from inside his shirt and from behind his belt. She gasped a soft famine sound of joy and thrust her two hands out to caress the shiny bar. After seeing Sarah’s excitement over the gold bar John’s enthusiasm perked right up.

Both Sarah and John’s eyes widened when Jake told them of the other two bars that had been discovered. Jake related the story of the discovery and of how, when and where in great detail for Sarah and John. After the excitement of his storytelling had calmed down Jake asked John if he would go with him to see if the three cowpokes would consider helping the gold hunters in their canyon search.

The two men found the cowpokes shoveling horse and cattle poop in the stock yards at the livery stables. John invited the three men to lunch at the nearest eatery. He told them to meet him and Jake at the eatery at one o'clock sharp.

The cowpokes were early and were sitting on old wobbly benches in front of the eatery when John and Jake appeared on their horses. John located a table in a corner of the eatery where no one else was sitting close by.

"Boys, I have a proposition for Y'all to consider. Do you want to hear it?" John's matter of fact tone kind of startled the three young men. They looked a little bewildered and hesitated a second or two before answering. After looking at each other and shrugging their shoulders, they answered in the affirmative by shaking their heads up and down.

"First, and most important,….. and I mean extremely important." Now John's voice lowered and his eyes lids narrow and his brow furrowed into a facial growl. "What I'm going to say next must be a complete secret. …….understood?" Now the three men were getting a little concerned, but they agreed. "We want you all to work with us….not for us……..but with us in hunting gold!"

The three cowpokes were not only startled and bewildered, now they were confused at John's declaration and his unselfish request.

"Mr. McCrumb, we don't rightly understand what you're saying, hunting gold where? What do ya mean, not working for you?" Henry Edwards had just become the three young men's spoke person. "We would be happy to work for you. You have been very kind to us."

"Henry, we have discovered gold in a long lost and secret canyon not far from here. There's a lot of work to be done. And, there's enough gold for all of us." John really had the three Tennessee boy's undivided and penetrating attention now. "What we're asking is would the three of you like to be junior partners with us?"

"Mr. McCrumb, when do we start?" John got a quick and determined answer from Henry.

"Fellows, you'll start right now! Go with Jake, he'll take you to your new job". John had finished his part of the new hiring mission, now he had to get back to Sarah. She and John had an appointment with some doctors in the hospital.

Jake took the three cowpokes to the livery stable where he bought each a fine horse and saddle. Their next stop was Denver's finest gunsmith. Each of the cowpokes picked out a new Colt 45 caliber side arm with simple holsters. Jake insisted that each one of them needed a new Remington 30/30 rifle and shells.

Sarah's pains were worsening even though she wasn't passing any more blood than she normally passed. But, the blood coloration had changed just a bit. It seemed to be just a little darker in color.

Sarah had an examination the day before John came back from the canyon. The meeting today was for the results of that examination. Sarah knew the results would not be good ones. She was mentally and spiritually prepared for the results, it was John's wellbeing she was more concerned about. She knew that emotionally he would take the results in the worst way possible.

Two doctors were waiting for John and Sarah at the hospital. The doctors and a nurse took the couple into a consultation room where they could have a private discussion. The doctors got right to the heart of Sarah's increasing pain. They told her and John that her cancer had gotten much worse. They told them that there wasn't anything that could be done medically for cancer, only for the pain. In the most delicate words possible the doctors told Sarah that her life was quickly ebbing away. Both doctors and the nurse had tears in their eyes. John broke down in a wash of tears as he took Sarah in his arms. He never wanted to let her go, never ever again. He cried because his heart was breaking. Sarah tried to console him with the comfort of her love.

"John, I promise you that the gift of our love will take us through this to a better reward." Sarah kissed John and positioned his head on her breasts. "John, you have been my strength many times during our blessed marriage. Now I need that strength more than ever. John, my heart will forever be with you."

The nurse had to leave the room because all of the emotions overwhelmed her. The doctors were also moved to teary eyes. They had never encountered such faith as Sarah's. John finally gained some control of his emotions with the help of Sarah's continuing soft comforting words. John slowly regained his composure as he looked into her eyes. He was trying desperately to find the right words to say, but no words would come. He couldn't find the courage to say anything. If he did find the right words his heart would burst and the tears would drown out any words he spoke.

Sarah smiled into John's eyes and gently placed her fingers on his cheeks. "John, you don't have to say anything..........my heart knows that your heart is hurting.........My heart knows what your heart is trying to say...........John, there is no love stronger than our love for each other..........I will always be here for you........ you must always believe that..........look at me John, look into my eyes.........every time your heart beats, my heart will beat with it......".

John and Sarah just sat there looking at each other holding each other's hands. The love they had for each other surpassed all worldly bonds because they each considered it was a spiritual love from God Himself.

Sarah wiped the tears from John's face and cheerfully said, "John, I'm not gone yet, sweetheart.........." Sarah started to chuckle with that little girl like sweet chuckle that always made John laugh. "John, I'm hungry, take me to my favorite eatery and feed me."

Both of the doctors and John were now smiling through all of their tears because of Sarah's request for food. It was typical Sarah's faith driven humor and it worked.

Jake had left the gold bar with John and Sarah. That night by the light of a coal oil burning lamp Sarah examined and re-examined almost every inch of the gold bar, being a female she even tried smelling it. John started to laugh when Sarah put the gold bar to her nose. Just holding something that valuable with an unsolved history was really fascinating to Sarah. When she had finished her examination of the bar she looked at John and informed him that she wanted to see the secret lost canyon. John's brow sort of wrinkled, he wasn't sure if he should really believe her request or not. But it didn't take him long to get the message; one thing was certain, Sarah was going to see this famous gold producing canyon. And soon!

The same morning that Jake had left the canyon to inform John of the gold bars, Jock had promised to show the men a discovery he had made when he first found the canyon. Jock was the first person up after Jake had ridden off for Denver that morning. The old prospector had fried bacon and his special mountain fried pancakes for the rest of the crew. Coffee was always boiling in the coffee pot. Sometimes the coffee was so strong Jeremiah said it could almost pour itself.

After everyone had their fill of Jock's mountain heavy pancakes he told them to prepare the lanterns with coal oil. He told the guys they were going to do a little cave exploring. Any time a seasoned mountain man explored a cave he would definitely have either his side arm hooked to his belt or a powerful rifle in one of his hands. Caves were wonderful homes for the giant brown bear. Jeremiah knew what cave Jock was leading them to; he had seen the cave his first day in the canyon. He was sure this cave was not the home of any bear. He had not seen any signs of bear poop or bear rubbings on any of the trees and more important, no bear sightings. Besides, the dogs would have warned everyone with their barking if a bear had roamed the camp at night.

The men made their way through the twisted mahogany trees and large heavy thick tangled berry bushes to the entrance of the cave. The dogs and the baby buffalo had followed the men to the cave, but it was decided that the dogs should stay out in the open. The depth of a pitch black cave for a lost dog would be too dangerous to chance. Everyone carried a lit lantern. A couple of feet into the cave Jock stopped the men and pointed to the cave wall on their right-hand side.

"Look over there at that wall……. What do you see?" Jock was pointing to some strange markings and writings on the cave wall. It was the same markings that John thought he had seen when he and Jake first discovered the cave their first day in the canyon. John wasn't sure at that time he was actually seeing writings because of shadows or maybe his eyes were just playing tricks on him.

"These are Spanish writings." Jock continued. "And over here is what I believe is a date, I believe it reads 1738. It could be 1728 or even 1718……..There are more writing a little further in the cave……..I've only been back in the cave,……..maybe a hundred feet…….didn't want to get trapped in here by myself"

"Well, Jock….this a good as time as any to explore this sucker…… what do ya think?" Jeremiah was ready for the adventure.

Jerald and Jacky were having a difficult time taming their enthusiasm. They were ready to run into the thick darkness that lay ahead of them to the back of the cave at any given word of encouragement. Jeremiah told the boys to be real careful because there could be hidden pits, holes or "hollow-outs" in any location in these old caves. The boys noticed the further they went into the cave the colder it got. In fact, it was quite cold. The cave was about ten to twelve feet wide, sometimes a little wider. It was a good ten foot high; Jeremiah never had to bend down. The crew moved slow, examining almost every foot of the cave. At about one hundred feet into the cave, there was nothing unusual, other than more strange writings could be seen on the cave wall.

Jock wanted to sample the rock wall every twenty or so feet. He would chip some chunks off of the wall with his mining hammer. The loose chunks went into a leather bag he had tied to his belt. At about two hundred feet into the canyon cave, both Jerald and Jacky was losing their enthusiasm for this cave exploring stuff. They had lost sight of the cave's entrance sunlight a few feet back. Now, it would really be pitch black without the lanterns. The cave was damp and getting colder. There was some water seepage on the cave walls which gave the cave's dimension a sense of eeriness. Neither boy wanted to be the one to suggest that they all go back. But both boys would be happy to do just that, go back.

The cave floor was graduating at an upward level and the cave's temperature was getting a little warmer, but still cold. Jock figured they were somewhere near five hundred feet into the mountain when a large room like a giant bubble was before them. They couldn't really tell how large the cave room was, but it appeared to be huge. The lanterns light were not powerful enough to flood the whole room. Jock warned the explorers that they should be very careful because of pits and holes, especially in this large "bubble" room as he dubbed it.

Just a few feet into the strange "bubble room", Jeremiah who was in the lead tripped over a large object he thought must have been a large rock, or maybe a boulder protruding out of the ground. After he had retrieved his lantern he crawled back to the thing he had tripped over and he discovered it was some type of a large metal chest. It was extremely heavy, either an iron or bronze box. Its size was at least a couple of feet in all directions, maybe a little bigger. The box turned out to be iron and was heavily encrusted by age. Jeremiah held the lantern close to the box, but couldn't determine much about it because of the lack of good lighting. He could just barely make out a highly detailed marking what looked like a royal crest; maybe it was a rich guy's chest. At least it had important looking characteristics.

At about the same time Jeremiah had tripped over the iron box Jock had made an incredible discovery of his own. Lying next to the wall of the cave was the remains of an ancient decomposed skeleton in a metal vest and a metal helmet. It was without a doubt a sixteen hundred century Spanish conquistador warrior's paraphernalia.

The metal armor was dirty and dusty, but still in solid condition. The design on the vest armor was just barely visible. There was a broken end tip of an Indian stone point lying inside the armor vest. Jock could see other armor type forms but those forms were at the farthest range of the lanterns glow and hard to recognize with little light. He would explore those areas another day under more lantern light.

Both Jock and Jeremiah decided it was time to leave the cave and finish their exploration later when they had more help. They also needed more lantern light power to properly get a better visual look at this large bubble in the mountain. Jerald and Jacky had silently decided that they should have retreated from the cave about two hundred feet ago. The box was too heavy for two men to carry and they had too far to go to the cave's entrance. There were large iron rings on two sides of the box. The men could carve out two long poles, place them through the rings and four men could carry the box to sunlight. They would need the sunlight to examine the box's contents anyway. The cave's air was musty and the guys needed to breathe some fresh air. It didn't take the four men long to really appreciate fresh air again and in the sunlight too. Within a matter of a few minutes, the gold seekers were at the cave's entrance. They knew that Jake and the three cowpokes would be in the canyon to help with the next cave exploration. They were happily greeted by the four dogs and a buffalo at the cave's entrance.

Jeremiah told Jerald and Jacky if that buffalo grows any faster they'll be able to ride it in a month. Jock started laughing watching the buffalo running with the dogs. He commented that the damn buffalo thinks it's a dog.

The four cave explorers had lost track of time while they were in the cave. What seemed like only a couple of hours, in reality, they were in the cave over five hours. It was well into the afternoon when they emerged from the entrance of the cave. They went back to the campsite to relax and gather their thoughts, eat and drink coffee. They had much to discuss and talk about after the day's experience. There were a lot of questions to be asked and some answers to be understood before further evaluation of the next action in exploring and removing items from the cave.

Jake and the three cowpokes rode into the campsite in time to share some food and strong coffee. Jeremiah related the day's events to four sets of a very attentive pair of ears. Jake kind of expected or at least was hoping that the cave would give the explorers some kind of significant historical treasures of its past. The three cowpokes were flabbergasted and could hardly believe what they were being told. Jock handed them the two gold bars to examine.

"Jock, we appreciate you sharing your good fortune here in the canyon with us ......and Jeremiah; we really want to thank you, John and Jake for bringing us into this group, but..." There was a long pause before Henry could finish his question. He was fighting back tears. "but why are you doing it? You certainly don't really need us."

"Son.......life is hard.....and when that great man way up there in the heavens sends a great blessing.....well...we just need to share it with someone we think deserves a portion of that blessing." Jeremiah was not only a very big man in physical stature; he also had a very big sharing heart.

"Now Henry," Jeremiah continued with a question, "What in the sam hill are these other two cowpokes names? Guys, we're still going to call Y'all cowpokes, but we still need to know your Christian given names"

"OK, this tall one is called Red," Henry was laughing now and the other two cowpokes were brimming with pride during the introductions. "Red Montgomery and this other character with the beard is Jasper Higgins. Red and Jasper and I have been friends all of our lives in Tennessee. My mom and pa were killed a few years ago and Red and Jasper's families have helped me to take care of my two brothers and blind sister."

Red Montgomery was almost as tall as Jeremiah, but not nearly as big. Jasper Higgins was about six feet tall and quite stout, especially around his middle.

"Why did ya come out west fellas?" Jock didn't know the answer to that question, Jeremiah and Jake did.

"Most all of the folks in our hometown back in Tennessee are poor people…..we just thought we would come out west and get some of that gold we kept hearing about... Then we could bring some of it back to Tennessee and help our families. When we did finally save enough money to get here there wasn't any gold to find, others had found it first. We ended shoveling horse and cow poop so we could at least make enough money so we buy food. Couldn't find any of that gold we heard so much about and now we don't have any money to get back home. I need to make sure my sister is well taken care of. My brothers will do fine but my sister "Bright" needs my help." Henry wasn't laughing anymore.

The gold hunters were delighted to have these three cowpokes part of the canyon team. They would be a huge help to lighten the workload that was ahead of the gold hunting team. After Henry gave his answer to Jock's question Jeremiah thought maybe it was the time that he and John needed to have a conversation about Henry and his sister "Bright".

When Lucy and Amy heard that their momma was going to some hidden canyon with their pap they wanted to know what hidden canyon they were talking about. Neither John nor Sarah had told the girls about any gold hunt or the hidden canyon.

Amy had accidentally overheard a conversation where her mom told her pappa that she was going to some mysterious canyon. Amy told Lucy and now the girls were a little confused over why all the mystery over this secret canyon. The girls didn't know anything about any canyon let alone their mom wanting to visit it. John had told the girls not to say anything to anybody if they should inquire why their pa's frequent visits to the mountains near Denver. Lucy just thought her pap was thinking about buying some land near the mountains. Maybe he wanted to be a farmer again is all she thought. But now, for two days all John heard from his two daughters was about this secret hidden canyon.

"Why can't we go to the canyon with you? We want to see the canyon too. The boys got to go.........and I'm older than the boys." That was Lucy's standard answer when the boys got to do something and she didn't. That is when the debates broke out into begs, pleads and appeals of going to the canyon.

Finally, John and Sarah broke down and gave into the girl's constant pleading and begging. Now John would have to tell Lucy and Amy about the gold and possible treasures. The boys knew so now it was only fair that the girls were told also.

Neither Lucy nor Amy could scarcely believe the story of the gold and the hidden canyon, it sounded like some fairy tale. They had never met Jock nor heard of any conversations about him. Their fascinations with the gold bar were exhilarating and captivating to the sisters. Neither sister wanted to put the gold bar down once they got it in their hands. Their desire to go to the canyon grew even more intense when they were told the cowpokes were helping in the canyon to look for gold. Lucy let her pap and momma know that she was just a little annoyed that Amy and she were the last to be told about this adventure. John apologized to his daughters and told them that they had the right to be a little upset that they had not been told about the gold and the canyon before now. But, he also informed them in short terms that he was not going be tolerant if their whining continued.

After church services that next Sunday morning Sarah and the girls told their friends that John was taking them to look at some farming property that he was considering buying northwest of Denver. They would be gone all day Monday and would see everybody sometime on Tuesday. The ladies of the church took turns checking on Sarah's well-being almost every day. Clair and Mary had a habit of showing up at Lucy and Amy's room at the boarding house just about any time of the day. They had to tell the church people a reason why the McCrumb would be gone for the day or panic would overcome the small congregation of Christians because of Sarah health problems. The McCrumb's were well thought of by those who know them as a Christian family. John and Sarah couldn't tell anybody about the gold or the hidden canyon; not yet anyway!

John had rented a buggy with a shade top on it for the trip to the canyon, he didn't want Sarah riding a horse and this way Lucy and Amy could ride with their momma. Sarah and the girls put on comfortable new-fangled riding trousers for ladies. These were not the usual type of clothing that a woman would normally wear in public, but there would be no public to see them in the desert or in the canyon. The sisters thought that these newfangled duds were super and even talked about wearing them in Denver; their Ma shook her head in a very determined way that indicated "that will never happen"! The clothes were actually almost like men's loose work pants but with a few frills. The women in the western gold fields wore these types of clothes without the frills.

John and his family left early Monday morning and reached the canyon entrance about an hour and a half later. Finding their way to the hidden canyon was an exciting adventure for Lucy and Amy. It was tiring for Sarah and she was in some moderate pain, but she never once complained. When they walked through the natural rock opening into the hidden canyon Sarah and the girls were amazed at the splendor that was between the majestic canyon walls. The first things Lucy spotted was the waterfall cascading out of the canyon wall. Amy was fascinated with all of the strange looking bushes and trees. John led them to the small stream in hopes that the men would still be working the stream for other gold bars.

The sisters were almost bowled over by four tail-wagging pooches and one rambunctious buffalo. The five animals were jockeying for attention and petting privileges. The little Buffalo was winning because of her size.

Jacky was the first person to see his momma and sisters. He tripped and fell a number of times trying to get out of the stream to hug his momma. Jerald followed just as fast. Jeremiah and Jake were surprised to see Sarah and the girls here in the canyon but were very pleased to see Sarah's bright smile. The two cowpokes spoke to Ms. Sarah and the sisters, Henry spoke to Ms. Sarah and Lucy. John introduced Jock to his wife and two daughters.

Lucy and Amy wanted to get in the stream of water and look for gold, but their pa wanted to show them the cave first. Jeremiah said that he would go to the cave with them but first he needed to tell John about what was found when the men explored five hundred feet of the cave. Lucy and Amy thought Jeremiah was just joking around with them with the cave story. When they finally realized that Jeremiah was telling the truth they couldn't wait to get in the cave. John didn't think it was a good idea for the girls to go deep cave exploring, at least not today. Jeremiah agreed.

When they reached the cave's entrance Jeremiah lit four lanterns, one for each of them. John said they would go into the cave for about a hundred feet, that far in the cave would give the girls a reality check just how dark and lonely a cave can be. At about one hundred and fifty feet into the cave, the sisters were ready to welcome some good old sunlight. That was enough cave exploring for Lucy and Amy, at least for this cave and on that day. They would rather hunt for gold in the stream. Jeremiah told them if they didn't mind getting those fancy girl duds wet and their mom didn't care it was OK with the guys.

Sarah told the girls to go ahead but be careful and don't hurt themselves. Lucy found a convenient spot in the stream next to Henry. Amy lasted in the cold rocky creek water for about fifteen minutes. She described a number of excuses to exit the water; the rocks hurt her feet, the water was too cold and it was just too hard standing up straight. She fell twice, the second time she bruised her elbow. Lucy didn't last much longer than Amy in the water, especially after falling backward on her pride. Henry had to help her up and out of the stream. Hunting gold in a cold rocky creek bed sounded glamorous but it turned out to be a pain in the elbow, a pain on the feet and in Lucy's case a pain in the posterior.

Jock fixed the guests a good old fashion prospector's meal; beans, bacon and mountain pancakes. Sarah and the girls had a fun and enjoyable day in the canyon except maybe for Jock's mountain pancakes. Sarah was happy to get back to the boarding house later that afternoon so she could rest. Lucy and Amy wore themselves out exploring the valley. They had plenty of company with four dogs and a buffalo while looking for lost treasures. Jock had given each of the sisters one of the small gold nuggets that had been found in the stream. It was going to be tough for the girls not being able to tell their friends about this hidden valley and the adventure they had roaming through it. They particularly wanted to tell their friends about their adventure in the deep dark beer cave and the small gold nuggets. Keeping that part of the canyon adventure a secret was really trying the sister's promise of silence to their pa.

John told Jeremiah that he would be back to the valley Wednesday morning to help with further exploration of the great "bubble" room and the removal of the gold and anything else that was discovered.

John brought Jake and Jock into in the discussion for their input. It was decided to abandon the hunt for gold in the stream for the present and concentrate on the pond where the cascading water from the crack in the canyon wall hit the canyon floor. Jock figured there might be a possibility, even if a slim one, of finding some large gold nuggets in the pond. If there was gold in the mountain behind that cliff wall the power and force of the waterfalls could force nuggets through the crack in the canyon wall. Jock's experience in prospecting had taught him that it was by the force of water that had placed gold nuggets in every river where gold had been found in the first place. This pond could be a natural for a gold deposit, or it could just be a water pond loaded with plain old rocks. They would start working the pond after the men had taken their booty from out of the large domed "bubble room" in the mountain.

John was in the Valley by nine on Wednesday morning. This Wednesday was June 30th in1875 and the day was bright with almost no clouds in the sky and there was a sharp nip in the air where a light weight coat felt good to keep a chill at bay. John, Jeremiah, Jake, Jock and the three cowpokes were ready to invade the cave for the second time. This time there would be plenty of light radiating from nine or ten lit lanterns. It was decided that Jerald and Jacky would take a watch at the cave entrance and keep the dogs and buffalo company.

It took the seven men about thirty minutes to reach the large mountain cavern after leaving the cave's entrance. Jeremiah had named the large underground mountain room the "bubble". Everybody started referring to it as the "bubble". This was John's first time in the bubble and he was amazed at its size. With the added lantern light the men could see the room's domed ceiling. The ceiling was close to fifty feet above the bubbles floor and from wall to wall was about one hundred fifty feet wide. Even with the added light, the depth of the room couldn't be detected. It just appeared to be a deep black hole. To get the maximum use of the lanterns the men stayed together as they explored the bubble. They found two more ancient skeletons clothed in Spanish armor. The breastplates and helmets were in good condition. One of the remains must of have been an important leader. Next to his remains was an engraved broadsword that had a gold handle that was encrusted with rare gemstones. His breastplate was inlaid with gold designs.

Next to the remains of the man that John had determined was a man of some kind of distinction was a neatly placed mound of one hundred and ninety-two bars of gold bullion. These gold bars were the same type the guys had found in the stream. Jock sank to his knees in disbelief, and in a low but excited tone of voice said that the mound of gold bars could be worth maybe close to one hundred thousand dollars.

All of the guys in that caves bubble were astounded and stunned with disbelief. One of the cowpokes softly asked John if he and his friends were really going to share this gold with the three boys from Tennessee. John looked at the kid and shook his head in a yes manner. Now Jeremiah was on his knees trying to grasp some reality in his amazement. John got on one knee and told the others that they need to thank God for this bounty. As John started to pray, every man there went to their knees and bowed their heads.

"Almighty God in His heavens, we bow to Your Mercy and Your Grace. Our God, we are blessed by Your love. Thanks to You our Heavenly Father for Your bountiful blessings. Guide us as we use this good fortune. Guide us to share in humility and love. In Jesus' name, Amen"

There were six other, "Amens."

The explorer's found two other iron boxes and other smaller objects like knives, swords and Indian arrow and spear points. There were a number of other strange markings and writings on the walls of the bubble room. They didn't try to explore any deeper into the depth of the large mysterious mountain bubble. The depth of the bubble room would have to be explored another day and at another time. Both Jock and John felt that this cave probably did hold many other secrets and other treasures to be found. It was well into the afternoon when the last item that had been found in the cave was brought into the light of day. Jeremiah figured it had been almost two hundred years at the least since these treasures had last seen the sunshine. The skeleton remains were left in the bubble.

Around the supper fire that night it was decided that Jock, Jeremiah, and John would go back to Denver in the next couple of days and file for the "U S Homestead Act" to secure the ownership of the area. They wanted to examine the contents of the iron boxes first and then they would file for the land. The U.S. Homestead Act of 1862 allowed any American citizen to file for a 160 acre Homestead on any Federal land, especially in the west. Both John and Jock would file. John would file his 160 acres homestead in front of the hidden canyon and Jock would file his 160 acres homestead in the canyon itself. It was agreed that Jake would also file for the allotted 160 acres next to Johns further out into the desert. The Homestead Act allowed each claimant six months to build a dwelling on the property. The dwelling could be of any size. It just had to have four walls and a roof. On the last day of the sixth month period, the property would officially be owned by the petitioner. John and Sarah had acquired their 160 acres in Kansas under the 1862 "Homestead Act". Scott Walker who was an important attorney in Denver was also a member of the small church of Christ where the McCrumb family went to church services each Sunday. John had already talked with Scott about helping with the homestead applications. Scott told John he would be happy to help; that part of lawyering was one of his preferences. With the precise directions and with the proper paperwork the "Homestead Act" could be buttoned up and officially stamped within days.

After John, Jake and Jock's land filing were confirmed and legitimized the men would then start liquidating the Spanish artifacts to eastern antique dealers. At the same time, they would establish serious contacts with the big northeastern United States wealthy gold buyers. Dealing with gold buyers could become a real and dangerous problem at times. Cheating. stealing and too many fingers in the negotiations was always a big problem.Their biggest problems would be keeping the human vermin off the land they were homesteading.

Once they applied for the homestead act it would become public record and bad people would hear about it. The four older men found no problems in dealing harshly with interloping vermin. One dead vermin just means one less vermin to hurt any another decent human. The cowpokes would eventually learn that lesson just by watching their new partners. Early the next morning, Jock, had the three cowpokes dig a hole so they could bury the hundred and ninety-five gold bars for safe keeping. After the gold was buried and covered over the hole would be camouflaged with dead tree debris.

Only one of the iron chests was sealed with a large heavy padlock, the other two were minus their padlocks, probably still undiscovered somewhere in the mountains bubble. John had to pry open the first iron box without a padlock. In fact, it took both John and Jeremiah to break the lid free from the main part of the chest. It took them almost twenty minutes before they were able to raise the heavy lid and expose the chests secretes. When they finally managed to free the encrusted metal lid the box revealed gold coins, lots of gold coins, hundreds of gold coins, thousands of gold coins. The heavy iron chest was chocked full of gold coins of many different shapes and sizes. All of the men stood in stark silence, just staring at the golden treasure horde with gaping mouths and gawking expressions. This was like a dream in reality with two more boxes to open. No one could ever have a dream this big!

Jock reached down with both hands and dug two fists full of coins and gazed at a forty year dream finally realized right there in the palm of his hands. Over forty years of failure wiped away with the opening of one iron chest, and two more to open. There wouldn't be any more bad jokes and humiliating stories about that crazy old fart, Jock, and his hidden canyon failures.

Everyone was jolted back to reality from out of their hypnotizing trance over the brilliant glimmer of gold coins when Jerald asked about the other two chests. The second chest was just as hard to open as the first one was. More gold coins in the second chest, the same shape and size coins as the first chest held, but this chest was only half full of the solid gold coin currency. The first chest was full to the brim with the glittering gold.

Now it was time to open the mysterious chest with the royal crest engraved in the lid. This chest for some reason had the only large chunky lock that fastens together the lid to the main part of the decorated iron container. This chest was larger than the other two and the intrigue surrounding it was mounting as the gold hunters deliberated on the best way to dislodge the intimidating looking lock. The lock was so encrusted with decades of age; even maybe centuries of age the only way to separate it from the chest was to, as Jock put it. "Beat the hell out of it." And, that is just what the men did, beat it until the lock fell apart under the constant pounding of a hammer and ax.

John hesitated a moment before he slowly lifted the lid to unveil the chest secrets that had been hidden from human eyes for well over a hundred years, possibly two hundred years.

"A king's ransom!" Jake declared in utter amazement! With those three words, Jake had actually described the chests contents Astonishment and bewilderment overpowered everyone's presence of mind when the lid was fully opened and the chests secrets were finally revealed.

There was a long silence before anyone spoke. No one wanted to break the spell binding moment of disbelief of what lay before them in one single iron box.

Jock knelt beside the chest, with misty eyes and quivering hands. His entire body was trembling with emotions he had never experienced before. One part of those emotions was telling him that this moment wasn't real, only a dream gone badly. Other emotions were effectively expressing the truth of this very moment in Jock's life; not only had he become a successful gold hunter, he was among the most successful treasure hunters of all time. John and the others not only could see Jock's emotions in action they could also feel his pride in finally snatching victory right out of many years of constant defeats mouth. John laid his hand on Jock's shoulder and gave him credit where credit was generously due.

"Jock, this is your party, the party you have been missing for almost fifty years. Many hard years ……..but….. I would say the wait was worth it. No other prospector can claim a greater find than all of this … allow me to shake your hand." John extended his hand and clutched Jock's hand as old friends would.

"John…….none of this would never have happened if I hadn't met Jeremiah and Jake. And if you hadn't grubbed staked me………… John,……… I would still be just digging empty holes……….. I want to thank all of you……….. for having faith in this old broken down gold hunter." Jock was sincere and meant every word of his "thank you" dialog.

After Jock had thanked everyone the attention went back to Jake's three-word declarations, "A king's ransom".

The mysterious ancient chest was full of precious gold jewelry of all makes, sizes, and shapes. There were gold necklaces with precious stones encrusted in the correct places. There were gold chains of many sizes and shapes. There were gold pins encrusted with diamonds, rubies, and emeralds that had adorned the wealthiest queens, princesses, royalties and upper-crust ladies of Europe at an earlier time in world history. There were gold rings and bracelets that had bejeweled the richest of the utmost aristocracies and nobilities in Europe. There were medallions and rarest coins of the finest gold found in the old world. There were smaller gold bars with royalty stamps of the Crowns of Europe. There were diamonds of all sizes with many different cuts of brilliance.

Yes, the chest did hold a King's ransom. In fact, it held the ransom of many Kings and Queens. It was the mother lode of any mother lode ever found in the western hemisphere. And, the men still had other possibilities to find more gold in Jock's hidden canyon.

Each chest was buried in separate locations and then camouflaged over in secret from any meddling two legged vermin. The Spanish armor and smaller artifacts were buried in a separate hole. Each partner would carry a hand-written map of each hole where the treasures were buried.

The next morning, Thursday, July 29th, 1875 John, Jock and Jeremiah rode back to Denver to meet with Scott Walker in his law office to file and sign papers for homesteading the four hundred and eighty acres in and around the hidden valley. John also wanted to get back to Sarah's side because of her health problems. By the end of the day, the filing of the homestead papers had been completed and John was back into Sarah's arms.

John told Sarah that the homestead paper had been completed and filed with the proper authorities. John and Sarah had discussed the necessity of building a house on the 160 acres because of the requirement that was regulated by the Homestead Act of 1862. John wanted to have the construction of the house completed by the end of September of 1875 which would give the builder a construction timeline of two months. The first couple of days of July he and Sarah looked at some of the homes in Denver. When Sarah had chosen one she liked John hired a recommended carpenter and his crew to build their new house. John had already selected a building site for the house. It was next to a small stream and directly in line with the entrance to the first blind canyon; the canyon before Jock's hidden canyon. All of the cut lumber would be provided by a large Denver lumber cutting mill. The mill would furnish everything needed to build the house. John hired a Denver mule team firm to haul the lumber from Denver to the house building site. He hired extra workers to hunt and provide large rocks for the houses foundation walls. When all of the construction contracts and the agreed date lines were firmed up John would get back to caring full time for Sarah and visiting the hidden canyon periodically. With those timely visits, he could also keep tabs on the house construction progress.

Jake had contracted with the same lumber cutting mill for the lumber for his house. A separate construction crew would build Jake's house not far from John's and Sarah's. Building both of the houses this close together would give the families added comfort and peace of mind.

During the days just after he signed the Homestead Act papers John could tell a vast difference in Sarah's appearance. She had the look of exhaustion and her pain was more intense than usual. Her attitude never changed even with the increase in pain. Her strength and faith never wavered from her attitude towards God, her friends or her family. Lucy and Amy would cry to their papa about their momma's sickness. They were trying to understand why God would allow their momma to suffer like this. They needed their momma to be well and always be there for the family. John tried to explain this part of life to his daughters, but there was so much he didn't understand and it was so hard for him to be convincing. To see Sarah like this was placing his faith in jeopardy. He didn't want to live life without Sarah living it with him. Sarah had always been his one constant stabilizer in life. What would he, or how could he possibly go on without her by his side; that was his constant fear.

John told Jeremiah of Sarah's condition and asked him to send Jerald and Jacky back to Denver from the valley. Jeremiah wanted to stay and help but agreed to send the brothers back to be with their mom. He assured John that either he or Jake would ride back to Denver every two or three days to check on Sarah and to see if they could help in any way.

Jeremiah left early in the afternoon for the canyon, he wanted to get there before dark. Sarah wanted to go to the family's favorite eatery that evening for supper. She wasn't at all hungry but she wanted John and the girls to feel assured that everything was OK.

But it wasn't OK; Sarah was sensing a mild stomach sickening along with a worsening pain. She had told John earlier in the day that she needed to see one of the doctors in the morning. Sarah hardly ever requested a doctor's visit. It was always John who insisted that Sarah either visit the hospital or see a doctor. Her request for a doctor's visit really had John worried.

Sarah tried to keep the conversation around the supper table light, airy and in a positive mood. She would ask Lucy and Amy optimistic questions about their day or how were their friends doing. The sisters understood what their mom was doing and they tried to give cheerful answers. Their part wasn't working because of their grief-stricken feelings and they knew it. But, the two sisters didn't want to weaken their mom's resolve so they put a loving effort forward in making this supper time a pleasant time. Sarah would take a small bite every now and then and in doing so she would mess the food up on her plate to give the illusion that the food was disappearing. She knew she wasn't fooling anybody, but it gave her comfort knowing that no one said anything about the messy plate.

The next day the sisters tried to beg their way in going to the doctor with their mom and pa, but no amount of begging worked to their satisfaction. They did follow their parents for a while but decided it would be a useless adventure. They turned back towards their friend Clair Squibb's home.

The doctor's honesty is exactly what Sarah wanted or putting it more plainly, honesty is what she demanded. Doctor Dan Bancroft and Doctor Samuel Shiese met Sarah and John in the hospital's conference room. Doctor Shiese was new to Sarah and John. Doctor Shiese was new to the Denver hospital. He had previously practiced in a Boston hospital treating female cancer patients. He had closely studied Sarah's examination records from the Denver hospital. He was a kindly and soft-spoken elderly gentleman from the old school of doctoring.

"Mrs. McCrumb I have studied with diligence your historical cancer reports that Doctor Bancroft was kind enough to allow me to examine." Doctor Shiese spoke softly with a sincere sensitivity of caring for Sarah's emotions.

"You have two cancers; one of the Cervix and one of the Uterus. The tumor of the Uterus is also cancer. I know that you are well aware that both are very serious and not treatable. I am well aware by observation from the hospital staff that you are a very honest and an extremely strong woman. I am convinced because of what I have been told concerning your faith; you already know that God is going to bring you to His home soon."

“Yes...I do know that............I pray for my dear family’s strength and faith.” Sarah had a loving smile and tears of sadness in her eyes.

John could not stop the tears from rolling down his cheeks. He clutched Sarah’s hands tight to his chest as he lowered himself close to her side.

“Doctor Shiese…….how close is my time?............ Will I………. Will I get…very sick? And the pain……….. How bad will the pain be?” Sarah was demonstrating a resilient dignity of her strength of character and a steadfast faith in her questions.

“And…Please, Doctor Shiese…..call me Sarah…….. That’s who I am.”

“Yes Sarah, Thank you. One cannot say with any certainty about the pain or sickness. They can become acute or they could remain moderate. We do have medicine for both pain and sickness and we will make sure you have both and as much as you need. And as for time………only God can answer that one.”

After Doctor Bancroft had asked Sarah a couple of questions, both he and Doctor Shiese turned their attention to John’s needs. When John was asked if he had any questions, his mind went totally blank. The distressing news of Sarah’s condition was overwhelming and he could not contain his grief. Without any questions from John, both doctors talked to John in ways they believed he needed to hear. Sarah was controlling her emotions for John’s sake. John was desperately trying to control his emotions for Sarah’s sake, but he just couldn’t do it.

Thru his tears and gasps for breath John finally, manage to ask a truly hard question.

"What and how are we going to explain any of this to Lucy and Amy? Or….Jerald and Jacky…….they all worship their ma…..… .Sarah… you are their gift to life." John was having a difficult time getting the words to flow because of his emotions being challenged.

"You have always……….always been their pillar of strength...Oh God….what are we going to do? Help us, God……..Please God….. help us!" John completely broke down and gave in to his emotions.

Sarah took John into her arms and whispered comforting words to him. She looked at both doctors with begging eyes for help. The doctors had one of the nurses give John some pills to calm him down. It took a couple of minutes to relieve John of some of his emotional grief. The nurse gave Sarah a small bottle of the pills.

Sarah's positive demeanor was and will forever be a strength that John will call on many times in his life. This day was one of those times. John took Sarah to her favorite Denver eatery for lunch after leaving the hospital.

Doctor Bancroft and Doctor Shiese further discussed with Sarah her condition and her strength of faith and character.She and John left the hospital for the eatery.

"Dan, (Dr. Dan Bancroft) you were absolutely correct in your description of Sarah McCrumb. What a remarkable lady! I have found the pioneer women of the west to be so much more resolute of faith and determination than I experienced in Boston……….It is so sad to know such a lady as Sarah whose life is in her last days and yet she shines so brightly on this earth." Doctor Samuel Shiese's heart was truly touched by Sarah McCrumb.

"I think we might be able to help Sarah and John if you and I could talk to their children. If you would agree, I will ask Sarah if she is agreeable." That was Doctor Shiese's suggestion.

Doctor Dan Bancroft shook his head in agreement. He also knew that Sarah's days on this earth were very limited; only a few months or weeks or perhaps only days away. Both he and Dr. Shiese would use Sarah as an example of courage to help other distraught patience's for the rest of their doctoring lives.

For the first few days of August in 1875, John stayed in Denver with Sarah. When he did go out to the canyon it would only be for a couple of days at a time. Sarah and her wellbeing was the constant and an overriding purpose for John's current concerns. Sarah enjoyed mostly good days in August of that year. Her sickness was not very distressing and the pains were controlled with medications. Sarah kept to her normal activities, not wanting to upset her ever watchful family.

Jerald and Jacky came back to Denver the day after their momma and papa were at the hospital. Sarah had suggested to John that they explain her condition to the children in a quiet and secluded spot away from the bustle of Denver. John thought of a spot near a small stream a couple of miles outside of Denver.

"Then why not make a picnic out of it?" Sarah proposed.

The next morning the McCrumb family geared up in a one horse stable buggy and traveled the short distance to the small trout stream away from the activities and bustle of Denver.

The family spent the next five hours trying to comprehend and struggling somehow to understand the inevitable fact that Sarah was dying and very soon. Lucy, Amy, Jerald, and Jacky were devastated with profound emotional anguish at the thought of losing their momma in death. Matters were even made worse when John could not give the children a cohesive answer to any of their questions. His own grief made the majority of his answers incoherent. It was Sarah herself that brought coherence and some serenity to the discussion.

"I have always accepted what God has given me in this life……. John, He blessed me with you………Lucy, my first born...You were born in the middle of a raging storm on a small ship in the middle of a vast ocean. Lucy, your lungs and spirit of a new life were strong during that birth, now I need you to be even stronger in spirit during my rebirth to God." Sarah took Lucy in her arms and kissed her gently on her forehead.

"Amy, you were an answer to a prayer……to one of my prayers… .….You came to your papa and me in strength…………..Now I need you to be strong for me once again………Now I need your prayers." Sarah took her youngest daughter and cuddled her next to her breasts.

"Jerald...Jacky……..you were both birthed in agony of labor pains ………You both came into this world with the great strength of resolving…………You both are my Scottish gifts to this new world of ours………..You are the future heritage of our proud Scottish name………..To be strong in your days on this earth, you must show a greater strength now……….for me……..be strong for me……..It is now that your papa and I needs that strength……..I am so very proud of you both….My sons are now men."

With many other words and soul searching discussions spoken that day the McCrumb family rode back to Denver in silence, but with a fervent new resolve for the future. Early the next day the McCrumb children were taken to the Denver hospital to discuss the dilemma concerning their momma and the future without her.

The discussion between the McCrumb children and doctor's Bancroft and Shiese lasted almost two hours. After the hospital visits that same resolve that had been forged the day before with their momma was now strengthened and solidified for Sarah, her love, and the McCrumb family's future.

Jake had ridden to Denver to be with John and Sarah during Sarah's meetings with the hospital's doctors. Sarah and John were close to Jake in a number of ways, as close as a father and mother could possibly be to an adopted son. As a matter of fact, Jake considered them as his second parents and much closer to them than to his original parents. His birth mom had died giving birth to Jake. He never knew his real father; his father had died in a fire when Jake was just an infant. His aunt had reared Jake that is until he enlisted in the Union Army when he was sixteen years old in the early part of the Civil War. Sarah was a very special lady in Jake's life. As far as he was concerned she was the only real mother he had ever known. He loved Sarah as much as any son could ever love a mother. Even in that short period of time, he had known her, Jake felt like he had known Sarah all of his life.

A couple of days after Sarah's hospital visit Jake asked Sarah and John to have lunch with him at Sarah's favorite eatery. Jake had never really opened up his innermost feeling to either John or Sarah and he felt it was the time he did. This was the reason for the lunch meeting.

"Sarah.... and John...please forgive me if I blunder or muddle up what I am about to try to explain. I've wanted to say these things ever since we left Alma. I feel so at a loss for the right words.........

Let's see........how do I start?.........You two…or both of you........ are so very special to me... You both have made me feel….so much of a part of your family...John…. I have loved you like a father ever since you saved my life at Chancellorsville. You were so caring and I felt a special father and son bond that I had always prayed for. When I heard you were going west I wanted to be close to you even as an adopted son…….. Which I reasoned would never happen……….. Sarah……...you warmly accepted me, even as an outsider into your family without question or judgment. I felt the untiring warmness of your love towards your family. That was a feeling I had never felt before…..That was a feeling I have always wanted for myself." Jake was not just fighting for the right words he was combating a breakdown of his emotions. Tears were welling in his eyes and the quivering in his speech was disturbing the flow of his words as he wished them to flow.

"I guess….what I am trying to say……is……..I want to be more to your family than I am……or what I think I am now. I want to be like as a son to both of you...There….I said it!" Jake's heart was breaking because of Sarah's condition and this was his way of telling her that he loved her.

"Jake…you are as close as you possibly can be……as a son to John and me, and without the labor pains, and I do thank you, Lord, for no labor pains that came with Jake." Sarah was gently laughing. All three started to laugh because of Sarah's "labor pains" comment. Jake felt more a part of the McCrumb family now and that feeling would follow him, even to his death.

Jeremiah had discussed with John the situation of Henry and his sister Bright. Both men agreed that it would be best if they sent Henry back to Tennessee and brought Bright back with him to Denver. Bright was going on twenty years old and she could be a great inspiration to Lucy and Amy. She could also be a comfort to Sarah, which was Jeremiah's pitch to John. Jeremiah told John Henry and Bright could be back in Denver by the end of the month of August if they left by train now. John agreed with Jeremiah assessment and suggested they talk to Henry about the possibility of bringing Bright to Denver. But first John had some important business to discuss with Jacob Baskins.

John had taken Jacob Baskins into his confidence concerning part of the gold discovery in the hidden canyon. Jacob Baskins was the husband of Sarah's friend Clara Baskins. Jacob was the Vice President of the Denver Mercantile Bank and he and Clara were members of the small church of Christ in Denver. Jacob had assured John that he could exchange good American hard cash for the equal value of solid gold. The bank would assay the gold and handle its transfer to a federal gold exchange. He also assured John the transaction would be kept locally confidential; just between John and the bank.

Henry was excited when John and Jeremiah told him that they wanted to bring Bright to Denver. John had exchanged $20,000 of gold bars for hard American currency. John bought Henry and Bright's tickets and paid their traveling expenses with his own money. Henry was sent on his way and was instructed to communicate by telegraph back to John as often as possible. John gave Henry the $20,000 in cash and instructed him to give each one of his two brothers $10,000. The twenty thousand dollars would give his brothers a fair start to a good life in their home state of Tennessee. Henry could not believe the generosity of John McCrumb.

John and Sarah had talked about the possibility of bringing Bright to Denver. Sarah was delighted with the plan and even suggested the possibility of the doctors in the hospital examining Bright's condition of blindness. They were not sure of the extent of Bright's condition with her eyesight. There was that possibility her type of blindness could be medically helped.

After Jake and Jeremiah was convinced that Sarah would be OK for the present they traveled back to the canyon to begin exploring the pond that had been created by the waterfalls for possible gold. Jerald and Jacky stayed in Denver to be near their momma. Lucy and Amy divided their time between being with their momma, their two friends, and volunteering as "helping aids" in the hospital. The four friends, Lucy, Amy, Clair, and Mary were very excited about meeting Bright, the blind sister of Henry Edwards, "the cowpoke who had a crush on Lucy."

Exploring the small lake or "the Pond" as the men had labeled it would start in earnest when Jake and Jeremiah returned to the canyon. The pond had been formed by the cascading water from the crack in the canyon wall. The crack was approximately two hundred and fifty feet above the canyon floor. The widest width of the water flowing from the crack was about seven feet and that was just before it reached the water in the pond. There wasn't any way to measure the amount of water that was flowing from the crack in the canyon wall, but it was enough to keep the stream in the valley flowing with gentle rapids. The final descent of the falls was moderate enough for the men to take a quick cold shower under the pure mountain water.

The deepest part of the pond was maybe four to five feet depending on where you were standing. The bed of the pond was a mixture of loose soil, a type of volcanic clay and a mountain of moderate to small rocks. There were some larger boulder size rocks where the water falls collided with the pond water.

Jock suggested they start exploring the bottom of the pond in an area somewhere at the outer edge of the pond. They could work their way around the perimeter of the pond. After the outer perimeter had been completely explored they could cut the pond in sections like a pie and work their way to the center of the pond. The plan which included filling large buckets with the rocks and sediment off of the floor of the pond, then pulling the buckets to dry land and dumping the contents in a prepared area for separating any gold from all other pond debris. Only two to three inches of the bottom of the pond would be excavated for extraction of possible gold. It was a simple plan, but it would be a labor intense exercise. The men realized from the beginning it would be a difficult task and they approached the program knowing it would be an exhausting endeavor.Possibly, it just might become an impossible endeavor.

The process was being made even more difficult because of the depth of the water in the pond. The two cowpokes, Red Montgomery and Jasper Higgins would be the first ones in the pond filling the buckets with the ponds bottom material. Jeremiah would pull the buckets from the pond and dump the material on a large prepared wooden platform with narrow wire meshing at one end for Jock and Jake to filter the pond material through the mesh. It was an extremely slow and tiring process. Everyone had determined that draining the pond was completely and totally out of the question and impossible to achieve.

By the end of the first day, very little progress had been accomplished. Filling the buckets with the ponds bottom material was difficult and frustrating because of the depth of the pond. That evening around the supper's camp fire the discussion was about any ideas on how to get the ponds water level lower so the two diggers, whoever they might be would have an easier and more tolerable working arrangement.

Red suggested that they could dig a wide trench on the north side of the pond for about forty to sixty feet to an area where the canyon's terrain took a significant downhill dip into the canyons valley floor. The trench would have to be at least five foot wide and three or four foot deep. It would be a rough dig, but it just might be their answer to a difficult dilemma. It could create another small lake on the floor of the valley if the trench was left open.

The next morning the five men took a good look at the north side of the pond to see if Red's idea had any merit. After about fifteen minutes into the evaluation of Red's idea, Jock blurted out a few irreverent cuss words. It was a rare occasion to hear Jock cuss. He seldom used profane language.

"Damn it, Jeremiah, I think the kid has just solved our problem. It sure as hell isn't going to be easy digging that damn ditch, but it'll sure work for our needs."

"You're right Jock, it will work." Jeremiah was shaking his head and a smiling. He slapped Red on his back and shouted, "OK, gang, let's get digging!"

They mentally surveyed the landscape on the north side of the pond and then mapped out the area to be dug. The digging would start where the land took that steep downhill dip into the valley below then the men would dig the trench at an upward angle towards the pond. They knew the digging would be very difficult because of the rocky ground.

After seven days of long hours and hard labor with pickaxes and shovels, the five men were within two feet of the pond's water. The trench was a good five feet wide and three to four foot deep; three feet deep near the end of the trench and four foot deep next to the pond. At noon on the seventh day of what seemed like an impossible feat, Jake tossed his shovel to the bottom of the trench and sat down to rest. The other guys started to laugh at him with some good-natured barbed comments. Jake just smiled and started to throw some small rocks at his tormentors.

All of a sudden Jake leaped to his feet and then back down on one knee. He was frantically moving stones around until he found the stone he wanted. He grabbed it in his hand and shoved it high in the air towards Jock.

Jock took the bright colored stone out of Jake's hand and exclaimed in a half choking and half laughing voice, "Great gobs of goose grease, this is one of the biggest gold nuggets I've ever seen, let alone held in my hands! This dang thing is just about as big as a chicken egg."

The confusion over the discovery of this one gold nugget ended the days digging. The first thought on everyone's mind was just how many other nuggets have the diggers tossed out of the trench during the past seven days of digging. Jock told them maybe none. He explained to them that it wasn't unheard of to find a lone nugget all by its "lonesome" in unusual situations. His better explanation was the fact they were getting very close to the pond itself and maybe the pond had been larger at one time, and maybe this area had been filled in over the decades, possibly caused by an ancient earthquake. They spent the remaining hours in the day scouring the area where Jake found his nugget and the discarded trench debris of the past week. Nothing else with the color of gold was found.

John made a surprise visit to the canyon and was there in time for breakfast the morning after Jake's new gold nugget discovery. John was delighted when he was shown the large gold nugget that had been found the day before. He asked Jock what he thought it all meant. Jock explained to John what he had told the others about the possibility of the size of the pond maybe a century ago.

John was amazed and delighted with Red Montgomery's suggestion how to drain the pond. He told Red that he deserved a bonus of extra food for his brilliant suggestion. Red thanked John and blushed with a self-satisfying laugh.

The men spent the next hour examining the remaining two feet of the landscape to be removed before opening up the waters in the pond to the new five-foot wide trench. The water in the pond was mere inches below the land surface separating the pond water and the trench. Jeremiah suggested that they dig away another foot of land, then dig a hole to the pond at the bottom of the trench wall separating the trench and the pond water. This way he explained the pond water would wash away the remaining trench wall from the bottom up until the wall would be finally shattered and spoiled into the trench and transferred into the designated valley floor where they initially wanted the water to rest.

Before they started the trench project everyone had agreed that if the opening of the trench impeded the flow of the water in the original Small River, or "stream" as they called it, in the beginning, they would or could back dam the trench to restore the original streams flow. Damming the trench at the edge of the pond would be a very simple and quick project.

Jeremiah's plan worked perfectly. By mid-afternoon, the trench was working as designed. The pond's water was quickly receding to desired levels. Exploring the bottom of the pond would be much easier now with the new water depth in the pond. The north end of the pond where the trench had been dug was about a foot higher than where the valley stream was taking water from the pond.

The original stream would continue to flow but at a much narrower dimension and not as deep as before the trench's existence. Much of the pond now only had an inch or two of water. The prospectors went to sleep that night with renewed expectations and a few grandiose desires for future rewards. But, none of them were absolutely sure about the grandiose or the rewards.

By the middle of August John McCrumb and his friends were ready to search out the centuries of accumulated debris that had collected in the ancient pond. Over those centuries there had been billions of gallons of water that had been forced from the bowels of the mountain through the crack in the canyon wall into the pond and the mysterious valley with its hidden treasures. John wanted to be with his friends on that first day of the exploration of the drained pond. He would go back to Denver to be with Sarah on the next day. He also wanted to be in Denver when Henry arrived back from Tennessee with his sister Bright.

The first day of exploring the pond for gold nuggets proved to be promising. They found a little less than eight ounces in gold nuggets on that first day. The going price for an ounce of gold in 1875 was just a little over $23.00 for a troy ounce. The men always weighed their gold in regular standard ounces and not troy ounces. A troy ounce was just a might heavier than a standard ounce. When they sold their gold they sold it by the troy ounce. Their total monetary take in gold that first day was about $185.00. The average yearly income of an American worker in 1875 was from $150.00 to $195.00. The men found monetarily in one day what the average worker would make in dollars in 365 days.

By the first week of September in 1875 a little less than one-quarter of the pond had been adequately searched for its hidden gold. In those first ten days of prospecting for gold in the pond, the men had found close to twenty-five pounds of gold nuggets which calculated into about four hundred standard ounces of gold. The American hard currency value of those four hundred ounces was over $9,000.00 in standard ounces, more by troy ounces. That amount of money was the average yearly wages for about fifty American family wage earners.

John only stayed a couple of days in the camp; he wanted to get back to Denver in time to welcome Bright, Henry's blind sister from Tennessee. Before he left the camp he warned Jeremiah there were some less than desirable characters back in Denver that were taking notice of the activities surrounding the construction of his new house. John felt that he had been followed on this last trip to the valley. He didn't have any hard evidence of being followed. He promised Jeremiah that he would be more observant of his surroundings on his next visit. On his way back to Denver he spent a few hours inspecting the progress of his and Sarah's new home. The construction was going well and the house should be finished on time by the middle or the last days of September.

Jeremiah told Jake, Jock and the cowpokes of John's concerns of possible interlopers. Jock told Jeremiah that he was surprised that there hadn't been any unscrupulous visitors long before this. Jock suggested that they create some evidence traps in the outer canyon next to John's new house. Jeremiah's scowl exhibited a definite, "I don't have the slightest idea what you're talking about Jock!"

Jock explained that they should place items in a crisscross pattern at the mouth of the outer canyon that would have to be moved or disturbed if anyone undesirables tried to enter the canyon. They could also rearrange ground debris that would be disturbed if a person or a horse should walk on it. They could check those prepared areas every couple of days. If anything appeared disturbed than they would be certain they were having unwelcomed visitors. Everyone agreed that it should be done and soon. The next morning Jock and the cowpokes executed some of Jock's "vision traps" as he called them. They used small size rope, twine and string, long narrow branches and loose soil to create these "vision traps".

The next morning the guy's booby-trapped a larger area at the outer canyon entrance with different clever device arrangements of material that an unwelcomed intruder would have to disturb if they were trying to enter the canyon. They checked their deceptive human vermin traps twice the first week, with no positive results of any intrusion.

Working through the pond's debris in hunting for gold nuggets was progressing at a fever pitch. There was a good reason for the fever and the pitch. The fever was "gold fever" and the pitch was finding a gold nugget to pitch it into the pile of already accumulated gold. In the next four days, they had unearthed another twenty-five pounds of gold nuggets. It took the same crew six days to accumulate the first twenty-five pounds of gold. At this rate, they were finding nuggets in the pond Jake calculated the pond could be holding somewhere around a hundred thousand dollars of gold nuggets. Jock agreed!

By the last week in September John and Sarah's new house was just about completed. Henry and Bright wouldn't arrive in Denver from Tennessee for another week and a half. Henry had wired John of their arrival date. John wanted to check on the gold hunter's progress in the hidden valley. There were some finishing touches he wanted to be done inside of the new house. He figured he could accomplish all of these tasks in this one visit.

He brought Lucy and Amy out to the house with him so they could hang curtains, arrange furniture and create a women's touch to the living area of the house. The sisters had ridden in a one-horse drawn stable Surrey with a sun top. John wanted all of this done before he finally brought Sarah out to see the finished house. Sarah had ventured out to the house just one time while it was under construction. She had been too weak to make the almost two hours round trip to the construction site.

John would ride to the hidden canyon while the girls womanized the new house with all of the frills that would give a home that delicate ladies frosting on the cake look, so to speak.

John couldn't shake a strange feeling that he was being watched by some unfamiliar characters. He couldn't determine whether it was human or maybe an animal. He knew that there were mountain lions and large brown bears that roamed the Rocky Mountains and many of both species had been seen in these mountains and around the surrounding areas. The feeling was just too strong to ignore. He decided to double back and survey the area around the house for a while from a hidden position. It wasn't long before he saw some riders off in the distance, that's when he pulled his Henry rifle from its scabbard. The riders were coming down from the side of the mountain that bordered the west side of the hidden canyon. They stopped behind some large boulders a couple hundred yards from the house. There were at least four of them. They watched the house for a spell, and then they rode off towards Denver.

John knew that there had been some talk in Denver about the McCrumb house that was being built near the "Blind Canyon" a few miles outside of the city. Samuel Squibb, the owner of the livery Stables and a member of the small church of Christ in Denver would tell John of any gossip that would come his way if it was about John's activity at the house or canyon. Samuel knew that John and some mysterious partners had filed for three different homesteads near the canyon. The filings were made public when the filing papers were signed. The three homestead filings and those unknown McCrumb partners had raised a few eyebrows among two groups of folks in Denver. The first group was the elite; politicians and city leaders who were very interested in this McCrumb person. They knew of Sarah McCrumb and her many visits to the new Denver hospital. They had determined and rightly so, that the McCrumb family had a very private nature. But John and his inner circle of friends coming and goings out to the house and canyon had a lot of other folks in Denver scratching their heads. Some of those folks were the second group; the riff raft of Denver's dark side.

This group of Denver's less desirable population had become increasingly interested in John McCrumb and his friend's constant travels to and from the "Blind Canyon". This group was from the old and sleazy part of Denver. That was the group who had been watching, calculating and scheming to discover John's secret of the canyon. They suspected it had to do with gold because of the old stories of gold and treasures lost in some part of those mountains near Denver. They were not sure of how many men were involved with John or what they had found, but they were determined to have it for themselves if it had anything to do with gold. But not knowing how many men were with John McCrumb this group of desperadoes had to be very careful how and when they played their cards.

John rode back to the house and helped the girls finish with their house warming details. Lucy and Amy had ridden to the house in one of the liveries stables one-horse buggies. They had brought some small furniture along with the drapes, curtains, and other pretty lady items in the buggy. John was riding his horse Thunder. Before they rode back to Denver Lucy was the first to mention to her pap what he had already observed.

"Pap, I think somebody followed us to the house this morning. I *know* that somebody followed us!" Lucy was determined in her statement. "I saw at least two men when we were at the house today. I saw them way out yonder by those big rocks next to the Juniper trees. I could just barely make them out." Lucy was trying to be nonchalant as if somebody was right next to her and she didn't want them to know she was talking about them.

"Poppa, I had that same feeling and I saw them too," Amy added her observation right after Lucy.

"It's OK, I know who they are. I'll talk to them when we get back to Denver." John didn't want to upset the girls. He really didn't know who the men were or what they were up too. He was sure whoever they were they was not up to any good. Samuel Squibb had warned John to be careful because he was being watched by some of Denver's low life characters.

John didn't think the men who were spying on the house had followed him and the girls back to Denver. Once he felt assured that the girls were safe back with Sarah he got Jerald and Jacky to ride back with him to the house and the hidden canyon. Before they left for the canyon they stopped by Samuel Squibb's home to ask Samuel if he and some other members of the church's congregation would watch over Sarah and the girls for a couple of days, just until John got back into Denver.

It was still light when they reached the house. He didn't see any signs that the house had been entered or disturbed. He did detect a number of strange horse tracks around the mouth of the canyon. He wasn't sure, but it looked like maybe five or six horses had made the tracks. The tracks were only a day or two old. He told the boys to be careful and be on the lookout for any strange movement or anything out of the normal as they approached the canyon's entrance. The three men had their six shooters strapped to their sides.

The three entered the hidden canyon with extreme caution not knowing if trouble had been there before them. Relief was welcomed when they saw Jake, Jeremiah, Jock and the cowpokes at the camp site. John had told his sons to act normal, not to telegraph their concerns to any unwelcomed guests that just might be watching. John engaged in a normal conversation with his companions not wanting to raise suspicions just in case he was being watched by unfriendly forces. As the evening advanced toward bedtime he had managed to warn everyone about the possibility of uninvited guests visiting during the night. But, the events of that night were normal and proved to be uneventful.

When the rays of the morning sun finally did break in the eastern skies everybody went about their daily ritual, eating breakfast, then shifting rocks and dirt in the pond on their quest to finding more gold nuggets. Everyone was on the extra vigil and common sense alert, but they maintained a demeanor of causal calm not wanting to telegraph their apprehension of possible danger lurking behind every rock, bush or tree. The next couple of days and nights were just as uneventful as that first day when they expected possible trouble.

By the fourth night, everyone's nerves were raw with anticipation of unresolved waiting and nothing occurring that even resembled danger. John was beginning to think that maybe he had overreacted in warning his comrades.

During that fourth day, Jeremiah told John that he had an uneasy feeling of appending danger. John had learned that Jeremiah's premonitions usually had substantial merit and he was not about to disregard the big man's instinct on this day. That night John cautioned his sons and his colleagues to be extra alert. Under the dark of night John, Jake and Jeremiah abandoned their bedrolls to sleep a few feet away from their normal sleeping spot using other blankets to keep the chill away. It was a cautionary move to surprise any foreign troubling vermin's that might visit the campsite during the night. Jeremiah's huge one hundred and fifty-five pound dog Ammo always slept by Jeremiah's side. Jerald and Jack's three pooches, Kick, Tubby and Buster were always by the boy's feet at night. The Buffalo always laid her massive head anywhere she wanted at night as long as it was near the dogs. Lucy and Amy had secretly named the female buffalo "Patsy". Jerald and Jacky knew what their sisters had done, so "Patsy" it was.

Long after everyone had settled in for the night Jeremiah and Ammo quietly made their way closer to the entrance of the hidden valley. Jeremiah wanted to be in a better position to counteract any nefarious night time intruders if they did show their presents. His uneasy feeling of impending trouble was stronger than it was earlier in the day. When he had found the position he felt would give him the upper hand in a gunfight he settled in with Ammo and his arsenal of weapons.

Jeremiah's premonition of danger was weighing heavy on John's mind too. He was taking Jeremiah's warning extremely seriously. Right after midnight John accumulated his weapons and moved further to the west of the camp site. There he would be in a much better position to see the camp and discharge his fire power at anyone approaching the camp from that particular angle. His adrenalin was high; he knew there would be no sleep that night.

Jake and Jock, even the brothers and the cowpokes were all wide eyed with their guns and knives resting just fractions of a second from their grasp.

“Jerald…are ya asleep?” Jacky was whispering so low Jerald had a hard time hearing the question.

“No, I’m ain’t asleep…….can’t go to sleep. Are you asleep?”

“No, I can’t sleep either……. Jerald, …we should have brought our rifle too.” The annoyance in Jacky’s voice over the rifles that had been left home was very evident.

“Are ya afraid?” It was Jerald’s turn to ask a more pertinent question.

“Well, maybe…..just a little…..Are you?” Jacky didn’t want to be afraid, but he was.

“I am too…..just a little…….I think.” Jerald had kept his six-shooter as close to him as possible. “Jacky…..if we have to start shooting……….we have to make………to make sure we don’t shoot at our friends.”

“How are we gonna tell who we’re shootin at?” Jacky’s question was perplexing but was making sense.

“I don’t know…….we need to help each other….don’t shoot until we’re sure who we’re shootin at. This isn’t like the Indian raid…….. we can’t see who’s shooting at us”. Jerald was beginning to revive some of the memories of the Pawnee attack.

Both brothers were beginning to have flashbacks of the Pawnee assault back in Kansas. The bizarre shadows contrived by the moonlight contrasted against the many dark canyon objects in the night and not being able to see anything within just a few feet in front of you because of the black darkness was distressing in an already impossible dangerous situation. Just waiting for some possible unknown treacherous adversary to shoot at you would cause debilitating stress on the strongest of men. The men in the hidden canyon were strong and they were expecting the worst to happen, they just didn't have the slightest idea of when and what that worst would be. They weren't even sure if there was even a worst.

The night had seemed to be really long for the nine gold prospectors. Throughout the night ghostly shadows seemed to be moving in different directions and each shadow presented itself as a possible enemy. Both John and Jeremiah had inched their way during the night closer to the valley's entrance. The first rays of sunlight in the east brought some relief to John and his companions. But none of them had abandoned their anxious watch for danger. As the sun made its presence in the canyon valley life began to come alive. Even Patsy was chewing on the dew sprinkled valley vegetation. Jeremiah managed to attract John's attention with low tone whistles. John cautiously crawled to where Jeremiah had camouflaged himself behind some small boulders. After a few guarded moments, the shadowed valley floor turned into bright sunlight. The three cowpokes slowly rose from their hiding spots only to find that Jerald and Jacky were not more than fifteen feet from where they had been hiding. Jake and Jock left their hiding places and headed toward Jeremiah and John.

The men gathered around Jock's steaming hot coffee pot. The conversation was dominated about the vigilance watch of the night. Jeremiah still had that premonition of pending danger. John felt the same way. He cautioned everyone not to let their guards down. John decided to head back to Denver. Jeremiah wanted to accompany John, at least part of the way back to Denver because of the possibility of him being alone and ambushed. John was adamant that Jeremiah stays with the men in the valley.

After John and Thunder had left the camp in the hidden canyon Jeremiah told the brothers to quickly saddle their horses and follow behind their pa at a reasonable distance. He sternly made sure that they understood his wishes; if there was any trouble or any indication of trouble one of them was to ride back to the valley and let the men know.

John had gotten as far as his new house when he realized that someone or somebodies had been there during the night. He was extremely cautious as he rode up to the house. He didn't see any signs of life around the house. When he got to the front of the house he readied himself to dismount Thunder when a rifle shot splintered the stillness of the early morning with a deafening sound. John heard the shot and the felt the blistering pain all at the same instant. When he finally regained his senses he realized that he was lying on the hard ground. It was difficult for him to move. He tried to look for Thunder, but couldn't see him. He could make out some men coming towards him on horses from behind some large boulders about a hundred yards from the house. He couldn't quite make out how many horses there were because his vision was blurry. He tried to draw his 45 caliber side arm but just couldn't seem to find it or feel it.

John was having a difficult time focusing visually and mentally. He could feel himself fading in and out from reality. He was desperately trying to focus on the shooters as they rode towards him. His worst thoughts were he was about to die. Just before he passed out again he thought he heard a barrage of gunfire all around him. It was a strange sensation; he continued to fade in and out of consciousness. For a split second, he thought he was back in a civil war battle at Chancellorsville, but then reality would resurface. He was confused because of all of the gun explosions and the loud yelling. He wasn't sure how long he had been on the ground, but it seemed like a long time. In reality, he had only been the ground for a few minutes.

The barrage of gun shots John heard after he had fallen to the ground was the exploding cartridges from the rifles that Jeremiah had given to Jerald and Jacky after he had told them to follow their pa. The next barrage of gunfire was not only from Jerald and Jacky but was exploding from Jeremiah's buffalo gun. Jeremiah had followed close behind the brothers.

Within a very short period of time, there were three dead outlaws and one wounded lying between John and the boulders where the gunmen had been hiding. Jeremiah on his horse "Mountain" and his dog Ammo never slowed down when they came into the clearing from the canyons yawning entrance. He was firing his buffalo gun while riding Mountain at a full gallop. Jeremiah had only one thing on his mind and that was catching up to the ambushers and killing all of them. When he passed by the house he was not far behind the bushwhackers that had shot John. Jeremiah thought he saw at least four of the gunmen that had ambushed John.

Not far from the house one of the gunmen's horses stumbled sending the outlaw tumbling in the hard desert dirt. He managed to right himself and he drew his six-shooter and took aim at Jeremiah as the big mountain man and his horse Mountain charged toward him. His first shot missed Jeremiah. He never got a second chance at another shot. Ammo had slammed into the outlaw at about forty miles an hour causing him to sprawl backward for yards. Jeremiah kept right on charging after the other desperados. After Ammo had mangled the downed shooter almost to his grave the big dog continued the race for Western justice not far behind Jeremiah.

Jerald and Jacky got to their pa as quick as possible after the ambushers had been driven off. John recognized his sons and smiled at their bravery. The boy's first action was to try and stop their pa from bleeding. John had been shot in his back on his right side just above his right lung. The bullet had exited from the right side of John's chest. It was a clean shot missing all of his vital organs. The bullet had missed his right lung only by of a fraction of an inch. The boys did manage to stop the bleeding, but they knew that their pa needed a doctor to treat him. John was in a lot of pain and he had lost a considerable amount of blood. They helped their pa back on Thunder and started the critical ride back to Denver. Before they left they did check on the wounded outlaw. His wounds were bad but their pa was more important to them at the moment. Jacky did try to stop as much bleeding as he could on the guy. They would tell the sheriff to come and get him when they got to Denver.

The brothers knew that their ride back to Denver with their pa would be dangerous and critical because of the possibility of their pa's wound starting to bleed again. They also realized that if they didn't get him to the hospital quickly he could die of other complications.

Jeremiah had managed to bring down another one of the killers with a blast from his buffalo gun. He knew that there were at least two more shooters and he was determined that they would pay dearly for their monstrous deed of ambushing and shooting his friend John McCrumb. He vowed that they would die before the sunset on this night. When he reached Denver he stopped at the livery stables and asked if anyone has seen any riders coming through in a hurry in the last half hour. Not only had they seen them, they even knew who they were.

"Two really bad hombre, the brothers Jim Bass and Bill Bass." The stable man knew both of them. He told Jeremiah that those two were thieves and killers. He had heard that they had robbed and killed a man and his wife in a stage coach hold up a few years before.

"Do ya know where they might be hanging out?" Jeremiah took a long chance question.

"Yeah!" Samuel Squibb, the owner of the livery stable chimed in. "They hang out a lot at the "Crooked Nugget" saloon over on "Y" Street. But be careful Jeremiah, that's a bad place and it's in the old part of Denver. That part of town has a bad reputation. Our sheriff and his deputies have cleaned it up a lot but still a part of town I'll not venture in."

Before Jeremiah left to find the Bass brothers he asked Samuel to send a buggy towards the McCrumb's new house. He told him that John had been shot and he needed help.

Jeremiah, his Horse Mountain, and Ammo slowly made their way through the early morning dusty streets of the newer part of the city. Denver had made great strides in casting off its Wild West frontier image of gun fights in every street. At one time they could match the saloon and street killings of Dodge City and Tombstone, but that was in the past. Denver was trying to build its image as the "Gateway City" to the west coast and the Pacific Ocean. The leaders in Denver were less than a year away from having the Colorado Territory declared the 38th State in the Union and Denver as the States Capital.

Jeremiah reined Mountain to the hitching rail in front of the "Crooked Nugget". He checked the condition of the other horses that were tied to the long wooden pole hitching rail in front of the saloon. Two of the horses were heavy lathered from being ridden hard from a distance. It wasn't quite noon time so Jeremiah figured there wouldn't be too many drinkers in the saloon. He counted seven other horses tied to the pole. The odds in a gunfight in this saloon were not in his favor, but at this point, it didn't matter that much to Jeremiah. The big mountain man's mind was set on what he had to do and that is what he was about to do; kill the Bass brothers.

As he prepared to walk up the "Crocked Nuggets" dilapidated wooden steps he heard someone call his name. He made a quick turn with his buffalo rifle ready for action. It was Jake bringing his horse to an abrupt halt. Jake was off of his horse before the horse could complete its last stride.

"You're not going in there without me my friend." Jeremiah had never heard Jake use such a demanding tone in his voice before. It was almost like a threat. This was a side of Jake Jeremiah didn't know existed. Jake walked right past the big mountain man and went straight through the saloon's swinging doors. Jeremiah had to move quickly to catch up with him.

"We want the Bass brothers and if anyone else gets in our way we'll kill you too." Jeremiah's deep baritone voice shook the whole saloon.

There was a deadening silence that rippled through the bar's patrons. Everyone was momentarily stunned; some were just plainly petrified with fear. Two guys at the bar threw their arms up in the air and yelled they didn't want any part of what was about to happen. They were out the door and running down the street without any further discussions. They didn't even bother to unhitch their horses. That left seven men plus the barkeeper in the room. There were four cowboy's playing cards at one table and two bad looking characters drinking whiskey at another table and a lone drinker at the bar.

"Jim and Bill Bass….make yourselves known…….you ain't leaving this saloon alive. If you ain't Jim or Bill Bass…….I strongly suggest you get the hell out of here……..if you don't get out NOW…you can die with those two sons of bitches……they just tried to kill our friend." Jeremiah was at his wit's end and was ready to explode. With those last words, he cocked his buffalo rifle and drew his revolver all at the same time. Jake already had his six-shooter in hand. The two bad looking characters drinking whiskey threw their hands up in the air and made a fast retreat towards the swinging saloon doors and quickly disappeared with their horses fading on the horizon on one of Denver's dusty streets.

The cowboy at the bar suddenly went for his revolver that was strapped to his side. The instant his arm moved towards his gun Ammo charged and knocked him to the floor before he could bring the gun out of its holster. Jeremiah had whispered to his dog to "Watch him" before the two bad looking characters made their escape out of the swinging saloon doors. The guy on the floor underneath the bulk of the one hundred and fifty-pound Ammo found himself desperately trying to protect his flesh from being torn from his body.

The four card players already had their weapons resting in their laps out of their holsters. They leaped from their chairs with their guns blazing. In a matter of seconds, the saloon was filled with a thick smell of gun powder. The residue smoke from the discharging bullets caused a mystical and leery haze to fill the room. What seemed like minutes of exploding gunfire actually lasted less than twenty seconds.

The guy who had been standing at the bar was bleeding profusely as he withered from pain on the old wooden floor. Ammo had brought a successful ending to the pitiful looking ex-desperado with his canine teeth. Ammo had backed off and was just standing next to the gunman guarding over him as the beaten crook withered in pain. The four card players were sprawled in four different directions on the saloons worn wooden floor. Only one of them still had breath in his lungs. Jake and Jeremiah was standing side by side, where they had stood before the shooting started, neither of them moving. Both men were breathing with deep, heavy and laboring quick breaths. Jake surveyed the room, looking to make sure there wasn't any more danger lurking behind some chair, table or post. He remembered the bar keeper, but that guy wasn't anywhere to be found. He slowly holstered his empty six-shooter and turned toward Jeremiah. There was blood running down Jeremiah's right cheek and more blood oozing from his shirt on his left side. Jeremiah didn't seem to notice that he had been grazed to the side of his head with one of the outlaw's bullets. Nor did he know that another bullet had hit him in his side until Jake asked him if it hurt.

Samuel Squibb drove the one horse buckboard himself looking for his wounded friend. When Samuel finally met up with Jerald, Jacky, and their pa it was none too soon. John was having a very difficult time staying on Thunder. Jacky had to set behind his pa on Thunder to keep John from falling off of the horse. John was still dizzy and his breathing was labored.

Later, the doctors at the hospital would determine that John had a slight concussion that happened when he hit his head on the hard ground after falling off of Thunder during the moment he got shot. Samuel had brought a lot of blankets for John's comfort. Once they got John on the buckboard the travel time to the hospital was cut to just minutes. John's bleeding had completely stopped; the brothers had accomplished a superb job in binding their pa's wound.

At the hospital, the doctors cleaned John's wound, medicated the wound, bandaged the wound and declared John good to go. Sarah and the girls had been staying at the Squibb's home while John was away. After Samuel had gotten John to the hospital he picked Sarah and the girls up from his house and took them to the hospital to be with John. John would stay in the hospital for the night and Sarah and the girls would stay with him.

Jeremiah and Jake just stood in the same spot for a couple of minutes before Jake finally ask Jeremiah if his side was hurting.

The strong smell of spent gun powder left a deadly stench in the quiet saloon's ballroom. The eye burning haze was quickly dissipating into the old porous wooden walls of the once notorious "Crooked Nugget" saloon. Ammo was still watching over the gunman he had slammed to the saloon floor. The guy was bleeding from both arms, from the top of his head and from his shoulders. He looked like he had been through a meat grinder. The bartender was still missing.

Jeremiah wiped the blood from the side of his head. He stared at the blood on his fingers for a couple of seconds then walked over to a saloon chair and sat down. Jake followed Jeremiah and set down in the chair next to him.

"Jeremiah, are you alright?'

"Yea, just resting."

We need to check your side, Jeremiah.........I think you got shot."

"Yea........I think you're right....... I think I got shot too."

"Jeremiah....do ya think we'll go to jail?" Jake's question was asked with a lot of apprehensions.

"I don't think so, Jake.........I don't think there is anyone in this town big enough to put us in jail.

As Jeremiah was finishing his sentence Samuel was walking through the saloon's swinging doors. Samuel surveyed the saloon from wall to wall before walking over to the table where Jeremiah and Jake were setting.

No one said anything for a couple of minutes. Finally, Jeremiah broke the silence.

"Tell me about John Samuel!" Jeremiah never looked up from his hardened glare. Jeremiah's tone of voice was almost frozen in panic. The question was hard for him to ask. But, it was Samuel's anticipated answer that had caused the cold fear in his tone of voice.

"Jeremiah....John is OK. He's fine..... He's in the hospital...... Sarah and the kids are with him. They're letting him go in a couple of days. He'd love to see you, Jeremiah." Samuel smiled when he saw the big mountain man's tense body relax and the tears of relief in his eyes. Jake reached over and grabbed the big man's hands. Tears of relief were rolling down his cheeks too.

A crowd had gathered on the dirt street in front of the weather-beaten old saloon. Jeremiah and Jake wanted to wait for the law before they went out through the saloon's swinging doors. Sheriff

Edmund Willoughby and Marshall David Cook finally made their presence known as they entered the old saloon.

"Well, I see the Bass brothers finally met someone they couldn't bully, uh." Sheriff Willoughby spoke the words with a mocking tone. "It's about time! …………OK, somebody tell me what happened here."

Both Jeremiah and Jake were standing when the sheriff and the marshal walked into the saloon. Both lawmen were taken back by the size of Jeremiah and a little uneasy with the size of Ammo who was still guarding the guy on the floor. The whole scene caused the two lawmen to have a little apprehension. With four dead men sprawled on the dusty floor in different directions; another one on the floor covered with his own blood next to Ammo was somewhat disquieting to the senses. Both the sheriff and the Marshall knew Samuel Squibb and had great respect for him. Samuel was not only the owner of the livery stables; he was also in the city of Denver's governing board. After they heard the complete story of the salon's shootout and the ambush of John McCrumb earlier at his new house the lawmen concluded their investigation was done right then and there. Jake and Jeremiah were free to leave. Marshall Cook would send some men out to the McCrumb's house and gather the dead men and the wounded bushwhacker.

The story of the gunfight in the saloon and the bad guys being killed out on the prairie would soon spread all over Denver. The results of the story would produce a positive effect. Every outlaw and crook in the Denver area would surely think twice before messing with the McCrumb's and their gun-toting friends.

It took both Samuel and Jake to persuade Jeremiah to go to the hospital to have the bullet wound to his side taken care of. Jeremiah was anxious to see and make sure John was alright. If it hadn't been for John being in the hospital Jake doubted that they would have ever gotten Jeremiah to the hospital.

By the time Henry and Bright were to arrive in Denver from Tennessee in the "Iron Horse", a twelve wheel drive locomotive both John and Jeremiah were well on their way to complete recoveries from the ambush and "Crooked Nugget" gun fight.

The day that Henry and Bright did arrive at the chosen railroad station in Denver the whole gang of friends were patiently waiting outside of the small depot on an old worn wooden platform. John and Sarah were calm, but Lucy and Amy and their two girlfriends were fitful and fidgety. They wore a path walking up and down on the old wooden platform. Jake, Jeremiah, and the two McCrumb boys were nervous but tried not to show their eagerness for the train to hurry up and arrive. The two cowpokes were excited not only to see Bright again, but they wanted to hear about any news from back home.

A lone whistle announced the anticipated arrival of the two-hour late train as it was finally entering the freight yard's track system. They could see the billowing smoke before they saw the actual engine. It was slowly chugging its way around a long curve towards the depot. As the gigantic iron monster puffed its way to its final resting spot before thundering the final burst of huge white clouds of rolling steam created in the engine's massive boilers the McCrumb bunch was trying to figure out which passenger car to position themselves next to.

When the train finally came to a complete stop in front of the depot the first person out of the second passenger car was the conductor with his recognizable familiar uniform and cap. He placed the famous metal footstep on the ground so the passengers could descend the cars steps easily to the wooden platform. Henry was the seventh passenger to appear on the steps. As Henry started his descent down the steps he turned and took his sister's hand to help and guide her safely to the wooden platform below. Everyone on the platform stood looking in absolute disbelief at the beautiful girl who was holding Henry's hand. Bright stood in the sunlight almost like a picturesque statue from one of those famous European museums. Her long bright radiant auburn hair and sparkling green eyes made her five-foot-six-inch slender body a perfect picture of feminine beauty. Henry whispered in her ear and with a little guidance, Bright gracefully walked straight over to Sarah. Her first words were offered to Sarah McCrumb.

"Mrs. McCrumb I have not met you personally, but after hearing about you and your family from my brother Henry I do want you to know that I sincerely do love you and your beautiful family". Sarah started to cry and took Bright into her arms.

Both Lucy and Amy came running over to their mom and Bright. Both girls were crying with happiness and joy, all at the same time. They exchanged hugs and kisses with Bright. The cowpokes came over too and each one gave Bright a big hug. Henry took Bright by the hand and made all of the proper introductions to John, Jeremiah, Jake, Mary and Clair and the McCrumb girls and of course Jerald and Jacky. Bright was a little shy and reserved in her words and actions. She was not totally blind as everyone had thought. Her vision was impaired as if she had thick cataracts. Her eyes had a thin misty film that covered her eyeballs. Everything she saw was hazy to her vision.

If there was one person who was totally taken by Bright's beauty and personality it was Jake. He was captivated from the first moment he saw her walk down the steps of the train's passenger car. Jake had never married and never had a serious affair with any lady. He was somewhat shy and being very reserved was his nature. He was always considerate and very guarded never to offend the opposite sex. There was something very special about Bright and she had totally captured Jake's heart.

By the first week in October of 1875, The McCrumb house was finished. John and Jeremiah had recovered from their bullet wounds. The gold hunting in the hidden valley's pond was near completion. Bright had moved in with the McCrumb sisters in their new home. Sarah's health was deteriorating; she was weak and tired most of the time.

When Sarah saw the new house she gave John a big hug and thanked him for his love and devotion. Sarah's attitude had never wavered. She was just as loving, just as grateful and just as thankful for her family, her life and her steadfast faith in God as she ever was. Sarah had sustained that pioneer spirit, her devoted love for her family and that Scottish heritage of strength that helped to reinforce her family through many past difficult times. Her strength and faith of life and God are what will give her the strength and courage to face death. Her legacy was to be witnessed for generations to come. She will have passed her gift of courage, love, and strength not only to her children but to everyone who ever knew her.

It was on a Sunday, October the 17th in 1875 at four thirty-eight in the afternoon when Sarah Amy McCrumb peacefully passed away in her new house in Denver Colorado. Her beloved John was holding her hands. Her beautiful daughters and handsome sons (as she referred to them) were by her bedside. Jeremiah, Jake, Jock and the cowpokes were all there showing their devoted love for Sarah McCrumb. Sarah had asked that there be no tears because where she was going there were no tears. Bright was tightly holding hands with Lucy and Amy.

The small Denver congregation of the church of Christ had held their Sunday morning worship service that day in the home of Sarah and John McCrumb. They stayed until dark. The Denver city leaders paid their respects. The hospital staff was there out of love for Sarah and John.

No one could ever explain just how or why there were five noble looking Kiowa Native American Braves that had shown up on that particular day at the McCrumb house. They had brought gifts of sorrow and gifts of happiness on that day to the McCrumb family. Their reverence for Sarah the few moments they were with her was completely humbling and with deep sincerity.

When the Kiowa Indians left the McCrumb's yard that day all of the other guests stood in absolute wonderment as these magnificent noble Indian Braves finished their tribute to the white skin lady that they all had admired. Each of the Kiowa braves also paid their respects to Lucy and Amy with small gifts, and then to the McCrumb brothers with other small gifts. Their leader "Two Elks" stopped and turned facing John, he placed his right hand over his heart then extended his arm towards John. John understood this gesture of true brotherhood and friendship. The Kiowa left just as quietly as they had come.

Sarah had made John promise to do two things for her after she was gone. The first was to go to the hidden canyon immediately and finish what he had started. By doing that he would have less time to mourn her passing. The second thing she had asked John to do was get in touch with his brother James back in Pennsylvania, and bring James and his wife Hazel out west to be part of the McCrumb clan in this wonderful new frontier. Sarah would forever guide the lives of her beloved family in spirit as long as they had the breath of life.

Losing Sarah had a crushing effect on John and his family. If it hadn't been for Bright Amy would have withdrawn into a silent shell of despair within a couple of days after Sarah had died. Lucy would find a quiet place of sanctuary and cry for her momma until her eyes were swollen. Henry was always nearby trying to offer comfort to Lucy, even if it was in his usual awkward way. He didn't want to offend her by overcrowding her personal space. He didn't know exactly what to do, except just being there for her.

Jerald and Jacky would go into the hidden valley to work on Jock's house. Often they would find a quiet place to mourn the loss of their momma. John could see the despair that his children were experiencing. John was in deep anguish himself but he knew that he had to be strong for his children. Every night his world seemed to collapse just a little more. His solemn promise to Sarah that he would always be there for their children after her passing was always in his thoughts. John and Sarah had prayed together that her strength and faith in death would be John's faith and strength in life. John could see Amy's despair even with Bright trying to comfort her. Seeing Lucy constantly fighting back tears he realized that he had to do something to bring Sarah's strength and spirit back into his family.

Six days after Sarah had passed John had Bright, Lucy and Amy fix a picnic lunch. John and his family planned an outing like the one they had after hearing of Sarah's troubling health news from the Denver doctors. During this quiet time, they talked together. They cried together. They prayed together. They were strengthened together. When the family meeting was over and everyone had said a private prayer Sarah's spirit was once again in charge and the McCrumb family was once again united in their faith in God, with renewed strength. It would not be easy for the McCrumb family to overcome the loss of Sarah but with Sarah's spirit and prayers to God, the family would conquer the distress of her death. The anticipated long journey to the mystical Lost River Valley in the Idaho Territory could once again become the family's main focus with a new determination of strength and purpose.

Lucy, Amy, and Bright were getting comfortable living in the new house. Jerald and Jacky were really happy with their bedroom. Both brothers would stay with the girls at the house during the day for protection. They had a lot of outside work to do; building rail fences and horse corrals.

John wired his brother James who lived in Pennsylvania asking him to come to Denver to live. James agreed and John wired him the money for the train fare to the Colorado Territory. After the war, James had settled on a little farm in western Pennsylvania with his wife, Hazel. They didn't own any land of their own. James and his wife hired out as farming sharecroppers.

By the end of October, the gold that had lain dormant for centuries in the hidden valley pond had been mined almost in total. The men were sure that the pond still held some gold that had been missed, but at least ninety-five percent of the gold had been recovered from of the pond. Jock had calculated that the gold hunters had mined in standard ounces somewhere around $157,000 worth of gold nuggets from the pond; approximately four hundred and twenty-six pounds of gold. The gold was stored in wooden boxes then buried and camouflaged with tree limbs and other debris.

Jeremiah suggested to the men that maybe they should damn the trench back to its original origin. The valley stream was slowly disappearing and that is, "not how we found it", Jeremiah lamented.

Everyone agreed. It only took a couple of hours to restore the pond back to its natural configuration. Before the trench was damned Jerald and Jacky searched the stream bed for any overlooked gold nuggets. To Jock's surprise, the brothers did find four or five pounds of the gold; that glittering stuff that western dreams were made of.

When John asked the two cowpokes, Red Montgomery and Jasper Higgins if they were ready to go back home to Tennessee their response was a resounding, "Yes". John, Jake, and Jeremiah had discussed the possibility of the cowpokes wanting to go back to their homes in Tennessee. That had been their wish when Jeremiah had first hired them to help bring the wagons into Denver. When Jeremiah first saw them the cowpokes were shoveling cow and horse poop for money just for food and a bed at night. Now, they could go back home to Tennessee with money, lots of money.

Jeremiah and John talked to Red and Jasper about their train tickets back to their homes in Tennessee. John told them that he would purchase their tickets the first part of the next week. He also told them they would be paid some money for helping in the hidden valley, he didn't tell them how much money would be involved. The cowpokes were hoping for a few hundred dollars each so they could help with some of their Tennessee family's and friend's needs.

John took gold nuggets once again to Jacob Baskins the vice president of the Mercantile Bank in Denver. Jacob would take the raw gold, have it assayed and then exchange the gold for hard paper American currency. The gold would then be transferred to a Federal gold exchange house. As usual, the total transaction was kept strictly confidential.

When Red and Jasper were ready to board the train to Tennessee John, Jake, Jock, Jeremiah, Bright, and Henry were there to see them off. Lucy, Amy, Jerald, and Jacky got there in time to join in the hugs, handshakes, and kisses. After the second rounds of hugs, kisses, and handshakes John handed each cowpoke a large strong leather satchel.

"Well boys, thanks for everything. We'll keep in touch. Take good care of those satchels." John just smiled then said, "Enjoy!"

When the train had left the station both cowpokes knew what was in the satchels, they just didn't know how much. They were hoping for at least $500 each.

Red very slowly opened his satchel just enough to peek in it. Jasper was watching Red's eyes; he wanted to check his expression when Red saw what was inside the satchel. Red's eyes widened and his mouth opened wide and then his jaw dropped. In each satchel was $15,000 in good American paper currency. The cowpokes and their families were rich and set financially for life if the money was handled responsibly.

John and Sarah's initial destination was Salt Lake City in the Utah Territory. But after staying in Denver for these past several months and the hospital visits for Sarah and Sarah's passing John decided that Salt Lake City was never going to happen. He was more intrigued with the Idaho Territory and decided that the "Lost River Valley" in Idaho would be his and his family's next home. John had a number of discussions with Jake and Jeremiah about their plans of settling in the Idaho territory and not Utah. Now that Sarah was gone John was ready to get serious about those talks in a more direct and determined way. John knew that Jeremiah was not all that comfortable living on flat land. Jeremiah called himself a mountain man for a very real reason. He was fascinated with gold, but gold and wealth were not his passion. Breathing mountain air, listening to the wolves howl at night, drinking from a mountain brook and watching the stars at night from on top of a mountain was Jeremiah's passion for freedom. That's the way he wanted to live and that is where he wanted to die.

For Jake, there were two important desires in his life and they were paramount above all else. The first desire was to have a family someday with Bright like the McCrumb's family. The second desire was to always be near the McCrumb family. There were others things that Jake yearned for, but these two yearnings came far above everything else. Jake was trying to get up enough nerve to ask Henry if it was permissible to court Bright. Of course, that is if Bright would agree. Bright knew that Jake was sweet on her because of all of the attention he showed her. That attention was foreign to Bright and it came as a surprise. No one had ever paid her any attention back in Tennessee except her brothers. She was shy and backward because of her eyesight difficulties. She didn't think any man would want a wife who couldn't see well. None of the boys or men back in Tennessee "paid her no mind", as she put it.

After a lot of talks, the three men came to an agreement that by the end of February of 1876 if the snow wasn't packed high they would hitch up the wagons and travel the "Overland Trail" to Fort Laramie and there take the "Oregon Trail" into the Idaho Territory. John had an almost every night discussion with Jerald, Jacky, Lucy and Amy about another wagon train trip, this time to the Idaho Territory. The boys were excited and looked forward to the new adventure. Lucy was fine with the new plans as long as Henry and Bright were going. Amy felt the same as Lucy. The only problems that Lucy and Amy had were caused by their past experience with the Pawnee and Ute Indians. Both girls still had some bad nightmares and some of those dreams got a little more intense after their mom had passed away. The dreams were less frequent now, but still very disturbing. Even though their momma was buried close to their Denver home it was their momma's spirit of strength, love and precious memories that they would take with them to the Lost River Valley in Idaho or any other place, and that was what was important to the McCrumb sisters.

Jacob Baskins, John's friend and the Vice President of the Denver Merchantile Bank sent a message to John that Harold Blocker the bank's president needed to speak with John a soon as possible. John met with Jacob and Harold Blocker the next morning in the office of the president of the Denver Mercantile Bank. Harold Blocker and Jacob's were eagerly waiting for John on that cold November day in 1875. Mr. Blocker took the lead in the morning conversation.

"Mr. McCrumb, we have some vis……"

"Please, call me John, I don't go by Mr. anything" John was smiling as he spoke but he was quite firm with the reason for his interruption. "I do want to apologize for interrupting you Mr. Blocker, but I just can't handle the "Mr."."

"I'm with you John on the "Mr." part. I'll call you John and you can me Harold. We bankers do get stuffy sometimes."

"John, our bank is going to have some visitors from San Francisco in a couple of days. They are U.S. Government officials from the San Francisco coinage Mint. As you might already know the San Francisco Mint stamps out gold coins for the large gold producers In the State of California and for the surrounding territories such as the Colorado Territory. Of course, we hope to be recognized by the Federal Government as a new State in the Union by the end of next year. At that time Colorado as an officially recognized state will have its own coin mint. The mint and the gold is owned and regulated by the Federal Government.

I know that you have used our bank before to transfer your gold into paper currency. And we do appreciate your confidence in our ability to do that service for you. If you have other gold that you wish to transfer this would be a great opportunity to do just that. Other than dealing with individual gold buyers which could be a disgusting experience the persons from the Mint would exchange the gold for currency in only one transaction. They would also load it and transfer it to the mint in Sans Francisco at no charge. Of course, we here at the bank would also benefit. We would handle the entire transaction, then hand you the Federal backed paper currency, however you requested it."

John told the bankers that there was more gold, but he did not give a figure amount. He explained to them that he would talk to his partners and that he would get back to them the next day.

That evening Jock, Jeremiah, and Jake had their discussion at John's house. After a couple of hours of serious conversation, the four men decided to sell the nuggets, gold bars and one metal box of Spanish gold coins to the individuals representing the San Francisco Mint. Jock wanted to keep the one iron box that wasn't quite full of Spanish coins in their possession. The other men agreed that would be a good idea. Everyone knew the location where that one box had been buried. They were also keeping the larger iron box that held the gold jewelry. Each of the partners had made a hand-drawn map of the location of both boxes.

The next morning John told the bankers the decision that he and his partners had agreed to. The San Francisco Mint and the Mercantile Bank made all of the arrangement to pick up the gold in iron transport wagons with a bunch of armed guards. The gold was transferred to a secret location to be assayed. The bank had its representatives present during the assaying process. Jeremiah and Jock were also present when the gold was being assayed. That procedure of transfer, assaying and document signing took all of five days. The final hard currency figure after being assayed and stored in the Mercantile Bank before the final transfer to the San Francisco Mint was just a little under a quarter of a million dollars. The paper U.S. Government currency was left in the bank's vaults until John and his friends decided when their final plans were determined. The gold was transported in a special armored railroad train car from Denver to San Francisco. John counted at least sixteen armed guards that boarded the special armored train car that was owned by the San Francisco Mint.

"Good riddance, and maybe one day I'll have a gold coin in my pocket from some of that gold." That was John's goodbye speech to the gold as the train chugged its way from the station's depot and finally from the city of Denver to its destination in the state of California.

The McCrumb family was trying to be a normal family after the passing of Sarah. But, nothing was the same and any form of normalcy was just a state of mind and not actual reality. The nights were the worst time of the day. The dark of night seemed much darker and the minutes in the night seemed much longer. Many nights John would get up and go sit on the front porch until the sun would peak its rays over the mountain tops. Amy would subconsciously look for her mom in the kitchen, but the kitchen would be empty. Amy did not like being alone at night she would either sleep next to Lucy or Bright. She never wanted to be alone during the daytime, she always wanted to be close to somebody. Lucy would write sweet notes to her mom in a secret ledger. Jerald and Jacky would talk to their mom every night in their prayers to God. During the day when John and the boys were not working around the house or building something in the farm yards, they would go to the hidden valley and help with the construction of Jock's log cabin. There were trees to cut down then prepare the logs for cabin walls.

Building rail fences and corrals for the horses during the daylight hours on the farm helped to take John and the boy's minds from languishing over Sarah's death. They would start working at sunrise and quit at dark. Everyone dreaded to see the sun set in the west, that meant the night was upon them once again and Sarah would not be there with her precious smile.

John wanted to do something special for the hospital in memory of Sarah. He was very appreciative for the loving care that the doctors and nurses had shown towards Sarah. He was also thankful for the care they had given him and Jeremiah's with their bullet wounds. He called a meeting with Jeremiah, Jake, Jock, Henry and then his two daughters and his two sons to discuss his idea. Everybody was in agreement that the hospital and staff had played a large part in everyone's lives. Jake suggested that they donate enough money to add onto the hospital in Sara's name. Jeremiah proposed $10.000. Everyone was in favor of that dollar amount. John wanted everyone to be there when the doctors and hospital were told of the donation.

John contacted the hospital governing committee, all of the doctors that used the hospital and the hospital nurses to meet with John and his friends so the presentation of the gift could formally be given. John made a short talk how thankful he was that Sarah had such wonderful care while she was in the good hands of the hospital, doctors and the hospital staff.

Jeremiah made the presentation of the $10,000 check drawn on the Denver Mercantile Bank. The hospital representatives had not been told what the presentation was; they thought it was going to be a presentation letter of thanks or something similar. Everyone was thrilled but still did not understand what the $10,000 was for. John explained the money was for the expansion of the hospital facilities and medical equipment. The hospital governing committee was sitting in their chairs speechless. The nurses were crying and the doctors were shaking the benefactor's hands. The only stipulation was the new facility was to honor the memory of Sarah McCrumb.

A couple of days after the hospital check presentation Jeremiah suggested to John that they needed to go deer hunting. Jeremiah reasoned that a short hunting trip would help to take John's mind off of Sarah and maybe turn John's grief around to a more positive direction. John was having a very difficult time coping with the loss of his beloved Sarah. John agreed to the hunting trip, but he wanted to take his two sons with them. It took the exertion of everybody for two days to get the four hunters prepared for their trek into the wild mysterious world of this part of the Rocky Mountains. Actually, it was just a labor of love for John. Everybody wanted to see John back with that old spark of life that inspired his friends.

There had been light snow flurries off and on for a couple of weeks, but nothing real heavy and that were unusual for this time of the year. Most winters in the Rocky Mountains were inundated with blizzards that concluded with heavy snow falls. The winter of 1875 and spring of 1876 proved to be a mild winter, the first in decades. This type of weather would work in favor of the McCrumb's and their traveling companions in their journey to the Idaho Territory.

The four adventurers left early in the morning of the third day of their preparation for the hunt. They rode their horses and took three pack horses with them. The pack horses were in case they actually did shoot something. Of course, Jeremiah was hoping for a successful hunt, but his main purpose was getting

John's mind going in a different direction. Jeremiah had Ammo trailing by his side as the group left the McCrumb's house. They didn't take the other dogs because they were not trained for the mountain hunt. Patsy had to stay behind also; she didn't want any part of the cold she stayed in the warmth of the barn most of the time.

The expanse of the Rocky Mountains in the Colorado Territory was enormous. The majestic peaks of those rugged and jagged mountains were thousands of feet above the valleys of the earth and forever reaching for the dark blue hues of the heavens.

When the air is still and calm in the high mountains, the silence of those mountains was deafening. When there were sounds it was like God's orchestra of the mountain playing a beautiful lost symphony by some unknown author. The sounds are varied and at times mystifying. But, when the sounds are all composed in harmonization a person could close their eyes and listen to the beauty of that harmony forever. When the wind, which a human cannot see, but when the wind moves through the trees it creates many strange and wonderful sounds that please the mind. The screeching of the eagle and the owl added another blend of musical notes to enhance the sounds of the wind and the music of the trees. The crashing sound of water as it rapidly charges over the boulders of a river add even more sounds to the symphony as it reaches a crescendo. The lonesome howl of the wolf and the lone coyote even blends in with that ever increasing crescendo. Even the jackrabbit as it hops and the mountain lion as it gracefully and almost noiselessly moves from rock ledge to rock ledge add unique sounds to the forever ongoing inexplicable music of the mountains. This is what Jeremiah wanted John to experience and just maybe find himself again with Sarah's spirit tuning his heart and possibly adding to the mountains music.

In the far distance on another range of the mountains, the adventurers could see a large herd of elks migrating to better feeding grounds. The great golden eagles and the majestic bald eagle filled the skies as they hunted prey for substance.

Just after mid-day, Jerald spotted what he thought were deer in a stand of large pine trees not far from where they rode. John congratulated his son for having a keen eye; it was in fact, a small herd of whitetail deer. After the guys dismounted Jeremiah told the boys to take the first shot. Both brothers identified which deer they had in their gun sights, that way there would be no squabbling who actually had the better aim. The boys fired at the same time. Both boys missed their targets. The brothers looked at each other in total disgust. John and Jeremiah both laughed and mused, "Better luck next time." Jeremiah added, "Maybe!"

The sound of the rifle blasts sent the herd of deer deeper into the trees far from the hunters. The higher the hunters climbed up the mountain slopes the colder the weather. The guys were dressed for this kind of cold. Jeremiah had a lot of experience during the winter months in the mountains in the Colorado Territory.

It wasn't long before they encountered another herd of deer, this time it was a much larger herd. Jeremiah would never shoot a doe, always a buck and the biggest buck if he could. The men dismounted for the second time and chose their individual deer carefully in the sights of their rifles. It was hard to focus in the cold; their fingers would go numb in just a couple of seconds. But Jeremiah told them if they were going be men of the mountains they would have to endure the cold and hope their fingers didn't freeze to the trigger before they brought their prey to the ground. Everyone fired almost at the same time. Jeremiah's deer dropped immediately. Jacky's deer staggered for a brief second then dropped.

Jerald's deer lived to see another day. His dad's deer would also see another day and probably alongside Jerald's deer.

The hunters gutted the two large bucks and then tied them to the pack horses. Jeremiah wanted to camp a good distance away from where the bucks had been gutted. He was concerned with the entrails smell reaching the great brown bears of the mountains. It could even be a problem just with the gutted carcasses of the deer. But, Jeremiah had confidence that Ammo would warn the group if any bears came near their campsite. The day had been bright with just a few clouds and there was just a light quilt of snow on the ground. They made camp next to a large rock formation on the mountain. The rock formation gave them some secure protection on two sides from any prowling carnivorous animals while they slept. They built a large fire and gathered enough driftwood to stoke the fire all night long. The heavy wool bedding kept them warm through the cold of the night. Morning came really fast for the hunters. Jeremiah had the strong black coffee boiling and the bacon frying by the time the brothers had opened their sleepy eyes to a new day.

Jeremiah wanted the group to ride west over a long rugged ridge and then a slope down into a wooded valley where deer and possibly elk would be sleeping in the early afternoon after their morning feeding. This valley wasn't new to Jeremiah he had been here before a number of years ago hunting and trapping. That was the year Jeremiah had an almost disastrous encounter with a giant grizzly bear in this same valley. In his many years of living and hunting in the Rocky Mountains Jeremiah had numerous confrontations with the smaller size regular mountain brown bears, but much fewer encounters with the giant grizzly bears. The more common habitat for the giant grizzlies was further north in the Idaho territory and the country of Canada. But the Colorado Territory had its share of the giant brown bears.

That year had been a good year for the giant mountain man. He had trapped many beaver and muskrats for their fur. He had bagged three big horn mountain rams, two mountain lions, and three small brown bears. Those hides brought premium prices in trades. He had made all of these trades by late spring and early fall of that year. It had been a banner year for Jeremiah up until that September when he met with the great bear.

It was mid-September of that year when he and Ammo were preparing their campsite in the early evening. Ammo became agitated and began with deep and menacing growls when Jeremiah was finishing building the night's campfire. Jeremiah had just built a good blazing campfire. He turned to see what Ammo was getting so worked up over when out of the bowls of the early darkening of the night a huge and ominous form appeared just a few feet from where Jeremiah was standing. Jeremiah knew immediately what danger he was facing; a huge grizzly with massive teeth and huge claws. The grizzly let out a mountain shaking growl as it rose on its two hind feet. Jeremiah stood almost six feet and seven inches tall and that grizzly towered above him. He would later say as he told this story to John and the two brothers that the grizzly must have been at least ten foot tall standing there in the shadows of the darkest part of the evening's twilight. He must have weighed at least a thousand to twelve hundred pounds. Jeremiah had little chance of defending himself standing that close to this monstrous adversary. The giant grizzly took a huge swipe at Jeremiah with its enormous right paw with those two and a half inch claws determined to do damage. The grizzly's paw just barely caught Jeremiah's left shoulder, but it was powerful enough to send the big man sprawling into and over the fire he had just started. The bear's claws ripped open Jeremiah leather coat and caused a deep bloody gash across his shoulder and chest. Jeremiah knew that he could be facing death in a matter of seconds with those enormous paws and at the mercy of this massive beast. He mentally prepared himself for the bear's next attack, but it didn't happen, not immediately.

Ammo had attacked the grizzly from its backside. Ammo had sunk his large jaws into the bear's hind leg and ripped a large chunk of flesh and bear leg tendons. Ammo had to let go of the bear's massive leg to get out of the bear's range of destructive claws. The bear charged toward the big dog but Ammo was much quicker than the bear's movements.

Jeremiah was able to recover from the bear's blow to his shoulder as Ammo continued to agitate the bear's movements. Jeremiah was able to get to his rifle. The big man's quick movements attracted the giant grizzly's attention and the massive animal turned to attack that movement. The grizzly was almost over Jeremiah when Jeremiah discharged his buffalo rifle at the bear point blank. The grizzly whirled to the side of the mountain man almost falling on him. The giant bear recovered and quickly limped off into the darkness emitting a horrible sound of pain. The huge grizzly disappeared limping into the night's vastness with Ammo nipping at its heels. Jeremiah didn't get off the second shot because he was near passing out, maybe from his wound, but more likely from just absolute freight.

Jeremiah was sure that Ammo had done some damage to the bear's leg because of the bear's limping out of the campsite. But he wasn't sure if he had hit the bear when he fired his buffalo rifle. Jeremiah was on his back when he fired the rifle and if he had hit the massive animal it would have only been in the lower part of one of the bear's legs. Jeremiah was alive and that is all that mattered at the time.

Jeremiah had told the story of the grizzly to John and the brothers the night before as they eat their supper around the campfire. A conversation with questions was hurled Jeremiah's way following his story.

"Jeremiah, do you have a scar from the bear's claws?" Jerald's first of many questions.

"Yep, sure do!" Jeremiah opened his coat far enough so the boys could see the scars that the bear's claws had left. It was really a dramatic wicked looking scar.

"Did you ever see the grizzly again Jeremiah?" It was Jacky's turn to ask a question.

"Nah, never seen that Grizz again,"

Jeremiah…do you think the grizzly could still be in this region?" That was John's question.

"I doubt it." His answer was not at all convincing to any of the three men listening to the story. "Grizzlies can live twenty-five years, and that was almost four years ago…….. I don't know? …………..I guess he could still be somewhere in these mountains, ………..I don't know……he might have limped off to die…….Probably not here any longer…………maybe not"

Jeremiah's answer sort off drifted off into an indefinite uncertainty of doubts.

The next morning the hunters started out early for the valley where Jeremiah said elk and deer might be feeding. To get to the valley the four would have to maneuver a treacherous ridge. After the four hunters had ridden the peak of the rugged and sometimes difficult ridge they finished the ride in the valley where there could be sleeping deer and elk. John suggested they dismount for lunch before the hunt for those sleeping deer and elk.

While they were eating beef jerky and drinking black coffee Jeremiah pointed to a high cliff half way up the mountain they had been on that morning. They had to focus their eyes to catch a glimpse of what Jeremiah was pointing it was a herd of bighorn rams climbing and jumping around the rocky cliffs. Jeremiah indicated that the big horn was next on their hunting agenda.

The afternoon hunt for the sleeping deer proved to be a lost cause; no deer, no elk, no nothing. Jeremiah just shrugged his big shoulders and offered the lame reasoning, "Well…maybe tomorrow."

No one blamed the big mountain man because everyone was enjoying the much-needed outing. The mountain air was clean and crisp and the beauty of the Rocky Mountains was a marvelous comforter for a troubled mind. In those three days with his sons and Jeremiah in the grandeur of one of God's marvelous creations, John's attitude was having an astounding transition. John was smiling again and that look on his face of dismay was gone. Jeremiah was pleased with himself; he had made a good choice having this hunting trip for the McCrumb men.

The men settled in their new campgrounds early so they could get an early start in the morning. The weather was almost perfect for hunting this time of the year. It was cold but the skies were clear and the sun did give some warmth during the day. The lack of blinding snow blizzards was a blessing.

In less than an hour after they had started the hunt on the next morning, the hunters found themselves riding parallel with a large herd of elk. The hunters were riding in the valley about a couple of hundred yards above them on the side of the mountain was the herd of elk. John figured that there were at least seventy to eighty elk in the herd. It was an amazing site to witness, especially being this close to the herd. Jacky asked Jeremiah why they couldn't shoot one of them. Jeremiah explained to Jacky that it would be almost impossible to retrieve an elk's carcass down the mountainside to the valley. Jeremiah stressed to the McCrumb boys in no uncertain terms, that killing any animal for just the sport of the kill would never happen in his presence. Jeremiah told them you only kill an animal for three reasons; for self-protection for the protection of others and for food. Jeremiah told them to enjoy the wonderful sight of those magnificent animals because not many humans will ever get that privilege.

Just before noon, the hunters came across a herd of deer, about twenty-five or so. The deer were nosing the snow covered ground searching for the late fall grass stubbles that were still hanging on to life before the winter freeze kill. Jeremiah told Jerald and John to take their shots because he and Jacky had their limit. He admonished Jerald to take his sweet time and don't jerk his rifle. Dad and son took steady aim and fired on Jeremiah's count of three. Two of the larger bucks dropped to the ground in unison. Son and dad turned to each other with big grins.

John and Jeremiah had Jerald and Jacky gut the two bucks and prepare them for the pack horses. They found a good place for their night camp. It was next to a gigantic boulder that would protect them from a cold light northern wind. They found large strong tree branches to hang the four deer for the night. The trees were close to the huge rock and would give some protection from night time meat eating marauders. A good fire was struck for the evening meal of jerky and some of Jeremiah's hot venison stew. Of course, Jeremiah's strong black coffee was once again used to swallowed down their gullets the western gourmet meal.

The four hunters were well snuggled in their sleeping paraphernalia when Ammo started a deep menacing growl that Jeremiah recognized immediately as a possible approaching danger. Jeremiah scrambled from under his many layers of cold forbidding covers. He grabbed his buffalo gun and then shook John from a sound sleep and warned him that something was amiss. John took hold of his Henry rifle and woke his sons up.

The night air was motionless and there appeared a billion times a billion stars in the dark northwestern sky. Every once in a while if you looked to the north you could catch a glimpse of the northern lights. The supper fire still had a low-grade flame flickering brightly and was casting some really weird shadows around the hunter's camp sight. All four of the hunters strained to hear any strange sound that might indicate an unwanted intruder. Ammo continued his menacing growl but did not get up from his resting position. The horses seemed uneasy and were moving around with unsettling nasal noises. Jeremiah tossed some larger wood limbs on the fire.

Time went by slow, seconds seemed like minutes and the minutes seemed like forever. Jeremiah had John and the brother's crouch next to the large boulder, it gave them some protection, at least on one side. All four men were gripping their rifles so hard their fingers were turning numb. But, none of them noticed the numbness in their fingers. Ammo had gotten up from his resting place and was now lying in front of Jeremiah. He had stopped his growling but was still in a state of alertness. He finally got up and would walk to the edge of where the campfire light met the dark of night and just stood there peering into the darkness. The men tensed and the hair on the back of their necks stood up when Ammo began that growl again, this time with a more alarming snarl. Ammo started slowly to back up and almost backed into the fire but stopped short of burning his rear end. His growl was intensifying and giving the men real cause for alarm.

The men strained to hear any menacing sounds but there was not a sound coming from the vast darkness around them. Then suddenly a loud sound like a tree was being snapped into broke the silence of the stillness of the night. The sound was ear shattering and lasted for a couple of minutes then silence reigned once again. Ammo stopped his growling and he lay back down in his initial resting place. Jeremiah looked over at John and just shook his head as if to ask, "What just happened?"

There wasn't much sleep done that night. The guys took turns on watch until the welcomed first rays of the sun peeked into the valley.

With those first sun rays, all four of the deer hunters were scouring the area trying to identify the crashing sound of the night before. It didn't take them long to find the reason for the noise. An eight-inch diameter pine tree had been snapped in half like a twig. The huge claw marks told the story of how the tree was snapped in two pieces.

Jeremiah told John and the boys that it was time to head back to the McCrumb ranch. Everyone eagerly agreed. The experience of the night before had everyone on edge and full fear alert. The hunt for the Big Horn could wait until another day. They secured the four gutted deer's on the pack horses and began their rigorous journey back to Denver. The trip back would take at the least two complete travel days and maybe part of a third day. During the ride back Jeremiah would double back every three to four miles to check for ground tracks and trees for broken limbs. He was looking for any signs that the group was being followed by their unknown visitor of the previous night.

Their travel that day was uneventful except for riding back over that rugged ridge. Lose rocks proved to be a definite hazard for the pack horses. The shifting weight of the dead deer's carcasses was hampering the pack horse's ability to maintain steady footing because of the loose rocks on the ridge. Problems riding the ridge were costing the men valuable travel time.

With the dangerous ridge behind the hunters, John suggested that they stop, rest and eat. Everyone was mentally fatigued and physically tired dealing with the last couple of hours dealing with the treacherous ridge trail. Eating beef jerky was getting a little old to the hunters, so Jeremiah shot four rabbits and cooked them over the open fire. Even his black coffee tasted good with the roasted rabbits and a good old pot of beans.

One thing the ride over that miserable ridge did do, it took everyone's mind off of the invisible threat that had encountered them the night before. Jeremiah wanted to set up the night camp a little early after he found a well-protected site, not only for the men but also for the horses and the four deer carcasses. He had found a good spot where two steep embankments would protect them on two sides of the camp. They could hang the deer next to one of the embankments and tether the horses in front of the other. Jerald and Jacky gathered five or six large armloads each of dry wood for a large camp fire. Jeremiah placed the initial fire well out in front of the embankments which would keep anyone fairly safe that was between the fire and the embankments from most predators.

Neither John, Jeremiah nor the brothers were in a race to see who could get to sleep the quickest that night. Jeremiah told some of his adventures in the mountains long after the night had settled in. It was well after midnight when Ammo's ears went to full attention and a low menacing growl could be heard in the dark just out of reach of the light of the campfire. The horses also began with low-grade whinnies and were lightly hoofing the ground. Jeremiah quickly stood up with his rifle in his arms and pointed to the dark beyond the campfire. John, Jerald, and Jacky followed Jeremiah example and rose to their feet with weapons in their hands. Unlike the night before this time, they could hear the deep low growl and some twigs and branches cracking. Suddenly it was total silence again. All a person could hear were the results of the wind as it was rustling through the branches of the trees. There were four pairs of ears and four pairs of eyes straining towards the night's darkness desperately trying to hear or see the menace that was evidently stalking them.

The stillness was shattered with a deep and profoundly deafening roaring growl of what was surely in everyone's mind a giant grizzly bear of monstrous size. A very frightening chill overwhelmed all four of the hunters. The horses were violently wrenching at their tethers with fear of the enormous danger that was lurking just yards away in the dark. Ammo's hair was standing straight up in the air and his growls had changed to vicious sounds of snarling's. The ferocious sound of the ominous growling in the night's darkness continued and each time the growl exploded in the night air, it seemed more menacing than the one before.

Slowly a huge dark form began to take shape from the dark into the light of the campfire. It was indeed a giant grizzly bear. The grizzly had a definitely pronounced limp as it made its way to a full view of the campfire. It stood at least ten to twelve foot tall when standing upright on its hind legs. The grizzly's massive head waved in the air as the rumbling roar cascaded from its huge open jaws. Ammo stood his ground, not charging the bear, but like two fighters just standing their grounds nose to nose and spitting monstrous intimidating sounds at each other.

The gigantic massive bear just stood in one place roaring his growls towards Jeremiah and his companions. The grizzly made no motions or indications that it was going to charge the hunters. Jeremiah stood with an amazed and astonished look on his face.

"John.....this bear is not going to charge,...he doesn't want to harm us." Jeremiah had just re-met his old antagonist of five years earlier.

"What.......are ya saying, Jeremiah..........This bear is out for blood.....We need to shoot before he charges.......Jeremiah,... shoot him or I will." John could hardly talk he was so scared. His arms were frozen and he could barely feel his rifle, let alone fire it.

"NO JOHN..........Don't shoot........Nobody shoot .... This Grizz is not here to harm us.........This Grizz .....This Grizz is giving Ammo and me a second look........ Look at Ammo....... he senses the Grizz means us no harm this time."

The giant grizzly dropped onto all fours and indifferently sniffed the air as if to determine if he was satisfied with his surroundings. He slowly lumbered within a few yards of Jeremiah and Ammo and then stopped. The four men seemed to be frozen in time and space. No one dared to move or breath heavy. The grizzly stood motionless looking toward Jeremiah and sniffing the air. He slowly rose up again on his hind haunches to his full height of almost twelve feet. He let out one last earth shattering deep roar that shook the ground the hunters stood on. Then the gigantic bear dropped to his all four feet again and slowly turned toward the dark night beyond the light of the flickering fire.

Just as suddenly as the monstrous grizzly appeared he disappeared into the night's darkness. The hair on Ammo's back relaxed. The four men all let go of their weapons with huge sighs of relief. Both

Jerald and Jacky had peed in their pants. Their pa almost did the same.

"That Grizz will forever know us......He will remember each one of us as long as he lives...........My friends, we are now part of this mountain." Jeremiah spoke with passion and resolve. He knew and understood the ways of the mountains. The immense Grizzly had introduced the McCrumb's and Jeremiah to the secret union of the mountain. Jeremiah had said a truth and he sincerely believed in that truth. The giant grizzly and the four hunters were now one with nature.

The remaining two days of travel back to the McCrumb's house was uneventful but extremely tiring. The first thing the hunters did after they had unsaddled the horses and tended their needs they skinned and dressed down the four deer into quarters. The meat was salted and stored in a typical ice house of the period in the 19th century.

Jeremiah, John, and the boys had built the ice house weeks before the deer hunt. They dug a hole in the ground about six foot deep and twelve-foot square. Then they built thick log walls at ground level around the hole. The walls were about four foot high above the ground. A wood plank roof was constructed over the hole and log walls. The men then packed two foot of dirt on the wood roof and covered the walls with dirt. When they were finished it just looked like a natural dirt hill in the yard. That is, except on the south side of the dirt hill there were steps heading downward six feet into the hole in the ground where a person would encounter a strong wooden door when opened a person would walk into a cold and damp twelve square foot summer storage room.

When the ice house was completed John and the boys filled the bottom two foot of the room with sawdust and straw. Next, they cut large chunks of ice during the winter months from the frozen rivers and frozen lakes around the Denver area. Usually, the total weight of the ice yield would be around a thousand pounds. The ice would then be buried in the sawdust and straw in the "ice house". This icing process would be worked the same way every winter. The ice house would stay at a cold temperature all summer long. Meat, canned fruits, and vegetables would be stored in the hand dug and hand constructed a 19th-century cooling system for a year round storage.

The deer hunt worked as Jeremiah had hoped. John's attitude was much better and his emotional coping with the loss of Sarah was greatly improving with every new day. Spiritually the members of the small church of Christ in Denver were a tremendous support group for the McCrumb family during their grieving for Sarah. Different members would visit and bring food to the McCrumb's home at least twice a week. By Christmas of that year, the McCrumb's had finally accepted in a personal way the passing of Sarah. The girls had Bright to help them cope with their sadness. The boys and John kept busy with the help of their friends working around the farm, building a barn, sheds, and miles of fencing. Jake kept busy working on and around his new house with Bright by his side much of the time. Jock had finished his log cabin and was building sheds and fencing on his property in the hidden valley.

John's brother James and his wife Hazel Ann were due to arrive in Denver the first week in January of 1876. James and his wife would live in the McCrumb house after John and his family headed to the Idaho Territory in the early spring of 1876. James was initially scheduled to arrive in Denver before Christmas, but bad weather in the northeastern part of the nation canceled out that timetable of a departure.

The members of the church of Christ did not celebrate the 25th of December as the birth date of Jesus Christ. They celebrated Christ's birth and death every Sunday of the year. But, they did use that day as a traditional family day of gathering and a gift giving day. The McCrumb family was really big on the gift giving part of that day.

During the last week of November and the first week in December the McCrumb's had Bright go through some medical eye exams at the Denver hospital. The Denver doctors were in agreement that Bright's eyesight could be improved, maybe not a hundred percent, but much better than they were at the present. They had heard of new eye operations that had been very successful in France with cataract surgery and Bright's eye problems were a form of cataracts.

The Denver doctors contacted the larger hospitals in Boston and New York concerning the possibility of Bright having the eye surgery performed in one of those larger medical New England facilities. Boston's largest medical facility was the first to the respond and it was all good news. Sometime during the month of February in 1876, a French eye cataract specialist would be at the Boston hospital that month teaching the new procedure to New England doctors and Bright just might be a candidate for the operation. Bright and Henry were very excited with that possibility. Of course, Jake was really excited. He and Bright were favorably becoming a very close couple. John told everyone that he would make all of the arrangements for Bright and Henry's journey to Boston when the time was right.

Time seemed to be moving at a snail's pace at the McCrumb's house. John and Jeremiah were preparing for the journey to the

Idaho Territory. Bright, Lucy, Amy, Henry, and Jake were counting the days until the trip to Boston. The McCrumb boys were counting all of the days for anything to happen and it seemed like nothing was happening. They were bored out of their minds. They did go rabbit hunting a lot. Now, there were times when Henry was preoccupied with the presence of Lucy's beauty and flirting smile, which continually kept him off guard and confused. That was the way she liked it.

The McCrumb family had planned for a huge food banquet for the 24th of December at the McCrum's ranch and Lucy, Amy, Bright and some of the ladies from church were in the process of preparing for the feast. This banquet would be talked about for years to come. John and Jeremiah had killed three more deer and an elk for the feast. John wanted plenty of food for the large Christmas festival. He and Jeremiah had purchased eight hogs and fifteen steers from some of Denver area's farmers and had them butchered and dressed. There were always plenty of chickens to roast and fry.

Much of the meat from the butchered cattle, hogs and wild game were given to Denver charities so the cities less fortunate could also enjoy a fine December 25th feast. John and his friends also gave those charities money to be spent on clothes, toys and other essentials for those in need. John particularly wanted all of the children in Denver to enjoy a wonderful Christmas.

Many folks from Denver were invited to the McCrumb's home for the 24th feast. Even many who were not invited showed up and that was just OK with John. The doctors and hospital staff were invited. The Mercantile Bank personnel were all invited. Church members were invited. Lucy and Amy's friends were invited. Jerald and Jacky's friends were invited. In fact, anybody who even heard about the feast was invited. There were just too many people to count, so Lucy, Amy, and Bright gave up counting. There were gifts for everyone who showed up, especially for the children. Scott Walker, John's lawyer, and fellow church member gave John and Jock and Jake each a very special gift, one they had been anxiously anticipating for months. Scott handed each of them the deeds and the final signed documents stating that the land they had filed for under 1862 Homestead Act was now legally theirs. With the signed documents Scott presented them with the titles to their lands.

After the prayer was offered giving thanks to God for the food and all blessings, a special prayer was offered for Sarah and her beloved family. John said a very private prayer, thanking God for giving him the blessing of a wife such as his Beloved Sarah.

James McCrumb and his wife Hazel Ann arrived in Denver on January 10th 1876. It was a Monday afternoon and the skies were clear and the temperature was 36 degrees. John and the whole family were on the depot platform to greet them. John introduced the couple to Jeremiah, Jake, and Henry, Bright and their two nieces and two nephews whom they had never met. Both John and James had similar McCrumb features; you could definitely tell they were brothers.

Both brothers had enlisted together in the 134th Pennsylvania Volunteers in August of 1862 for the Union cause during the Civil War. They fought together in the August 29th and 30th, 1862 Battle of Richmond Kentucky. It was the second largest Civil War battle in the state of Kentucky. The Richmond battle was a huge Confederate victory for Major General Edmund Kirby Smith. John managed to escape from being captured along with 1147 other Union soldiers. But, James was one of the 4,303 Union soldiers that were either captured or missing in action during that battle. Other Union fatalities in the Kentucky battle were 206 killed and

844 wounded. James managed to later escape from a Confederate prison compound and rejoined the 134th Pennsylvania Volunteers by Thanksgiving of that same year.

John had rented James and Hazel Ann a newer house in the better section of Denver. They would live in the rented house until John and his family moved on to the Idaho Territory.

The third out building that was constructed after the McCrumb house was completed in early October was a good size bunk house where Jeremiah, Jake, and the three cowpokes would lay their heads at night. The outside walls of the bunk house were doubled built like the main house for better warmth during the winter months. There were two large iron coal or wood-burning pot-bellied stoves in the bunk house to enhance the winter's warmth comfort. John had enough coal hauled to the ranch in the late fall to last the house and the bunk house heating stoves through the winter months with some coal to spare. Coal was the better fuel for heating during the winter months because it burned hotter and burned longer than wood. The inside of the bunkhouse was finished for the working man's comfort, especially during the winter months. The McCrumb's bunk house was built better than most Denver houses were constructed. John had built the bunk house for the future. If he, Jake or James decided to grow hay or raise cattle and horses there would be a bunk house for the help to lay their heads at night. Jake spent some of his days at the bunk house and other days at his new house.

The first and second bunk house outhouses (toilets) were constructed after the main house had been built. Deep holes were dug and ordinary wooden toilet structures were constructed then gingerly moved and placed over the holes. Each outhouse (toilet) had at least three holes carved in the seat for the comfort of the user. The two large bunk house toilets were for men only. The two toilets were placed far apart from each other and that distance was designed on purpose. When the family house was built, John had a fancier and larger outhouse toilet built for the pleasure of Sarah and his two daughters. It was a three-holer and all of the holes were smaller and designed for complete female comfort. A second outhouse was constructed for the main house it was plain and suited for John and the boys. Jerald and Jacky couldn't understand why their bottoms were not just as important as the girls.

Jake told the boys, "Just live with it! Someday you might figure out the behavior and character of the bottoms of the opposite sex. Well, maybe you will!"

In January of 1876 Denver only had thirteen inches of snowfall. Six of those thirteen inches fell in a single twenty-four hour period, leaving the rest of the month with only seven inches of snowfall. Between Denver and the McCrumb's house, there were only two to four inches of snow on the ground at any one time. Many days in January of that year were sunny days with temperatures highs in the low thirty-degree range. The weather pattern for February of 1876 was just about the same as January. The way the weather pattern was evolving March would be a good month for the McCrumb's to begin their trek to the Idaho Territory.

In January of 1876, the Denver hospital received word from the Boston City Hospital that a German and two French eye doctors would be in Boston to train America doctors the delicate eye operation procedures and also to perform eye surgeries during the months of February and March. In that same communique was the "Ok" for Bright to have an eye operation in the Boston hospital during those two months if her condition warranted the operation.

Bright and her brother Henry and John held a couple of important meetings conferring with the Denver hospital staff about Brights trip to Boston. All of the discussions were positive. Through telegraph and letter correspondence the Denver hospital made all of the necessary arrangements for travel, lodging and Boston hospital prep time for Bright. John paid for everything through bank drafts. He also gave Henry and Bright spending money for the trip.

It was difficult for Bright to understand the generosity that John and his family had showered on her and Henry. Their lives in Tennessee had been so distressed most of the time. The folks in Tennessee were friendly and wonderful neighbors, but most of them were poor and struggling just to survive from week to week. Men worked hard from the sun up to sun down and for little wages. The women did whatever they could to help their men put food on the table. Most women would plant gardens and tend to them for the produce the garden would yield. A person's lifespan was shorter than most other surrounding states. There were very few doctors and no hospitals to serve the sick or frail where Bright grew up. Bright had a few girlfriends but none of the boys paid her any attention because of her blindness. Most girls in the town where she lived were married by Bright's age of nineteen. She never had store bought clothes, she made her own. She even made some of her brother's shirts. Her poor eyesight was not a hindrance with the peddle sewing machine. She could operate that machine blindfolded.

Henry and his two friends had traveled to the Colorado Territory in hopes of finding gold so they could make their families lives better back home in Tennessee. But their entire trip to Denver proved to be a total disaster for the three cowpokes. It didn't take long before they realized they had made a horrible blunder. There wasn't any gold left for them to discover. They didn't have any money to buy train tickets back to their Tennessee homes. They found themselves shoveling cow and horse poop just to make enough money so they could buy food and find a place to sleep at night in Denver. And that made things much worse back in Tennessee because the three men were not helping to put food on any Tennessee tables.

And now, because of one man's generosity, Bright and Henry's lives have been transformed like as if they were in a wonderful dream. But it wasn't a dream, it was real. It was difficult for Bright to understand that kind of kindness and liberality. Whatever was happening in her life she was quick to give God the credit. Maybe she reasoned that God was smiling down on her and Henry because of their new found faith. Both Bright and Henry had been baptized by the preacher of the small church of Christ in Denver. Bright was very humbled in this new world of hers. And for the first time in her life, she felt true love from a very special man. She could not understand why Jake would even consider her for his wife. She felt inadequate to be loved by a man of his qualities. Jake idolized Bright and he felt he was not good enough to receive her love. They would love each other for life.

There was a host of well-wishers on the depot's boardwalk to see Bright and Henry off when they boarded the train for their adventure to Boston. Lucy and Amy were crying for Bright's happiness. Bright was crying because she didn't want to be without Lucy and Amy's companionship. Just before she boarded the train Jake took her in his arms and told her for the first time how much he loved her. With that hug and a very long kiss, Bright and Henry boarded the train for their long voyage to Boston and hopefully better eyesight for Bright. Lucy and Amy's crying turned to happy giggles seeing Jake's "mile long kiss" that he had planted on Bright's lips. The "mile long kiss" was Amy's quote. On Thursday, January 27th, 1876 Bright and Henry began their adventure to Boston in hopes of better eyesight for Bright.

John had told Henry that he would telegraph him weekly of the happenings in Denver and the McCrumb's travel plans to the Idaho Territory. John also advised Henry that he would inform him later where he and Bright were to travel after Bright's eye operations.

By the end of February activity around the McCrumb's ranch was like a disturbed ant hill. Everything and everyone was in a hustle bustle mode with all activities geared towards the coming wagon train trek to the Idaho Territory. John had bought another covered wagon, or "Prairie Schooner" as Lucy preferred to call them. The original two covered wagons were brought out of storage and were being reconditioned. The large sign that Lucy had attached to her "chuck wagon" was still attached. The three covered wagons were being filled with the family's personal belongings. Many of the same items that had traveled from Alma Kansas to Denver were packed for the second time into the wagons with care.

Over the past couple of months, Jerald and Jacky with the help of Jake had taught Patsy how to be ridden like a horse. The boys found that the buffalo actually enjoyed being ridden. She would get excited when the specially build saddle was being carried towards her. Lucy and Amy loved the gentle rides on Patsy. Patsy was as tender and loveable as the girl's horses. Jeremiah still maintained that Patsy thought she was a dog and not a buffalo.

As the time of their departure drew close the nerves and anxieties of the travelers were running short. Last minute conversations between John, Jock, Jeremiah, and Jake were discussed in private. Each of the partners made sure they still had their maps of where the two iron boxes filled with gold and jewelry had been buried. Jock was certain he was close to discovering a new vein of gold in the treasure cave. That possibility of more gold had the four men excited. But, of course, the guys knew that Jock would always follow that dream of gold in just under the next shovel full of dirt. The adventure of a new gold find would never end for the old prospector. The trust that the four men had in each other was more valuable to them than the gold itself.

The four partners divided all of the gold that had been found in the valley after the initial find had been shipped to the San Fransico Mint. Each partner received an equal share, about ten pounds of gold which had a dollar value of about four thousand dollars to each of them. They all had access to the bank account in the Denver Mercantile Bank. Jock didn't want any of his money in the bank. He was satisfied with just having gold in his pockets or buried in some secret hideaway.

For their journey to the Idaho Territory, John took twenty-five thousand dollars in paper money and $5,000 in gold. The paper money would be for land purchase. Jeremiah had little use for paper money; he only took five thousand dollars of the "paper crap" and $5,000 in gold. Jake, looking forward to land purchase in the new territory took fifteen thousand dollars in paper money and $5,000 in gold. Jock and John gave Jeremiah extra gold because of his lack of love for the "paper crap".

Jeremiah and John wished Jock well and promised him that they would be back in Denver soon to check on him and the ranch. John told Jock that his brother James would go into Denver and get him supplies anytime he needed them. John knew that Jock didn't want to have anything to do with Denver, ever again. Jock told his two friends not to worry about the two iron chest filled with gold and precious gems, "I'll sleep over them every night". John and Jeremiah just laughed and shook their old friend's hand.

John and Jake purchased another three hundred and twenty acres of Denver land from the federal government. This new three hundred and twenty acres of land surrounded the originally homesteaded land grant of three hundred and twenty acres that the two men had purchased earlier.

John and his brother James discussed at length the future of the McCrumb's Colorado farm. The two brothers decided to grow hay and raise cattle on the Denver farm. John hired a line crew to build fences in a large portion of his and Jake's land. James would oversee the building of miles of fencing. John had put a certain amount of money in a separate account in the Mercantile Bank that James could draw from when needed. James and Hazel Ann for the first time in their lives felt free from debt and now with a real purpose to show for their labors. John had given his brother a new lease on life and James was determined to make good on this new life in the western frontier. After John would settle his family in the Idaho territory he would travel back to Denver and then consider how to stock the ranch with cattle. In the meantime, James could oversee the fence building and start clearing land for planting hay. John gave James enough money to buy a hundred head of good beef cattle. In their future plans were the purchase of more acres of Colorado land.

On March 6th in 1876 thirty-nine covered wagons left Denver and the Colorado Territory on the "Overland Trail" heading north towards the destination of Fort Laramie and the Oregon Trail. It was on a Monday about 10 AM in the morning. The skies were overcast and a lite snow was gently falling from the gray skies. The McCrumb's three covered wagons were part of that larger wagon train. The thirty-nine covered wagons and hundreds of brave pioneers were heading west with the determination to further build a great nation.

The day before the wagon train embarked on its precarious journey to Fort Laramie the McCrumb's, Jeremiah, Jake, and Jock attended church services in the little church of Christ building in Denver. Tears were shed, hugs were given and goodbyes were exchanged. To Johns surprise, both Jeremiah and Jake asked to be baptized into Christ's body. Jock indicated, maybe later for him. Before John left the Sunday services that day he gave the church's congregation $5,000 for their work in Denver. He suggested they might hire another minister to spread God's Gospel in the Denver area.

That evening John spent almost two hours sitting next to Sarah's grave. Her grave was close to the house he had built for her. What was said during those two hours was private and still is private after all of these many years. Lucy, Amy, Jerald, and Jacky spent their time at the grave crying and saying their good buys to their beloved momma. The McCrumb's didn't know what the future held for each of them, but they were sure of one truth; Sarah's memory and spirit would always be with each of them and would guide them however the future cards were dealt.

The night before the wagons was to roll towards the Idaho Territory Lucy and Amy gave their brothers a very special surprise gift. A gift that the brothers thought had been lost to them forever. Jerald and Jacky were dumbfounded when their sisters handed them all of the bear claws and bear teeth that had been taken from the bear that the sisters and their momma had killed back yonder on the Smoky Hill Trail. The brothers thanked their sisters and gave them big hugs. Lucy put her very special parfleche painted bag that Two Elks had given her in a very safe place in the chuck wagon. She still had not looked inside of the bag that held the answers to her three requests. She was satisfied just knowing the wonderful history it held.

When the wagon master yelled "Wagons Ho" the thirty-nine covered wagons began their approximately one hundred and eighty-mile journey on the "Overland Trail" to Fort Laramie in the Wyoming Territory. Usually, during the late 1870's, that was a safe journey because the Overland Trail was protected for the most part by the U.S. Cavalry. The Overland Trail was a famous and regular stagecoach route to Fort Laramie, the Oregon Trail, and the Mormon Trail from the 1840's to the 1870's. During the earlier years from the 1850's through the 1860's and a couple of the early years in the 1870's the Overland Trail was a dangerous ride, whether it was by stage coach, on horseback or on a wagon train. Marauders, stagecoach bandits, and Indians found the trail to be easy pickings for money, gold, and scalps and in that order.

John McCrumb, his family and companions had mixed feelings when they heard the wagon master's words of "Wagons Ho". They only lived in Denver for a few months, but Denver had become their home. So much had happened during those very few months. It seemed they had been there a lifetime. They had made so many new and dear friends. And most important, a wife and a momma were buried there.

The first two days on the trail were uneventful. There had been a light snow both days and the temperature was moderate. The days did seem to be so much longer. The skies were dark gray, gloomy and dreary. It was almost depressing with the dark skies and nothing but white snow no matter where one would look. There weren't any pleasant bright colors anywhere to be found.

A company of the U.S. Calvary had traveled by the wagon train for the first two days. Amy found the Calvary boys in their blue uniforms to be quite handsome and she managed to flirt with a couple of them with her artful and clever smile. She was learning how to do this by watching Lucy and Henry and especially watching Jake and Bright. The company of soldiers had to leave the wagon train at mid-day on the third day because of reports of an Indian uprising in a small white settlement just north of Denver. The captain told the wagon master he did not know how long they would be gone.

Late in the afternoon on the third day, there were ominous indications that a possible powerful snow blizzard with gusty winds was about to overtake the wagon train. The wagon master informed every wagon crew in the train to prepare for the blizzard the best they could. He firmly stressed the importance of protection for the animals and the wagon master strongly emphasized that bodily harm, even death can and does happen during these harsh prairie snow blizzards. He again highlighted the importance of staying in the shelter of the wagons during the blizzard and of more consequence maintaining body warmth at all times.

Some of the wagons formed a circle so the horses and cattle could be protected in the middle of the circle. Other placed their wagons heading into the blizzard so the winds could not blow the wagons over. John and his companions lined their three wagons up side by side with the first wagon facing the blunt of the wind. They expected the winds to be blustery and mighty cold with temperatures well below freezing. The positions that the three wagons had been placed would protect two of the wagons from the cold blast of the wind. The first wagon was situated so it would take the blunt of the blizzards freezing winds. The second and third wagons that were behind the first wagon would be spared that initial blast of cold weather. Those wagons would be the warmer of the three wagons and that is where the pioneers would sleep partially protected from the freezing blustery wind. The horses were tethered behind the third wagon protected from the brunt of the cold wind.

When morning finally did arrive it entered the new day with a full howling and blustery cold snowy blizzard cascading with rage from due north. The blowing snow was causing limited sight and causing huge drifts of snow against many of the wagons. The snow drift against John's first wagon that was facing north had almost covered the complete side of the wagon that was facing the blizzard. That actually was good; it helped to divert the wind and created some insulation against the cold for the next two wagons. The blizzard raged all day into the dark of night. By midnight, the snow had let up and the wind decreased down to a moderate breeze. The slight breeze was good for the pioneers because it would keep cold weather from becoming sub-freezing. There had been very little movement in the wagon camp the entire day because of the dangerous freezing conditions. It had been hard to check on any of your neighbors because of the dangerous cold and challenging winds.

The fifth morning brought bright blue skies and temperatures just below freezing. Human movement from the wagons was slow and cautious. John and his groups slept warm through both nights under mountains of blankets and coverlets. The dogs slept next to their masters in the wagons. After checking on his kids and friends John next checked on Patsy and the horses. The horses and Patsy fared well compared to some of the other stock in the wagon train.

Two of the wagons in the train lost a couple of horse's to the freezing weather. The biggest tragedy was two young children who froze to death during the night blizzard. A young bride died two days later from complications of the blizzard. After everyone had dug their wagons out from under the snow drifts and normalize their situations the wagon master prepared everyone for the funeral services of the two young children before continuing the journey. Three of the wagons turned back towards Denver. In one of the wagons was the young bride who later died. John and his companions had helped as many of those travelers in the train who were hit the hardest during the storm the best that they could. Lucy and Amy along with others tried to give comfort to the mother who had lost her two children. It was a sad day for all of those pioneers who had started that tragic journey together.

The fifth day of travel was slow and laborious trying to travel through the thick and deep snow that had fallen the day before. The train managed to travel only six miles that day. During the sixth day on the Overland trail, the remaining thirty-six wagons met up with a small band of friendly Cheyanne Indians. Jeremiah was able to converse with them. The Indians were hunting for deer, elk or moose. Jeremiah and John gave the Cheyanne an extra deer quarter that had been salted down for future meals. The Cheyanne were surprised and grateful for the gift. Jeremiah assured the Indians that a return gift was not necessary.

Beginning the seventh day on the Overland trail the wagon train was still about seventy miles from their initial destination of Fort Laramie. Their travel time was way behind schedule and there appeared there was nothing that could be done to make up any extra time. Right after mid-day, another incident occurred that was going to set them back another half a day. A covered wagon and it's a middle-aged couple from an earlier and larger wagon train had been left behind because of a broken axel and a completely damaged back wheel.

Any wagon train crossing the prairies, the mountains or from town to town, it was unforgivable and morally corrupt to desert a damaged wagon and the family that owned the wagon leaving them on their own in the desert to fend for themselves. Only a depraved and decadent wagon master or fellow travelers, in this case, would leave another human to suffer that kind of injustice.

The wagon master of the thirty-six wagon train told the couple with the broken down wagon that the people in his train would help to restore their wagon. John told the wagon master that he had iron plates to rebuild the axle and a new wheel to replace the damaged wheel. The men of the thirty-six wagons joined together and within three hours had the busted wagon ready to roll. Jeremiah had amazed everyone by holding the damaged wagon up all by himself while the new wheel was replaced. The grateful couple who owned the wagon thanked everyone for their kindness and generosity. Jack and Ila Bonner made a special effort in thanking John and Jeremiah for their help. With tears in her eyes, Ila Bonner hugged the wagon master, then hugged John, Jake, and Jeremiah. Without their kindness, the couple would have been left to the wild elements of the vast and empty prairie.

The wagon master, John, Jeremiah, and Jake made the couple a promise; when they reached Fort Laramie if the other wagon master was still there, he would be taught a lesson he would never forget.

Two more days on the Overland trail went without incident or problems. By nightfall, on a ninth day, the wagon caravan was almost within shouting distance of Fort Laramie. The Calvary had rejoined the wagon train on the day before. The horse soldiers were heading back to Fort Laramie for further instruction of any Indian disturbance. The problem they thought existed in the small white settlement north of Denver was a false alarm. Some folks swore they had seen a small band of Indians prowling and studying the settlement four or five nights in a row. The prowling Indians turned out to be a small herd of antelope feeding on the late winter stubble grass.

There was only a light blanket of snow on the ground and the temperatures were moderate during the day in the low forties when the thirty-seven wagons rolled within sight of Fort Laramie on March 15th, 1876. The Calvary detachment rode ahead of the wagon train past Fort Laramie's huge weather-beaten entrance doors.

The original Fort was built around 1833-1834 as a trading post for animal skin and fur trappers of the northwest. The American Fur Company purchased the fort in 1841. The trading post served a twofold purpose during those early years. It not only was the main fur trading center, but it also served as a viable location for a migration destination of the thousands of pioneers and their covered wagons as they trudged the trails to California and Oregon. The fort became a welcomed site for those traveling the Mormon and Oregon Trails during the pinnacle of the covered wagon migration to the West in the last half of the nineteen century. Until the early twentieth century, the fort was constructed of logs cut from the forest of the Wyoming Territory. Some of the original buildings were adobe. In June of 1849, the U.S. Government purchased the fort for the sum of $4,000. There were three companies of the U.S. Cavalry deployed to the fort and Fort Laramie became a permanent garrison for the U.S. military. The fort was never under any major siege from the Native Americans. Many of the more peaceful Indians erected their teepees next to the Fort's outer walls.

The thirty-seven covered wagons were parked to the west of the fort's outer walls. Other wagons from two other wagon trains were situated on the other side of the fort. The wagon master met with the fort's commanding officer and gave his report of their trip, their destination and the names of those pioneers in the train. When the names of John McCrumb and Jake Banks were mentioned the fort's commander jumped from his chair and almost tripped trying to get from behind his desk.

"Take me to McCrumb and Banks!" The commander's demand was a definite order to be followed.

When John saw the wagon master and the fort's commander walking towards him, he strained his eyes to make sure what he was seeing was really what he was seeing. To his delight, his eyes were not playing tricks on him. He gathered a big smile and walked towards the two with his right arm outstretched.

"Captain Jordan? Captain Wesley Jordan?" John was almost at a run when the two men clasp hands, then hugged each other.

After the hugs were done John turned and called to the wagons. "Jake!" Then he almost screamed the name. "JAKE, GET YOURSELF OVER HERE! NOW!"

When Jake saw Captain Jordan he ran to his old commander and gave him a huge bear hug. After the battle of Chancellorsville Captain Jordan took the young Banks under his wing and with his mentoring Jake grew in the ranks of the Union Army. It was with the recommendation of Captain Jordon and other superior officers that Jake became a personal courier for President Abraham Lincoln. The President had taken a sincere liking for the young courier and was planning a promotion and a more confidential position for the young man from Pennsylvania. Jake was devastated when Lincoln was assassination and he left the Union Army to drift from job to job. He spent most of his time as a wrangler on cattle ranches. Jake never forgot the kindness and help that Captain Jordan had shown him, but it was John McCrumb who had captured the young soldier's admiration. When John and Sarah moved from Pennsylvania to Alma Kansas Jake followed close behind them, just so he wouldn't lose track of the man who had saved his life. He didn't want John to know that he had followed him; he always stayed a safe distance from the McCrumb's. John had saved his life and he considered John as the father figure he had never known. It was always on the back of Jake's mind to someday tell John his feelings, but he had to manage his courage and chose the right time.

The excitement of past experiences re-discovered lasted the rest of that entire day. Captain Jordan took them to his office and their discussions covered fourteen years of personal past histories of each man. Captain Jordan invited Jake, Jeremiah, John and John's family to have supper with him that evening in the Fort Laramie's dining hall.

That evening the McCrumb boys could feel their boyish adventures swirling through their minds of cowboys, soldiers, Indians and glorious battles as they sat among those amazing Cavalry warriors in their dress blue uniforms and in the same room, eating the same grub and sharing their amazing stories and escapades.

Lucy and Amy were dazzled being the only females in the dining hall with so many brave and handsome soldiers of the U.S. Cavalry. Well, almost the only females, but the wife of Captain Jordan and a couple of older women of the Fort just did not count. Both Lucy and Amy just knew that all of those handsome worrier's eyes were directed their way. Both girls tried their best to be nonchalant and sophisticated as they paraded themselves at the dining table for the benefit of those handsome men in blue uniforms. Amy dropped a fork full of salad on the floor and Lucy knocked over her glass of milk. All eyes were definitely on the McCrumb sisters.

The next morning the wagon master and John told Captain Jordan of the wagon that been disabled with the broken axle and damaged wheel and that it had been abandoned by the previous wagon train.

They also told Captain Jordon the wagon master of that train was drunk most of the time on the trail. Captain Jordan was furious. He summoned four of his Officers to find the wagon master of that train and bring him to the Captain's office. Jeremiah went with the officers on their hunt.

When they finally located the wagon master he was still drunk and he became belligerent towards the soldiers. He refused to cooperate with them, but Jeremiah persuaded him that it was in his best interest to cooperate and follow the soldiers peaceably or be broken in half.

Captain Jordan had the drunken wagon master put in the fort's stockades. He informed the wagon owners that were on that particular train they were now without a wagon master. He also chastised them for not aiding the disabled wagon. The longer he chastised the group the angrier he became. He scolded them in the harshest of terms for leaving the couple alone in the desert without help or hope.

The McCrumb's and their wagon train stayed at Fort Laramie for two more days before continuing their journey west on the much traveled Oregon Trail. John had decided months before, about the same time he and Sarah had entered Denver, to abandon his desire to go to Salt Lake and the Utah Territory. That was about the same time he had queried Jeremiah about traveling to the Rocky Mountains in the Idaho Territory. Both the Oregon Trail and the Mormon Trail made Fort Laramie a valuable mid-point destination for wagon trains heading west. The two wagon trains that were at Fort Laramie when John and his wagons arrived were traveling the Mormon Trail. A third wagon train that reached Fort Laramie the day John and his group left was also heading for the Great Salt Lake via the Mormon Trail.

On that last day at Fort Laramie Captain Jordan, John and Jake shook hands and wished each other the best of everything in this life. It had been a wonderful reunion for the three northern Union comrades. They shared memories during a time in their lives when each depended on the other for not only for their safety but for a comradely that requires a deep brotherly trust. These past few days would forever bond the three in heart, spirit, and mind. Captain Jordan sent a detachment of Fort Laramie soldiers with the wagon train as far as the edge of the Wyoming Territorial boundaries. Ila and Jack Bonner joined the thirty-six wagon caravan making the wagon train now thirty-seven strong. The journey of the thirty-seven wagons would travel the vast area that would later develop into southern Wyoming. The long awaited journey began early morning on March 20th, 1876. Over a thousand miles of the Oregon Trail lay before them on that chilly Monday morning.

The Bonner's were headed to Oregon but decided to stay with the McCrumb's to the Idaho Territory. They eventually ended up in what is now Boise, Idaho. They purchased a large block of land which later included one of the three main Boise future boulevards, Broadway. The Bonner's became very wealthy and influential Boise residents and always kept in touch with the McCrumb's until the day they died.

The Oregon Trail had been heavily traveled since the early 1840's by tens of thousands of European immigrants, the Midwest, and eastern U.S. poor folks, all searching for the rewards of a dream and a better life in the unknown and mystical west with its stories of gold, silver, adventure and storybook endings. But, for many that storybook ending turned into pages of thousands of tragic endings. The trail holds thousands of untold stories of those who braved the deep wheel ruts that marked the trails destinations. There are many more thousand Oregon Trail stories of tears, desperations, heartaches and death that will never be told. The trail is lined with unmarked graves for a thousand miles of those who never saw their dreams or a better life come true. But those pioneers who are buried in those unmarked graves played a huge role in the founding and building of a great nation, because of their pioneering spirits of adventure.

By the late 1880's the Oregon and Mormon Trails were less traveled than in earlier times. The mighty eastern railroad companies were determined to push their massive iron horses chugging towards the ever-changing Western Frontier. Thousands of miles of iron rails were replacing the worn out old wagon trails as the new iron roadway crossed over the midwest plains and vast western prairies, then through and over the rugged Rocky Mountains into the new and uncharted west. By 1880 it was much easier to travel to the west by railroad then with the drudgery and hardship and the danger of the wagon train. A person could travel from the east coast to Colorado, Salt Lake City or on to California by railroad in just a matter of a few days depending on their destination. Traveling by wagons it could take months with the traveler facing dangerous situations every day. By the year of 1900, the wagon train was almost a thing of the past, slowly, without fan fair, no cheering crowds waving flags and with no tears of remorse had lost its past pseudo glamor and had faded into the history books of the old American west.

Captain Jordan had drawn a map for John of the trails in the Idaho Territory. To reach the Idaho Territory and the "Lander Cut-Off" in western Wyoming and then to Soda Springs in the Idaho Territory was close to three hundred and ten daunting miles of mostly flat lands and Indians. Captain Jordon told John and Jeremiah that the Lakota Sioux, the Northern Cheyenne, the Arapaho and possibly the Blackfeet Indians were to be feared and avoided if possible.

From the "Lander Cut-Off" to Soda Springs was about another seventy-five miles. John and Captain Jordan calculated without any major obstacles the McCrumb's should make Soda Springs in the Idaho Territory within twenty to twenty-three days. That would put the wagons in that target destination of Soda Springs about the 8th to the 10th of April 1876.

Captain Jordan said the 7th Cavalry in the Montana Territory was having some problems with those four different Indian nations. He also told them the 7th Cavalry was under the command of a fellow Union Officer that they all had known personally. That Union officer was Lieutenant Colonel George Armstrong Custer. When they knew Custer during the War Between the States he was a Second Lieutenant. They thought he was an arrogant jackass back then and they hadn't any reason to change their opinions of him now. As far as they were concerned he was still an arrogant jackass. Jake first met Custer during the battle of Gettysburg. According to Jake Custer brought his men to the battle late and then tried to take over command of some men from another officer's unit. Jake said the other officer had to be restrained from shooting Custer. A couple of days after the battle when the Union army had won a decisive victory over the Rebel army that officer did knock the hell out of Custer with just one blow from his right fist. Custer went into hiding for a couple of days with a bloodied nose and puffy lips.

Three months after the three Union soldiers had their conversation about Custer at Fort Laramie with Captin Jordon Custer would be killed in the battle of the "Little Bighorn" in eastern Montana Territory. The Lakota Sioux, Northern Cheyenne, and Arapaho Indians sent Custer to his death in one swooping decisive Indian charge. Even though the "Battle of the "Little Bighorn" has been glamorized in many stories Custer's arrogance and miscalculations of the Indians war chief's, Setting Bull and Crazy Horse, most certainly caused the deaths of many in the 7th Cavalry.

The Cavalry detachment that Captain Jordan had sent with the wagon train was welcomed with glad hearts. The detachment would be a huge deterrent to any wayward renegade Indians from attacking the wagon train.

It took Bright and her brother Henry almost a week and a half of exhaustive travel by way of the railroad to reach their destination of Boston. The giant steam engine and its trailing cars of cargo and human passengers lumbered its way across the vast American prairies, the infinite food producing lands of mid-America plains, then plodding its way through the bustling industrial manufacturing world of the mid-west and finally inching its way toward the establishments of wealth and Revolutionary War produced aristocracies of the Robber Barons in the American northeast.

Boston was a completely foreign world to Henry and Bright Edwards. The glamor of the tall architectural structure buildings, the well-kept cobbled stone streets and the ladies in beautiful and colorful long bustled dresses with their strange feathered and flowery hats and dainty umbrellas was intimidating to the Edwards. Bright couldn't see the unique veracity that was all around her because of her poor eyesight. Henry had to describe those extraordinary figures and colors to her. The sounds, the features, and the colors were blurry and muddled to her sight. Cataracts kept Bright from seeing things as they really were. She could usually distinguish who she was talking to by their features most of the time if those persons were close enough to her. Henry had taught her numbers and the letters of the alphabet by writing them on paper and making the figures about three inches high and very dark. He would write a sentence in those large letters for her to read and that is how she learned to read and write.

This new world was strange and scary for Bright. She wished that Jake was there beside her to give her comfort and confidence. She loved her brother, but for the first time in her life she loved someone else more, but in a very much different way. She missed the strength of Jake's companionship and comforting words. The feelings toward Jake were new and perplexing for her. She thought about him all of the time. At night she would silently weep for this new felt love that he showered her with. She was afraid that being away from him would cause him not to feel the same about her when she returned back from Boston. Her love for him grew with every thought of him. Now, more than ever in this strange place, Bright wanted him beside her for his reassurance. The fear of losing Jake's love was a fear she needed not to fear.

Jake was just as miserable without the company of Bright. He was fearful that while in Boston she would fall in love with one of those rich and highly educated college type men. Bright was constantly in the back of his mind. He would ask John or Jeremiah if they thought she would still like him when she came back. Jeremiah made the mistake of teasing him one day that she just might stay in Boston to live. That really screwed up Jakes mind for a while. It took both John and Jeremiah a couple of days to convince Jake that Jeremiah's comment was just in jest.

Every day they would reassure Jake that Bright loved him and just couldn't wait to be back here to be with him. Jake believed them, but there was still this tiny doubt that continued to gaw at his confidence.

After a number of examinations and numerous doctor consultations, it was determined that Bright was a perfect candidate for the new revolutionary European eye surgery to replace, repair or remove eye cataracts. In many of the European eye operations, there was never any deadening procedures or anesthesia used before the operation. In the Boston hospital, there was a very new procedure to offer a light anesthesia and medicine to deaden the area that was to be operated on. The dilemma with Bright's operation was whether they could or should use this very new anesthesia solution before her operation. It was finally concluded that the new procedure would be used.

Both of Bright's eyes were operated on the same day. The doctors told Henry that they felt the operation was a tremendous success, but the final results would only be known when the bandages were removed a week later. Bright was in some moderate to lightly severe pain for the first four days after the operation. After the fourth day, the pain began to disappear. The doctors changed the bandages and medicated her eyes every two days in an almost complete dark situation. When the bandages were removed for the last time on the eighth day after the operation in a dimly lit room Bright was excited and frightened all at the same time. She was excited to have the bandages removed but frightened the operation had not been successful and her eyesight would be the same or even worse. When the last gauze was removed from each eye and she opened her eyes a sensation of fear and dismay spread over her entire body, everything was cloudy and gray. She wanted to cry out. She wanted to just die right there, right then, that very moment.

The doctors could see her emotional dismay. One of them took her shoulders in his hands to comfort her. He told her everything was going to be OK. He told her that it would take a few moments for her eyes to adjust. After fifteen minutes her surroundings began to appear and slowly started to come into focus. Her eyesight was beginning to materialize. After a half hour in that dim-lit room Bright for the first time in her life saw things and items as she had never seen them before. Each day for the next five days the doctors would allow a little more light to enter Bright's hospital room. On that fifth day, she really saw her brother normally for the first time. She never really knew what her brother looked like until that day. Her brother was handsome and had green eyes. She knew that he had green eyes, but she had never seen his green eyes.

Slowly at first, with the natural sunlight that had entered the room, Bright saw her handsome brother as he was seen by others for the very first time. Tears started to slowly roll down her cheeks and she extended her arms towards her brother. Henry took her in his arms and both brother and sister cried in each other's grateful embrace.

"I want to see your green eyes." Bright whispered to her brother.

But that wouldn't happen for a couple of more days. Bright would have to spend another seven days in a controlled dim atmosphere for her eyes to heal properly. The soreness was gently fading away and cloudiness that had covered her beautiful green eyes for so many years had over ninety percent disappeared. There would always be some cloudy residue, but Bright would hardly ever notice that small percentage of residue that was left. Each day for those last seven days in the dim room a little more light was introduced each day.

It was on the twelfth day when Bright really knew and understood the provenance of God. That was the day she walked out into the sunlight and for the first time saw the different shades of green in her brother's eyes. Bright was suddenly in a different world now with her new restored eyesight. She was seeing things and colors that she didn't know existed. She knew that blue was blue, but what she didn't know there were a thousand different shades of blue. This new world of sight was beautiful, but also a little strange and confusing for Bright.

After the successful eye operation and total recovery, all Bright could think about was getting back to Jake, where ever he was. John had kept in constant contact with Henry over the past months via the Telegraph. Before he left Denver for Fort Laramie John had wired Henry train tickets for him and Bright from Boston to Soda Springs in the Idaho Territory. A new train company had constructed a rail line from Ogden Utah to the small settlement of Soda Springs. That would be the quickest route for Bright and Henry to travel back west to rejoin the McCrumb clan. The ticket schedule was for Henry and Bright to leave Boston on the 5th of April and the McCrumb's wagons would be at Soda Springs waiting for their arrival during the last weeks of April.

Miles of new rail lines were being constructed every day forging further into the west and great northwestern territories allowing the wealthy central and east coast money investors who saw the great potential in capturing the immense commerce that the western and northwest territories offered.

Henry and Bright had arrived in Boston on February the 8th, 1876. Bright's operation was performed after many days of tests on the 14th of February. The brother and sister left Boston for Soda Springs in the Idaho Territory on the 5th of April of 1876. They arrived in Soda Springs on the 13th of that same month.

The McCrumb's left Denver for Fort Laramie on the Overland Trail on the 6th of March 1876. They arrived at Fort Laramie ten days later on the 16th of March. The McCrumb's wagon train departed Fort

Laramie four days later for Soda Springs on the 20th of March. The McCrumb wagons arrived at Soda Springs on the 11th day in the month of April, two days before Henry and Bright were to arrive. All of those travel plans worked to a grand conclusion.

John's three wagons and his neighboring thirty-four other wagons along with the cavalry soldiers that Captain Jordan had deployed from Fort Laramie to accompany the thirty-seven wagons to the Idaho Territory met no resistance for the first four days of their journey west. The weather was pleasant just a might cool. The deep wagon ruts that had been sculptured in the Oregon Trail by the thousands of wagons that had gone on before them were sometimes damaging to a weak wagon wheel or axle. Their immediate destination was the huge granite rock that had been created eons ago and now famously named "Independence Rock".

This gigantic granite boulder that could be seen for miles before a wagon train could finally repose beside it was about 130 feet tall, 1900 feet long and about 850 feet wide. It was between the years of 1800 and 1830 when the first fur traders and the first wagon trains were introduced to this magnificent boulder. The Red Man had revered this wonderment of the Wyoming Territory desert for hundreds of years. It was in 1830 when a pioneer named William Sublette dubbed the Boulder "Independence Rock". It was on the 4th of July of that same year when he and about 80 other pioneers in his wagon train celebrated Independence Day at the base of the large granite monument. From that time forward every wagon train that traveled the Oregon Trail or the Mormon Trail looked forward to reaching the celebrated "Independence Rock". The large piece of granite was in the Sweetwater Valley and next to the Sweetwater River in the Wyoming Territory.

Pioneers for almost a hundred years had been carving their names in the granite walls of "Independence Rock". The McCrumb young'uns wanted theirs and their momma's name carved in the rock for history's sake. They wanted everybody in the future to know that they had been there.

It was late in the afternoon when the wagon train came to a halt and made camp for the night at the base of the renowned "Independence Rock". After camp was settled it was getting too dark to visit the massive rock. Further investigation would have to wait until morning. After the supper had been concluded and everyone was settling down for the night Lucy asked her pap if she could talk to him in private.

They found a quiet, private, and warm spot next to their campfire. John had noticed that Lucy and Amy had been kind of placid and withdrawn ever since they had left Fort Laramie. He just assumed they were lonely and missing their momma. He was partially right, but Lucy was experiencing another type of an emotional problem. This new challenge for her was a phenomenon called "growing into womanhood". This new experience for Lucy was, for the most part, going to be out of John's curriculum. But, for this evening's chat, John would be able to understand and help with Lucy's question, to a point.

Not having their momma beside them on this journey was causing some melancholy and gloomy moments for Lucy and for Amy. But, Lucy was experiencing a new kind of feelings, ones she had never felt before.

"Pap.....I know that you miss momma a lot.......I cry sometimes because I miss her too......but......" John soon realized that Lucy had other things on her mind, not just her momma.

"Pap...... when did you........I mean....did you love momma the first time you saw her?........Did momma...........when did you know.....I mean.....when did momma tell you she loved you?" Lucy was developing herself into a quandary of confusions. She knew what she wanted to ask, but the stumbling with her words was aggravating her.

"Sweetheart, I think I loved your momma the first time I saw her........I think it took your momma a few weeks before she had any feelings for me. Lucy....your momma was a very practical woman.........she wanted to know all about me before she committed her feelings."

Remembering how he had met Sarah brought fond memories back to John and a smile of satisfaction on his lips quickly spread to his grinning eyes.

"Lucy your momma knew when she knew and when she was sure she knew.......... that was the time I knew....that she knew."

"Pap....you're not making any sense..........Well....maybe a little sense....I think?" Lucy thought she understood what her pap was saying, but wasn't quite sure. But John knew exactly what he was saying and his smile finally convinced Lucy that she also understood, whether she did or not.

"Lucy....this is not just about your momma is it?" John was trying to help his daughter to explain the problem she was endeavoring to talk about.

"Pap........" There was a long silence before Lucy could finish the question she had started. "Pap........ do you like Henry......Or I mean .....do you think Henry is a........ is a nice boy?"

"Lucy……Henry is not a boy……Henry is a young man." John was now starting to understand in which direction this conversation was heading. "Yes….I do like Henry. He is a solid young man. He is going to make some lady a fine husband someday."

John's last comment about Henry making some women a good husband really threw Lucy's train of thought off balance. Now, she was almost too embarrassed to ask her pap any other questions about Henry.

"Lucy, how do you feel about Henry?" John's question just took a load of anxiety off of Lucy's shoulders. His question opened the door for her to openly discuss her feelings. Now, she could vent and really ask for her pap's help in trying to understand these new emotions that have invaded her feminine feelings. These new sensations only started after Henry and Bright left for Boston. Lucy did miss Bright, but all she could think about was Henry and wishing he was back here near her.

"Pap, I really miss Henry. I think about him all of the time. I even dream about him, am I being young and foolish? Poppa, Is this just a little naïve girl flirtation thing that I'm going through? I'm really confused." Lucy rarely calls her dad Poppa and when she does it usually indicates she is in some degree of distress.

"No Lucy, you are not being foolish, naïve and you're not a little girl anymore. You are a beautiful young women. Your feelings for Henry are real and important. Is it love? I don't know. I can't figure that one out for you. Just stay you and who you are. Those feelings will work themselves out to a right and real conclusion. I think Henry is going through the same problem with his feelings about you. If it is the right thing for both of you, you'll know when the time comes. Until then let your feelings take their natural course. Don't force them."

"But Pap………what if Henry doesn't like me when he gets back from……………what if he has found another….."

"Lucy, Luuuucy…….." Lucy's poppa interrupted her in the middle of her question. "Stop! Right now!" John cupped Lucy's cheeks in his two big strong hands, kissed her on her forehead and started to chuckle before he finished his fatherly humor.

"Lucy, I'll bet ya Henry still remembers who you are……..I'll even bet ya he still remembers your name is Lucy…….He'll probably still remember what you look like ……Well, Maybe?........But….I'm not sure of all of those pretty girls that are in Boston…… He might have………I'm not sure, but maybe he………"

"Poppa stop it!……now your poking fun at me…….Am I really being that silly?" Lucy was laughing at herself now.

John looked at his precious daughter with a smile of pride. She was blossoming into a beautiful young woman. Both Lucy and Amy had Sarah's attractive and stunning features of a true Scottish beauty. Their bright and striking auburn hair and their captivating clear emerald green eyes that seemed to be able to hypnotize a person was indeed inherited from Sarah. Both of her daughters had given Sarah a proud sense of her Scottish heritage. John's memory drifted back to a time many years before: to a time when he met his beautiful Sarah in the Scottish Highlands.

Both John McCrumb and Sarah McGregor were born in the Highlands of Scotland. John McCrumb's immediate family was the last of the Scottish McCrumb's to still live in Scotland. The McCrumb's were never a renowned Clan of the Highlands; they made their living farming, raising sheep and working for the larger Highland Clans. In the seventeenth and eighteenth centuries, the McCrumb's were also mercenaries and fierce warriors who would hire out to fight in Clan battles. The McCrumb's were an extremely tight Scottish clan that was very protective of each other and unyielding of their Scottish background and their family traditions. They were a very private and straightforward clan that kept to themselves and seldom troubled outsiders. They would defend their beliefs and their clan family to the death. The McCrumb's in the late seventeen hundreds and early eighteen hundreds refused to recognize any type of English rule. They refused to pay homage to any king that was not of Scottish heritage. The majority of the McCrumb families had migrated to Canada by 1840, then into Pennsylvania. John McCrumb was the last of the McCrumb's to leave Scotland.

Sarah McGregor was a descendant of Charles Edward Stuart, better known as "Bonnie Prince Charles". Sarah was a proud member of the "Gregor Clan". Her family was wealthier than most but very humble in appearance. The McGregor's were strong in the Scottish family tradition. Sarah was the pride and joy of her momma and father: she was their only child. When her parents were killed in a tragic accident Sarah was fourteen years old. After the accident, Sarah went to live with her favorite Aunt and Uncle in the northern Highlands. That was where she met this very handsome fellow who worked for her Uncle herding sheep and laboring in the hay fields. Sarah was seventeen years old when her Uncle hired the young John McCrumb.

When Sara's uncle introduced her to John, it was love at first sight for John McCrumb. During that first meeting, Sarah all but ignored John but spoke politely. Of course, it was all intentional on her part. She did find this young man delightfully handsome but didn't want him to appreciate the fact that she noticed. The aunt and uncle invited John to enjoy supper at their well-supplied supper table a couple of nights each week. They thought well of

John and recognized his good McCrumb Scottish background. He was a hard worker and very intelligent. His demeanor and character were beyond reproach. He was never backward to say what he was thinking but was always considerate when he spoke. He never backed away from a good argument or proper debate. He was a respectable match for their reserved and aloof niece. During the supper engagements, Sarah tried to be demure and uninterested in John's company at the table. But John being the McCrumb he was, he wasn't going to let Sarah get away with her little girl games. At the supper table, John would constantly direct comments and questions at Sarah. He was forcing her to recognize and speak to him. Sarah's aunt and uncle found John's tactics enjoyable to watch.

After a few weeks of having John to their supper table twice each week Sarah's uncle stopped inviting John. Her uncle was going to discover Sarah's true emotions about this John McCrumb fellow. Her uncle was also a little conflicted with Sarah's conduct at the supper table. After a couple of weeks without John at the supper table, Sarah was becoming discontent over John's absence. She would try to be inconspicuous and elusive when asking her aunt if John was OK. At different times during the day, Sarah would take little walks, "for exercise", that was the excuse she would use. She would walk in the fields trying to catch a glimpse of John. In one of those walks, she thought she might have seen him away out yonder in the vast field, but was not sure. After the third week with no John at the supper table, Sarah broke down and asked her uncle why John had stopped coming to enjoy supper with them.

"Well Sarah, I was beginning to think you didn't want him at the table with us. I think John felt the same way, so I quit inviting him." This was her uncle's way of teaching Sarah a very valuable life lesson.

"I don't care if he comes." Sarah's face became very flushed, almost the same color as her hair. She became very agitated and frustrated to a point she had to go outside to be by herself. She found a quiet spot and started to cry. After she had composed her emotions she went back into the house. She finally got up enough nerve to approach her uncle with further conversations about John and the supper table.

'Uncle Eon ....it's OK with me if John eats supper with us......I mean...please, don't stop asking him because of me.........because it is really OK with me..........I really don't mind him eating supper with me......ah, I mean us." Now Sarah was flustered and quite upset with herself. She kept asking herself, "How stupid can one girl be?"

"I'll tell you what Sarah if you would like John to eat supper with us again you invite him." Sarah was totally numbed by her uncle's request. How could she possibly ask John to supper after the way she had treated him?

"But Uncle Eon, I don't know how I................."

"Sarah, if you want John McCrumb to eat at our table again, then you have to ask him. Sarah, John is a very good person and if I were you I'd ask now before he leaves to go back to his family............... He is leaving in the morning.............Right now he is with the sheep in the sheep pasture." Eon turned and walked away from Sarah. She could not see him chuckling under his breath. John was not going anywhere, but Sarah did not know that.

Sarah hurried out to the sheep pasture where John was tending to his job. John saw her running towards the gate to the pasture. He turned to walk towards her. When Sarah saw John starting to come in her direction she slowed down to a leisurely walk. She didn't want him to think she was doing anything but a relaxing walk in the fields. John met her at the gate.

"Good afternoon Sarah, can I help you?" John was trying to be polite and not wanting to seem to be assertive to Sarah in any way.

"John..........John....AH.....please forgive me for being such a snot.......Please, John......will you please come and have supper with us tonight?.... Please!" Sarah blurted out the words without even thinking. She even surprised herself with this gush of humility. She grabbed her mouth with both hands not believing what she had just done. Sarah started to cry and again apologized for her rude behavior.

John climbed over the gate and held Sarah close in his strong arms. He held Sarah's chin up with his left hand and looked into her beautiful green eyes.

"Sarah McGregor....I love you....Will you be my beautiful Scottish wife?"

When John's mind and memory returned to the present, he was still holding Lucy in his arms. It was time to tell her the story of how he met her beautiful momma.

Lucy was intrigued with her pap's story of how he and her momma had met. Now she knew something that Amy didn't know and that made her feel absolutely empowered. She could dangle this incredible information over her sister's head. She could taunt and tease Amy until Amy begged her to divulge this wonderful and very private story about their momma and poppa.

"Pap...I have gallons of love for you and momma.......Pap.... did momma say "yes" when you ask her to marry you by the gate? ....Or did you have to ask her again at another time?" Lucy's eyes were really wide open now, waiting for her poppa's answer.

"I don't know Lucy....What do you think?"............There was a long pause than Lucy smiled at her pap.

"Ok Lucy, it's time to get some sleep."

Everyone in the McCrumb's wagons had a restful slumber that night anticipating exploring and carving their names in the huge "Independence Rock" on the next day.

The wagon train spent the following day at the massive boulder while the pioneers explored the monolith and carved their names at its base. By late afternoon the thirty-seven wagons prepared to continue their journey on the following morning. Their next destination would be "South Pass", which was located in the southwest corner of the Wyoming Territory. The Pass had served as a natural wagon train route to the west between the Central Rocky Mountains and the Southern Rocky Mountains. The South Pass was situated on top of the Continental Divide between the two ranges of mountains. It was referred to as the "Saddle" to the west. The famous "Landers Cutoff" was located northwest of the Pass.

Fur traders, Pioneers, and explorers had been using the South Pass for decades before the McCrumb's wagons passed through on the ancient wagon wheel ruts that were created by thousands of wagons before them. Whenever the wagon train did reach the South Pass a major decision would have to be made by each individual wagon owner. The wagons could either journey to the north and then follow the "Landers Cutoff" to Soda Springs and Fort Hall or they could head south to Fort Bridger than travel to Soda Springs and Fort Hall in the Idaho Territory.

The "Landers Cutoff" would be a rougher passage because of its altitude and steep incline, but it was almost ninety miles shorter than the Fort Bridger's route. The cutoff would take the wagons over high mountain passes almost nine thousand feet above sea level. South Pass and the Fort Bridger Trail was about seventy-five hundred feet above sea level. Over the "Lander Cutoff," the wagons would have to travel about fifteen hundred feet higher in the mountains, then down the western slope of the Central Rocky's to fifty-five hundred feet above sea level to reach their Idaho Territory destination of Soda Springs. "Landers Cutoff" was the shorter route to Soda Springs it was also the more hazardous route to Soda Springs. Most wagon trains avoided the cutoff route because of the steep and dangerous mountain passes.

When the wagon train was fifty miles east of "South Pass" a once in a lifetime spectacular phenomena waited for the thirty-seven weary wagon train travelers. It was a dream come true for John McCrumb. He had mentioned this dream or wish, if you please, to Sarah a number of times after they had left Alma on their quest to the west. It was early morning in late March of 1876 when the lead wagon suddenly stopped and all of the occupants climbed out of the wagon and started pointing to the northwest. At first, John and his group could barely see what was causing all of the excitement with the lead wagons. When John finally did recognize what all of the enthusiasm was about a broad smile swept over his lips. In the far distances north of the wagons he could make out a massive herd of buffalo.

The closer the wagons got to the herd the more the pioneer's amazement turned to astonishment and bewilderment. The landscape was disappearing under the hooves of thousands of buffalo. When the wagon train came alongside the herd, about two of three hundred yards from the grazing herd the landscape beyond the herd was totally blanketed with tens of thousands of the massive majestic beasts.

After the wagon train had moved alongside the grazing sea of buffalo for a half of an hour no one could see the end or the beginning of these wonderful animals. Jeremiah told John that he had never seen this many buffs at one time. He estimated that there could be as many as a hundred thousand animals in this one herd of bison. After traveling almost an hour alongside the herd there still was no end or beginning in site.

Lucy and Amy found this adventure incredibly wonderful. They were walking beside their "chuck wagon" with Patsy by their side. At first, they were afraid that Patsy would run and join the herd, but Patsy didn't want anything to do with that massive mess of buffalo. Jake told the sisters that Patsy still thinks that she is a dog.

Jerald and Jacky couldn't understand why they couldn't shoot the buffalo. Jeremiah tried to explain to the brothers the danger of causing a massive stampede of thousands of these giant beasts. The boys weren't convinced that it would cause a stampede. It finally took their poppa to end their "whiny" and "stupid" quest. For a second or two it would appear that their poppa could be more damaging to the boys than a thousand stampeding Bison.

After an hour and a half the herd was thinning out and the end of an era was slowly fading into American History. Within twenty years the American bison was almost gone from the Western Plains. The white man was slowly succeeding to rape the great northwest of its grandeur. The same untamed and mysterious northwest that President Thomas Jefferson had sent Meriwether Lewis and William Clark to discover and map out in May of 1804. The Wild West that President Theodore Roosevelt loved and coveted to conserve its culture, its landscapes, and its Buffalo. The old west was slowly turning into a strange infancy of a new birth and the immaturity of a new nation.

After its amazing encounters with one the west's most amazing animals, the wagon train continued its trek towards "South Pass" and the Idaho Territory. After four more days of uninterrupted travel, the wagons were nearing the eastern mouth of the "South Pass" and the "saddle" of the pioneer's gate to the far western frontier and the Pacific Ocean.

South Pass is where the Mormon Trail twisted south to Fort Bridger, then on to Ogdon Utah and finally the destination of thousands of Mormon wagon trains, Salt Lake City in the Utah Territory.

Fort Bridger, as were most Cavalry Fort locations in the West started out as a trading post. Jim Bridger started his fur trading post in about 1842. By the early 1850's the trading post became an important wagon train outfitting point on the Oregon and Mormon trails. The history of the trading post between 1850 and 1856 is somewhat convoluted and becomes a little muddy and confusing, depending on who is telling the story.

One story goes that Brigham Young confiscated the post from Bridger and drove Bridger from the territory. Another story states that Brigham Young purchased the trading post from Bridger for $8,000 in raw gold. There are no records or facts validating the latter story. A sure fact is; Brigham Young and the Mormons did end up with the trading post. Bad tensions over the trading post did fester between the Federal Government and the Mormons and by 1857 Brigham Young called up his guerrilla army, the Nauvoo Legion to defend or seizure back Fort Bridger and if all else fails at the least burn it down. The Federal Government had taken possession of the trading post and transferred it into an Army compound. The feud boiled over into an almost war between the U.S. and Brigham Young and the Mormon population in Utah when the Mormons did burn the Fort down. The Mormon War against the Federal Government ended in 1857 when President Buchanan sent U.S. troops into the Wyoming Territory and recaptured the Fort and deposed Brigham Young from his self-appointment as Governor of the Utah Territory. Under the command of the U.S. Government, the Fort became a station for the Pony Express and the Overland Stage Routes.

By the time the thirty-seven wagons had camped on the Continental Divide in the region of the South Pass John and his companions had decided to continue their journey to Soda Springs through the Landers Cutoff. The Bonner's and two other families also elected to stay with the McCrumb's three wagons traveling to the Landers Cutoff route. When the wagon train reached the South Pass the cavalry detachment that Captain Jordan had sent with the McCrumb's wagons would return to Fort Laramie. John gave each soldier a hundred dollars in money currency and a gold nugget for good luck. Those soldiers were the happiest soldiers in the United States Military. The remaining thirty-two wagons in the original wagon train continued their western journey using the Fort Bridger route. The wagon master chose what he considered the less dangerous land trail. His choice would prove to be a fatal decision.

The McCrumb's started their five wagon journey on the Landers Cutoff to Soda Springs on the first day of April of 1876. The other thirty-two wagons continued their trek to Fort Bridger. The spring weather was beautiful with clear skies. The days were warming; the nights were still very chilly. All of the Landers Cutoff on the east side of the Central Rocky Mountains was in a vast level land prairie of sage and a large variety of Wyoming brush. There were a few twisted trees here and there, but mostly an easy travel for wagon trains. There were five medium size rivers that they would have to traverse before climbing in the steep mountain passes. None of the rivers were going to be a big challenge, but every river crossing will offer its own particular dangers. One river crossing in the Colorado Territory that had instigated a couple of threatening moments when one of the McCrumb's two wagons had its wheel collide with a large boulder that was hidden under the water. An incident like that can cause the wheel to snap in half. Luckily that didn't happen to the wheel in Colorado.

The first two days of travel went without problems. In fact, it was the best two days of travel time for distance since they left Alma Kansas a little over a year ago. For those two days, the wagons covered a little over sixty miles of Wyoming Territory land. Wild game was plentiful; there was deer, antelope, and thousands of rabbits. The rivers were full of fish. The pioneers eat well during this western Wyoming journey. They found wild asparagus growing everywhere and wild rhubarb growing along the trail. They were careful not to eat the leaves of the rhubarb plants because the leaves were poisonous. Sweet berries such as currants, raspberries, sweet and sour gooseberries were plentiful. The only really dangerous problem the pilgrims encountered were rattlesnakes. This Wyoming prairie was full of the large western diamondback slithering critters. The snakes were just coming out of their winter hibernation. Jacky killed one that was almost eight foot long. Keeping the dogs from being bitten was an all day job.

Jeremiah reasoned that by the evening of the third day the wagons would be at the foothills of the Central Rockies. John figured that they were days ahead of the wagons that had gone on to Fort Bridger. Jeremiah's prediction was right on the money; on the evening of the third day, the Central Rockies were opening their gates for the McCrumb's passage over to the Idaho Territory.

During supper around the campfire on the night before the wagons began their trek over the Central Rockies all of the families of the six wagons had gathered to discuss the mountain crossing. Lucy and Amy were by themselves all cuddled in heavy blankets talking about their momma, Henry, Bright and what the future might hold for them. Amy asked Lucy if she was in love with Henry. Lucy didn't know how to answer her sister because her feelings were so very confusing.

"I don't know…….I really miss him………I have never felt this way before……..I talked to pap about how I felt and he told me I would know the time when my feelings were feelings of love."

Lucy had told Amy of her conversation with their Poppa the day after she had talked to him. She had also hinted to Amy about the time her pap had asked their momma to marry him.

"Lucy, did poppa really tell you of the time he proposed to momma?" Amy wasn't sure if she had completely understood that part of their conversation when Lucy's told her about her talk with her poppa concerning her feelings for Henry.

"Well……..he did tell me a little bit when he asked Momma to………" that is all the further Lucy got before being interrupted by Jacky.

"Poppa wants you two over by the big fire."

"Lucy…….come back here…………..Lucy…..I want to know what poppa told you about when he proposed to momma", Amy was becoming very agitated because of Lucy's stalling tactics in answering that question. She had asked Lucy that question in a number of subtle ways, but she only received slippery answers. Now she was getting provoked with Lucy evasiveness.

Lucy just smiled, then got up to see what her pap wanted. Amy scowled at her sister and mumbled under her breath something that sounded like, "You Just wait until tomorrow sister". Or, was it, "You will hate the sorrow tomorrow with your sitter!"

The first mountain pass was a gradual climb with large rocks that had to be avoided. The going was much slower now because of the incline and the rough terrain. John was hoping to be on the western side of the mountains by the third or fourth day of travel. He wasn't sure of any time schedule over the mountain passes. Captain Jordan didn't have any reliable information about the Landers Cutoff. He thought John and his wagons were going to travel the Oregon Trail through Fort Bridger. The further the wagons climbed the narrower the pass became. By the evening of that first day on the mountain, the pilgrims found a level spot of land where they could camp for the night. At the elevation where they decided to camp the weather was turning really cold.

Jeremiah asked Jake and the brothers to be on the lookout for the giant bighorn sheep. He told them that these mountains were full of the big horn. Jeremiah also cautioned them to be vigilant of the big cats that roamed the Rocky Mountains. The Rocky Mountain cougar or mountain lion as some called them could grow to a really large size. Jeremiah saw one a few years back before it was skinned. It measured from the nose to the tip of its tail almost twelve feet and weighed one hundred and ninety pounds. One on one no man would be a match for a cat that size without a gun. He had heard of one mountain man who did kill a smaller cougar that weighed about a hundred and fifty pounds with a knife, but the guy took a painful beating from the cougar's deadly claws and piercing fangs before it died. He lived to tell the story, but the price was pretty steep.

Jerald and Jacky spent the whole night dreaming about mountain lions and giant bighorn sheep. Because they were this high in the mountains at least they didn't have to worry about rattlesnakes, it was just too cold for the cold-blooded critters.

Amy had ignored Lucy all day and that pleased Lucy because she knew that she had gotten Amy's goat. The more Amy ignored Lucy the more Lucy ignored Amy and that really infuriated Amy. Lucy decided she had taunted her sister long enough and it was time to tell Amy the story of their poppa and momma's first meeting. She was pleased with herself for irritating her sister with her secret, but it was time to end the amusement. It was late and the night was bringing in a cold wind. The sisters had partially made up even though Lucy still had not told Amy the story of their momma and poppa's first meeting. The sisters were snuggling up really tight in heavy woolen blankets to fight off the nights bone wrenching chill. Lucy snuggled up to Amy and kissed her on the forehead.

"Amy, have I got a juicy story to tell you about pap and momma." Lucy was using her sweetest tone of voice.

Amy was grinding her teeth and wanted to bop Lucy on her nose, but she wanted to hear the story more than bopping her sister on the nose, so she returned Lucy's sweet tone with her own charming sweet response.

"Really?.........Is it how Poppa proposed to momma?" Amy was still aggravated but wanted to hear the story so she played along with Lucy's little game. There would be a payback time in the future. Thinking about the payback time Amy just wrinkled her nose and smiled.

Lucy told the story but added just a little more romance and glamor to it so as to heighten the intrigue for both of the sister's benefit. The romance in the original story was beautiful enough, but it appeared that Lucy and Amy appreciated just a little more allure. They both went to sleep and dreamt all night long about love, romance, and glamor. Just before Lucy closed her eyes for sleep, she said her nightly prayers, she prayed for Henry and Bright's safe journey back to the wagon train. She also managed to get in a request that Henry would still feel the same towards her as he did before he left for Boston.

Jake in his prayers to God that night asked for the safety of Bright, as well as everybody else, but Bright had become a new special joy of love in his life and she was always in his thoughts. Jake was the thankful type that was always counting his blessings, especially the blessing of being with the McCrumb's. Ever since the battle of Chancellorsville Jake's one hope was to someday call John his chosen father. Jake never thought he would ever be with the McCrumb's going west, and now, here he was. In his wildest dreams he never anticipated that someday he would be wealthy, and now he was. He had lost all anticipation of ever finding the women of his dreams, and now he had found her. Jake was always counting his blessings.

Sarah's strong spirit of love for John and her strength of adventure was the driving force that kept John from emotionally breaking down to the point of giving up. Her love of life was constantly the essence controlling the mind of her beloved John toward a better tomorrow. His constant prayers for a new life in the Rocky Mountains in the Idaho Territory will be his tribute to his beloved Sarah.

The second day of trying to traverse the Central Rockies and another pass separating the eastern Landers Cutoff trail from the western Landers Cutoff trail was going to be even slower and more dangerous than the day before. The incline on this pass was steeper and there was still snow on the ground making the incline more hazardous. The individuals holding the reins of the horses and steers that were pulling the heavy wagons had to constantly keep their one foot on the wagons brake pedal. Sometimes both feet were needed. If a teamster (driver) would lose control of the brakes and the wagon started to roll back down the mountain it would be catastrophic for that wagon and any wagons behind the runaway wagon. John was beginning to doubt his judgment and decision in taking the Landers Cutoff. Every yard forward was a treacherous yard forward.

When a wagon had rolled a hundred feet or so large rocks or wooden blocks were placed behind the wagon wheels to keep the wagons from rolling backward. Those times were used to give the horses and steers a rest break. Every foot accomplished towards the summit of the mountain was met with potential disaster. If the summit wasn't reached by dark the future of the seven wagons would be in serious doubt.

By late in the afternoon the six wagons did reach the summit of the mountain. The flat area at the summit was a surprise and a welcomed relief for the Pioneers. This mountain pass and the flat surface had been a critical and decisive element to make the Landers Cutoff an alternate route to Soda Springs in the Idaho Territory.

The large flat area at the summit was about thirty acres in size which made that empty space a perfect camping spot. There was very little snow at the summit. There were a couple of small water ponds and plenty of foliage for the animals to munch on. The complete scene was a little weird. It looked like a giant had taken a large shovel and shoveled out a section of the mountain top to make the pass friendlier for weary travelers. On both sides of the flat part of the pass the mountain rose another thousand feet into the air and continued on for hundreds of miles in both directions.

Once the wagons were situated and a camp fire was started the pioneers started to settle in for the night. Jake and Jeremiah wanted to search the area for clues of animal inhabitants or possible Indian artifacts or items that other travelers had left behind. Jeremiah did identify fresh bighorn sheep poop, dried large cat poop and really old dried up human poop. He was sure that he and Jake had discovered a couple of old sunken human graves, they left them undefiled. There were some unidentifiable Indians drawings. Parts of old weathered wagon parts dotted the landscape. Jeremiah told John of their findings and was certain that this pass had been used by fur traders and Indians for hundreds of years.

Jeremiah told John that he could feel the presence of the bighorn sheep. "Those Rams are really close John. We're going to get one of those twisted horn critters before we leave this mountain."

John agreed to go on the hunt with Jeremiah. He told Jeremiah that the folks and the wagons needed a few days of rest anyway. Also, all of the wagons would have to be checked for damage and possibly some minor repairs made. Jake and the boys declared their God-given right to go on the hunt for the big horn too.

The next morning after the sun had created a little warmth on the mountain's summit Jeremiah, John, Jake and the brother's donned heavy clothes and with rifles in hand began their climb up the north slope of the mountain next to the flat summit. It was a fairly easy climb, kind of steep, but the slight difficulties were easily overcome. This part of the mountain was mostly rocky ledges, the kind of ledges that the bighorn loved to venture over. The bighorn were sure-footed animals that could maneuver on the worst rocky ledges and most dangerous crags on any mountain. They could rule over the most treacherous mountain crags and ledges as easy as a man could walk on the level ground. After an hour of climbing Jeremiah's quest would soon be rewarded, but not in the way he could have ever imagined.

It was Jacky who cautioned Jeremiah to look towards a higher ledge just a few yards to the right of him. Jeremiah was stunned at the magnificent animal that was staring down at him. It was the largest bighorn ram he had ever seen. Its immense shoulders rippled with power and strength. The huge horns were a full one and a half turn. This ram was the king of all bighorns. The massive animal didn't move a muscle, nor did it appear to be frightened by the men with the devastating rifle. The ram just stood its ground staring down at Jeremiah with a staunch look of determination. This incredible animal was no more than thirty feet from the giant mountain man. John and Jake marveled at the two perfect warriors as they tried to stare each other down. Neither gave an inch nor flinched before the other. Jacky asked his brother how long was this strange scene going to last? For the moment Jeremiah didn't even attempt to raise his buffalo gun. He did turn to look at his companions who were watching him in wonderment. Then Jeremiah turned his head toward the vast beautiful expanse of the western landscape that lay before him on the western side of the Central Rockies. He was captivated by the magnificent breathtaking vastness of a creation that he never imagined existed. Jeremiah gazed what seemed like minutes, but it was for just a few seconds. Slowly he turned back to observe the spectacular Bighorn that was also viewing the western expanse that Jeremiah had just been observing. The big sheep had not moved a muscle. Slowly the animal brought its gaze from the western landscape back to eyeballing the huge man that was on the ledge just below him. The two giant warriors of the mountains continued their observation of each other marking a true western epoch snapshot in time for all ages.

Back at the wagons Lucy and Amy decided to explore the other side of the pass. The sisters were a little aggravated that their two brothers were allowed to venture off with their poppa discovering one part of the mountain and leaving them behind. This mind fantasy of neglect caused their thought process to kind of work in the reverse. If the boys get to explore one part of the mountain, "we girls have the right to explore the other part of the mountain."

Amy was a little concerned about their safety, but Lucy pooh-poohed the idea of any danger. The girls fixed themselves a lunch and started up the slope on the south end of the flat summit. It was an easy climb; the incline was gradual and not rocky like the northern climb. The sisters had gone a couple of hundred feet when the terrain became drastically altered. The mountain suddenly became rock walls with narrow cracks and crag passageways through and around huge boulders and ledges. Amy was getting nervous, but Lucy convinced her to go just a little further. They found a ledge where they could stand and look out over the vast plains and mountains to the west of the Central Rockies. The two sisters just stood in fascinating wonderment of what was before them. What they were viewing seemed to Lucy and Amy to be an unknown and undiscovered world. It seemed like they could see forever; they had never been in a position before where they were so high and could see so far in the distance. Neither girl felt the chilling of the mountain breeze as their amazement was captivated by the beauty of the world before them.

Amy suggested they set on this ledge and eat their lunch that they had fixed back at the wagon. As they ate their lunch and enjoyed the wonderment of a stunning view the sisters could not envision the danger that was stalking them. It was such a beautiful day and everything had gone so well for the sisters during the past three weeks, so how could anything go wrong on a gorgeous day like this day so high in the mountains and away from the dangers of the past.

Back at the northern end of the flat summit neither the giant mountain man nor the magnificent ram had moved from their piece of the mountain they each had staked out for this contest of wills. What seemed like hours only lasted a matter of five to ten minutes.

Jeremiah finally turned to John and shook his head. He shrugged his shoulders and laid his rifle against the ledges wall.

"I can't do this John… I can't kill this magnificent king of this mountain." Jeremiah turned back towards the beautiful bighorn ram and softly uttered the words of absolute adoration. "You win ………you magnificent warrior of this mountain, you deserve to win!"

"Jeremiah, you both win… you both stood your ground!" John was fascinated watching these two guardians of the mountains.

Jeremiah slowly backed down from the ledge he was on and began walking back towards the wagons. John and Jake looked at each other in total amazement and understanding of Jeremiah's regards for the bighorn that now completely owned the mountain. Both Jake and John kept their eyes on the incredible animal as it watched Jeremiah descend the mountain. After a few moments, the giant sheep slowly turned and then disappeared into its kingdom.

Jerald and Jacky were really confused at what had just happened. John recognized their confusion; it was all over their faces.

"Boys, what you just witnessed is the soul of a giant of a man. Please, try to learn what you just saw. There's also an enormous lesson to be learned from the strength of will from that mountain sheep. But, there's a greater lesson to be learned from the actions that Jeremiah demonstrated today. Learn those two lessons and learn them well.

"But poppa.... I don't think I understand." Jerald was trying to understand but had not quite grasped it, yet.

"I don't either poppa; will you help us to understand?" Jacky asked the right question.

John smiled at his sons, patted them both on their heads and shook his head in the affirmative. Then they followed Jeremiah and Jake back down the mountain, back to the flat summit and the wagons.

The nearer the men got to the wagons, a complexing feeling came over John. He couldn't quite comprehend the feeling, but it was becoming more intense mixed with the anxiety of fear. When they finally reached level ground John immediately went to the wagons looking for Lucy and Amy. He didn't see either of them anywhere. He asked the folks in the other wagons if they had seen the sisters. Ila Bonner told John she had seen them earlier walking towards the other end of the flat summit. She supposed that they might be going on a picnic, but wasn't sure. All five men took off in the direction where Ila had seen the girls go.

John was angry with himself; he should have been more firm with Lucy and Amy by telling them NOT to go climbing on any part of this mountain without him or some of the other men. He had told them not to follow him and the other men where they were going to hunt the bighorn sheep. John kept telling himself that he should have been more specific with his instruction to Lucy because of her adventurous and free spirited ways.

He kept telling himself that they were OK, but he was still irritated at himself and with the girls just the same. When they came to the rock walls on the south side of the mountain pass John's heart started to pound just a little harder. If the girls were climbing around in these cracks and crevasses there was danger everywhere. Some of the crevasses seemed to have bottomless pits in them. If a person were to fall off one of a ledge's they could end up thousands of feet below. Then there was the dilemma of which crack or crevasses to follow. Jeremiah let out a thundering, "LUCYYYYYYY….AMYYYYY". Almost at the same instant that Jeremiah called the sister's names a blood-curdling childlike piercing scream sounded somewhere higher in the maze of cliffs and ledges.

Jeremiah started to climb towards the cracks in the rock wall where he thought the sound was coming from. He shouted at the others to follow him!

"It's a cat John….it's a mountain lion!" Jeremiah had a distinct dreaded fear in the tone of his voice that sent terrifying chills all over John's body. Jeremiah knew that they were close, but would they be in time to prevent any harm or carnage to them or the sisters.

Crawling through the cracks and trying to avoid the crevasses was difficult and challenging, especially for a man the size of Jeremiah. John was having his own difficulties climbing and then running into dead ends. Jake was the fastest climber and was above Jeremiah, but seemed to be going in the wrong direction. Jerald and Jacky were both finding their own routes over through the rough rocky cliff walls.

Jeremiah continued to shout out the names of Lucy and Amy, but there was no answer from the sisters. He was certain that they could hear him. He yelled to John trying to determine where John's position was. When John yelled back the two seemed to be going in the opposite directions.

The still cold air was again broken by a shrill piercing cat growl and this time it was a more chilling and terrifying sound. John was in a blurring frenzy, a feeling of complete helplessness and his fear for his daughters could not be quenched.

"Everybody…….. STOP RIGHT WHERE YOU ARE! LET'S GET OUR POSITIONS COORDINATED!" Jeremiah needed to get everyone to cooperate in the effort to find Lucy and Amy. After each person had identified their position by voice Jeremiah instructed them to keep in voice contact. No one noticed at the time, but Jerald didn't answer Jeremiah's voice request.

A couple of minutes after Jeremiah had gotten everyone's attention, Jacky was yelling so everybody could hear.

"OVER HERE…….OVER HERE……I THINK THEY'RE OVER HERE………..HURRY……I THINK I JUST SAW THE BACK END AND A TAIL OF A MOUNTAIN LION!" Jacky's body and mind were almost in shock. Fear had gripped his whole body. He was shaking so hard he was having a difficult time holding on to his rifle.

Jeremiah told Jacky to keep talking so the other men could work their way towards the sound of his voice. It seemed like hours before John finally caught sight of his youngest son, but it had only been minutes. Jake and Jeremiah finally met but was still a short distance from Jacky's voice. Jerald had got his foot caught in one of the small narrow crags in the rocks, and the only way he could escape was to pull his foot out from his shoe. He finally managed to free his shoe from its rock captor. But Jerald appeared to be above everybody else. He worked his way towards where he thought Jacky's voice was coming from, but he had this strange feeling he was going in the wrong direction even though his brother's voice was getting stronger and closer. But, Jacky's voice seemed to be coming from well below where Jerald was climbing.

Lucy and Amy had been enjoying their picnic lunch and relishing the fabulous view of a new world they would eventually be calling home. They were not aware of any immediate danger that could possibly confront them on this beautiful mountain and especially on this wonderful cloudless day. They had set on the rock ledge for about an hour enjoying the food and talking of silly girl things and the adventures that were before them in the days, weeks and months ahead. Amy started to giggle when she told Lucy that she had to pee. Lucy started to laugh and admitted that she had to pee too. It gave the sisters a sense of empowerment and freedom to be able to urinate in the open and on a mountain top with the whole beautiful universe watching.

"Amy... I bet I can squat on that boulder over there and pee further than you can." Lucy jumped up on the large rock and maneuvered her undergarments to a peeing position. When Lucy had finished she pulled her panties up and scrambled down as Amy climbed up on the rock and positioned herself to outdistance Lucy in this whizzing contest. Before Amy could begin to win the contest an ear piercing scream of a mountain cougar deadened the sound of the mountain all around the two girls. Amy peed all over herself as she fell from the rock and tumbled against Lucy knocking Lucy down. The sisters scrambled to get under a low hanging rock ledge in a corner of the larger ledge where they had just enjoyed their picnic. They weren't sure what kind of an animal it was that made the ear shattering and terrifying sound, but they knew that it was above them on another ledge in the rock wall of the mountain. They also realized this animal was big and it was an immense danger to their lives. When they heard Jeremiah's calls for them they were too frightened and too terrified to answer him. The girls could hear and almost feel the animal's heavy breathing and low gutter snarling sounds coming from somewhere just above their heads.

Both girls had huddled themselves as close together as possible. Lucy couldn't tell how hard she was shaking because Amy was shaking so hard. The sisters were holding each other's hands and didn't even realize that they were holding each other's hands.

"I don't want 'a die, Lucy.......I don't want 'a die." Amy was trying her best not to cry or talk loud. But the hushed tears just kept flowing anyway from both girls. Lucy just knew that the animal could hear her and her sister breathing and their shaking.

Both Jeremiah and Jake found John at the same time. John held his finger up to his lips as a sign of silence. He pointed towards Jacky who was maybe twenty feet from his poppa. Jacky was hiding behind a large boulder that was next to the ledge where Lucy and Amy were cowering under the lowest part of the ledge. John also pointed to a ledge that was about seven or eight feet higher than the ledge that he felt Jacky had seen the cat and heard Lucy and Amy. Jeremiah, John, and Jake could hear the big cat's low snarling sounds. Jeremiah wasn't sure, but he would swear that he could distinguish the growls of two different cats. He whispered those concerns to both John and Jake.

Without any warning, the mountain lion jumped six feet to a lower ledge behind some rocks that were out of view of the men. The sisters were on the next ledge below the cougar. John couldn't hold it any longer, he yelled to his daughters to let them know that he and the others were close.

“Lucy...Amy… if you’re on a ledge and can hear me you need to let us know. Don’t be afraid….just say something so we’ll know where you are.” John knew that the cat would be warned by his voice, but his daughters needed to know that he was here to help them. There were about thirty seconds of silence and then:

“Poppa we’re here….please come and get us.” John couldn’t tell which daughter had called out because of the freight in the voice.

A few seconds later the cougar came from behind a boulder and jumped on the ledge that the girls were on. The big cat was eight feet from the sisters and appeared ready to spring when Jerald came out from a seven foot higher crag in one of the rock walls and jumped those seven feet onto the cougar’s back knocking the cat for a tumble. Jerald went sprawling and hit his head on the rock ledge when he landed. The three men lost sight of Jerald and the cat. They couldn’t see the girls, but they could hear them screaming. All three men scrambled to climb over the remaining rocks and ledges that were separating them from Jerald, the cat, and the girls.

As Jerald landed on the big cat’s back Jacky jumped from where he was hiding to the ledge that his sister’s, the cat, and his brother was on. It took the cat less than a minute to recover to a standing position and now its intended quarry was Jerald. With lightening speed, the cougar sprang towards the older McCrumb brother. Jerald had regained his senses enough to see the big cat coming at him. Jerald curled up into a fetal position with his back towards the charging cougar. Just as the cougar landed on Jerald Jacky took a hefty swing with his rifle butt and cracked the lion on its back with the stock of the gun. The cougar recoiled and hesitated before turning on Jacky. That slight hesitation by the cougar gave Jacky the time he needed to aim his rifle and shoot the big cat.

It took John and his companions a couple of minutes before they managed to cross over the maze of rocks and crags to get to the ledge. Lucy and Amy were still huddled in the corner under the low ledge, crying and shaking. Jerald was setting up holding his bleeding head and right shoulder. Jacky was beside his brother wiping the blood from Jerald's eyes. The huge mountain lion was lying next to the brothers, dead, with a fatal bullet in its head.

Lucy and Amy were too terrified to move. They were shaking so bad they wouldn't have been able to walk if they had gotten up. John ran over to his daughters and forced both of them into his strong arms of protection.

Jeremiah and Jake went to Jerald's aid. The mountain lion had clawed Jerald's head and right shoulder and arm when it leaped on him. Thanks to Jacky's quick action the wounds caused by the big cat were not life threating. Jerald's scalp, forehead, and shoulder took the brunt of the cat's claws. Luckily the claws missed Jerald's eyes by a couple of inches. The men managed to stop the flow of blood from Jerald's head and shoulder wound.

John had managed to calm his daughters, their crying was reduced to sobs of fear. Between the mountain cold and their shock of the event, the girls were still shaking uncontrollably. Jeremiah and Jake handed John their heavy coats to wrap the girl in. Jerald was still a little dizzy from the blow to his head when he fell after jumping on the cats back.

Jeremiah still had this weird feeling that he had heard the scream of two cats and not just one. He advised everyone to be cautious and alert.

The men carefully guided Lucy and Amy back down the rocky cliffs to the safety of level ground and the familiarity of the wagons. Ila and the other two pioneer ladies took charge of the two girls. They helped to clean and redress the sisters in warmer clothes. John stayed close to his two daughters. Jacky helped his brother clean and treat his head and shoulder wounds. Jerald was hurting pretty bad, but he had to stay a man and not show too much of the hurt. Looking back, neither brother had shown any signs of fear during the cougar incident. Their adrenalin of protection was so high fear was totally out of the question.

Jeremiah and Jake made their way back up the difficult climb over crags, rocks, and ledges to retrieve the remains or the cougar. Jeremiah wanted the cat's skin and Jake thought that Jerald and Jacky should have part of the cat as a trophy for saving the girls and the pride of the kill. The cougar was larger than an average mountain lion. It weighed about a hundred and sixty pounds and it wasn't going to be easy getting the dead cat down over the rocks and cliff that were below the two men. Both men decided it would be much easier and safer to skin the cat on the ledge where it was killed and leave the carcass to the buzzards.

Before they made their first attempt to move or skin the mountain lion Jeremiah told Jake that he had to clear up a matter of confusion that had been bugging him. Jake followed Jeremiah as they made their way further up the ledges. After twenty minutes of difficult and rigorous climbing, Jeremiah would finally be able to put his mental doubts aside once he reached a high ledge. On this ledge, the two men could stand and look almost forever at the vast landscape before them. Jeremiah pointed to some moving objects well below them on some lower rocks. It was another mountain lion and two young cubs making their way to a safer spot on the mountain. Jeremiah knew that there was more than one cougar posing a threat to the girls. His mountain man instinct had severed him well.

Lucy and Amy were still having a difficult time hours after the cougar encounter. Both girls would start shaking with sporadic bursts of sobbing and wanting their momma. It was extremely painful for John watching his daughters suffer this kind of trauma. Ila told John the girls were still in some shock. It was her opinion the cause of the shock was not so much because of fear of the mountain lion hurting them, but it was caused by watching their brother possibly being killed by the lion. She thought it might be a possible healing moment if Jerald and Jacky sat and talked with their sisters for a while.

After Jerald had his deep claw wounds treated with a healing balm and bandaged he was told to rest in one of the wagons. Jacky had stayed with his brother for moral support. After the discussion with Ila Bonner John went to Jerald and explained to him the condition of his sisters. John asked his son if he was feeling up to talking with Lucy and Amy. Both brothers wanted to go to their sister's right then.

When Lucy and Amy saw Jerald and Jacky walking towards them both girls started to cry and ran to meet their brothers. The hugging lasted for a good five minutes. After Lucy and Amy's emotions had been reassured, they, their brother's along with the entire pioneer group sat together by a huge campfire and talked about the day's event.

Jacky made a joke about Jerald's funny new hat; he was referring to the multi-colored bandages on his brother's head. The bandage had been quickly assembled from different available rags found in the wagons. He also commented that Jerald might be handsome now, and not so homely. It was a good joke in many ways; it allowed Lucy and Amy to laugh at their brothers and that was a perfect way for the girls to vent their fears. The two sisters cuddle with their brothers until it was time for some well-earned sleep. Sleep would not come easy for Jerald; he was experiencing some extremely coarse pain to his head and shoulder.

John and the other three wagon owners decided to wait a few more days before descending the west side of the Landers Cutoff pass. This would give everyone a much-needed break from the experience of the mountain lion episode. Lucy and Amy would be feeling much better and Jerald's wounds would be a couple of days closer in the healing process. Jake wanted to get to Soda Springs ahead of Bright's arrival. Jeremiah's last thoughts before the wagons were to move out and descend the western side of those beautiful Rockies was reliving those moments with that magnificent mountain ram and the eye ball to eye ball standoff between himself and that magnificent bighorn. Jeremiah would forever be connected to the mountain ram in a strange brotherly way. John's concerns were about his two daughters and two sons. It was troubling for John thinking about the moments when Lucy and Amy were crying for their momma days before. Some nights John would wake up calling out "Sarah's" name. He silently wondered if those traumatic emotions over losing a mother and a wife would someday diminish where the hurt wasn't so hard to endure.

After Jake and Jeremiah had carried the cougar skin down to the wagons they hung the hide in the sun. Jeremiah gave the cat's skull to Jacky and the claws to Jerald. He told Jacky that he would help him to preserve the skull when they arrived at their final destination.

Ila and Jack Bonner decided to settle in the Treasure Valley; the area of Boise Idaho. Mr. and Mrs. Haney joined the McCrumb's wagon train at Fort Laramie and were going to follow the McCrumb's into the Lost River Valley. Mr. and Mrs. Beverlander who had also joined the McCrumb's wagon train at Fort Laramie were not sure where they were going to settle. There were three settlements that they had under consideration; Idaho Falls on the banks of the Snake River, the Blackfoot settlement near Fort Hall and the Shoshone-Bannock Indian Reservation under Chief Pocatello or a smaller settlement called Shelley just west of Idaho Falls. The Beverlander's was even considering following the McCrumb's to the Lost River Valley. They had even discussed dropping the "ER" off of the end of their Norwegian name.

The six wagons began their downward decline on the western slope of the summit of the Landers Cutoff on April $8^{th,}$ 1876. Soda Springs was about seventy miles northwest of the small wagon train. The land was flat and the travel time to the Soda Springs should be an easy three or four-day journey. The weather was dry and the temperature was getting warmer. John was anticipating arriving at Soda Springs a few days ahead of Henry and Bright's arrival. Lucy and Amy were in a better frame of mind and the sisters were emotionally improving from the encounter with the cougar.

Lucy found some inward solace in studying her painted pouch that held her three wishes from the Ute Indian incident. Her family had saved her from that potential tragedy and now once again her family had saved her and her sister from potential death from the mountain lion attack. She still had not opened the pouch. Jerald's lion claw wounds were healing but he still had some pain to remind him of the attack. Jerald and Jacky were working on stringing bear claws and bear teeth on small strips of tanned leather for necklaces. They were still very grateful to their sisters for such a wonderful gift of the teeth and claws from the bear the sisters had helped kill. Now the boys could add the cougar claws to the necklaces. Amy was even helping her brothers string the teeth and claws.

The journey down the western slope of the cutoff was more difficult and demanding than the pioneers had anticipated. Both feet on the wagons brake pedals was absolutely essential all the way down the slope in order to keep the wagons from over running the horses and steers that were certainly not pulling the wagons. John told Jeremiah that all of the brake shoes would have to be checked and probably some replaced after the wagons had finally once again reached the flatlands of the prairie.

When the pioneers finally reach the floor of the valley they were not prepared for the strange landscape that laid before them.The topography and the geography between the base of the mountain and Soda Springs was a totally different world that the weary voyagers had ever encountered before. There were strange looking trees in every direction. There were perplexing grasses and green foliage everywhere the pioneers looked. The strange phenomenon that had startled and amazed the travelers in the most bizarre way was the sporadic and at times very large volcanic lava rock beds that had been violently belched from volcanoes thousands of years ago. The wagons could travel for a few miles and without warning, other massive lava beds would appear on the horizon. The lava formations were grotesque and at times frightening looking. There was evidence where the lava had bubbled up and then fiercely burst open causing deep cavities in the lava mass. Some of the bubbles that had not burst were as big as a large house. The further west the wagons traveled the lava beds became more massive and closer together.

Another bizarre phenomenon that was ominous and menacing to the pilgrims were geysers of hot steaming water that would spurt out of the ground and spray a stream of scolding hot water skyward. The geysers varied in size. Small geysers would just bubble up out of the ground and spray the hot water only a couple of feet in the air, while other geysers would spit scorching hot water a couple of hundred feet skyward. To say the least, the travelers were unnerved, anxious and extremely apprehensive in this new environment. None of the travelers had ever been in this type of ecosystem before. It was new to them and at times quite astonishing but more to the point it was stunning but forbidding.

John had to keep reassuring Lucy and Amy that a volcano wasn't going to erupt at any moment nor a huge geyser wasn't going to materialize under one of the wagons sending the wagon high in the air resting on a body of hot steaming water. The closer they got to Soda Springs the more geysers they encountered and the larger the lava beds became.

None of these pioneers had ever heard of the Great Yellowstone of Wyoming, Montana and the southeastern section of the Idaho Territory. The Great Yellowstone was nearly 3,500 square miles and was a massive volcanic hot spot. The Yellowstone consisted of alpine rivers, captivating canyons of great beauty, gushing geysers and thousands of pools of hot springs. Many of the pools of hot water were displayed with hundreds of magnificent different colors caused by the Yellowstone's diverse clay and ground compounds. The Yellowstone was home to hundreds of species of animals. The elk, grizzly, antelope, deer, bison, wolves, coyote, moose and the golden and bald eagle ruled in the massive Yellowstone. The Indians called the Yellowstone the sacred ground of "Mother Earth".

It was early afternoon on the 11th of April when the six wagons rolled into Soda Springs and camped next to the brand new train station. Soda Springs was a small, but important junction of the

Oregon Trail between Fort Laramie to the east and Fort Boise to the west. In 1863 the "Oasis of Soda Springs" was better known as Fort Conner, making the small settlement the second oldest settlement in Idaho.

Soda Springs was situated in the vicinity of the Bear River Valley and the Aspen Mountains. Ancient volcanic activity had shaped the landscape with hot bubbling soda springs, therefore its name. Ancient large lava flows covered the land north of the settlement creating enormous and strange lava beds and mysterious lava caves. Two primeval large volcanic cones to the north of Soda Springs were the culprits that had belched the lava over much of the landscape.

The small wagon train had managed to arrive at Soda Springs before the arrival of Henry and Bright from their Boston journey. That had been John's initial plan but he wasn't sure when the couple from Boston would finally reach this destination. He would just have to wait and pray that Henry and Bright made all of the right connections. The next regular scheduled train arrival was on the 13th of April, just two days away. Jake was anxious and praying that Bright would be on that train, but John told him not to get his hopes up to high. It could be days or weeks if ever before Henry and Bright would reach Soda Springs. Everything was so unpredictable in this ever changing western frontier.

John told the exhausted travelers it was time to make camp and check the wagons for any needed repairs. John inquired of the station-master of news of any travel difficulties towards the west or any news of Indian problems in the territories. The station master would be the person who received all important news via the singing land telegraph. There were no problems for the western travelers. There was news of Indian unrest in the Wyoming Territory. It seemed that the Lakota Sioux, Northern Cheyenne, and

Arapahoe were defying the U.S. government by not returning to their government appointed reservations. It was Chief Setting Bull and Crazy Horse of the Lakota Sioux Nation that was leading the Indian rebellion against the white man's demand. It was on June 25th of 1876, just two months after John's inquiry from the station master that the Indian uprising lead by Setting Bull and Crazy Horse came to a bloody highpoint at the Battle of the Little Bighorn and the defeat and death of George Armstrong Custer.

The station master gave John some personal tragic news concerning the wagon train that had split from the McCrumb's and the three wagons that chose to follow the McCrumb's to the Landers Cutoff. The other thirty-two wagons had split at the South Pass and taken a different route from at the South Pass. The McCrumb's three wagons and three other wagons left South Pass for the Landers Cutoff while the rest of the wagon train traveled from the South Pass on to Fort Bridger. That wagon train had been attacked by an unidentified band of renegade Indians and the majority of those pioneers were massacred. The few that were saved were rescued by a company of soldiers from Fort Bridger. John hesitated from telling his group of travelers of the disastrous news but decided that they should know and then count their blessings.

During the two-day wait for the next scheduled train to Soda Springs, the McCrumb party of pioneers spent that time recuperating, tended to their personal needs and doing necessary repairs to their wagons. Lucy, Amy Jerald, and Jacky wanted to explore the many weird and fascinating natural wonders that surrounded the small settlement. Everyone in the camp took warm baths in naturally heated earthen pools that were near the campsite. The sisters and brothers stayed together during their exploring adventures. No one wanted to get lost in the maze of lava caves and treacherous trenches.

Lucy had to catch up her journal that she had been keeping since they had left Alma over a year ago. She took these relaxing times to fill in all of the blank pages that were not written on during the difficult times. But, she could easily fill them in now; they were still fresh on her mind.

The McCrumb group was heavy hearted with pain and sorrow when John finally told them of the tragic news of their past companions on the Oregon Trail. They all knelt in prayer for the loss of lives of the wagon train. They thanked God for their blessings of safety. It was hard to understand that the Almighty wasn't with both groups of pioneers. John stated that he believed that God was with both groups, it was the band of renegade Indians that had caused the tragedy. John said that he believed God would be merciful to the pioneers that had their lives taken from them and that God would take vengeance on the killers. Everyone shook their heads in agreement.

On the 13th of April 1876, Jake was a nerves wreck anticipating the scheduled train's arrival. If Bright wasn't on this train John feared that Jake would jump in some hot steam pit and drowned himself. John had tried every reasonable tactic to calm Jake down. If John were a drinking man, and if he did have any liquor he would give it Jake and get him drunk for a week, just so there would be some calm in the camp. John anticipated that Bright was having the same feelings for Jake.

Lucy was trying to hide her feelings from her pap, but she was terrified in her mind that Henry would not remember her. John knew that his oldest daughter was having the same feelings that were driving Jake crazy, but being a young woman he also knew that she didn't want those outside of the family to see her panic with anxiety.

"Foolish female pride", she kept muttering to herself.

Finally in the late afternoon on the 13th the small gauged steam engine puffed its way passed the lava beds and steaming geysers to the tiny railway station. There were many bundles of pelts and furs on the station platform to be placed in one of the rail cars to be shipped back to Ogden Utah, then to the east coast. As the engine belched out its excess steam the platform and the wooden station disappeared in the white billowy puffs of hot white steam. As the steam dissipated the lone passenger car became visible to the McCrumb's and friends. There wasn't a conductor; a brakeman came from the caboose to open the passenger cars door. He entered the car and returned to the platform a couple of minutes later.

Jake walked to the door of the passenger car as if he already knew that Bright was about to walk down the cars iron steps. After a couple of intense moments, a big smile crossed Jake's lips and Bright appeared on the top step.

When she got to the last step Jake picked her up off of the step and whirled her In his arms to the platform. Bright was crying when she wrapped her arms around Jake's neck so tight she felt she could have hung there forever.

"Jake I love you...I love you so much…." Bright found the time between the kisses and hugs to get those few words out. She was perfectly in love for the first time in her life and as it turned out, Jake was the perfect partner for her.

"Bright… I will never let you out of my sight again……… never…. Never ever again. I have loved you from that first moment I saw you get off of the train from Tennessee." Jake felt like his heart was about to burst. He would not let Bright out of his arms. Jake never wanted this feeling of love to ever escape from him.

"Bright….. Will you marry me and be my beautiful wife forever and ever?" The words flowed out of Jake's mouth as easy as eating some of Sarah's home baked apple pie. He would put Bright on a pedestal and there she would stay all the rest of her life

"YES!" Bright screamed her answer for everyone to hear. And everyone did!

When Henry reached the platform he watched his sister in her wonderful moment of bliss. He was smiling for his sister's chance of happiness. Henry had great admiration for Jake and he had already told his sister that he approved of her choice in husbands. He was sure that Jake was going to ask Bright to marry him. He was proud of Bright and was happy that she finally would have a chance to a truly happy life thanks to Jake and the McCrumb's.

Henry had another important matter on his mind; Lucy. For the past two months his attentions have been two-fold; his sister's eyesight, her wellbeing and his strong feelings for Lucy. He was sure that Lucy had some feelings for him, but he wasn't sure if those feeling were deep or just a friendly girl crush. On the train from Boston Henry had made up a hundred ways how to approach Lucy when he saw her again. But, none of them made any sense after he had designed them. Everything he would come up with just seemed more stupid than the previous one. Henry finally gave up and decided to just play it by ear.

When Henry turned from watching his sister he walked over to John and shook his hand. Henry thanked John for everything that he had done for his family. Then he looked for Lucy. Lucy was standing next to the depot. She was shaking and afraid to say anything in fear that Henry would not recognize her intentions. Maybe he would be indifferent to her now since he had been in

Boston. Lucy feared that Henry might have found other interests while he was in Boston. Maybe now he would consider her just another little "smart allick" girl. Henry walked over to where Lucy was standing and stopped just shy of touching her. Lucy felt as if she would faint before either said the first word.

"Lucy….. I don't want to offend you…and if I seem to be bold, please forgive me……but Lucy… I ….ah…..I love you very much……" Henry was starting to sputter and twist his words in nonunderstandable dribble. He was beginning to doubt his own ability to speak coherent words. His only option was to just blurt out what he was thinking and trying to say. "Lucy may I hold you and maybe Kiss………." Henry never got the other words out of his mouth. Lucy jumped into his arms and kissed him long on his mouth.

"Oh Henry…you silly man…..I have missed you so……I love you too." Lucy managed to get those words out between her and Henry's hugs and kisses.

Jeremiah walked over and put his huge arm around John's shoulder and just smiled.

"Well, my friend…..it looks like our family is just about to change and get bigger……For the better, I think."

"Yep….Jeremiah, I think you just might be right……..I wish Sarah was here to see Lucy's beautiful glowing smile." John had a mixture of tears; tears of happiness and then those tears of sorrow for Sarah's sake.

"Sarah is here John…..You got to believe that she is here, John….. You just got to believe." Jeremiah was determined to make John realize that Sarah's spirit was here with him and Lucy.

Amy was laughing and bawling all at the same time. First, she was hugging her sister than she would be hugging Bright. In a few minutes, she would be back to hugging Lucy and then back hugging Bright. Both Jake and Henry were getting their share of hugs and teary kisses from Amy. Jeremiah and John got their turn with Amy's teary and mushy kisses during her round of hugs.

John took his first daughter in his arms and told her how much he loved her. He reminded her of their conversation about her feeling that they had a few weeks earlier. Through loving tears, she told John how much she loved her pap. Lucy was no longer a little girl; now she was a beautiful young woman. Sarah would have been so proud of her first daughter.

Sarah had told Lucy more than once that Henry was a good boy and he would make a wonderful husband for some deserving women someday. Sarah realized Henry's character that first night at the supper table when she had asked him personal questions. That was the night he told the McCrumb family that he had a blind sister named Bright. That was the same night Lucy learned a very valuable "on the spot" momma lesson in life.

Jerald and Jacky tried very hard to look happy and really interested in all of this hugging and kissing and the rest of the happy "going's on", but the surrounding "going's on" was just a little too much for their heart strings. They would really be happier if they were out there exploring the lava beds. Besides that, Jerald's head wound was hurting and all of this noisy celebrating was not helping. They shook Jake and Henry's hands and scurried off to the lava beds.

Later that evening when all of the pioneers were huddled around the camp fire for the evening meal the conversations varied, depending on which group you might be with at that particular moment.

Jeremiah and Jake were telling Henry about the mountain lion incident. Because they were some of the main characters in this cougar story Jerald and Jacky were intently listening to every word not wanting to miss hearing their names mentioned along with the words "bravery" and "courage". John and the pioneers of the other three wagons were discussing their decision and their blessings for not traveling on to Fort Bridger and being part of the Indian massacre. Lucy, Bright, and Amy were, of course, wagging their tongues about Boston, eye operations, marriage, babies, and other secretive girl things. Amy was the one who was really digesting all of this girl talk of marriage, and baby stuff for her future reference.

In a couple of days, the six wagons would be leaving Soda Springs and heading west again. Their next destination would be Fort Hall and the magnificent Snake River. The Snake River was the thirteenth largest river in America, almost eleven hundred miles long. The six wagons were going to have to "FORD" the "SNAKE". John and his wagons had crossed many streams and rivers on their quest for a new life on the western frontier, but the mighty Snake River would be their greatest challenge. In past decades before the McCrumb's hundreds of covered wagons had been destroyed and hundreds of pioneers lives were lost trying cross over the wild and treacherous torrents of the rampaging waters of the mighty Snake.

Fort Hall was about forty-five to fifty miles northwest of Soda Springs. It would take John and his traveling companions a little over two days to reach the fort. The original Fort Hall was first a fur trading post along the Snake River in the Idaho Territory. It was established in 1832 by one Nathaniel Jarvis Wyeth. The trading post was converted to an Army post in about 1852. A new Fort Hall was built in 1870 about twelve miles from the Snake River. The old Fort was torn down after a number of tragic mishaps including being damaged by the Snake River in a devastating flood. It has been estimated that over a quarter of a million of immigrants and pioneers had traveled through Fort Hall on their way to a new western adventure during the eighteen hundred's. Fort Hall was the key Post for the Overland Stage, mail and freight lines to the surrounding settlements and the mining frontier in the Pacific Northwest. The Fort Hall housed an Army Garrison for traveler's protection until the late eighteen hundred's. The large Shoshone and Bannock Indian Reservation actually encompassed the Fort by treaty.

The six wagons arrived at Fort Hall on the eighteenth of April 1876 just in time to eat their noonday meal. As the sixteen weary travelers made camp they became aware of their extremely unusual surroundings. There were much more Indians at the Fort than there were white people. That one small detail of "a lot more red men than white men" as Jeremiah properly summed it up caused considerable anxiety with the ladies and a foreboding feeling for Jerald and Jacky.

If you could believe Jacky's description, there were Indian teepees as far as the eye could see and there were at least ten thousand Indians. He was sure he could see scalps hanging from almost every teepee. John told his son's to get used to the landscape because they were going to be there for a few days. When Jerald asked his poppa what a few days meant, John just smiled and walked away.

After a couple of days at the Fort Jerald and Jacky were getting familiar and relaxed towards the Indians who were very friendly towards the brothers. Lucy and Amy were still standoffish because of their experience with the Ute. The sisters wanted to know and learn about these people but it would take a little time for them to adjust to the fact that these Indians were friendly and peaceful. Lucy, with Amy tagging along, would begin talking to the elderly

Indian ladies and would inquire concerning their handmade bead work. The beadwork fascinated the sisters and had captured their imagination. As those discussions increased the nagging remembrance of the experience at the hands of the Ute began to fade.The sister soon realized that these Indians were noble and friendly.

The Shoshone and the Bannock nation's had been on this reservation since 1868 and were at peace with the white man and had been since "Pocatello", the Shoshone Chief had signed the Treaty in 1868 at Fort Bridger. Chief Pocatello and the Shoshone had kept their part of the treaty since the treaty's signing. The US government had welched on their part of the treaty constantly. Washington was deficient on honoring the important elements of the treaty; food and livestock. It was the Shoshone that had suffered year after year. They lacked the promised food, livestock and the assistance of seed and medicine that was directed in the treaty as long the Shoshone stayed on the reservation. Even though the government faulted year after year on their part of the treaty Chief Pocatello had kept his people peaceful and on the reservation.

Chief Pocatello had met with the Utah Mormons earlier seeking assistance and hoping for any kind of help for his people. The Mormon leadership wanted to help and even tried to help the Shoshone people but the rank and file Mormon membership rebelled, "not wanting anything to do with the red skin savages".

Jeremiah wanted to learn more about the Shoshone Indians. He made his presence known on the reservation and met with the Shoshone Chief. Jeremiah learned from Chief Pocatello about the tribe's problems with the US government. He learned of the bad winter the tribe had just experienced with their lack of food and medicine. He became aware that the Indian's would willingly trade for any type of crop seeds that would help them through the next winter months.

Jeremiah talked with John about the possibility of trading with the Shoshone. John had kegged many different types of vegetable seeds before leaving Alma. The seeds had been for John and Sarah's future; their future in their new western homestead. John had kegged many hundreds of pounds of seeds of many varieties of vegetables. There was corn, different beans, squash, peas, wheat, regular beets, sugar beets, cucumber and other types of seeds. Jeremiah had advanced a potential meeting with Chief Pocatello and other Shoshone leaders with himself and John to discuss a possible trade. The Shoshone had endured a bad winter and it had left many of the tribe members lacking in sustainable foods and in poor health. Many of the young had lost their struggle for life. John could not comprehend the government's treatment of the Shoshone people, not only was it deplorable it was a plain disservice of human justice.

Jeremiah, John, Jake, Henry and the two brothers were invited to a POW WOW at Chief Pocatello's teepee. This would be a great once in a lifetime event for Jerald and Jacky, one that they would never forget. It would be a lifetime experience that would serve the brothers well in the future with the Idaho Redman. Jeremiah did all of the preliminary negotiations, which were going to be in the Indians favor according to John. To John's utter surprise the Indian called Pocatello could speak good broken English. John turned to look at Jeremiah and Jeremiah raised his eyebrows, smiled and shook his head and shrugged his shoulders in the affirmative.

John told the Chief that he would have a railroad train box car shipped from Salt Lake City to Fort Hall filled with staple foods, vegetables, dried and salted meats and cattle and what medicine he could find. He told Pocatello that another train car would be filled with hay, blankets and planting seeds of all kinds and other necessities to help sustain them after their devastating winter.

Jeremiah told John that the chief told him in the Shoshone dialect that he preferred that these new friends call him "Buffalo Robe". He favored the name "Buffalo Robe" over the name Pocatello. In fact, the word "Pocatello" did not even have a meaning in the Shoshone dialect. Jeremiah told John that is was a great honor that had just been bestowed on them by the Shoshone Chief allowing them to call him "Buffalo Robe".

Jeremiah told Buffalo Robe that Jerald's birthday was just a few days away and that Jacky's birthday was just one full moon away. The Shoshone Chief smiled at the boys and placed his hand on their heads one at a time. The Chief was also interested in the brothers encounter with the mountain lion. Jerald had taken the bandages off of his head for the POW WOW. The scars were still very prominent and hurtful looking.

Both John and Jeremiah had noticed a very pretty young half-breed girl maybe about thirteen or fourteen year's old hanging around the chief's teepee. She was tanned skinned with dark blue eyes. Buffalo Robe noticed that both white men had noticed the young girl, but said nothing.

The boys spent the next two days on the reservation with Buffalo Robe and some of the reservations young Indian boys. Both Jerald and Jacky became blood brothers to four of the Shoshone young Braves. They were cut at the base of their palm of their left hand because tradition says there is a line at the base of that hand that runs to a man's heart. When the blood reaches the heart that will bond the two together for life as brothers here on Mother Earth and forever beyond the skies.

That evening Jerald and Jacky told their sisters about the exciting couple of days they had spent on the reservation. Of course, they were very proud to show off their "Blood Brother" scars. Immediately Lucy wanted a blood sister scar, even if it had to be with her own sister.

The biggest news the brothers had to tell their sisters was about the half-breed Indian girl that they had seen on the reservation. The sisters were shocked and wanted to know more; what did she look like, what color was her skin, what color was her hair and was she tall, short, fat or skinny. Jerald and Jacky thought the questions would never end. Jerald got tired of saying. "I don't know?"! Lucy was determined to find out for herself the truth behind her brother's strange story. She wasn't sure if they weren't just telling another big whopper. The brothers enjoyed putting whoppers over on their sisters.

It was not a common practice, but Lucy wanted to know why she couldn't become a blood sister to one of the Shoshone girls. Jeremiah had a troublesome time trying to convince Lucy that it just wasn't done and that it would never be done. Lucy complained that wasn't a good enough explanation and she still couldn't understand, "Why not! If it was good enough for boys, why not girls."

After their POW WOW with Buffalo Robe John and Jake took the train to Salt Lake City to order the supplies that he had promised to the Shoshone Chief. The two men were back at Fort Hall six days later. While John was in Salt Lake City he purchased sixty head of cattle and had the cattle shipped back to the Indian reservation by train in a cattle car. The second railroad box car was loaded with wooden barrels and kegs full of all kinds of food staples such as grains, flour, salt, and sugar, dried and salted meats. There were kegs of planting seeds, blankets, bundles of hay and other sustainable items for health and welfare. These extra two railroad box cars would also be shipped to the Shoshone Reservation at Fort Hall. John paid for everything with a bank draft drawn from his account in the Denver Mercantile Bank. John advised the Chief that four box cars, not just two would be delivered to Fort Hall within seven to ten days.

Lucy, Amy, and Bright were invited and welcomed to the reservation by the Shoshone Chief and his daughter, "Shinning Star". The women of the reservation, both old and young were gentle, friendly and educational towards the three white girls. Some of the young Indian girls were fascinated with the three white girl's clear deep green eyes. Both of the sisters kept looking for a glimpse of the half-breed girl that their brothers had told them about. They had not told Bright about the half-breed girl because they did not want to look stupid if their brother's had pitched them another farfetched story. After a while, Lucy came to the conclusion that the boys were just pulling their legs and telling a big black whopper of a tale concerning a half-breed Indian girl. This was probably just another really big incredible brother fabrication.

Buffalo Robe invited the three girls to his teepee which really excited the girls. Lucy, Amy, and Bright sat on vividly colored rugs with bizarre zig-zag designs in the Chief's buffalo hide "house" teepee. Also in the tee-pee with Buffalo Robe was his daughter and some of the elderly women of the Shoshone tribe. There was also three older women of the Bannock tribe, but the girls couldn't tell the differences between the different tribes. The girls asked many questions and Buffalo Robe was gracious enough to answer all of them.

After the girls had asked many questions and had answered many others questions from Buffalo Robe the three girls had lost track of the time. Buffalo Robe spoke to one of the Shoshone women and she quickly left the teepee. The Shoshone chief had wanted to hear and understand the character of the McCrumb sisters before he made his important decision to send the Shoshone women from the teepee.

It wasn't long before the tent flap opened and a beautiful young tall girl entered the teepee. This had to be the girl that Jerald and Jacky had told their sisters about a couple of nights before because she resembled their descriptions of the half-breed girl. The Chief introduced the girl as "White Antelope", a daughter of the Shoshone. The girl walked over and sat next to Lucy and Amy. Both sisters sat there in complete mystified silence. Neither of the girls knew how to act or what to say, so they said nothing, only smiled and nodded their heads. "White Antelope" setting next to them made Lucy, Amy and Bright uneasy, tense and just a little awkward and frightened. They just sat there with silly and confused looks on their faces. Some of the elderly Indian ladies did show slightly amused smiles after watching the girls with their silly confused expressions.

The tall Indian girl wore a typical Indian buckskin dress with buckskin leggings and beaded moccasins. The dress was fringed and adorned with delicate designed multi-colored beadwork. Her hair was black and her eyes were a subtle deep blue to lite blue hues. Her skin was a very light tan color, not as dark as the other Indians in the teepee. Her slim build didn't resemble the sturdier built bodies of the other Indian girls that the sisters had observed on the reservation. Her facial features were strong and resembled the features of Caucasian women more than the facial features of Indian women. She was just about as tall as Amy; five foot five or five foot six inches. She was very picturesque and very beautiful. All three of the white girls were stunned by her presence and charisma.

White Antelope smiled at the girl's and said something to Buffalo Robe in the Shoshone dialect and all of the women in the teepee laughed. The Indian Chief shook his head, smiled and agreed with her in Shoshone. After he had agreed with the tall girl there were a few moments of silence before the Chief spoke again.

"White Antelope wishes to show you some our land." With that said he arose and led the girls out into the open sunlight. Waiting outside for the girls were four horses without saddles, only horse blankets that would be between their rear ends and the bouncing horse. A couple of the Indian braves had to help the three white girls on their horses. White Antelope grabbed her horses mane and whirled herself on her horse with graceful ease. Lucy was just a little jealous and it showed. White Antelope took the girls out to see the great Snake River.

On the way to the river the three white girls had varying conversations between themselves dealing with the beautiful landscape, the Indian's hospitality and of course the conversation finally turned to a discussion about White Antelope. White Antelope seemed not to understand their words nor did she pay any attention or speak a word of Shoshone.

When the girls finally reached the magnificent and imposing power of the mighty Snake River White Antelope finally spoke her first words to the three white girls.

"Isn't it beautiful?" All three of the white visitors looked at White Antelope in utter amazement. The three girls were flabbergasted, dumbfounded and a few other surprising astonishments.

Without saying another word White Antelope continued her gaze at the grandeur of the most extraordinary and fascinating river west of the Continental Divide. On the east of the Divide, it was the mighty Mississippi but here in the west, it was a thousand miles of the roaring Snake before dumping its tumultuous waters into the Beautiful and wide Columbia River made famous by the 1804 Lewis and Clark expedition.

"You speak English!" Bright was the first girl to corral her bewilderment.

White Antelope turned towards the white girls with a huge smile and an expressive look of, "I want to be your friend." "Yes, my father was a Mormon explorer and my mother Shoshone women. I was born on the reservation and lived in the Great Salt Lake City until my parents were killed when I was twelve years old."

White Antelope slid off of her beautiful brown and white pinto pony and asked the girls to sit with her on the soft grass. The girls got comfortable in a circle under the warmth of the Idaho sun.

"How did your mom and dad die?" it was Lucy who had regained her sense of reality.

"They were killed by a raiding party of renegade Blackfeet Indians." White Antelope gave the impression that she did not want to discuss her parent's death in detail.

"Do you like living on the reservation?" Bright got her question in before Amy could ask hers.

"Yes, but I would like to live like my mother and father did in the Great Salt Lake, someplace where I could continue my schooling. Where I could fix my hair and wear the feminine girl clothes like I used to, like the ones you have on. The Shoshone people and Buffalo Robe are a special and wonderful family, but I miss a close family of my own; like I think, you probably have."

The rest of the day was spent with girl talk, riding and exploring parts of the reservation. White Antelope was delighted to be in the company of her new friends. It was an instant feeling of the family closeness that she missed after her family was killed.

At the end of the day, White Antelope's new friends were showered with gifts of bead necklaces and beaded leather work. There were a couple of young handsome Indian braves that caught the eye of Amy. Amy also caught the watchful eyes of a few of those handsome braves.

The girls thanked their host, Chief Buffalo Robe for the wonderful day. They were especially happy with their new friend. The girls hugged White Antelope and told her how much they loved her. She told the girls that her English given name was Mary Armstrong and please call her Mary. Bright told the girls including Mary that she would make a wonderful sister. The three white girls now understood why the white man use saddles on their horses. Three white sore rear ends would be a great reason.

John wanted to camp at Fort Hall for a couple of weeks. That would give him and Jeremiah an opportunity to investigate and prepare for the crossing of the Snake River. There were only a couple of areas where the river could be crossed in this part of the Idaho Territory with some degree of safety. The further west a wagon traveled along the Snake River it would become impossible to cross the river's treacherous rapids. By the time the river had thundered its way into central Idaho the mighty Snake River had created huge, wide and deep gorges in the earth. If the gorges weren't wicked enough to totally destroy a wagon, extreme and deadly waterfalls awaited any unsuspecting boater traveling on the river. At the western end of the Idaho Territory, the colossal river dumped its rampaging and roaring waters into the mighty Columbia River of Lewis and Clarke fame, then on to the majestic Pacific Ocean.

At one of the possible areas near Fort Hall where the river could be forded the wagons would have to be partially floated across the river. Ropes secured to horses then strapped to the wagons would guide the wagons parallel from shore to the opposite shore praying that the horses and rope could sustain the wagons from being swept downstream towards the waterfalls. This more difficult crossing was just a little over three hundred feet wide.

But there was an added danger at that crossing. Some of the earliest wagon trains met with disaster at this river crossing. Some of the wagons could not withstand the sudden surge of the rampaging river waters and they were capsized and swept down the river and over monstrous waterfalls. Anything going over the falls would either be killed or totally destroyed. Hundreds of pioneers had lost their lives going over those ravaging falls, while others lost all of their worldly possessions. After those first few disasters, the wagon handlers of future caravans were more cautious at attempting to ford the river at that crossing. No matter how careful a wagon was handled during any crossing it was not guaranteed that it would be a safe crossing without tragedies as other earlier pioneers had learned.

The other less dangerous crossing was a few miles upriver northwest of the Fort. The river at this point was considerable wider and shallower with gentler rapids which made the crossing much safer and quicker. The river bed at this juncture of the river had been crossed thousands of times over the past decades making for a solid foundation for the wheels of a covered wagon. John and Jeremiah chose this crossing for their further quest of the west.

After the four train box cars filled with the supplies that John had ordered for Buffalo Robe and the Shoshone arrived from Salt Lake City and were unloaded at the Shoshone reservation, it was time for the six wagons to continue on their journey to their individual destinations in the Idaho Territory. All of the travelers were rested and their covered wagons restocked for the final journey of their quests for a new beginning in the western frontier. President Thomas Jefferson had started this western discovery adventure seventy years earlier with the Lewis and Clark expedition. The McCrumb's had that same valued spirit of adventure in their heritage and was following the same dreams and desires to forge a new nation for those generations that would follow after them.

The last days before the wagons rolled west once again there were a lot of goodbyes to be said. The Shoshone Nation and Chief Buffalo Robe had honored all of the travelers with a traditional Indian "Good Journey" Ceremonies. It was a humbling experience for the white settlers. The colorful ceremony was truly from the soul of the tribe. It was an experience that none of the pioneers would ever forget. The involvement with these Native Americans with their distinctive culture and true friendship turned a new page of understanding for the sixteen white western-bound travelers of the McCrumb wagon train.

John, Jeremiah, and Jake met with Buffalo Robe privately a number of times. The most important and meaningful private discussion sessions between the four men would affect the lives of a number of people for years to come. These important meetings were instigated by the Shoshone Chief himself.

The Shoshone Chief had great respect for the McCrumb family and their friends. John's generosity towards the Shoshone Nation had placed him in their hearts as a special white father of their People. This solemn respect that Buffalo Robe had for John and John's two daughters and two sons caused the Shoshone chief to reflect on a promise that he had decreed to a friend four years earlier. Up until this time the Chief had not been able to fulfill that promise to his friend. The McCrumb family could be the catalyst in allowing the Shoshone Chief to finally fulfill that solemn pledge he had made. Buffalo Robe explained to John in great detail the reasons leading up to the promise that he had made to White Antilope's father before he died at the hands of the Black Feet Indians. Buffalo Robe explained to John why John and his family could fulfill that pledge. Now, It was up to John and his family to determine their help to Buffalo Robe. John and his two daughters and two sons would have to deeply study the ramification to their family if they agreed to the fulfillment of the promise that the Shoshone Chief had made to his friend. Their conclusion would have to be made before they crossed over the Snake River.

John and his family would fervently pray over Buffalo Robes' request, but right now there was another very important and family altering event that was happening just five days before the McCrumb wagons were to cross over the mighty Snake River to continue their adventure west. That extraordinary event was the marriage of Bright Edwards and Jake Banks!

Bright's eye operations in Boston were considered a complete success. As far as Bright was concerned the operations were a miracle from God. She could see things now that she had never seen before. Everyday colors that most folks just took for granted still amazed and fascinate Bright. She knew that her brother's eyes were green, but she could only imagine what the color green really looked like. Now she could see the hues of the light green to the deep greens of his eyes. She could actually see for the first time what her brother really looked like. For nineteen years Bright only saw blurred and hazy imageries that were real to her but not real to the world. Her eyesight was not one hundred percent perfect, but no one could convince Bright that they weren't perfect.

Bright fell in love with Jake Banks the first time he spoke to her. It wasn't his looks that mattered; she couldn't see what he really looked like. It was his soft manner in how he spoke and treated her. She felt his warm personality with his first words. Jake touched her heart in a way that no other man nor boy had ever affected her. Looks did not matter to Bright, true affection and honest love did matter.

Bright saw for the first time a truly handsome man as she was walking down the train's steps when she arrived at the train station in Soda Springs. That was when that beautiful handsome man picked her up off of train steps and hugged and kissed her on the train station's platform. She was in Jake's arms, the only man she would ever love.

And now, she was going to marry that beautiful handsome guy!

The Fort Hall commander agreed to perform the wedding ceremony if Jake and Bright were willing to "git hitched" as he phrased the words. It was going to be a modest ceremony filled with love, passion, and friendship. Jake and Bright were only expecting maybe twenty folks at the most to attend the ceremony. They knew that Buffalo Robe and White Antelope would be there. The ceremony was filled with love, passion, and friendship but the attendance was totally overwhelming to the bride and groom, almost two hundred well-wishers attended the merriment of the marriage shindig.

There were three other wagon trains at the Fort that were preparing for their continuing journeys to the west. Most of those pioneers couldn't turn down the happiness and gaiety of a true pioneer wedding. Lucy and Amy had picked and gathered as many wildflowers as they could find. The sisters made a garland crown of flowers for Bright's head. The rest of the wildflowers the sisters threw at Bright's feet.

The unexpected large wedding jamboree crowd decided to have a full-blown hoedown wedding festival. Some of the men brought harmonicas while others dug out their fiddles. There were even a couple of mouth harps and a bunch of musical whiskey jugs.The ladies quickly prepared a large bountiful feast and the celebration began. During the exchange of the wedding vows both Lucy and Amy blubbered. Henry was holding Lucy's hand all through the ceremony and her blubbering. The fiddle playing with the musical backing of the harmonics and musical jugs, howling dogs, feasting, and dancing lasted well into the night. Bright and Jake's Prairie wedding was one that grew more magical in legend and myth as each year passed on that part of the Oregon Trail.

Bright was radiant and Jake was a handsome guy and very proud of his beautiful wife. Everyone congratulated the couple and wished them happiness forever. Neither Bright nor Jake could have ever imagined happiness such as their happiness on that wonderful day of their marriage. What seemed so impossible for the newlyweds years ago, became a beautiful reality because of the love and care and generosity of true caring humans such as the McCrumb's. It is strange how one or two people like the McCrumb family could cause an everlasting effect on so many other people in a wonderfully positive way: people like Jake and Bright because for a split moment in time, they all crossed each other's paths during that precise special moment in time. Jeremiah Austin, Jock, the cowpokes,

White Antelope are beautiful examples of that "precise moment in time" when all of their paths crossed at that special moment in time with the McCrumb family. It also worked in reverse for the McCrumb family. That one moment in time can change so many lives for the best and for a better world.

Buffalo Robe and some of the Shoshone friends were at the wedding. White Antelope stood next to Lucy and Amy during the ceremony of vows. She didn't blubber, but there were tears slowly rolling down her cheeks.

Jeremiah and John had secretly bought another covered wagon for the newlyweds and the girls had prepared it for Bright and Jake's wedding night. Jeremiah had the wagon pulled far away from the other wagons for the newlywed's privacy. It was an embarrassing moment when the crowd escorted the couple to their new wedding night quarters. It was a good thing that the ceremony lasted well into the night; no one could see the red and flushed faces of Bright and Jake as they hurriedly climbed up into the wedding night prepared wagon, hoping the crowd would silently and very quickly go away, go anywhere, just go somewhere else.

It was the first day of May of 1876 when the seven wagons of the McCrumb's wagon train reached the eastern banks of the mighty Snake River. There were a few clouds in the sky and the sun was warm. There were over a hundred Shoshone braves, women and children there to wish them well on their western journey. Buffalo Robe was there and White Antelope was at his side.

John rode Thunder over to the Chief and thanked him for being a true friend. The Shoshone Chief took his knife and made a cut at the base of his left palm. John took his knife and did the same. They would forever be blood brothers. The pioneers cheered and the

Indian Braves whooped and yelled. Buffalo Robe gave Jerald and Jacky each a gift for their birthdays. He had remembered Jeremiah's words.

Jerald and Jacky, Lucy and Amy walked over to the side of White Antelope's brown and white pinto pony and took her hand after she got off of the horse. The two brothers and the two sisters hugged and welcomed their new sister and one beautiful brown and white Shoshone pinto pony into the McCrumb family. Again the pioneers cheered and the Indian braves whooped and yelled. Buffalo Robe's promise to Mary Armstong's white father had been fulfilled. The McCrumb family had accepted Buffalo Robe's wish and Mary Armstrong became a daughter and a sister into the McCrunb family. The Shoshone people, White Antelope and the McCrumb's would meet again many times in the future, as true friends should.

Crossing the Snake River was challenging and at times harrowing, but the seven wagons made the crossing without any disastrous calamities, just minor mishaps. The last leg of the McCrumb's yearlong journey from Alma Kansas to their new western home was coming to a conclusion and the enigmatic end would soon be revealed. This amazing and at times sad and tragic journey was about to be understood to its fullness. John wanted to be settled in the Lost River Valley before Jacky's fifteenth birthday which was on the fifteenth day of May. Throughout this ultimate venture of the journey west, John's beloved wife Sarah was always on his mind and was always with him in spirit.

Mary Armstrong would ride with Lucy and Amy in the chuck wagon. Lucy's original weather-beaten and torn sign that read "LUCY CHUCK WAGON" was still attached to the back of the wagon. White Antelope had always been aware of the promise that Buffalo Robe had made with her father before he died from the wounds he had suffered from the Blackfeet Indians. She had escaped injury during the marauder's raid. A Shoshone counter attack drove the Blackfeet away and rescued the young girl, but was too late to save her parents.

White Antelope had requested that the McCrumb's call her by her Christian given name which was Mary. After her parents were killed Mary missed the close family unit that she was familiar with. She loved the Shoshone and the reservation, but it was not the family she desired. Buffalo Robe understood her feelings and had made her a promise that if he ever located a sound and suitable white family that deserved and loved her he personally would help her to become part of that family. The McCrumb family was that perfect family. After almost five years Mary had given up hope of ever being a part of a family unit again that she so desperately desired.

When the McCrumb family came into her life her hopes swelled to a new high. Her love for the McCrumb's was instant, even before she actually met them. Her admiration for John and his generosity was overwhelming. She watched John and Jeremiah's first meeting with the Shoshone Chief with intent to learn more of this gracious white man. She was enthralled with the McCrumb boys when they visited the reservation. She found them to be polite and shy, but eager to learn about the Shoshone way of life. She was particularly interested and fascinated with the oldest McCrumb brother. After sharing a day with the McCrumb girls and after learning the story of Bright, Mary told Buffalo Robe this was the family she desired. And as the old adage goes, "The rest of the story is history.

After John's last private meeting with the Shoshone Chief concerning Buffalo Robe's promise to White Antelope John had a meeting with Lucy and Amy, Jerald and Jacky. In the meeting, he included his extended family; Jeremiah, Jake and Bright and Bright's brother Henry. Lucy, Amy, Jerald, and Jacky were extremely excited with the possibility of having White Antelope as a sister. They thought of it as being only something that happens in fairy tales. The McCrumb's extended family knew of the Chief's promise and the thought of including Mary into the McCrumb family all agreed it was the right thing for the McCrumb's to do.

Lucy and Amy couldn't wait until the three girls could go shopping for clothes for Mary. Mary was already trying on the two sister's dresses. Both Lucy and Amy told Mary she could have any of the dresses she wanted, the sisters had plenty of them. Mary did have one small problem with the sister's undergarments and that was the apparel which she was not accustomed to. Those older girl things were awkward, itchy and uncomfortable at times when they ended up in unwanted places. John had told his daughters about a trading post in a settlement called Blackfoot and it probably sold clothes. That little bit of information really got the girls excited. The Blackfoot trading post was less than a day's travel time after crossing the Snake River.

It was at the river crossing when Ila and Jack Bonner would take their leave from their new found friends and fellow pioneer travelers. Ila and Jack would continue on the Oregon Trail west until they reached the Boise basin near the southwestern part of the Idaho Territory. The goodbyes were emotional and sincere. The Bonners were extremely grateful for the help that John and his companions had shown them when their wagon had broken down between Denver and Fort Laramie. The Bonners and the McCrumb's would become lifelong friends.

A couple of hours after the crossing of the mighty Snake River the six wagons converged on the settlement of Blackfoot. Blackfoot was still in the immediate area of the Shoshone and Bannock Reservation. The pioneers could stock extra items before the trek to the Lost River Valley. The six wagons would travel north from Blackfoot to the Valley of the Lost River on an old stage coach and wagon train trail. Much of the trail was called the "Goodale's Cutoff". The Goodale's Cutoff trail was established in 1862 north of the Snake River where it spurred off of the Oregon Trail and headed due north. The cutoff was used in earlier days as a pack trail by Indians and fur traders. The cutoff headed north from Fort Hall and Blackfoot toward the enormous lone standing mountain called the "Great Butte". The Great Butte was a classic landmark that was between Blackfoot and the Lost River Valley. The valley was five or six days travel by wagon from Blackfoot.

While the other pioneers checked their gear and added supplies the four girls happily and eagerly invaded the local trading post. The girls were not disappointed, there was a small, but ample supply of ladies and young girl garments of several kinds. The girls had a fun time finding pretty dresses for Mary and of course a few items for themselves. Some of the wearing apparel was the unmentionables around the men folk. The girls really got excited when they saw the pretty feminine hats. Before they left the trading post the girls spent a few minutes at the candy counter.

The land north of Blackfoot looking toward the McCrumb's final destination of the Lost River Valley as far as the eye could see was immense, flat and seemed infinite in space. It appeared to be a vast sea of nothing but sagebrush and open space. This vast open prairie has for centuries been the home of the coyote, the jackrabbits, prairie dogs and rattlesnakes, pheasants, sage hens and at times an elusive wolf. Way off in the far distance a tiny dot of a lone mountain seemed to be breaking through the earth in the beginning of its birth.

The wagons got a late start on the day of the Snake River crossing, but no one complained because the end of a long journey was coming to a final conclusion. Many more new future journeys would begin for each of the seventeen travelers, but this voyage had been exhausting, strenuous and at times distressing, demanding and heartbreaking. The voyage had challenged the total character of strength and moral will of each of the pioneers. Each one had endured the test and gave their all for a new future in this new land. They had survived the journey and a new future lay ahead for each of them. Daylight was lasting longer now, which gave the Pioneers more traveling time, but on this day they camped early.

Mary had grown up next to huge buffalo herds, but Patsy was unique for her. She was never able to get close to a live buffalo and now she could ride one if she so desired. She found it to be a pleasure to pat and rub the course wiry hair of Patsy. Patsy would nuzzle her nose against Mary's face and then give her a giant buffalo tongue wiping kiss. Mary was also fascinated with Ammo. She had never seen a dog as large as Ammo. Ammo was larger than the size of some of the reservations baby horses. Mary had never seen a man as big as Jeremiah and she was intrigued with this giant white man and his many fascinating tales of adventures.

John treated Mary as if she was one of his own daughters. Jerald and Jacky treated her as if she was their sister. Mary wasn't quite sure of Jake yet, but she thought he must be a gentle and good man for Bright to love him so much. She was extremely happy to be a part of this wonderful family. She had never had the same companionship with the Shoshone families or the Shoshone girls as she was enjoying with Lucy, Amy, and Bright. Mary was smart enough to realize that there would be times when she might be on the outs with someone in the family, but she also knew that she would still be loved by all of them and that was what would be important to her during those times.

On the first night out from Blackfoot, the four girls would set up in the dark wagon and have a long heart to hearts girl talk until the early morning hours. Bright would leave the groups talk-a-thong early long before the last tongue wagging ceased. She needed to get back to Jake, the love of her life. The girls had so many questions to ask each other. Mary wanted to know everything about Bright, Lucy and Amy. Lucy, Amy, and Bright wanted to know everything about Mary. The girls would soon learn that Mary's story was a story most fascinating. Her academic brilliance was demonstrated during the time she spent at the Mormon higher learning classes in Salt Lake City before her parents were killed. The tragedy of her parents being killed by the Blackfeet Indians. Her adventures of being adopted and reared on the Shoshone Reservation was absorbing and captivating for Mary which gave her a charismatic charm that touched anyone who had the pleasure of knowing her.

The morning of the second day of May greeted the seven wagons as they started rolling with a light chilly drizzling rain. The sky was overcast with light gray water saturated clouds. The whole day was spent dodging raindrops. Finally, John called for an early camp to prepare for the event of a possible heavier rain through the night. Wagon tarps were put in place so camp fires could be lit and a meal cooked. Everyone was inside their wagons before the soaking rain settled on the wagons. The three girls were relaxed and comfy in one wagon preparing for an extensive tongue wagging event.

Before midnight the rains came heavier, but only lasted a couple of hours. By sun up the rain had stopped and the blue sky was gaining ground on the clouds. The pesky dust was gone, but the ground was unstable and muddy in more places than John would have liked.

There hadn't been much ground covered by the wagons the day before and the ground covered by the wagons on this day wouldn't be much better. It would be slow going because of the muddy trail. Rain storms were rare in this part of the Idaho Territory, maybe only two to three inches a year. But you could always count on mud after a heavy rain.

The landscape was the same every morning; it was boring, desolate and dismally forsaken looking. There was nothing but sagebrush as far as one could see. There was maybe the appearance of mountains in the very far distance to the north, but nothing but sagebrush to the east and sagebrush to the west. The muddy trail was drying and the ground covered by the wagons was getting better to travel over as each hour passed by.

Jacky commented to his poppa that the tiny lone mountain they saw in the far distance on the first day of their journey after leaving Blackfoot was getting bigger each day of travel. On the third day of the journey that tiny looking lone mountain had grown to a gigantic size. It was huge and the wagons were still miles from its foothills. Also far to the northwest, there was an ominous and menacing looking landscape that seemed to be familiar to the pioneers. It appeared to be like the lava beds that they saw at Soda Springs, but these new lava beds were massive in size and seemed to go on forever.

Everyone in the wagon train was captivated with the mammoth size of this lone mountain butte. The fur traders, Indians, and pioneers for the past seventy years had used the butte as a landmark on their march to the great Northwest Territory. It was called the "Great Southern Butte" to those who were familiar with this gargantuan lone mountain. This single one mountain stood alone in the middle of a vast flat waterless wasteland of sagebrush. Its regal majesty would one day find its place on the pages of history books recording the exploration and conquest and the building of the Great Northwest territories. It was indeed a strange looking monument sitting there alone in the middle of the open prairie. It was a landmark that had endured the centuries of time. It must have been a majestic sight when this lone mountain was being thrust up through the earth's crust in the vast vacant prairie during its creation. What secrets it held in its beginning are still secrets, they have been lost to time.

All of the travelers wanted to camp at the base of the Great Butte. The Butte rose out of the earth towards the sky another two to three thousand feet above the desert floor. It was four to five miles long from east to west and one mile wide from north to south. It would take almost a day for a covered wagon to travel completely around it. The Butte was large and extremely impressive. Near the summit of the butte, the pioneers could determine a number of interesting looking caves. Of course, Jerald and Jacky could imagine Indians, treasure, and adventure in each one of the caves. John told the boys that those caves didn't hold any adventure for them, so don't even ask. But, they asked anyway.

After setting up the base camp was completed everyone in the train took some time off to explore some small parts of the eastern end of the buttes foothills before supper. Jeremiah warned everyone to be wary of rattlesnakes. Jerald and Jacky took their shotguns and went jackrabbit hunting. They didn't have to hunt very long, there were hundreds of jackrabbits everywhere they looked. The boys even saw two red foxes. The foxes were hunting small rodents for their night's supper. The red foxes regular stable meals were mice and desert rats. The brothers ended their hunt with a bounty of twelve rabbit's, a red fox and one seven-foot western diamondback rattlesnake wth a seven button rattle. Jeremiah told the boys that rabbit pelts were worth twenty cents each in trade at any trading post. The red fox pelt would bring fifty cents in trade. He told the brothers that he would help them skin the snake and make a belt from the skin. The roasted rabbits were one of the main items on the campers menu for that night. The brothers kept the rabbit skins for future trades.

Jake alerted everyone's attention toward the northern skies that were brilliant and captivating with a night show of the beautiful Aurora Borealis (Northern Lights). The myriad of colors of the Aurora Borealis was flooding the northern sky, dancing and swaying in an amazing choreographed order that seemed to be coming from heaven itself. The beautiful and brilliant nighttime sky opera in the northern hemisphere lasted all night long. Some of the pioneers tried to stay awake watching the dazzling show of amazing colors of greens, reds, yellows, and blues, but they soon gave way to sleep.

Lucy was concerned about her pap. He was intensely involved daily with the wagon train and its everyday functions, but he would find reasons to be by himself at times. He never neglected Lucy, Amy or the boys, but his attention seemed to be detached in other directions. Lucy asked Jeremiah and Jake if she was just imagining things that weren't real about her pap. Jeremiah assured her that she was not imagining a fantasy, what she assumed was real. Jeremiah tried to explain to Lucy as best he could what her pap was going through.

Jeremiah told Lucy that in a few days they would be arriving in the valley where her momma and poppa had dreamed about a new life together. A beautiful valley where they had prepared to live their lives with their children and their grandchildren. Now, her momma was gone and her poppa was feeling the pain of her passing all over again. Even though John had all of his family and friends right there beside him, he felt alone without Sarah. Jeremiah told Lucy to just be there for her poppa and let him knew how much she loves him. Lucy partially understood everything that the big mountain man was telling her, but she was still confused at what to do to help free her papa from of his deep despair.

Lucy told Amy, Mary and Bright about her confused feelings about her pap and his despair. Amy started to cry because she felt the same way but didn't know how to tell anyone. Lucy hugged her sister and wiped the tears from her cheeks. Bright suggested that maybe the sisters should set with their poppa more in the evenings and ask him to tell them happy stories and delightful tales about their momma and poppa before the sisters were born. Mary agreed. By doing this John would be forced to talk about Sarah more and out in the open to others. "Maybe that is just what your poppa needs", Mary observed. That next evening the girl's put their plan to the test after the camps evening supper and the Pilgrims had settled down under a beautiful western evening sky.

John was a little surprised but it was a very pleasant surprised when Lucy, Amy, and Mary sat next to him by the warmth of the nightly fire and ask him to tell them stories about their momma before she and their poppa move to the Americas. The three girls ask John dozens of questions that brought back wonderful memories for John.

After many weeks John began to look forward to his nightly discussions with the girls and anyone else who joined the discussions about Sarah. The girls had carried out their plan faithfully and their plan was a great success. John's attitude and dispirited feelings changed drastically for the better and everyone was pleased, especially John. Just by sharing stories about Sarah verbally to others John's depression was vented and he was better able to cope with his loss of his beloved Sarah.

Leaving the Big Butte signaled that the long journey to the Lost River Valley was nearing a conclusion. After over a year the McCrumb's and their friends could see in the far distance the Rocky Mountains that were protecting the Lost River Valley from the outside world. Two or three more days and their quest would become a reality.

But before they could enter the valley the six wagons would have to navigate around and at times through the edge of the massive earth catastrophe that had happened thousands of years earlier. What was before them now were hundreds, maybe thousands of square miles of nothing but grotesque and enormous lava flows that had been spewed from the yawning jaws of three volcanos that were situated side by side eons of years ago. The pioneers would have to confront this last obstacle before entering the Lost River Valley. This lava flow made the lava beds they had encountered at Soda Springs look like a tiny infant in diapers. This lava flow near the Lost River Valley was hundreds of square miles in all directions and nearly impossible to penetrate from any of the directions. The old stage and fur trading trail skirted the eastern edges of the massive ancient volcanic flows. The trail wasn't meant for this type of large covered wagons in the beginning just horses and small stage coaches. Over the years new partial trails were maneuvered around the lava pits and large lava bubble beds to accommodate larger wagons. It was slow going but with determinations and a more compatible trail, the wagons could negotiate the area to a more friendlier landscape. John did stop a couple times next to the massive lava flows so the pioneers could explore some of the three volcanoes mysteries. These massive lava beds would invite numerous mystifying adventures for the McCrumb clan in the future.

On the tenth day of May of 1876, the McCrumb's wagon train was just a couple of miles from the entrance to the valley of their destination. When the six wagons entered into the Lost River Valley they were met with an enormous surprise. Scattered along the banks of the mysterious Lost River were many teepees and hundreds of Native Americans.

The Indians didn't seem to be surprised or concerned to see these white strangers in covered wagons. In fact, the Indians were very friendly and came forward to graciously welcome the settlers to the beautiful valley.

John and Jeremiah soon learned that these Indians were the Lemhi's of the Shoshone Nation. Their leader was Chief Tendoy. Tendoy was a nephew of the famous Lewis and Clark Indian squaw "Sacajawea". Tendoy became Chief of the Lemhi in 1863 after Chief Snagg was killed by some renegade miners. Tendoy was highly respected by the white settlers throughout the Idaho Territory for his work as a peacemaker. He kept members of his tribe from joining other bands of Indians in attacking the whites. Tendoy refused to settle his Shoshone followers on the reservation at Fort Hall. The government finally agreed to Tendoy's demands for a reservation in the Lemhi Valley in the Idaho Territory. That reservation was about a hundred miles north of the Lost River Valley. It had been a long tradition that the Lemhi would camp along the Lost River from early November to early spring. By the middle of March, the Lemhi would pull up camp and head back to the reservation in the Lemhi Valley. They were late this year on their trek back to the reservation. The past winter in the Lemhi Valley had been bitter cold and devastating for the Indians. That was the reason the Lemhi would winter in the Lost River Valley. Chief Tendoy and the Lemhi became fast friends with the McCrumb's over the next thirty years. John continued to allow them to camp on McCrumb land over the winter months. The Lemhi first encountered the white man when missionaries visited the Lemhi lands in the 1850s and 60s. Thy had learned to speak the English language. Chief Tendoy died in 1907 almost a year to the day after John McCrumb died in 1906.

The six wagons made camp next to the Lost River in the area that boasts of the tallest peak of the Rockies Mountains in the Idaho Territory. Jeremiah stayed in the camp for a couple of more months before he bid the pioneers a, "So Long for a while". He wanted to explore the Antelope Mountain Range of the Rockies. That range of mountains was the western border of the valley. He promised John that he would be back in the valley before the first or second snow of winter. It was a tearful "So Long" for Lucy and Amy and the brothers. It seemed to them that they had known Jeremiah all of their lives. Now, he was a big part of their lives and that is how they wanted it to stay. It was just as hard saying goodbye to Ammo, he also was a big part of the McCrumb family. Everyone was positive that Patsy would really miss Ammo. Jeremiah told the sisters that Patsy still thinks she is a dog. Jeremiah finally convinced the girls and their brothers that he would always be a part of the McCrumb family. He promised them that his frequent sojourns in the mountains would only be two or three months at the most then he would come back to the valley.

When John and Jake filed for homestead lands in the Colorado Territory near the "Hidden Canyon" in 1875 they also inquired from the US Government Land agencies about acquiring lands in the Idaho Territory. Most of the land in the region of Idaho was wilderness and was readily available to anyone who wanted to homestead it. All an individual had to do was stake out their claim and file a vague handwritten description of their claim by post with the US Office of Land Management in Denver. There was only one other obligation the individual who was filing the claim must do; either he or she would have to build a livable structure that could endure the winter months. It was as simple as that, the land was there for the asking.

John had claimed for five thousand acres and Jake had claimed for one thousand acres. In future years they both would increase the size of their land holdings in the vast Idaho and Colorado Territories.

It was early on a Sunday morning, the 21st of May in 1876 when all of the pioneers gathered for church services on the banks of the Lost River. Many of the Lemhi had gathered with the worshipping pioneers. The Lemhi believed in God and His Son. They had learned about God from earlier missionaries. This was an important opportunity for the McCrumb's to further the Lemhi's education about the Great Creator.

After the final prayer was offered in that early morning worship service and the large noonday lunch had been served Jake and Bright walked for a while in one of the lush fields beside the Lost River. They held hands and thanked God for their magnificent surroundings. Jake told Bright that their future was before them in this beautiful valley. Henry and Lucy set on the banks of the river after the prayer service and meal, in low tones talked about their future together in the valley. Jerald and Jacky saddled their horses and rode off for adventures that would last a lifetime.

After the services and the Lord's Supper had been taken and the last prayer uttered and the last noonday meal is eaten John kissed his daughters and excused himself from the gathering. John found a quiet and secluded place next to the river. He closed his eyes and whispered softly, "Sarah my beloved darling, I love you". John thanked God for all of his bounties. He opened his eyes and slowly surveyed his beautiful and wonderful surroundings. He again whispered softly, "My beautiful Sarah, we are home."

John's mind drifted back to long ago memories until he was completely lost in the past.

His thoughts wandered back to the time when his family's trek from Alma Kansas to the Idaho Territory in prairie schooners had begun a little over one year ago. It was on March 17, 1875, when the McCrumb family began their hazardous journey into the unknown of the western frontier. He reflected back to the time when Jake Banks had ridden his horse to the corral fence on the McCrumb's farm and then joined the family on their quest to the vast western frontier.

The journey had not only been difficult and dangerous, but heart-rending and tragic at times. Maybe now the McCrumb's could start a new life in this beautiful valley that had been shaped at creation five miles above sea level and surrounded on three sides by the majestic Idaho Rocky Mountains. Those spacious mountain peaks were towering several thousand feet above the valley floor desperately searching and reaching upwards trying to find the pinnacle of the heavenly skies. The "Pioneer Range" as it was later named, was the tallest range of the Rockies in Idaho.

The McCrumb family had begun their long and difficult journey to this largely unknown and mysterious valley in the Idaho Territory a few years after the finale shot of the devastating War Between the States was silenced. The war was a time in his life that John McCrumb was desperately trying to forget. It was nothing more to him now than just a fleeting whisper in history. He wanted to leave behind the horrors of that war and move on to the future with his family. Discovering the Lost River Valley was truly a gift from God and the McCrumb family was firmly convinced of that truth. If only his beloved Sarah was here by his side. She would have loved the beauty of this valley. Sarah's pioneering love of nature's wonderment would have brought a unique blossoming beauty to this valley.

John's memory was slowly fading back to the reality of 1876. His mind had lost the value of time; it had journeyed back to the beginning of his and Sarah's adventurous trek from the early days of Pennsylvania. What seemed like a lifetime of memories were only a few valuable moments in time. John realized that his thoughts had gotten away from him. He again surveyed the grandeur and beauty of this wonderful and mystical valley.

With tears clouding his eyes John once again turned his head upward toward the blue cloudless sky of the heavens. He thanked God and then in a soft whisper he uttered those precious words once again.

"My beautiful Sarah, we are home."

THIS FIRST PART IS FINISHED, BUT THE ADVENTURES CONTINUES!

SARAH'S BLESSINGS

By Jerald Beverland

Printed in the United States
By Bookmasters